The Cowboy Who Loved Texas

Enemies to Lovers Romance & Small Town Saga

Three Rivers Romance™
Book 3

Liz Isaacson

Reader Note

Hello Fabulous Christian Cowboy Readers!

I'm thrilled you're back in Three Rivers with me!

This is a second chance romance between Dawson and Caroline. In it, you'll get sweet and swoony kisses and nothing more. Lots of grumpy cowboy banter and fun farm pets, which are totally amazing.

Caroline is five years out from a disastrous marriage, where she was gaslighted and slightly controlled. There are brief, non-graphic references to this previous marriage and husband; nothing more.

All of my books address real life situations without fear or shame, because I believe we all make mistakes, our Savior suffered for all of us, and we can all repent, be healed, and come back to God.

So are you ready for true-to-life romance, family saga, and the small town goodness you might've come to expect from me?! I hope so! If you're new, you're in for a treat!

xoxo

~Liz

The Small Town of Three Rivers

Welcome to Three Rivers! There have been three complete series here already - Three Rivers Ranch, Seven Sons Ranch (Walker Brothers), and Shiloh Ridge Ranch (Glover Family).

That's 37 books. Loads of characters. I'm going to list them here, but you don't need to know them all comprehensively for this book. I just know some of you like seeing these amazing small towns and who lives here!

. . .

Three Rivers Ranch:

Frank and Heidi Ackerman - patriarch and matriarch. Frank died 15 years ago; Heidi is remarried to Malcolm Rust.

Squire and Kelly Ackerman

Son: Finn - 31
Daughter: Libby - 26
Son: Michael - 23
Son: Samuel - 19

Pete and Chelsea Marshall (Chelsea is Squire's sister, and they own Courage Reins, which is housed at Three Rivers Ranch)

4 sons:
Paul - 26
Henry - 24
John - 21
Rich - 18

. . .

Reese and Carly Sanders: They're the admins for Courage Reins, Pete and Chelsea's equine therapy unit at Three Rivers Ranch. They have no children.

Garth and Juliette Ahlstrom (former foreman; vet technician)

    Son: Jake - 23

    Son: Carson - 21

Cal and Trina Hodgkins (he's the full-time vet at Three Rivers Ranch)

    Daughter: Sabrina - 34

    Daughter: Abby - 26

    Daughter: Olive - 21

Ethan and Brynn Greene (they own Bowman's Breeds, which is housed at Three Rivers Ranch)

    Daughter: Carolina - 23

Son: Tyson - 21
Son: Bryan - 19

Beau Peterson (foreman at Three Rivers Ranch), single

Bennett and Ellie Peterson (he's a cowboy, she works on the finances on the ranch with Kelly)
Daughter: Joy - 9
Son: Jaxon - 6

Tad and Sandy Jorgensen (he's a cowboy, she owns the pancake house in town)
Son: Nathaniel (Nate) - 21
Daughter: Helen - 18

Kenny and Taryn Stockton (he's a

cowboy, she works for a local online newspaper in town)
Daughter: Joelle (Jo) - 20

Jon and Grace Carver (he's a cowboy, she helps Heidi run the bakery in town)

Andy and Lawrence Collins (he's a cowboy, she owns a clothing boutique in town)

Summer and Tanner Wolfe (he's a cowboy, she's a nurse at the hospital in town)

Gavin and Navy Redd - they own their own single-family ranch on the northeast side of Three Rivers

. . .

Boone and Nicole Carver (Squire's cousin) - they own and operate the full time veterinary clinic in town

Camila and Dylan Walker (he's a cowboy and an electrician, she owns a plumbing shop in town)

Seven Sons Ranch:
Momma & Daddy: Penny and Gideon Walker
1. RHETT & EVELYN WALKER
Son: Conrad - 22
Triplets: Austin, Elaine, and Easton - 18

2. JEREMIAH & WHITNEY WALKER
Son: Jonah Jeremiah (JJ) - 20
Daughter: Clara Jean - 18
Son: Jason - 16
Daughter: Emily - 14

Daughter: Hattie - 11

3. LIAM & CALLIE WALKER
Daughter: Denise - 26
Daughter: Ginger - 22

4. TRIPP & IVORY WALKER
Son: Oliver - 34 (and married to Aurora Glover)
Son: Isaac - 22

5. WYATT & MARCY WALKER
Son: Warren - 19
Son: Cole - 17
Son: Harrison - 16
Daughter: Rachel - 13

6. SKYLER & MALLERY WALKER
Daughter: Camila - 19

Son: Sawyer - 17
Son: Gideon - 14

7. MICAH & SIMONE WALKER
Son: Travis (Trap) - 18
Daughter: Daisy - 16
Son: Jensen - 12
Daughter: Laurel - 10

Shiloh Ridge Ranch:
Lois & Stone (deceased) Glover, 7 children, in age-order: (Lois is now married to Donald Parker)
1. Bear — Sammy, wife

- Lincoln (26), adopted son
- Stetson (Smiles, 16), son
- Russell (Rock, 15), son
- Heather (13), daughter
- Sunnie (12), daughter

2. Cactus — Allison, ex-wife / Bryce, son (deceased) // — Willa, wife

- Mitch (27), adopted son
- Cameron (22), adopted son
- Kyle (20), adopted son
- Charlie (Chaz, 18), son
- Lynn (17), adopted daughter
- Melissa (14), daughter

3. Judge — June, wife

- Lucy Mae (32), step-daughter
- Birch (15), son
- Willow (12), daughter
- Linden (9), son

4. Preacher — Charlie, wife

- Betty (16), daughter
- Hank (13), son
- Daisy (10), daughter

5. Arizona — Duke Rhinehart, husband, living at the Rhinehart Ranch, just south of Shiloh Ridge

- Shiloh (16), daughter
- April (13), daughter
- Dwayne (11), son
- Dallas (8), son

6. Mister — Libby, wife

- Belle (13), son
- Marley (11), daughter
- Hazel (8), daughter
- Brantley (6), son

7. Bishop — Montana, wife

- Aurora (34), step-daughter and married to Oliver Osburn
- Robbie (20), son
- Georgia (14), daughter

Aurora and Oliver have 3 children, who are Bishop and Montana's grandchildren:

- Jewel (7), daughter
- Laramie (Lara, 4), daughter
- Mason (almost 2), son

Dawna & Bull (deceased) Glover, 5 children, in age-order:

1. Ranger — Oakley, wife

- Wilder (17), son
- Fawn (16), daughter

2. Ward — Dot, wife

- Glory Rose (17), daughter
- Silver (14), son
- Flint (12), son

3. Ace — Holly Ann, wife

- Gunnison (16), son
- Pearl Jo (14), daughter
- Ashton (11), son

4. Etta — August Winters, husband

- Hailey (24), adopted daughter
- Joey (14), son

- Nash and Nellie (twins - 12), son and daughter

5. Ida — Brady Burton, husband

- Johnny and Judy (twins - 17), son and daughter
- Riggs (12), son
- Sonora (9), daughter

Bull and Stone Glover were brothers, so their children are cousins. Ranger and Bear, for example, are cousins, and each the oldest sibling in their families.

Chapter One

Dawson Rhinehart pulled into the parking lot at the Three Rivers community center, coming to a stop right beside his parents. He got out and opened the back passenger door to collect the two pans of breakfast casserole his mama had made for this morning's New Year's Day breakfast fundraiser.

His father labored to get out of the truck only a pace away, and Dawson fought the desire to abandon the food and help his daddy. He succeeded, and he moved at the pace of a sloth behind his father as he took slow, stilted steps up to the sidewalk. He used the hood of the truck to help him get up that step, and then Daddy looped his arm through Mama's and used her strength to stabilize himself.

Inside, a flurry of activity told him where to take the food, and he handed it off to Ramona Whitely, who smiled and said, "Thank your mother, Dawson."

"Yes, ma'am," he said, wishing he could turn around and walk right back out to his truck. He didn't care about this fundraising breakfast for the fire department, and he figured they'd already gotten the money for his ticket whether he ate or not.

He did want a bigger, nicer truck, as sometimes the wildfires out here in the Texas Panhandle could throw flames twenty feet in the air, if the summer season was long and dry and people didn't take proper precautions around their homes, farms, ranches, and vehicles.

Stuffing down his irritation at something that hadn't even happened yet, Dawson paused in the doorway and waited for a family to go by him. He had some errands to run after this breakfast, and because he couldn't put it off any longer, he joined the flow of people moving past the entrance to the kitchen and into the big gymnasium where he'd played basketball as a child.

His sports career had lasted until third grade, when he'd realized he didn't have the greatest hand-eye coordination—and his daddy wasn't going to drive him down to town for multiple practices each week, plus games on Saturdays.

He'd stuck to farm work after that, inventing games with his younger brother in the equipment shed, the barns, the stables, and simply the wide open land on the Rhinehart Ranch. Technically called Hidden Hills Ranch, Inc for the taxes, Dawson loved working his family land that they all called the Rhinehart Ranch.

They had good neighbors and good soil, and Dawson would rather be up there than down here. He wasn't exactly a people-person.

Still, he moved to the doorway of the gym and looked inside. People teemed around the long tables set up for the breakfast buffet.

People moved along all the circular tables set up for eating. People laughed; people talked; people people people.

Dawson took a steeling breath and took the first step into the gymnasium. He couldn't see his mama or daddy, but he figured they'd saved him a spot. Perhaps if he just wandered around, they'd find him.

He nodded to family friends, then Judge Glover and his wife, then he veered over to Micah Walker. He was a decade older than Dawson, but they'd worked on building Mama's cabinetry together, and Micah had rebuilt the barn on the ranch after the summer flooding from a couple of summers ago.

"Howdy," he said to perhaps the one person he'd call a friend in Three Rivers. He had brothers, and Duke was married to a Glover, so Dawson had never hurt for company if he wanted it.

"Dawson." Micah half rose and shook his hand. "Are you looking for a place to sit?" Each table held eight, and Micah and Simone only had three children. No one else had sat with them, and Dawson nodded over to their oldest. Trap had finished high school last spring, but he'd been working with his father for years even before that.

"My folks are here," he said, glancing around. "Somewhere." He looked at Micah for a moment. "I was just wondering if you got that new cherry wood in. I want to try a cutting board with it."

"Not yet," Micah said. "Simone's been selling a lot of our checkerboard charcuterie boards at her shows lately."

"Yeah?" Dawson glanced over to Trap, who nodded.

"Cherry and oak," he said. "One lady bought one to use as a checker board."

"Light and dark," Dawson said, smiling at the younger man. He knocked on the table and straightened. "Good to see you guys."

He looked over his shoulder and found his mom with her hand in the air. "There's my mama. Enjoy breakfast."

"It's cold pancakes and burnt bacon,"

Micah said, to which Simone swatted him and said, "Shh."

Dawson chuckled as he walked away, because Micah had just vocalized his feelings about the breakfast. He moved over three tables and took his seat beside his daddy. "You're in the back," he said, working hard to keep the question mark off the last word. He managed too, in his mind.

"Yep," Daddy said. No further explanation. He never said more than necessary, and Dawson had definitely inherited that trait from his father.

No buffet ever had the back tables start first, and Dawson settled into his seat and folded his arms, ready to deal with his grumbling stomach until he could get it some flaccid bacon and cold pancakes.

"You savin' any of these?"

Dawson shook his head at the Bellamores while Daddy said, "Nope, all yours." He immediately started engaging Brit Bellamore in conversation about their winter crops, and Dawson listened with vague interest.

"We're ready to begin," someone said into a microphone. "Please raise your hand if you have seats at your table, as we have more people coming in."

Dawson dutifully raised his hand, and a woman pointed toward him. She turned a little girl in that direction, and another woman came behind her. He put his hand down and nodded at the woman, whom he didn't recognize.

"These are open?" she asked.

"All yours," he said, and she pulled out the chair next to Gabi Bellamore. As she shifted, the woman behind the little girl came into view, and Dawson's flesh and muscles dang near flowed out of his skin.

Caroline Thompson.

Dawson felt everything inside him blazing, and as their eyes met, he wondered what she saw. Him, obviously, as she froze. The little girl, who was probably six or seven years old, took the seat in the middle of the remaining three available while the other woman took her seat next to Gabi, and that left the only open seat next to Dawson.

Caroline's eyes narrowed then, and she practically stomped over to the chair and yanked it out. "Hello, Dawson," she clipped out.

"Caroline," he said easily. He hadn't seen her since their impromptu breakfast together at the diner a few months ago. He hadn't filed any paperwork either, which was probably why Caroline now shot ninja stars at him from her eyes.

She'd also texted him a time or two—not about owls or paperwork—that had left him confused, and he hadn't answered her. Maybe she was surly about that too.

Their breakfast together had been fine, in his opinion. They hadn't talked much once the food had come, and he'd managed to maintain his dignity as they'd walked out together. He'd tipped his hat at her and gone to his truck while she went to hers. She'd sent him her half of the bill before he'd even gotten the air conditioning blowing in his truck, and she hadn't pestered him again about the missing paperwork.

They didn't have owls at the Rhinehart

Ranch, plain and simple. And she couldn't make him file without proof of the endangered animals. She'd tried to say the ranch was prime habitat for the burrowing owls, and she needed him to file paperwork saying he wouldn't disrupt their habitat, but he'd ignored her.

In fact, he'd looked up the law, and he didn't have to file anything about a habitat, not even for an endangered animal—until the animal was there. Then, they couldn't remove the animals and destroy their habitat, but until the little owls chose the Rhinehart Ranch as their home, Caroline couldn't force Dawson to do anything.

"Thanks for coming to the firehouse fundraising breakfast," someone said. "We're going to go ahead and get started. Thank you for your support of our firemen and our efforts to improve our emergency services for the people of Three Rivers."

After a quick prayer, where silence descended on them, the noise broke out as people stood and started talking. And talking, and talking, and talking.

Dawson should have something to say to Caroline, but for the life of him, he couldn't think of a single thing. He looked at the little girl next to her and found they had the same hair color.

"Your daughter?" he asked, not sure why he'd gone there. If Caroline Thompson had a daughter, she could have a husband, and that would mean Dawson's fizzing crush on the woman indicated he'd gone insane.

He glanced over to the other woman sandwiching the girl, and she looked like Caroline too.

"No," she said, but she didn't offer up any information about who the girl was.

"Niece?" Dawson tried again.

Caroline glared at him. "Yes, Mister Rhinehart. This is Judy. She's my niece."

He managed to smile at the girl as she looked at her aunt and then him. "Nice to meet you. I'm Dawson."

"Hi, Dawson," Judy said in a cute, high-pitched, little-girl voice. She looked over to her mama and back to him.

"I'm Dawson," he said again as he reached his hand across the table to Caroline's obvious sister. "You must be—"

"My sister," Caroline barked, cutting him off. "Belle. She's going to be living with me for a while."

Another smile manifested itself. "That's great," he said, shaking her hand. He pulled it back and noticed the two sisters exchange a glance. He ignored it and indicated his mama and daddy. "My parents. Wade and Abby."

"Great to meet you," Belle said. "How do you know Caroline?"

"Well, uh." Dawson shifted in his seat, wishing they'd somehow call their table up to get food. His eyes tracked over to the table where people had just gotten up, and they still had three to go until he could reasonably stand. "We had breakfast together once."

"No," Caroline said. "He's one of the ranches who won't file the endangered habitat paperwork."

Dawson looked over to his father, whose frown lines had deepened between his eyes.

"*Ranches* can't file paperwork," he said quietly. "*People* file paperwork."

Caroline scoffed, but she didn't correct herself.

"Where are you guys from?" he asked Judy and Belle.

Belle didn't seem to have any of the tight-lipped qualities of Caroline, and she started telling him and everyone at the table about their move from Phoenix. She never mentioned a husband, and Dawson didn't have time to ask before their table became eligible to go get in line for breakfast.

He expected to be separated from Caroline then, because his parents didn't move fast at all these days, and he wouldn't just leave them in the dust. But Judy didn't move fast either, and with all the tables and chairs and people, they ended up joining the line in the same order where they'd been sitting at the table.

Which put Dawson right behind Caroline, with his frowny father hot on his heels. He wanted to say something to her, but all of the things that came into his head would embarrass him greatly.

Do you want to go to breakfast again? My treat.

Couldn't say that.

Your hair sure is pretty down like that, Caroline.

He hallucinated and pictured himself reaching up to tuck it behind her ear just before he kissed her. Certainly couldn't say or do that.

I'll file the paperwork, okay? Just don't be mad at me anymore.

But he'd been stubborn for too long about the paperwork, and he couldn't back down now. Caroline was a smart woman, and she'd want to know why he'd suddenly decided to file. He couldn't tell her it was because he found her gorgeous, even as unrelenting as she was.

She clearly didn't like him, though he'd never known someone to get so worked up over burrowing owls and paperwork before. She wasn't the first Wildlife Conservation Officer he'd worked with, for crying out loud.

"Oh, my goodness," she muttered ahead of him, and Dawson blinked to get himself out of the fantasy where he and Caroline held hands and shared intimate things about their lives— like the real reason her sister had come to stay with her in Three Rivers.

"This is a crime against potatoes," she muttered, some limp shreds falling off the spoon. They were white and obviously cold, not a stitch of browned, crispy goodness anywhere.

Without thinking, Dawson looked up and handed his paper plate of cold scrambled eggs to the woman standing there. "Can you take this?" he asked. She did, a squeak of surprise coming from her that wasn't really a protest.

He took Caroline's plate and handed it to her too. "Thank you." Then he took Caroline's hand, his skin burning where it touched hers, and said, "Come with me."

Chapter Two

"Come with you?" Caroline Thompson stumbled after Dawson Rhinehart, because she had no other choice. The man had a grip on her hand she wouldn't be able to break even if she wanted to.

By some miracle in heaven, she didn't want to. His hand was big, warm, rough, and absolutely amazing surrounding hers. She just hadn't held hands with a man in a while, that was all.

She did not like Dawson Rhinehart. The man had been nothing but a stubborn mule for months now, and no one needed to know she'd often sat on her back porch, the sun sinking into the evening with her flipping her phone over and over and over, a text to him started but never finished and sent.

She'd tried a couple of times, and when he hadn't answered, she'd given up.

Now Belle was here, and she needed help with Judy. They both needed a lot of support as Belle navigated the divorce process and tried to keep herself and her daughter safe from her abusive ex-husband. Thankfully, Chuck hadn't followed them to Three Rivers, and Caroline hoped and prayed it could become a sanctuary for her sister and niece the way it had been for her.

"Where are we going?" she demanded as Dawson took her outside in the New Year's temperatures.

"I can't eat that garbage," he said. "We deserve a good breakfast." He cut her a look out of the corner of his eye, and how he looked so sexy and strong doing it, Caroline would never know.

"I'm not going to the diner with you," she said. "They have—"

"Home fries," he said. "I know." He clicked something on his key fob, and the closet truck to them beeped. He opened the passenger door for her, and Caroline simply looked at him.

He kept his head ducked down, his eyes barely able to meet hers past the brim of that deep, dark black cowboy hat. "Are you hungry?"

"Yes," she said without thinking.

"I'm not going to hurt you." He let go of her hand. "I can't stand breakfasts like this, and I'm starving, and we deserve to start the day with a good, hot meal."

Sparks popped through her blood, and she wondered if someone had poured baking soda into her veins, hoping for this kind of explosive, chemical reaction. "Where's the best place for breakfast in this town? Because it's my favorite meal, and I have yet to find somewhere that does what you speak of."

He grinned at her, and oh, that thing should

be criminal. Just like those cold, rubbery hash browns in the community center. "That's because you haven't eaten breakfast at my house."

Pure nervous energy ran through her, but Caroline thought it might actually be adrenaline. Excitement. She had the very distinct thought that this man could introduce some color and life into her existence, and she wanted that very, very badly.

"Okay," she said slowly. "I'll see where this goes, but I need to drive myself."

Dawson's face fell. "Can your sister get home without your car?"

Caroline blinked at him and said simply, "No, sir."

"I'll bring you back the moment you say," he said, and she didn't detect an ounce of dishonesty in him.

She still gave him a side-eyed look and squeezed past him to get in the truck. She honestly had no idea what she was doing. The Rhinehart Ranch sat forty-five minutes south of town. She couldn't just leave Belle and Judy at the community center.

Panicking, Caroline pulled her phone out of her pocket and started texting frantically. Dawson slid into the driver's seat and backed the truck out. He drove in silence, and Caroline had learned that he was familiar and comfortable and best friends with silence.

She wasn't sure how she felt about it, but she took the opportunity to text her sister where she'd gone and that her keys were sitting next to her plastic cup of water on that table.

I am going to get the whole story when you get back, Belle said. *Or I will fake a heart attack and interrupt whatever it is you have going on with Dawson.*

Caroline scoffed, which drew Dawson's attention. "You okay?" he drawled.

Okay, she tapped out quickly, and then she shoved her phone back into her pocket. "Yes," she said. "Just telling Belle what's going on."

"Mm. What did she say?"

"What are you going to tell your parents?"

"That something came up on the ranch." He grinned at her, that lopsided smile so adorable. "It's not exactly a lie."

"Do you regularly tell little white lies?"

"Technically, I haven't told either of my parents anything yet," he said. "So no." His smile remained as he turned to get on the road that led south. Caroline knew the area pretty well now that she'd been in town for nine or ten months, as she had to drive to a lot of the ranches and farms in Three Rivers for her job.

"Besides," he said. "I'm thirty-two years old, and if I want to take a pretty woman home for breakfast, I don't need to tell my mommy and daddy."

Ah, there was that familiar bite and fire. "Wait," she said as her brain caught up to her ears. "A pretty woman?"

Dawson's jaw jumped in that tell-tale way Caroline had seen in other men. He might not be a big talker, but he had plenty of non-verbal cues she could read just fine. Maybe she hadn't seen another man's jaw jump like that for her in a while, nor had she been called pretty by anyone but Belle or Judy in longer, but she wasn't new to dating and relationships.

"Yes, ma'am," he said. "I think you're pretty."

"Well...thank you," she said, not sure what else to say. Her momma had taught her that she could always be grateful, so "thank you" seemed appropriate.

"You ordered over-easy eggs at the diner a few months ago," he said. "Is that your favored way to take eggs?"

Caroline swiveled her attention toward him again. "Favored way to take eggs?"

"Yeah," he said without missing a beat. "Eggs are the most versatile food there is. You can—"

"Besides potatoes," she said.

He looked over to her. "Besides potatoes." He drove with one hand on the top of the wheel and the other draped lazily over his thigh. He seemed at-ease on this road, in this truck, with her. "So...how do you take your eggs?"

Caroline relaxed into the leather seat behind her. "I do like a really good over-easy egg.

They're hard to do, and I'll admit I usually break mine on the flip."

"I've done that too," he said.

"If I'm going to be real honest, though, I'd go with a poached egg. Over a nicely toasted English muffin, with hollandaise sauce."

"So an impossible task," he said.

"So far in Three Rivers, yes," she said. "There was this cute little bistro in Sweet Water Falls that made the best Eggs Benedict I've ever had." She smiled, the morning sunshine of this New Year streaming in through the windows. "Gonna be a nice day."

"Yep," he said. "Good day to be outside for sure."

He made the turn to go west from the highway, and they bumped along a nice dirt road and onto the Rhinehart Ranch. The homestead, a shed, and a barn sat straight ahead, with another much newer, nicer, and bigger house to her right.

Dawson didn't make that turn, and Caroline wondered who lived there. Obviously not him, and he went past another dirt road that went south again.

"Main house and barn here," he said. "Big vegetable garden back there my mama tortured us with." A smile cracked his face. "That place up front is my brother's. He's the foreman and runs the ranch. When Daddy dies, he'll own it outright."

"You won't share ownership with him?"

Dawson shook his head. "Daddy says it's just easier to have one owner. We have other clauses and whatnot in place to give us all a place here on the ranch."

"How many brothers do you have?"

"Two," he said. "One full sibling, one half. My daddy's first wife passed away, and he married my mama and had two more boys."

Caroline's heart expanded with emotion, because it seemed like Dawson had a good relationship with his family members, but she knew better than most that families were so complicated. Even when things were good, they were twisted and knotted and never simple.

"You?" he asked. "You've got Belle. Who else is in your family?"

"We have another older sister," she said. "Her name is Abigail. And I have a younger brother—my daddy's pride and joy." She heard the slight tang of bitterness in her tone as it landed on her tongue. "His name's Davy."

"A, B, C, D," Dawson said.

Surprise once again struck her right across the throat. He'd picked up on the alphabet in her siblings' names? Tall, handsome, and smart. A dangerous combination for her heart.

"Where do they live?"

"I grew up in Colorado," she said. "We're all over the Mountain West these days. Well, I mean, we were. Belle's here now. Davy's still in the Colorado Springs area. Abigail is in Boise."

"All good country," he said.

"Have you ever lived outside of Texas?"

He shook his head. "No, ma'am." He went around the shed and barn and continued down the road. "My brother, Brandon, and I live together. We've got a cabin out here. We have a man who works with us. Kevin Bentley. He had to give up his farm a bit ago, and he lived at Shiloh Ridge for a few months. His sister-in-law is a Glover. But we had a need, and he wants to work, so they moved up here. Him and his family. They've just got the one daughter."

Caroline had never heard him say so much, and it made her smile. "Is that everyone?"

"Yes, ma'am," he said. "We're not nearly the size of some other ranches. Five hundred and fifty acres. The four of us work it just fine."

She liked how he made a one-syllable word into two. "Just *fiy-yine*," she echoed, grinning at him.

"Are you gonna poke fun at how I talk?"

"Only when you make short words into long ones," she said, well aware of her flirting.

He pulled up to a cabin that bore blonde-wood logs, a sturdy roof, and bright blue shutters. He parked out front and killed the engine. "This is it. Don't be thinkin' it's gonna be nice. Two men live here."

"Give me a minute to prepare myself." She drew in a deep breath, as if she needed the oxygen as a shield against what she'd find behind that black door. Caroline held it for a silent count of four, then released it. "Okay, I'm ready."

"Dust and shadows," he muttered as he opened his door and got out of the truck. He slammed the door and glared at her through the windshield as he went round the hood. He dang near pulled her door off its hinges and looked at her again.

"Dust and shadows?" she repeated.

Dawson said nothing as he turned and headed for the cabin. She scurried after him, her stomach an empty well of nerves and hissing snakes. The cabin had a porch that ran the width of the house, with a swing built-in on one end and a rocking chair with a small round table on the other. Something sat on the table, and it took Caroline a moment to recognize the pocketknife there.

Shoes that obviously didn't belong to him or his brother sat on a mat a few feet from the door. Something fit for a teenager—or even younger. Not as young as Judy, but definitely not Dawson's age.

A couple of opaque rocks sat among the shoes too, along with a penny, a nickel, and a spare bit of metal.

What in the world?

A football, a Frisbee, and several dog toys waited neatly in a bin, indicating more to Dawson than grumpiness and veiled invitations.

Caroline's interest piqued, and while Dawson had longer legs than her and a massive angry stride, he'd left the front door open for her. She entered and stopped to take in his space.

"Close that, would you?" he asked, his voice almost a growl. "I don't need to be heatin' the outside."

"Sure, right." Caroline moved out of the way and pushed the door closed behind her. She'd stepped into a living room, where he and his brother had a sofa and love seat set in brown leather. A coffee table sat in front of the couch, and it all faced the front window. No TV.

Caroline couldn't see one of those in the room at all. In fact, a radio sat on the back counter, and she watched almost in slow motion as Dawson reached over and switched it on. Something low warbled out of it, but it wasn't loud enough for her to make out words or a discernible melody.

A dining room table sat pushed against the wall in the kitchen, with the back door of the house behind that. Curtains hung on all the windows. Matching curtains in plain blue fabric.

The carpet at her feet looked clean, as did the kitchen when she reached the counter and leaned against it. Dawson had already started getting out breakfast foods, and he loudly put two pans on his stovetop and flipped on the burners.

The flames whooshed as they came to life, and Caroline took a seat at the bar to watch the show.

His fridge had colorful drawings and notes attached to it with magnets. This man had children in his life, and for some reason, that made Caroline's heart soften toward him.

"I'm gonna do over-easy eggs," he said

without looking at her. "I don't have English muffins, and I'm too hungry to go to the trouble of hollandaise sauce."

"Sounds fine," she said, not teasing him this time. She enjoyed watching him work in the kitchen, and he could apparently only focus on one task at a time, because he made no effort to speak.

She took in the hat rack with jackets and hats on it next to the back door, and she couldn't help wondering who'd given him the potted plant in the window above the kitchen sink.

A niece? Nephew? Sister-in-law? His momma?

Fifteen minutes later, he held two plates, one in each hand, and nodded over to the table. Caroline slipped from the stool and went to join him. She gave him a side-eyed look as she sat and he placed a beautiful plate of hot, perfectly cooked over-easy eggs—the yolks still whole—several strips of bacon, and a whole pile of crispy, browned, perfectly shredded hash browns.

"Do we get to talk over this breakfast?" she asked as he sat down.

"If you'd like," he said. He nudged the salt and pepper shakers closer to her and picked up his fork.

"No pancakes."

Dawson met her eyes, pure fire raging in his eyes. Blue-green fire was something she'd never seen before, but it felt like she could dive into the aquamarine color of it and swim around. Or get scorched.

She was up for either.

"Next time," he said, and he dropped those beautiful eyes to his plate. She hurried to pick up her fork too, her mouth watering for want of crispy potatoes with ketchup.

"Oh." Dawson got to his feet and went around her to the fridge. He returned with the ketchup she'd been about to ask for and set it in front of her. "Here you go."

"Thank you." She squirted it onto her potatoes and mixed them up a little, her smile growing. "This is so amazing, Dawson. Thank you so much." She took a bite, and instant rejoicing sang across her taste buds. They had the right amount of crunch to soft potato, salt, and pepper.

"Oh," she moaned, the ketchup adding the right amount of tang to the party already happening in her mouth. She swallowed and immediately scooped up another bite. "These are the best hash browns I've ever had."

Dawson smiled slightly, the left side tipping up higher than the right. "I'm glad you like them."

She liked every bite she put in her mouth, and she sat back when her plate had been emptied and pressed one palm to her belly. "Dawson, that was incredible. Thank you."

He'd already finished, and he picked up his plate and hers and took them over to the sink without accepting her gratitude. She twisted and watched him wash the dishes they'd just used. "Are you always this grumpy?"

"About," he said.

She got up and went to join him at the sink. She gently inserted her hands into the water and took the plate from him to rinse it. He looked over to her, and in that moment, everything softened between them. Caroline could certainly get her ire up too, and she'd been plenty irritated and frustrated with this particular cowboy.

But that melted away under the heat of his look, and Caroline forgot how to rinse a dish and set it to dry. All she knew was his eyes, that blue, the scent of his skin and the lingering scent of bacon in the air.

He leaned toward her, and Caroline tensed, ready to receive his kiss. Her eyes drifted closed, only to rudely fly open again when a shrill noise pierced the air between them.

Dawson likewise jumped away from her, and she winced at the sound of the plate clattering against the sink. She'd dropped it, and she hastened to pick it up while Dawson's phone rang again.

"What?" he barked into it, his back turned to her.

Caroline's nerves felt like flapping bat wings against her inside organs as she finished the dishes quickly and turned off the faucet. She grabbed a towel from the handle on the stove and faced Dawson.

He wasn't holding the phone to his ear any longer but staring at something on it in front of him. "This is not happening," he said.

"It's happening," a man said on the other end of the line, his voice echoing through the cabin as Dawson had put the call on speakerphone. "Where are you? I need you back at the ranch ASAP."

Dawson didn't answer, and Caroline was actually glad she wasn't the only one he stayed silent with.

"Daws," the man barked. Probably his brother. "Get up here. We need to deal with these burrowing owls."

Ice flowed through her, and she stepped right over to Dawson's side. She looked at his phone while her legs locked, and she couldn't remember if that was good or bad. Was she about to pass out?

His phone showed a picture, and Caroline had plenty of experience with the animal she saw. It wasn't a great picture, but she knew a burrowing owl when she saw one.

"Dust and shadows," she whispered, and Dawson finally looked at her. Only his eyebrows rose, slow and steady. In any other situation, Caroline might have given him a flirty smile.

"Dawson," his brother said. "I can see you're at your cabin. Get out to the West End Fence immediately." His brother sighed. "And call that wildlife officer. She's going to be the death of us, but we can't put her off any longer."

The call ended, and still Dawson held his phone in front of him.

Caroline plucked his device from him, which caused a growl to come from his throat. "I didn't think today was a good day to cause death, but it looks like it might be." She offered him his phone back, which he swiped from her. "Let's go."

Then she led the way out of his cabin with the longest strides she could.

Chapter Three

Dawson really had no choice but to load up with Caroline and head out to the West End Fence. If he didn't go, Duke would just call again and get barkier and barkier.

Sometimes Dawson really hated that it was a ranch rule to have his location on. It did keep them safe, but it also gave Duke the ability to see where Dawson was at all times.

"No privacy," he muttered to himself.

"What?" Caroline asked.

Dawson had almost forgotten she rode with him. Of course, that was nigh to impossible, as the woman's perfume seemed tattooed inside his nostrils, and the shape of her in his life had already started to become familiar.

Which in and of itself was insane. He'd had two meals with her, one where she hadn't wanted to be there, and one where he'd almost kissed her.

Obvious much? Dawson thought. But at the same time, he'd never really beaten around the bush. Not even for the women he asked out.

"I'm sending you the paperwork you'll need," Caroline said from the passenger seat.

He didn't detect any malice or teasing or glee in her voice, and he glanced over to her. "Thank you."

She lowered her phone to her lap, something nervous edged in her eyes. "I'm really sorry the owls have moved onto your ranch."

The road narrowed and worsened, though they kept things in tiptop shape. They simply didn't need as good of roads this far out on the ranch. In fact, Dawson usually rode a horse or an ATV to go out to the West End Fence.

"I am too," he said with a sigh. "So what do

I do? Are you going to have cake tonight to celebrate that you were right and I was wrong?" He hoped she might smile and duck that pretty face, tuck her hair, and say, *Of course not, Dawson.*

Instead, the redheaded-ness inside her shot fire in his direction. "No," she said. "Believe it or not, I don't get joy out of you having owls here." She folded her arms and stared out the windshield. "Which we don't even know if you do yet."

Dawson wished he could recall his words. "You saw the picture. Did those look like bunny rabbits to you?"

"No," she bit out again.

"They were burrowing owls," he said, glancing over to her. "Even I know that, and I didn't go to school to identify them."

"I did so much more in school than that," she said.

Dawson didn't want to fight with her. He was just irritated. "I know," he said. "What else did you do?"

She eyed him warily. "In school?"

"Yeah," he said. "In school. How does one become a Wildlife Conservation Officer?"

"A lot of classes," she said. "I got a degree in wildlife management, with a lot of courses in natural resources management as well."

Great. So she was far smarter than him. Dawson reminded himself that he'd gone to college too. Earned a degree and everything.

"And we're required to take some law enforcement classes," she said. "It's done through the State, but I'd taken some classes in college too." She shifted in her seat, seemingly uncomfortable talking about this.

"Sounds like it kept you busy," he said.

"Yes," she clipped out. "It was a good escape for me, studying and classes." She cleared her throat. "At that time in my life."

Dawson's interest perked up, and he looked over to Caroline fully. Her face pinked up with a beautiful blush he didn't quite understand, and she blurted out, "It won't be so bad, having the owls here. You just can't destroy their dens or try to run them off." Her words rushed over each other, and Dawson wondered what she was trying to cover up.

Her schooling? He shook his head, unable to deal with all the thoughts currently in his head. He could find out more about her later, when he wasn't facing the wrath of his brother, an unknown number of texts as he sent out messages to the surrounding ranches about the owls, and who knew what else.

Oh, right. The paperwork in his inbox. That had to be done too.

"They'll multiply and never leave," he said darkly.

"What do you do out on the West End Fence?"

"It's farmland," he said.

"I hope it won't be a great loss."

"You tell me," he said. "Are these birds going to spread all over the place?"

Caroline took a moment to answer, and she sighed first. Not a good sign. He also caught sight of a couple of crows flying alongside the truck, and they at least buoyed his spirits.

"It depends on how many there are," she

said. "Where they came from, how mature they are, that kind of thing."

"Great," Dawson said, and he realized that she'd apologized about the owls roosting on the ranch. He glanced over to her, trying to make the pieces of her line up.

A couple of hours ago, she'd given him a terrible glare in the community center, and now, she rode alongside him in the truck, saying she'd get him paperwork and apologizing about the owls.

Dawson rounded a corner and caught sight of his dog, waiting down at the other end of the road, where it bent again. Ruffin got to his feet, and his tail started to wag. Then he turned and ran down the road, most likely back toward where Duke waited for Dawson and Caroline.

A sudden thought made his fingers tighten around the steering wheel. How in the world would Dawson have Caroline with him already? "That Wildlife Officer," Duke had called her. And the Rhinehart Ranch sat forty-five minutes south of town.

There was no way she could've gotten here

this fast, and Dawson needed a reason for why he'd had Caroline with him at his house.

You left breakfast with her, he told himself. Momma and Daddy would know something was up, and Dawson's mind blanked.

He'd been driving for enough years of his life that he kept doing that, and he eased the truck to a stop next to his older brother's.

Caroline didn't wait for him to come open her door, because this wasn't a date. Dawson dropped to the ground too, and it wasn't two seconds later that Nugget cawed and glided down, with Rocks coming in hot too.

The two crows landed on the hood of his white truck, their black feathers standing out against the pale paint.

Nugget voiced his welcome again with a, "Caw-aw!" and Dawson slid a look over to Caroline, who'd come to a complete stop at the corner of the truck on the passenger side, her eyes wide as she stared at the big black birds only a few feet from her.

"Hey, you guys," he said, deciding everything in his life was about to be blown wide open anyway. Might as well start with the crows.

Rocks, in true fashion, clicked forward, a rock in his right claw clunking against the hood. "What did you bring me?"

Dawson stepped over to the crow and held out his hand. He'd learned not to try to take anything from either crow. They were highly intelligent, and if they wanted to give him something, they'd give it to him.

Rocks jutted out his foot and deposited a stone in Dawson's open palm. And Dawson swore the crow wore a proud look on his birdy face when he looked up at him. "Oh, this one is glinting with silver." He grinned at the gifted rock Rocks had brought him.

Sometimes he kept them, and sometimes he just pocketed them and tossed them back out with the other stones when the crow wasn't looking. He wondered if Rocks had ever found the same shiny rock again and brought it to Dawson for a second time.

Ruffin arrived and put his paw up on Dawson's leg. He looked down at his cattle dog and bent down to greet him to get a brief reprieve from the shocked look on Caroline's face.

"Hey, you. You workin' with Duke this morning?" Dawson looked over to his brother's truck, but Duke didn't manifest himself. "Where is he, huh?"

Ruffin barked, because he'd just caught sight of the crows, and Nugget fixed his beady bird eyes on the dog and barked back. Just barked on back, his crow voice almost the same as Ruffin's.

Dawson grinned, because while he hadn't been thrilled with the crows seeking him out in the beginning, they brought him joy now. He'd learned a lot about the birds, including that they could imitate sounds—including dogs barking.

"I didn't realize you had a zoo here," Caroline said, and Dawson straightened to face her.

"Uh, well, no cowboy is worth his hat if he doesn't have a dog. This here's Ruffin." He looked from her to the dog, who seemed eager to please as usual.

Caroline smiled down at him and then

crouched in front of the canine the way Dawson had. "He's just so handsome." She took his face in her hands and smiled at him the way Dawson wanted her to grin in his direction. "I bet you can round up cattle, bring back that Frisbee I saw at your master's house, and keep his feet warm at night too."

She trilled out a laugh Dawson had never heard. He'd actually never dreamed she could even make such a noise. She looked up at him, and Dawson's hormones fired through his body. Hard.

The sun haloed her, making her blonde hair shine like spun gold. She beamed radiance at him, and he somehow managed to offer her his hand to help her back to standing.

She took it, and the whole world came to a complete stop. Sure, the New Year's Day sun shone overhead, though it wasn't too hot today. It wasn't terribly cold either, but the temperature would nip in the shade.

His skin sizzled against hers, and he wondered what Caroline felt. What she thought. What might happen next.

"He refuses to sleep on the bed," he said. "So alas, I sleep with cold feet."

"Alas," Caroline said, and if Dawson had to classify how she'd said the word, he'd label it as flirty. She was *flirting* with him. Wasn't she?

Nugget cawed, and that made Dawson flinch and then press his eyes closed in a long blink meant to infuse some patience into his system. Now he'd never know if Caroline had been flirting or not, and suddenly he wasn't so happy to have the crows around.

"Introduce me to your birds," she said.

Dawson caught the look of delight on her face as he opened his eyes. "First," he said as he turned toward the two crows still standing on the hood of his truck. "They're not *my* birds. These are wild crows."

"Yes, they look positively feral."

Dawson pulled his hand back and indicated the bigger, closer crow, appreciating her wit. Of course, when that wit turned to ire, he better watch out. But that only made him want to stick around to see what would bring out that fire in her, what would make her laugh, what would make her lean toward him again, her eyes falling to his mouth, like she maybe wanted to kiss him too.

He cleared his mind, focusing on the nearly blue-black quality of the crows' feathers as they glimmered almost holographically in the sunlight. "This is Nugget. He likes to sing and talk and imitate other animals." He glanced down to his dog. "Especially Ruffin."

"Do they get along?"

"Yeah, they don't give him any trouble; Nugget just likes to use his voice."

"And the other one?"

"Rocks," Dawson said, clearing his throat. "He likes to bring me shiny things."

"I see." She didn't say anything else, and Dawson wasn't going to be all, *Rocks and Nugget, this is Caroline. Don't be swooping down to peck her eyes out or anything. She's a friend.*

Friend.

The truth was Dawson didn't know what Caroline was. Enemy, friend, woman he'd made breakfast for, or simply the person he'd have to deal with when it came to these owls for who knew how long.

They both faced the truck and the fence beyond it, and Dawson got himself to move in that direction. "Duke?" he called.

He went past the truck and walked along the fence, searching down it toward the horizon for his brother. When he didn't see him, he turned around and found his tall, boxy-shouldered brother striding toward him with a storm shooting thunder and lightning from his eyes.

"Daws," he called, lifting his hand.

Dawson raised his hand too, just as Caroline came to his side and faced Duke as well. His brother came to a complete stop as if he'd run into a glass wall.

"Let the explanations begin," Dawson muttered under his breath.

Chapter Four

Caroline's cells vibrated with the tension now zinging through the air. Part of her wanted to slip her hand into Dawson's as he lowered his arm, but the louder, more professional part of her told her to actually put more distance between her and the cowboy.

She did that as the brothers continued to look at one another. Caroline's memory came forward then, and she remembered that Duke was Dawson's half-brother.

Duke finally started walking again, his eyebrows drawn down and his mouth a thin line before he said, "What's going on?" He finally moved his eyes to her. "Who's this?"

"Caroline Thompson," Dawson said, his voice a perfect diplomatic growl. "The Wildlife Conservation Officer."

Duke's irritation barely lifted, but he did arrive and stick out his hand. "Right. I'm Duke Rhinehart."

"Great to meet you." She shook his hand and looked along the fence line. "Do you want to show me where the owls are?"

"How did you get here so fast?"

"I—" Caroline sucked in a breath as Dawson's hand slid along her waist, no skin-to-skin contact and no heat, but the intimate pressure still made her body flood with tingles.

"We were at the fireman's breakfast," Dawson said. "Same table, and when we saw the food, I nearly upended everything." He made a sound that sounded like the crow barking, and it took a moment for Caroline to realize it was a laugh.

"I figured that wouldn't be good, so we came back to the ranch, and I made breakfast."

He cut Caroline a look out of the corner of his eye as he said, "we," his gaze quickly returning to his brother.

Duke met his eye again, held it for a moment, and then switched his gaze over to her. "What a lucky coincidence."

She turned toward Dawson, who wasn't going to be any help at all. He simply looked at her with those gorgeous aqua-marine eyes and gestured vaguely for her to go with Duke.

"They're down here," he said, and he'd already started to walk away. Since Dawson wasn't offering up any other options, Caroline moved to follow his brother.

She didn't want to work today, but sometimes she had to do things she didn't want to do. Owls didn't know what day it was, and Caroline didn't have to keep track of her hours. She got paid to get the job done, no matter when or where that happened.

Duke had just as long of legs as Dawson did, and he didn't slow his stride to allow them to keep up, despite the loose terrain at her feet. Caroline spent a lot of time outside, walking through dirt or down dirt roads or dealing with dirt. After all, that was what the burrowing owls lived in, and they'd become her whole life here in Three Rivers.

No one said anything as they walked, and Caroline's mind went on the fritz. Dawson had introduced her as the Wildlife Conservation Officer, not his girlfriend.

Which would've been weird, she told herself. She and Dawson were not dating, even if it had seemed like he might kiss her in front of that kitchen sink.

She now knew the dog toys belonged to a cattle shepherd named Ruffin, and the coins and shiny objects had come from a pair of crows he'd named Rocks and Nugget.

She twisted and looked behind her, but the crows had flown off. Ruffin trotted along beside Dawson, his tongue hanging out, and Dawson raised his eyebrows.

Caroline faced forward again, because it wasn't exactly even ground here, and she didn't need to trip and fall flat on her face. She wasn't even wearing her boots, so she minded the way and kept following Duke.

Due to her experience, she found the burrowing owls before Duke started to slow and stop. "Here they are," he said.

Caroline stepped past him and crouched down again. Ruffin came right to her side, and she looped her arm over his back. "You can't chase them off, buddy."

Only a few holes existed here, and she only saw two owls. She glanced around and found evidence of their tracks and inhabitation, and she sighed. "We'll need to cordon off this part of the ranch," she said.

"Can we keep them from spreading?" Duke asked. He seemed darker than Dawson, though when she looked up at him, she could see some of the same features in him that Dawson possessed. "Or do we have to just let them have complete run of the ranch?"

Caroline looked back to the burrowing owl den, ignoring the tightness in Duke's jaw. "Well, Duke, burrowing owls are actually quite fascinating. They don't actually dig these burrows themselves; they use holes abandoned by other animals, like prairie dogs or even armadillos here in Texas."

Dawson, who had caught up to them, listened intently, his aquamarine eyes reflecting a mixture of curiosity and concern. "How long do they usually stay in one place?" he asked, brushing a hand along the side of his face, as if he had something there he didn't like.

"They're somewhat nomadic, depending on the availability of food and the safety of their environment," Caroline explained, her eyes scanning the sparse landscape that stretched beyond the burrows. "They can stay in a suitable burrow for several years if it remains undisturbed. But they're also capable of moving on if they feel threatened or if the area becomes unsuitable. It's part of their survival instinct."

Duke crossed his arms, looking over the land that had been planted with winter wheat. "And expanding their nests?" he pressed, his voice tinged with a hint of worry.

Caroline nodded. "They can expand their

nesting area, yes. As their population grows, they'll need more space. It can lead to a larger colony if left unchecked, which isn't necessarily a bad thing unless it conflicts directly with your ranch operations."

Which of course it would. One look at these two grouchy cowboys confirmed that in a single breath. Ruffin whined softly and edged over to her, nudging Caroline's hand with his nose. She gave him a reassuring pat but remained focused on the brothers as she stood. "The presence of these owls can be a sign of a healthy ecosystem," she finally said, attempting to sound smart and tell them that their ranch had a healthy environment. "I know it's not what you want, but we'll need to be careful with land management here."

Dawson nodded, his gaze drifting towards the horizon. "It's God's creation, after all. We're just stewards," he murmured. His words hung in the air, a gentle reminder of their responsibility to the land and its creatures.

Caroline's pulse tripped over itself, because while she'd suspected Dawson had a lot of deep thoughts he didn't let come out of his mouth, she hadn't expected to be touched by one of them. She hadn't expected this man who'd caused her so much anxiety and grief over the past several months to be...soft. She hadn't expected to *like* him.

Duke also didn't seem to share the sentiment, because he asked, "But what if it comes down to choosing between the crops and the owls?" in a gruff, growly-bear voice. "This land isn't just our livelihood; it's our legacy."

"I honestly don't think it'll come to that," she said. "There's usually a breeding pair with some other solitary birds. This is a small space; they won't be able to stay if their flock is very big, and there are only two of them here." She glanced around as if another few owls would come swooping in.

"I'm not sure how long they've been here," she said. "They could have bones and such inside the burrow." She sighed and looked over to Dawson, then quickly rebounded her attention to Duke. "We really don't need to do much but make sure this habitat doesn't get disturbed. I can bring out some fencing and mark it off properly, and then you can keep doing what you do out here."

Her stomach vibrated a little bit at what she needed to say next. She wished she'd brought a bottle of water with her, as the sun beat overhead, and talking to these two men had left her mouth dry. "You'll have to be more conservative during breeding season, as loud machinery and whatnot can disturb that."

"When's breeding season?" Dawson asked.

"Starts about March," Caroline said, glancing over to him. "Runs through the summer months. We find a lot of owls move on after their chicks are raised."

"You're talking almost a year," Duke said. "Of us tiptoeing around these owls."

Caroline fixed him with her best law enforcement look. She'd had to take courses in law enforcement to become a Wildlife Conservation Officer, and she'd once been awarded a certificate for having the sharpest glare. "Yes, Mister Rhinehart," she said. "That's right.

These owls are protected by the State of Texas, and—"

"I know," Duke said, cutting her off. He held up one hand. "I'm sorry. It's not you I'm upset with." He looked over to the little brown owls with the bright yellow eyes. "Like my father says, if it's not one thing, it's another."

Duke looked over to Dawson. "You're in charge of this. Brandon, Kevin, and I will stay away from whatever gets marked off out here."

"Yes, sir," Dawson said, and Caroline wasn't sure why those words and his acquiescence to his brother made her heartbeat quiver, only that they did.

"Okay, well, I have to keep checking this fence. We've got predators coming onto the ranch somewhere, and I'm determined to find the break in the line today." With that he walked away, leaving Caroline with a very silent and very straight-faced Dawson.

She wanted to say something to cheer him up, but she didn't know what. She wanted him to smile at her and act like he'd had a good time at breakfast. She wanted him to *see* her.

No, she *needed* him to see her and respond to her.

She hadn't had that in her previous relationship, and she would not allow another man to look through her, ignore her birthdays, forget their anniversary, none of it. She would not make herself smaller to spare his feelings. She would not make her own special dinners.

She blinked, and the sun shining in her eyes reminded her she no longer lived in the Hill Country, married to a man who barely seemed to know she existed.

If she was going to start something with Dawson that went beyond unanswered emails and bickering, she simply wouldn't tolerate him falling silent and shutting down. She also couldn't believe she'd actually thought about starting something with Dawson—it was amazing what a good, home-cooked meal could do to a woman.

So you'll tell him if the time comes, she thought as he nodded back the way they'd come. "Should we go?"

"Yes." Her voice came out craggly and

rusty, and she cleared it, so she could speak in a stronger, more authoritative voice. After all, she was not going to fold herself into a box to make anyone else feel good about themselves. Not again. Never again.

"Yes, let's go." As she walked back to the truck with Dawson and his dog, she wondered if he'd ever ask her to do that, and she started praying that he wouldn't. Because she found herself interested in getting to know him and perhaps even becoming friends with him—and more than friends? —and that couldn't happen if he couldn't handle her coming back at him every once in a while.

Or if he never asked her out.

* * *

"Left here," she said, and Dawson dutifully flipped on his turn signal.

"You live in Crescent," he said.

"I what?" Caroline's heart beat strangely in her chest the closer to her house Dawson drove. She wasn't sure why, other than once he'd dropped her off here, he'd know where she lived.

Which was fine. She now knew where he lived.

He looked over to her, and it seemed several things had shifted by the simple act of driving out to the West End Fence and seeing all the animals there, even the ones that weren't threatened.

"You live in the Crescent neighborhood," he said. "See, all the old neighborhoods in Three Rivers, before the town started getting bigger, have names."

"I didn't know that."

"We have some great history in Three Rivers," he said, but he didn't offer anything else. He didn't volunteer to be her tour guide and then take her to dinner.

Just the fact that she wanted him to do that made a pinch of unrest settle between her ribs. Something foamed between her and Dawson, and he'd have to be a robot not to feel it. *Surely* he'd felt the electric buzz when he'd held her hand, even if it was only to steady her as she stood after loving on his dog.

In fact, he didn't say another thing until she said, "It's that red brick one on the left," to which he murmured, "Okay."

A few seconds later, he turned into her driveway and parked behind her SUV, which meant Belle and Judy were back from the fundraising breakfast. Of course they were. Caroline had been gone for hours.

She exhaled as she turned toward him, nothing to collect and take with her. No purse. No keys. Just her phone and herself. "Thanks for breakfast, Dawson." His older brother called him "Daws," but Caroline wasn't going to do that. "You make the hash browns just how I like them." She gave him a tentative smile she hoped would earn her a real date with this man, but he simply nodded in a very grumpy cowboy way, no twitching upward movement of his lips at all.

She wasn't sure if he was going to say anything, so she turned and opened her door. She used the runner on his tall truck to guide her feet to the ground and added, "See ya," as she hurried to close the door.

She turned and walked up the sidewalk, cursing herself and pressing her eyes closed for a step or two as the words *See ya* ran through her head.

Caroline scoffed. "See ya? Who says that?" She wasn't twelve and making a left on her bike while her friend went right after a lazy morning of fishing.

The curtains fluttered, which meant Belle had spotted her already, and Caroline would have to tell the whole story of that morning. She wished she had a more exciting ending— like a dinner date with Dawson tomorrow night —but at least the morning hadn't been a disaster.

Chapter Five

Dawson sat there and watched Caroline walk away from him. She had to be adding an extra sway to her step, because she hadn't walked like that as they'd gone toward the owls. Or maybe she just walked in this sexy way when she had perfectly even ground beneath her feet.

Either way, she was dangerously close to being swallowed by her house, and Dawson wouldn't see her anymore. Panic darted through him, because he didn't know when he'd see her again at all.

Without thinking, he jumped out of the truck, calling, "Caroline?"

She turned back to him as he rounded the hood of the truck in a jog, and he chastised himself. He didn't need to be an overeager puppy, or like Rocks, showing up with something shiny every time she left the house.

"Yeah?"

Dawson's hands felt like bricks attached to the end of his arms. His throat had turned to dust, and he coughed to clear the way for the words he wanted to say. "Uh, I was wondering...what are the next steps for the owl thing?"

She came toward him a couple of steps and stopped, once again becoming an angel in the midday light. "I already emailed you the paperwork. I'd look over that, and I'll bring out the fencing supplies and other things you need to protect the area."

She'd said all of this already, and Dawson hadn't been too blinded by rage to not hear her. He nodded and looked away. "That wasn't really what I was wondering."

She cocked her hip and then her head in

the opposite direction, making her body into a slight S he found so attractive. "What are you wondering?"

"How busy are the owls making you?" He shifted his feet and focused on her again, trying to push down his nerves. He'd asked out women before, and he told himself he could do it again. "Maybe if you're not too busy with the owls or your sister moving in." He gestured toward the house, which sat in the mid-day silence. "We could go to dinner sometime."

Sometime was not good enough for him, but he didn't want to push for tomorrow or anything.

Caroline watched him, those pretty pink lips turning up into a smile. She laughed and ducked her head, and when she raised it again, she said, "All right."

Dawson's own grin finally burst onto his face. "All right."

She moved over to him, something stern entering her expression. "I have one condition."

The smile slid right off his face. "You do?"

"Yes, sirree, and I'm afraid it's a deal-breaker."

She could flirt all right, and something in Dawson's chest warmed that she was flirting with him again. "Lay it on me then."

"You have to smile when we go out," she said. "You can't act like you want to be back home by yourself or that you might blow up if they don't have the soda you like, or that you want to stab my cat when you drop me off."

He raised his eyebrows. "I would never harm a cat." He rolled his shoulders as she cocked her eyebrows at him, clearly challenging him on the rest. "I mean, they're not dogs, but I still wouldn't hurt one."

He quirked up one side of his mouth, the other following quickly. "I'll smile."

"Thank you," she said. "I mean, if you aren't happy to be with me, you don't have to, but otherwise, I'd like a sign that you want to be with me."

"Yes, ma'am." He tucked his hands in his pockets so he wouldn't grab onto her. "Should I text you for your schedule?"

"What about tomorrow night?" she asked. "I'm still not working until Monday, so I'm free."

Dawson nodded, wondering what it would be like to have a job with real vacation days. "Tomorrow night, then. Six? Seven?" He hated his tongue and vocal cords then, because he kept saying too much.

Caroline smiled at him again, this time putting her palm flat against his breastbone. "Six would be great. Is that enough time for you to get here?"

"I'll be here," he promised, already sifting through ideas for their first real date. Based on what he knew about Caroline, she liked eating out and specific foods were very important to her. Dawson hadn't spent a lot of time dating, but he had friends, and he could text Finn, Alex, and Link to get some ideas.

He nodded again, forgot to smile, and headed back to the truck. "See ya tomorrow," he said, almost imitating her when she'd gotten out of the truck.

He buckled in and looked at her, and still

she stood there watching him, a somewhat incredulous look on her face. Or maybe that was annoyance. "Something not good," he muttered.

He left before she could break their date, though surely she could do that with a text any time between now and six p.m. tomorrow night.

"Lord, I've had a bad enough day already, okay?" he prayed. "She doesn't need to cancel the date and make it worse."

* * *

"Uncle Dawson!" The front door burst open with all the energy of a seven-year-old boy. "I lost a tooth! Uncle Dawson, look at my tooth!"

Dawson sat at the kitchen table with his brother, and they both looked over to Dallas, Duke and Arizona's youngest boy.

Two dogs came into the cabin next, followed by Dwayne, then April, and then Shiloh. The girls carried plates in their hands, and that only meant one thing: cookies.

"Has your mom been baking today?" Brandon asked, already on his feet to receive the nieces and nephews.

"Yep," Shiloh said as she reached the counter and slid the plate of cookies onto it.

"Uncle Dawson, look." Dallas arrived in front of him, pressing in so close, Dawson had to back up to see him properly. He pulled down his lip to show Dawson the gap in his teeth, and then he held up the lost tooth.

"Holy hole in your mouth," Dawson said, his smile in full force whenever the kids came over. "What are you gonna do now? You won't be able to eat those chocolate chip cookies your momma made."

"I will too." Dallas grinned at Dawson. "I had two of 'em this morning."

"What are you gonna do with that tooth?" Dawson asked, glancing up as April put a couple of cookies in front of him. "Thanks, missy."

She grinned at him, and Dawson's heart expanded with love. April was Duke and Zona's second child, and she had a wild streak that probably stemmed from both of them. It gave her parents fits sometimes, and she'd come to work with Dawson on the ranch anytime any of them needed a break.

She flirted with a lot of boys, which worried her parents, and she hated homework, reading, and doing anything her momma and daddy asked her to do. Dawson hadn't been old enough to understand why Duke had left the ranch for over fifteen years, but he knew his half-brother had run into some trouble—the kind that had driven him from town, from his family, for years.

Zona could be all smile or all thorns, so it wasn't all that surprising that the two of them had a daughter with all the same qualities as they did.

She pulled out the chair beside him and sat down. "Can I go out and see the owls with you?"

"In the morning," he said. "After my run, I'll stop by and knock, and by the time I'm ready, if you're here, you can."

She nodded and bent down to pat Ruffin

while Brandon exclaimed over the lost tooth and what the Tooth Fairy might bring for Dallas that night.

"Can I take Ruffin out to throw the Frisbee?" April asked.

"Of course." Dawson got up with her, took his cookies, and followed her back to the front porch. She collected the Frisbee from the mat beside the front door, and Dawson moved over to the small table where he kept his pocketknife and whittling wood.

Since it was a holiday, they'd done their skeleton chores and nothing more, and his hands itched to get a really beautiful piece of wood and shape it into something special. But he had texts to send, and Dawson was nothing if not dutiful.

So while April laughed and praised Ruffin every time he caught the Frisbee and brought it back, Dawson tapped out the news that they'd found the threatened burrowing owls on the ranch.

Lincoln Glover lived just north of the Rhinehart Ranch, and he'd become the junior foreman on his family's much larger piece of land earlier this year. Finley Ackerman had a one-man operation north of Three Rivers, and Alex Baxter's place sat the furthest from where Dawson and the blasted owls lived.

You've got to be kidding, Link sent back almost instantly. *I'm coming down there in the morning. Whereabouts are they?*

West side, Dawson told him as a couple of messages came in from Finn and then Alex.

Unbelievable, Finn said. *I guess I'll have to really keep my eyes out now.*

What do you have to do? Alex asked.

The owls had been sighted at a couple of other ranches, but further south, not anywhere near Three Rivers. Until now. So it wasn't surprising that no one in his friend group really knew much about them.

Perhaps Duke would have more experience and wisdom, and the men he worked with and collaborated with might know a lot more too. They'd been farming and ranching in the Texas Panhandle for a lot longer than Dawson, but as the rising generation, he had to learn what they already knew.

He spent the next several minutes telling them what he had to do, including the paperwork from Caroline, and the fact that she was bringing "supplies" to the ranch tomorrow to basically keep them away from the owls so they could have their habitat.

I'll send pictures, he said. *Maybe it won't be so bad.*

My daddy isn't going to like it no matter what, Link said.

Dawson smiled, because no, Bear Glover would not like the owls encroaching on his land. *And the west side?* he sent, chuckling now. *Can you imagine if Cactus finds those owls first?*

Link sent a long string of laughter, though annoying Cactus Glover was not an activity any of them would do willingly.

April's boots thunked against the porch as she came toward him, and she looked as sweaty as Ruffin. If dogs could sweat. "I let him in to get a drink." She sighed as she sat down at the only other seat at the table.

Dawson flipped his phone over and set it on the table next to his pocketknife. He watched April for a moment, and she reached up and finger-combed her hair back into a ponytail. She used a tie from around her wrist to secure it and looked over to him.

He cocked his eyebrows, and she rolled her eyes.

"Oh, so it's something," he said.

April heaved the biggest sigh ever heaved by a human being on the planet earth. Dawson worked hard not to chuckle, because he could only imagine Duke's reaction to his daughter. He ducked his head and focused on keeping his expression as neutral as possible. If she sensed any danger at all, she'd shut down. Rather, she'd stomp away in a fit, and Dawson wanted to be a safe place for her.

He knew what it was like to have nowhere to go, no one to turn to, and parents who meant well but simply didn't understand. In his eyes, at least.

"Momma says if I don't get my stupid grade up in algebra, I can't go to the Valentine's dance."

"Mm."

"It's really stupid. No one uses algebra."

Dawson was sure some people did, but he didn't say so. Someone like April? No, she probably wasn't ever going to use algebra. She wanted to herd cattle and wrestle goats out of the mud when the rain turned torrential and they needed help.

She'd gotten her love of the saddle, of horses, of dogs, of ranching, from both of her parents too. Her older sister, Shiloh, definitely had more feminine qualities, though she could saddle a horse and get a job done around the ranch too.

"What're you at now?" he asked.

"A C-minus," she muttered.

"And where does your momma want you?"

"B-minus."

Dawson didn't want to say that seemed fair, though it did. "Is that even possible to do before the dance?"

"I have to get it up before the end of January." She sighed. "Or she won't take me to buy a dress." She looked over to Dawson. "They're dumb anyway. Dresses."

He gave her a smile she didn't return. All at once, he knew why Caroline wanted him to smile when they were together. "Are you going to ask Aurora to make you something?"

"I think I could slay in a denim jumpsuit," she said.

Dawson laughed, straightening his back and letting himself relax into the conversation. "I'm sure you could, sweetheart." He got a grin from her this time. "Sounds like you better get your grade up to a B-minus."

"I can do it," she said with another sigh, this one not as pathetic and irritated as her previous one. "I have a test in a couple of weeks that'll do it."

"Do you need to come study with me in the office?"

"Maybe," she hedged.

"You could have your Valentine's dance date do it," Dawson suggested, trying to keep his voice casual. He was really asking her who she was going with, for he might agree with Zona about getting her grade up.

"Yeah, that would be a hard pass," April said. "Rusty is like, a genius. The last thing I need him thinkin' is that I'm stupid."

"Well, he could never think that," Dawson said. "Because it's not true." He gave April a pointed look, and she ducked her head.

"Okay, Uncle Dawson."

"Do you need to do the journaling? Or should we just talk through it?"

April didn't answer right away, and Dawson wouldn't let this go. Mental health was extremely important to him, as he dealt with some of his own issues. Even now, his fingers twitched to be doing something, and he forced them together to still them.

"I'm okay," she said finally.

"You sure?"

"Yes, sir." She took a big breath. "I can get my grades up, and Rory's gonna make me a denim pantsuit that is going to blow Rusty's mind." She grinned at Dawson. "Not that it matters. He's just a friend."

"Mm hm," Dawson said. "In his eyes? Or yours? Or for your momma and daddy?"

April's face colored quickly, which happened when she got angry or embarrassed, and the hint of Zona's redheaded genes betrayed her every time.

Dawson laughed and held up his hand. "I don't want to know."

"She just doesn't like him because he's sixteen already."

"Well, that is a fair bit older than you."

"Daddy is like, a million years older than Momma," she said bitterly.

"Yeah, and they met when your momma was in her thirties," Dawson fired back. "And they dated forever. Totally different, missy."

She said nothing, which was her way of admitting that what Dawson had said was right. He didn't need to rub it in her face, so he stayed silent too.

"I have a date tomorrow night," he said, clearing his throat as his niece swung her attention his way. "Maybe you could tell me a hip place to go."

She grinned and grinned. "Uncle Dawson, don't say 'hip.' You're too old."

"Ouch." He laughed, glad the mood had lightened. "She really likes potatoes in all their varieties. Seemed interested in a bit of Three Rivers history."

April was all-in now, as she did like hanging out in town. In fact, she'd complained more than once about how far away the ranch sat from where everything happened. "What are you thinking, Uncle Dawson?"

"I don't know, missy. That's why I asked you."

"I don't think the bowling alley or Wilde & Organic are for you."

"Wilde & Organic?"

"It's fun to walk around and find something to eat, then go back to someone's house and chill, watch movies, all that."

"Chill," he said, not even sure what that word meant. Asking his fourteen-year-old niece for dating help had been a very bad idea. He wanted that warm feeling in his chest while Caroline flirted with him, and he wanted that foamy, fizzy feeling flowing through his fingers once again when his hand touched hers.

So while they sat there in the evening stillness, only Ruffin panting at his feet to puncture the silence hanging in the air, Dawson prayed.

He figured if April couldn't help him on his first date with Caroline, the Lord could.

Chapter Six

Caroline hated the way the scratchy fabric of her shorts rubbed on her legs. She hated that she was even wearing her uniform today, but she was acting on official business this morning as she had to go into the office to get the supplies she needed to take to Hidden Hills Ranch.

In the kitchen, she still stumbled slightly when she saw Judy sitting there, a poured bowl of cereal in front of her, reading the back of the box. Pure nostalgia hit her, as Caroline had once spent her carefree childhood mornings doing the same thing. Except she'd had siblings, and Judy was an only-child.

"Morning, munchkin," Caroline said as she started making coffee. "Is your mom up yet?"

"Nope." Judy's skinny legs swung over the front of the chair. "Can you get more of this cookie cereal?" She bumped the box with her spoon. "This is almost gone."

Caroline looked over to her, so many things streaming through her. "Sure, baby. I can get some after I get done on this ranch I have to go to this morning."

"Thanks, Aunt Carol."

She smiled as she measured grounds and set the coffee to brew. Part of her wanted to march down the hall and get Belle out of bed. Her daughter needed her, and Caroline did have to go to work for a little bit this morning. *Perhaps Judy could come*, she thought but didn't say.

Her day wasn't mapped out or anything, and she wasn't meant to be in the office today at all. A quick check of her work email on her phone showed that Dawson had not filled out his paperwork and submitted it overnight, and she'd have been surprised if he had.

Still, a sting struck her in the bottom of her lungs. Ignoring it, she set about making a piece of toast to go with her coffee. Maybe, if she was lucky, she could get the supplies from the office and get up to Hidden Hills, get the fence built, and be done before lunch.

She loved eating out, and she didn't mind having lunch on her own. Then, she could come back here and see if Belle was going to get dressed today or not. "Maybe we can go to the petting zoo today," she said to Judy. "Do you think your mom would like that?"

"Yes," Judy said instantly. "Yes, she loves petting zoos." She appeared at Caroline's side. "I'll get her up and we can go."

"Oh, honey, it'll be later this afternoon. I have to go into work this morning."

Judy's face fell, and Caroline wondered if having Belle and Judy here was really the best thing for them. Her stomach pinched with worry, because she didn't know what to do. When Belle had called and said she and Judy were leaving Phoenix and they needed a place to stay, Caroline hadn't even thought about it. She'd simply said yes.

"Baby." Caroline bent down to be on the child's level. "It's just a couple of hours this morning. Then we'll get some lunch and go to the petting zoo." She watched her solo lunch disappear from her day in a poof, and she told herself family was worth it. Because they were.

The scent of coffee started to perfume the air, and Caroline pressed a kiss to the middle of Judy's forehead and then got down a mug for her coffee. "I'll go check on your mom." She glanced over to the table. "You're done eating?"

"Yes."

"Clean up your dishes then." Caroline gave her a quick look, and Judy went to do what she'd been asked. Caroline sighed and headed back down the hallway she'd already come down. Gondola came out of her bedroom and meowed, and Caroline smiled at the feline. "I'll get your breakfast in a minute."

She paused outside the door of Belle's room, leaning in to listen for any signs of life.

Hearing nothing, she knocked lightly and then pushed open the door. Belle lay in bed, her curtains drawn closed with only a sliver of the morning light trying to penetrate the darkness.

"Belle." Caroline stepped toward her with light feet, wishing she could just let her older sister sleep until the pain of her fresh divorce disappeared. But Caroline knew from personal experience that she couldn't.

A person had to live through that pain, learning how to manage it, how to deal with it when it snuck up behind them, and how to cope on really bad days. Caroline still had moments of extreme self-doubt and then pure preservation, making vows to never date or marry again.

She thought of Dawson and those pretty aquamarine eyes. She gently stroked Belle's hair off her forehead and said, "Hey, Belle. I have to go to work soon."

Her sister stirred, and then her eyes opened blearily. "You have to go to work today?"

"Just for a couple of hours," she said. She knelt down on the floor and gazed at her sister.

Such love filled her. "Judy can just watch TV. I just wanted you to know she's eaten breakfast, and I'm headed out in the next ten minutes or so."

"I'll get up," Belle said.

"There's some of that cinnamon chip bread," she said. "For toast."

Belle smiled, and that made Caroline's heart lift. Still, so much worry weighed her down, and she stroked her hand along her sister's hairline again. "What do you need today?"

Belle's eyes drifted closed again. "Nothing. I'm okay."

"Look through some of the menus for anything on the south side of town, and text me what you and Judy want for lunch. I'll get it and bring it back."

"Okay."

Caroline got to her feet, wishing God would ease this pain from her sister. She didn't understand why the world had to have so many problems at all. Couldn't the Lord erase the evil from the world?

She knew He could, but standing there in

her sister's dim bedroom, she also knew He wouldn't. No one could learn in a perfectly peaceful environment, and God needed her—and Belle—to exercise their faith and grow into the women He wanted them to be.

"Belle," she said, the confession about her date with Dawson that night about to spill from her. But she didn't know how to tell her. Would Belle be happy for her or disgusted and hurt?

She swallowed and said, "Coffee's ready," instead of telling her about her evening plans.

By the time she made the turn onto Dawson's ranch, her sister had texted to say she was up and showered, and she'd have Judy ready for their lunch and afternoon outing to the petting zoo. The wind blew across her SUV, shaking it enough to push her around a little bit, and Caroline gripped the steering wheel as she went up the slight incline and onto the ranch.

Duke's house sat out front, and this morning, a few kids were working in the yard while a woman sat on the front steps with a cup of coffee in her hand. She watched as Caroline drove by, and she'd never felt more scrutinized in her life.

She also couldn't remember her name, so Caroline simply kept going. She didn't need to stop by Dawson's cabin, because she'd texted him when she'd left the office with the supplies, and he'd said he'd be out on the West End Fence to help her erect the protections.

The wind continued to bully her as she drove past Dawson's cabin and onto the narrower road. She made the same turns Dawson had yesterday, and after she made the last one, she found his truck there, along with a pretty horse the color of ripe peaches. Semi-orange, semi-brown, semi-glossy.

"He's beautiful," she said to herself. He also didn't have a rider, but spoke to the fact that Caroline wouldn't find Dawson alone out here.

Sure enough, he and another man started approaching Caroline before she'd even come to a complete stop. The other cowboy stood a couple of inches taller than Dawson and had blonde hair peeking out from under his dark cowboy hat.

She got out of the SUV and nearly got blown right back in. Both cowboys pressed their palms to their heads to keep their hats on, and Caroline's hair whipped around until she could gather it all into one fist.

"Wow," she yelled above the wind. "This is insane." The air died on her last word, leaving her shouting into near stillness. Of course. Just her luck.

Thankfully, Dawson smiled at her and said, "Good morning."

"Morning." She glanced over to the other cowboy, who had two dogs orbiting him like satellites. "Hello." She stuck out her hand. "I'm Caroline Thompson."

"This is Lincoln Glover," Dawson said. "He wanted to come see what we're dealing with, as Shiloh Ridge is due north of here."

"Yes, Shiloh Ridge," she said, going into secretary mode. "You filed your paperwork a few months ago." She worked very hard not to look at Dawson, lest she wore any sort of accusation in her eyes. She gave Lincoln a clinical smile, which he returned in kind.

"Yes, ma'am," Lincoln said, his voice low and rumbly. "It's great to meet you. I think you originally sent paperwork to my uncle. Ward Glover?"

"That sounds about right," Caroline said. "I believe someone else too. Y'all have a couple of foremen at Shiloh Ridge, don't you?"

Lincoln grinned. "Three, ma'am. I'm the junior foreman." He shot a glance at Dawson. "Recently."

Dawson smiled at him and clapped his friend on the back. "Link helps steer a tight ship."

Lincoln shook his head, but his smile sat right there on his face. "I'm planning to ride our west side today and see where we are." He glanced over to Dawson and then back to her, an expression on his face she couldn't quite read as his smile faded. "I'm taking my prickliest uncle, so that should be fun."

Caroline didn't know any of the Glovers at Shiloh Ridge Ranch, so she couldn't speak to the fun-ness of Lincoln's upcoming task. She met Dawson's eyes again. "How are they looking this morning?" she asked, hugging herself.

"There are eight that I can see," Dawson said, his growly voice striking all kinds of chords inside her. They vibrated and hummed into a beautiful harmony, and heat rose past Caroline's lungs, tickling them as it eased into her throat.

"More than yesterday."

"Four hundred percent more," he said, looking past her to her vehicle. "Let's get the supplies out and get this done before it starts raining."

"Is it supposed to rain today?" She looked up into the sky as if she hadn't seen it yet. Clouds filled it, but they didn't look like the thick, dense, heavy gray ones that would drop gallons of rain in only a few minutes.

"Later, yes," he said. "I've got other work to do outside, so I just need this done."

So he was going to be Grumpy Gus this morning. Fine. She could play that game for now. She opened the back of her SUV and let the cowboys gather the wood, fencing, and tools they might need.

Shivering, Caroline reached into the back seat to get her jacket, and she quickly thrust her arms into the sleeves as the wind picked up again. She could wield a hammer and nails, but the cowboys were ten times faster and more capable than her, and it didn't take long for her to instruct them to build a fence around them with a perimeter of fifteen feet so the owls could still come and go from their new dens.

"There," she said. "And now it's up to the owls to decide what they do." Satisfied, she looked over to Dawson. He had a smudge of dirt on his cheekbone, and he struck her as rugged and sexy as he pulled off his gloves. Lincoln did the same thing, and the two cowboys shook hands.

"I better call Uncle Cactus and get goin'," Lincoln said, glancing up into the sky. "This doesn't look good."

"At least it's not a dry summer, so the ground won't soak up the rain."

Caroline looked between them. "What's... what's that about?"

"A couple of summers ago, we got so much rain," Lincoln said.

"The whole town flooded," Dawson said, and she liked the two of them telling this story tandem. She smiled at them both, her eyebrows lifting up.

"It wasn't bad up here," Lincoln said. "We're a bit higher, and the river doesn't branch until down in town."

"So much of the town flooded," Dawson said. "And yeah, the ranches north and along all the branches where Three Rivers actually branches into three rivers."

"Remember Alex's place?" Lincoln looked at Dawson, the two of them clearly close. "Those sinkholes?"

"Unbelievable," Dawson said as he shook his head. He looked back at Caroline. "I know we seem like a small town where not much happens, but you stick around a while, and you'll see."

Caroline tucked her hands into her jacket

pockets. "See what?" She looked over to Lincoln. "Floods? Fires? Snow?"

"I reckon," Lincoln said. "All of the above." He swatted at Dawson's chest. "Remember the year we couldn't get off Shiloh Ridge, because the snow caused a landslide?"

"And the fire in the apartment complex that brought Misty up to your ranch."

Lincoln laughed, his blonde head tipping back. The wind decided to kick up again, and it stole his cowboy hat from him. That cut his laughter short, but it didn't stop it completely. Dawson took a step closer to her as Lincoln went to chase his hat.

"Misty is his fiancée. They got back together a bit ago after a fire in her apartment complex." He glanced over to Lincoln, clear admiration and brotherly love in his expression.

"So you have friends," she said.

He met her gaze again, and she wondered if he could see the teasing flirtatiousness she felt racing through her bloodstream. "Of course I have friends. Did you think I wouldn't?"

"I'm still getting the bigger picture of you," she admitted.

Lincoln returned and said, "Hey, call me if y'all want to double. I bet we could get Finn and Alex too." He glanced over to Caroline, something uncertain in his eyes now. "But maybe that's too many."

"It's fine," Dawson clipped out, finally tearing his eyes from Caroline's. "I'll call you, brother." He threw one arm around Lincoln and gave him a quick clap on the shoulder. "Tell your momma and daddy hello. That mess of cousins and aunts and uncles."

"Yep." Lincoln embraced Dawson the same way and pulled back. "And you come get that pot of soup, or I'm gonna have my aunt blowing up my phone all night."

"I'll come get it."

"I ain't got time to be fielding texts from Etta," he said sternly, but his blue eyes sparkled as if someone had plugged them in and set them on fire at the same time.

Dawson laughed this time and said, "I'm not going to pass up free food from literally the best cook y'all have at that ranch." He cut a look over to Caroline. "I'll come get it."

"Oh, don't let Bishop hear you say Etta's the best cook." Lincoln chuckled again and settled his hat on his head. "Ma'am." He nodded his way away from her, and Caroline actually turned and watched him walk back to where he'd tied his horse. He unlooped the reins, then swung into the saddle like he did it every hour.

He probably did.

"He didn't drive?" she wondered.

"The Glovers are a special breed of cowboy," Dawson murmured back. "Great men and women there." He took a big breath, which seemed to break the quiet moment.

She inhaled too and turned to face him. Every time she looked at him, she saw someone and something different. The man had close friends, and things he'd been through with them. He had a past. He had different moods, and laughter she'd never heard before. He had family she hadn't met, and suddenly, she couldn't wait to do that.

"You know those shoes you have by your front door?" she asked.

Dawson blinked a couple of times, clearly surprised. "I suppose."

"Who do they belong to?"

He backed up a step. "You want to know who the shoes by my front door belong to?"

"They were too small to be yours or Brandon's."

He cocked up the corners of his mouth, like he knew something she didn't. "You haven't met Brandon. Maybe he's real short, with small feet."

She blinked too, a vein of cold shock filling her for a moment. Then everything in her body warmed when she realized Dawson Rhinehart could make a joke. "Just tell me who the shoes belong to."

He chuckled and ducked his head as he shook it. She doubted he knew how adorable that was, but she felt real feelings streaming through her at the mere sight of him.

Dawson raised his head, something blazing

in those oceanic eyes. "Can we talk out of the wind? Maybe on the way back to the ranch? I really do have things to do today if I'm to be showered and on your doorstep by six."

"I said—" She silenced when he reached out and brushed his fingertips along her cheek, finally giving true weight to his touch as he tucked a lock of her hair behind her ear.

"Six is just fine," he drawled.

She suspected he was saying more than that, but Caroline had gone numb and still at his touch. He nodded past her and said, "Let's go, Ruffin."

The dog went by her, and she let Dawson turn her back toward their vehicles. "I drove myself," she said dumbly.

"Can I hold your hand?" he murmured, but he didn't wait for her to say yes or no. He simply slid his gloves into his back pocket with one hand and with his other, he claimed her fingers with his own.

She pulled in a breath that another gust of wind thankfully stole the sound of, and somehow got her legs to start walking with him.

"I was thinking of doing a little sightseeing tonight," he said. "But we might have to raincheck that if it's raining."

"Sightseeing?"

"You seem interested in knowing some of the history of the town," he said, glancing over to her. "Unless I misread the situation completely. But—"

"No, you're right," she said, finally coming back to herself. "I wanted to be a history major in college, but I didn't want to teach."

"Is that all you can do?"

"No, but none of the job opportunities excited me."

"So you moved into wildlife management?"

"I don't like working at a desk."

Dawson didn't respond for a beat, and then he said, "I hate it too, and I think that might be the first thing we have in common."

Caroline scoffed, though her brain whirred through what else they might both like. "That's not true," she said. "We both like over-easy eggs."

He huffed out a couple beats of laughter.

"True." He exhaled and squeezed her hand. "I'll watch the weather, but it's not that fun to be out in the rain."

"Mm, no, it isn't." She watched the ground at her feet, existing in a state of excitement mingled with disbelief that she was holding someone's hand and talking about a date later that night. She'd never thought she'd be here again. In fact, she'd sworn not to put herself in this position again.

Her heartbeat throbbed painfully against her ribcage, her most vital organ feeling far too big for her chest. "So you'll watch the weather," she said as they reached the vehicles.

"Yeah," he said. "I'll watch the weather." He pulled open her door for her, and Caroline smiled shyly at him as she stepped past him and got behind the wheel. "See you at six, beautiful."

With that, he closed her door and moved over to his truck without a backward glance.

Caroline gripped the wheel with both hands and left the West End Fence ahead of

Dawson, her eyes straight forward but not seeing anything. "Dear Lord," she pray-moaned. "What am I doing? What am I going to tell Belle?"

Chapter Seven

Dawson glanced at the pair of tennis shoes as he went past them and into the cabin. They belonged to Dwayne, as the twelve-year-old could never find his shoes. Zona had simply started buying more pairs and leaving them wherever her son might go or be.

Therefore, Brandon and Dawson had some here; a couple of pairs waited at the homestead, and Dawson knew Zona had even put some in the back of every vehicle they owned.

He smiled to himself, because the soup pot he'd picked up from Etta Glover-Winters weighed a lot, and he didn't have the mental energy to smile, walk, and carry the soup toward the back counter. He made it, relief singing through the muscles in his arms and shoulders.

Brandon hadn't come in for lunch yet, and Dawson sighed as he took in the silence in their shared cabin. In that moment, something started clattering. It sounded like tires over rutted road, and it took Dawson a moment to realize what it was.

"Rain," he said, looking up at the ceiling. When he switched his gaze outside, he found the raindrops splashing angrily against the glass. "Great."

At least he wasn't outside, but Mother Nature had ruined his plans for that evening. "It's not the first time you've had to change things up last-minute," he muttered to himself and Ruffin. The dog looked up from his water bowl, decided Dawson wasn't talking to him, and went back to his drink.

He had modified his dates plenty of times in the past, but none of them had ever turned out all that well. His confidence level for this date already hovered near the bottom of the scale, and he desperately wanted to impress Caroline.

Why, he wasn't sure. And how? He had no idea.

The weather is making an outdoor walking tour of Main Street impossible, he sent to Finn. *Other ideas for me for tonight?*

Let me ask Henry.

Dawson looked up from his phone, trying to place Henry. *Your cousin?*

Yeah, and he dates a lot, Finn said. *Same age as Link. A year younger maybe. He'll know of something.*

I can text him. I think I have his number. Dawson started looking through his contacts while Finn texted back that he'd already asked Henry for something to do that night in the rain.

Dawson set down his phone and went to get down a couple of bowls. The front door banged open, and he dang near jumped out of his skin. "Bulls and broncos," he swore as he twisted and jumped away from the door at the same time.

"Whoo-ee," Brandon yelled. Or maybe he was just talking. He did everything louder than Dawson, that was for sure. "It is *coming down* out there." He brushed something off his shoulder that looked dangerously like hail, and with his adrenaline positively pumping through him, Dawson switched his gaze to the window.

Sure enough, he could *see* the rain more fully now, and the pounding on the roof intensified.

"You cooked?" Brandon didn't seem to care about the hail, but Dawson sure did. Hail ruined crops way more than rain did. Hail didn't seep right into the ground immediately. Hail meant the weather was more severe than one could tell from just looking at the flat, gray sky.

Hail could turn to snow. And while snow in the Texas Panhandle wasn't all that unheard of, it wasn't anything good either. Alerts would be sent out. Roads would get icy. More accidents. Heck, sometimes the over-anxious restaurant owners closed their doors for the safety of their employees.

"I didn't make the soup," Dawson said. "Etta did, and I went to pick it up."

"Even better," Brandon said, grinning his way into the kitchen. He lifted the lid and said, "Oh, boy. It's the tortellini kind. I love this stuff."

Dawson did too, but his phone had started chiming, one right after the other. Five, six, seven-eight-nine-ten times. The beeps crowded over the top of one another, and both he and Brandon looked at his device.

"That's not good," Brandon said. But he wasn't in charge of anything on the ranch, so he didn't have to carry that weight. Dawson did, but he tried to ignore it while he finished the task of getting down bowls and ladling up their lunch.

He couldn't avoid his phone when he sat down to eat, and he sighed as he pulled it toward him. The hail had softened back to rain that continued to lash out at the land.

"They've already issued a warning for the

river," he said, swiping those texts away. "Duke's sending along every text from the other ranch owners." Dawson frowned at his phone, wondering why his older brother was doing that. He never had before.

He tapped to call him, glancing over to Brandon. "I need to talk to Duke."

"Fine by me." Brandon had already eaten half his bowl of soup while Dawson hadn't taken a single bite yet.

"Hey, Daws."

"Hey," he said. "Why are you sending me all the ranch owner texts?"

Duke sighed, and Dawson didn't like the sound of that. He stared into the depths of his tortellini soup, trying to get that sigh to line up with texts he didn't normally get. Duke was a lot more like him than Brandon, in that he only said what was absolutely necessary and wore his inner grump on the outside. Such things must come from their daddy.

"Listen, Dawson," Duke said, and whenever he started a conversation with "Listen," it was something he didn't want to say. And something Dawson wouldn't really want to hear.

"Spit it out, Duke," he growled. "I'm at lunch, and I just want to eat in peace."

"I think it's time for you to take on some more responsibility for the ranch," Duke said. "I'm not going to be around forever, you know? I have four kids that need their dad, and you're more than capable."

Dawson didn't know what to say. Of all the times for this to come. Last week, he'd have welcomed it, for it would've given variety to his monotonous days. He'd work out a schedule where everything lined up just right.

But now? He didn't have time for this bomb to be dropped into his lap. He had a date with Caroline to deal with. A date with nothing to do.

"Are you still there?" Duke asked.

Dawson cleared his throat. "Yes," he said. "I'm here."

"What do you think?"

"What do you need me to do?" He glanced

over to Brandon, who looked at him with wide, blue eyes.

"I was thinking you'd handle things this winter, since the foreman and controller duties are less right now. And as they ramp up, we'll work on them together."

"I'm going to need your help in all seasons, Duke," Dawson said, his voice growing very quiet. "I—you know—you can't throw me to the wolves. I need to be walked through it at least once."

He hadn't spelled out everything for Duke, but he shouldn't have to. He knew about Dawson's challenges, and he'd always been kind and thoughtful with him, even when there'd been some resentment between them.

"Of course, brother," Duke said. "Maybe we can meet tonight to go over things like this."

"Emergencies."

"Right," Duke said. "Emergencies."

Dawson didn't want to say no, and Duke saved him from having to explain about his date by saying, "I'm getting a ton of texts. I'm going to forward them to you and then add you to the group text and let them know you'll be handling this for us."

"Duke."

"Don't worry, Daws. It's a lot of chatter about what's going on in various areas of town. If something happens up here, we report it. If it comes to organizing who needs help, we say we can come anytime. It's easy. This is something you can do."

Dawson took a deep breath, the knot in his throat starting to unravel. "Okay," he said, wondering how he was going to eat with so many nerves balled in his gut.

"And I'm right here if you need help." Duke wore a smile in his voice. "I hope you and Brandon are inside. Oh, you said you're at lunch, so you are."

"We are," he said.

"Come for dinner tonight," Duke said. "Zona and I will feed you like a king—if you can get here." He laughed and hung up before Dawson could protest.

Then he looked out the window. "If I can get there?" His brother and his family lived down the lane, around the corner, and past the homestead. All on dirt-gravel roads. Why wouldn't he be able to get there?

"Surely things aren't going to flood right now," he said as he got up and went to the window. His phone started going off in rapid succession again, which irritated Dawson to no end.

Outside, the rain continued to fall in a thick wave that blurred everything into something like an Impressionist painting. Or one of the watercolors of the ranch little Dallas had done as a four-year-old...that someone had poured even more water over.

"Come eat," Brandon said behind him, and Dawson turned away from the weather. He didn't see his phone sitting on the counter where he'd left it, and his younger brother nodded to the cooling bowl of soup. "The world isn't going to flood right now. Duke and the other ranch owners and controllers and foremen can wait."

"Where's my phone?"

"When you need it back, I'll give it to you."

Brandon used his spoon to push Dawson's bowl closer to him. "Now, eat."

Dawson picked up his own utensil and dipped it into the soup. No, it wasn't as hot as he'd like it, but it had a great tomato tang, with creamy cheese inside the tender pasta. His taste buds sighed into bliss, and the unrest about being separated from his device blipped at him but didn't shout.

He wanted to look up places to take Caroline for dinner that night, then reminded himself that he'd already chosen a restaurant. His heartbeat came to a sudden stop when he realized he'd agreed to meet Duke at dinnertime tonight.

"Brandon, I need my phone."

"You're not done eating yet," he said.

Dawson threw him the most murderous look he could muster on a half-full stomach. "It's not about the ranch."

"Then why do you need it?"

He couldn't see a way around telling Brandon about Caroline. He'd never really hidden any of his other dates or girlfriends, and he wasn't embarrassed. He'd already told his friends about her—not by name, though, and that felt intimate.

"I have a date tonight I need to rearrange," he said. "If you must know, Mister Nosy."

Brandon's expression turned to delight. "Who with?"

"I don't want to say. It's the first date, and I might not even get another one." Especially after this.

Brandon reached out and plucked the phone from the lazy Susan on the counter, where they kept salt and pepper shakers, napkins, a bottle of ketchup, and a basket for their keys and sunglasses.

"Do you really have a date?"

Dawson navigated to his text string with Caroline, his heart feeling like someone had filled it with wet cement and it was now drying and settling into the soles of his feet. "Not anymore," he said. "I'm going to cancel."

"Then just set up something else."

"Duke wants me to start doing more running of the ranch." Dawson rolled his head to stretch his neck. "I don't really know what that's going to do to my schedule."

"For the right woman, you'll blow up your schedule," Brandon said.

Dawson gaped at him, only a few words typed out to cancel the date with Caroline. "It's like you don't know me at all."

Brandon laughed, because he did know Dawson. "So you'll get out your pink sticky notes and you'll make arrangements to include whoever this is into your schedule."

"And what color will the new ranch duties be?" Dawson could see his sticky note board, and it was already full. "And the owls? I already had to add them." He went back to his phone and the few words he'd typed out.

"Caroline," Brandon said, and Dawson caught him with his neck craned to see the phone. He slapped his palm over the phone, but Brandon added, "Wildlife Officer."

Dawson looked at his brother, pure fire raging in his veins. "It's not—"

"You're dating the Wildlife Officer who made you stomp around like a raging gorilla?

The one who badgered you—your words—about the paperwork?"

Maybe he had used those words, and maybe he had paced in the cabin while ranting about her semi-abusive emails insisting he file the habitat paperwork. "She likes her hash browns a certain way," he said, which explained nothing.

He finished his text to her and sent it, hoping he'd get another chance with her. Instead of leaving it up to her or chance or God, he quickly sent her another text.

"Nice," Brandon said with pure appreciation in his voice, and Dawson slid his phone away a couple of inches.

"Can't be clearer than that, right?" Now he just had to wait for Caroline to respond. She seemed to have her phone surgically attached to her fingers, so it shouldn't take long. He prayed it wouldn't—and that her answer would be positive—while he nervously took another bite of soup.

Chapter Eight

Caroline kept stroking Judy's hair as she pressed her into her stomach. Belle hung on her arm, and Caroline wondered when she'd become the strong one. When people had started relying on her to know what to do and where to go.

They'd gone to lunch once she'd returned from the Rhinehart Ranch, and they'd barely finished before the sky had opened up. Since they'd gotten a seat in the garden, and it had a woven grass roof, they'd been able to weather the first ten or fifteen minutes.

Then the hail had started. That had forced

everyone to empty the outdoor tables, and now Caroline stood inside the restaurant, wondering how much longer it would pour like this. She'd seen others rushing by outside, and they were drenched to the skin. They'd parked down the street, and they'd all be soaked within two steps.

"It's going to let up soon," Caroline promised. A rumble of thunder decided right then was a good time to make its voice known, and she slowly closed her eyes. She needed more patience, but she didn't know where to find it.

She didn't mind standing at the window, looking outside, but she needed a jar of Biscoff spread and a spoon if she was going to do it for much longer. Crunchy Biscoff, not the smooth kind.

Her phone emitted a *bloopety-bloop* noise, and her heartbeat went wild. Dawson. Dawson had just texted her. Maybe he'd be in the area with a giant umbrella that would cover the whole block and everyone in this bistro could get where they needed to go without getting a single drop of water on them.

She tugged her phone out of her purse and angled it away from Belle, though her sister was engrossed in her own phone.

Hey, Caroline, I have some bad news. Not sure if you've seen the weather, but it's pouring, with some hail, and I've been summoned to an emergency meeting with my brother tonight, so I'm not going to be able to make our date work.

One big sentence, and she could only imagine the cowboy saying all of this in one breath. Literally, could only imagine it.

He'd texted again, right after that, and he'd said, *I don't want you thinking I don't want to see you. I do. Badly. So...I was thinking breakfast. My place. Tomorrow morning. Then I thought that was too cliché. Totally overdone. So now I'm thinking I can pencil you in for lunch, barring any other weather or brother emergencies. Let me know what you think.*

What she thought was that Dawson Rhinehart wanted to see her. Badly. She smiled, something like a soft sigh slipping from her lips. Then she let her fingers fly.

Too bad about tonight. But as luck would have it, I'm free all day tomorrow, what with it being Saturday and all.

She lowered her phone to her side, but she didn't put it away yet. She did press on the volume button on the side to get it to quiet, because Belle would eventually catch on that someone kept texting her. Someone with a specialized chime.

Her phone buzzed, and Caroline glanced down at it. *Great. At the risk of being that cowboy, I have to let you know I only get an hour for lunch.*

I'll bring something to your cabin, she typed out before she could think too hard about it. He wouldn't even be able to drive to her house and back in an hour. Then, feeling flirty and outside the boxes of what made her Caroline, she added, *You can't make your own schedule? Or take a longer lunch? It's the weekend.*

The ranch does not care what day of the week it is, Miss Thompson.

She giggled before she could stop herself, and Judy looked up at her. Caroline dropped the smile from her face, cleared her throat, and tucked her phone back into her purse.

"It's letting up a little," someone said, and she took that as her cue to leave. Then she wouldn't be able to look at her phone, even though it tempted her.

"Let's try to get home." She smiled down at her niece. "I don't think we'll be able to go to the petting zoo this afternoon."

Judy's face fell, but she hurried to look toward the window as another round of thunder rumbled through the sky.

"Belle," Caroline said, maybe a bit too harshly. But her sister had semi-disappeared into her device. When she looked up, her eyes contained a hazed layer that took a few moments to dissipate. "We need to go now."

"Okay." Belle moved with her just fine, but Caroline suspected that if she hadn't guided

Judy, Belle would've left her behind. Impatience and irritation threatened to kick their way up her throat, and then she reminded herself that Belle was only one month into a divorce that she hadn't wanted.

Caroline could be kind instead of snappy, and she took a deep breath as she followed someone out onto the sidewalk. The rain still drizzled, but she wouldn't have to drive home dripping all over her SUV. She wouldn't have to help Judy get out of her wet clothes—or Belle.

They made it to the SUV, and Caroline opened the back door for Judy with a "Up you go, little lady."

Her phone blooped again, and Caroline took a precious moment in the intensifying rain to silence it all the way. The last thing she needed was Belle noticing and offering to check it for her. Behind the wheel, she smiled over to her sister. "What should we do this afternoon now?"

"Hot chocolate," Judy said from the back seat. "Caramel popcorn. And a Barbie movie."

Caroline smiled at her niece, though the last thing she wanted to put on was a Barbie movie. Judy loved them, though, and she looked in the rearview mirror. "Do you want the mermaid one, or the princess one?"

"Mermaids!" Judy swung her legs that didn't quite reach the floor in the SUV, and Belle did smile over her shoulder to her daughter.

She leaned her head back against the rest and focused on Caroline. "I could make the caramel, and you can pour it over that rice cereal you love."

Caroline had just eaten plenty for lunch, but she did love her sweets. So she gave Belle a smile and said, "Absolutely."

Once home, Caroline got Judy and Belle inside, made sure Gondola had enough water, and left her sister to make the caramel-covered cereal. Then they'd all pile onto the couch, with the lights off, and put a movie on.

She didn't mind the simpleness of her life. In fact, it was something she'd desperately worked to achieve. A job she enjoyed and could do. A place to call home. A refuge. A sanctuary away from the storms her life had once been.

In the bathroom, where she'd barricaded herself so she could check her messages in private, she looked up and into her own eyes in the mirror. "If you're going to start dating Dawson, you have to woman-up and talk to Belle about it."

She breathed in, and her shoulders lifted. She'd been through a lot, and those shoulders had carried so much all on their own. She could carry her sister for a little bit too.

"Jesus will," she murmured. Jesus would carry them both when they needed it, Caroline knew that. She bowed her head and let herself just be for a few seconds. She just breathed, and appreciated that she still could. She let her mind think whatever it wanted. She pulled her shoulders back down as she exhaled, and the rest of her tight muscles followed suit.

And then, when she looked up, she prayed, "What's the right thing to do here?" She'd been divorced and rebuilding her life for five years, but Belle hadn't even made it five weeks yet. She still had a long road in front of her, and Caroline wanted to be there every step of the way.

Her phone fizzed in her palm, which indicated a text from Belle. Caroline switched her gaze to it, not sure what she'd find. *I'm not feeling like making anything,* Belle had said. *I can't stop crying, and I don't want Judy to see me like this. I don't want to do this. I can't keep living like this. I don't know how to do this.*

Caroline heard and felt the pure desperation, the pure agony, in her sister's texts. Tears touched her eyes, and Caroline didn't know how to console this hurt. She had no bandages for this kind of pain.

She had, however, experienced this exact torment, and she'd somehow made it through to the other side. *I know, my sweet sister. But you must.*

There was no other advice to give her. Caroline had experienced some very dark hours herself, and she'd hung on. She'd clung to certain truths that had somehow provided a pin-prick of light that had eventually grown brighter and brighter until she didn't feel so cold, so alone, so lost.

She left her bathroom and bedroom and went across the hall to Belle's bedroom, where her sister had already escaped. She sniffled and sobbed, and Caroline hurried to wrap her sister up in a tight hug. That had always helped her to feel like she wasn't about to splinter apart cell by cell.

"Hey," she soothed. She didn't say it was okay, because nothing was okay in Belle's world right now.

"I'm s-sorry," Belle said. "Everything reminds me of this beautiful thing I thought I had but didn't."

"I know, sissy. I know." Caroline stroked her sister's hair back off her cheek and forehead. "You take your time. I'll go spend the afternoon with Judy."

"She must be so sad too." Belle looked at her with a measure of hope in her expression. Hope Caroline didn't understand.

"I'll talk to her," she promised, finally deciding that perhaps Belle thought Judy wouldn't be sad that she didn't get to see her daddy anymore. But that wasn't rational or possible. Of course Judy—a real human being though she was only six years old—missed her daddy. She missed her friends in Phoenix. She'd been removed from the only life she'd ever known and brought to Three Rivers to live with her aunt.

She'd start at a new school next week. In a strange place. Everything unfamiliar.

Caroline had done the same thing when she'd left her marriage, and she'd done it all again when she'd taken this new position and had to come to Three Rivers.

She stayed with Belle for another minute or two, then carefully eased herself away from her sister, tucked her back into bed, and left the bedroom. As she walked, every step brought more strength to her mind.

Judy deserved someone to care for her, someone to see her and provide for her, and Caroline could do that while Belle grieved. As she moved into the living room, she didn't see her niece, and Judy hadn't camped out at the dining room table to color either.

Caroline called, "Judy?" and headed for the back door. She had a beautiful, fenced backyard that would've housed a dog so perfectly, and a pang of sadness hit her that she couldn't have the canine she wanted.

Although, with Judy and Belle here now, perhaps she could. The dog wouldn't be home alone all day with her sister here.

"Jude?" Caroline moved across the back deck and found Judy on the swing set that had come with the house and yard. "It's going to rain again, sweetheart. You can't stay out here for long." She looked up into the sky, with its angry gray clouds and the threat of more rain and hail and maybe worse.

"Okay," Judy called, seemingly unconcerned about another round of rain showers.

Caroline wrapped her arms around herself though she wore a pink sweater with a fox on the left side. She wanted to call Judy in right now, because she didn't want to stand on the back deck. "It's not about you," she muttered as she turned and went back inside. She also didn't have to stand outside and wait for Judy. The girl knew how to come back inside.

She put together the caramel popcorn, only reserving a bit of the sticky mixture to pour over her preferred crunchy treat—Rice Chex. Judy liked popcorn better, and Caroline settled her in front of the TV with the snack and the Barbie mermaid movie.

She didn't have to watch that either, but she did. She made dinner and fed Judy, neither of them seeing nor hearing from Belle again. Caroline stewed and stewed and stewed over Dawson, suddenly glad their date that evening had been canceled.

There was no way she could leave Judy with Belle tonight, and she had no words to tell her sister she was going to start dating again.

She took food to Belle, who didn't stir when she entered the bedroom, and she left the plate on her sister's nightstand. She fed Gondola and got Judy in the tub. She towel-dried the girl's hair, wondering how different tonight had been than she'd anticipated this morning, and she left Judy to color and read for an hour.

"I'll be back to tuck you in," she promised, and then Caroline sighed a ginormous sigh as she went into the kitchen only she had once maintained alone. Now, evidence of the two extra people living here sat everywhere, and Caroline pushed against the need to clean up.

She succeeded, and instead, grabbed the crunchy Biscoff jar from the cupboard, grabbed a spoon, and moved to stand in front of the front window. Her neighbors had been nothing short of amazing, each of them bringing her something treasured over the months.

A jar of grape juice, made from the Concord grapes lovingly grown all spring and summer. A pineapple upside down cake—an entire cake—leftover from someone's wedding. A loaf of honey sourdough bread, delivered in a brown bag with heat seeping through it.

Porch lights had started to come on as darkness lingered only minutes away. "My favorite time of day," Caroline said to herself. She loved dusk and twilight as it led another day into rest.

She liked to think through her day and what she'd done, what she could be grateful for, and what she could do better with the following day. She loved that God gave her multiple chances at some things, and she never ended a day without kneeling down and thanking Him for His great blessings.

So lost in her thoughts of that day—and how bored she'd been without a date to look forward to and only animated movies to occupy her time—was she that she didn't notice anyone pulling into her driveway.

She did, however, see the man as he crossed in front of her line of sight. With startling recognition, she said, "Dawson?"

The doorbell rang before she could move to open the door and tell him not to touch it. He moved like a ninja, that cowboy.

She'd barely slid the spoon out of her mouth from her last bite of Biscoff when Belle said, "Caroline?" She flicked her eyes toward the door. "Who's here?"

Caroline spun toward her, then back to the door, her boring evening and quiet contemplation suddenly anything but those things. "It's just...." She nodded to the plate of food in her sister's hand. "Go eat your dinner. I'll just... take care of this."

With that, she side-stepped over to the door and opened it, Biscoff and all.

Chapter Nine

Dawson had the distinct thought that he should've brought flowers to show up unannounced at Caroline's house. His heartbeat bounced like a tightly coiled spring that had finally been released.

The door opened, and anticipation drove through him. Anticipation of seeing Caroline. Smiling with her. Chatting for a few minutes. He'd worn a jacket as the evenings could be cool in the winter, and he was willing to simply sit on the front steps and talk with her for as long as she could.

His fantasies dried right up when he

caught sight of the fiery irritation in Caroline's eyes. And if he'd missed that, he did not mistake the way she flew from the house, barely opening the door wide enough to squeeze out, as she hissed, "What are you doing here?"

Dawson backed up a step, all of his defenses lifting right back into position. He'd had walls in place when it came to Caroline, and he should've known better than to think a single breakfast and some filed paperwork would change things so drastically between them.

"I had to come to town for groceries," he said. "Thought I'd stop by and say hi for a few minutes." He glanced to what she held in her hands. Cookie butter.

His smile grew as he raised his eyes back to hers. He caught her looking at her post-dinner treat too, and she quickly concealed it behind her back. That only made Dawson chuckle—and Caroline to go, "Shh."

She glanced behind her to the closed door and then gestured—with a spoon, mind you—for him to go down the steps and get off the porch.

He did, because he wasn't sure what she'd do next with that spoon. "What's going on?"

"Nothing," she said as she followed him. "Not that way."

Irritation fired through Dawson. "I'll just go."

"No, we can sit over here." She spoke a bit softer, and Dawson turned back to her. She gestured for him to go back down the sidewalk and onto the lawn. "You're standing right in front of the window."

He looked up to it, didn't see anything alarming, and heaved a sigh that he let out in a slow, hissing stream as he moved back toward her. "It's not warm out here, darlin'."

Caroline didn't go back into the house to get anything, and she did wear a pretty pink sweater with a fox on the front. Perhaps she'd be warm enough, and Dawson started fantasizing about loaning her his jacket in one great show of chivalry.

Yeah, and then you'll be cold, he thought. But it might be worth it too.

She led him over to a bench, and when she

turned back to him, she didn't try to hide the Biscoff. He nodded to the jar. "Crunchy or creamy?"

"Crunchy," she said, lifting her chin as if she had to defend her choice of cookie butters.

"I like it on graham crackers," he said. "My niece turned me onto it. It's her favorite snack." He groaned as he settled onto one end of the bench and waited for Caroline to do the same on the other side.

She hesitated, and Dawson wondered what he was doing here. He should've called or texted first. Before he could offer to leave again, she sat down, but she didn't lean back the way he did. Oh, no. She perched nervously on the very front of the bench, refusing to look at him.

He suddenly didn't know what to say. He'd thought they'd have some light-hearted conversation about what she'd done that day with her family, and maybe she'd ask him about how things had gone at his brother's that night.

Something that wasn't tense silence.

"Do you like pasta?" she asked out of nowhere.

"Yes," he said simply.

She nodded a couple of times. "I was thinking I'd bring pasta tomorrow for lunch."

"You're still going to come?" He and Brandon had plenty of leftover soup, and while Dawson hadn't anticipated her canceling their date when he'd arrived, nothing had been as he'd expected it to be.

She looked over to him, her eyes wide. "I—yes. Why wouldn't I?"

"Maybe because you didn't invite me inside," he said, cocking his eyebrows to challenge her. "And you didn't want me standing in sight of the window. But out here is okay." He looked across the street, where they sat in plain view of the neighbors on all sides.

With his heart sinking to his stomach, he added, "So it seems to me that you want to hide me from Belle and Judy."

"No," Caroline bit out, and oh, he now knew that her bark was so much harsher than her bite.

"Let's go inside, then. It's cold out here."

She shivered even as she said, "I'm fine right here."

He scoffed, wondering what to do next. His attraction to her slithered through him, teasing him and taunting him in a maddening way. "Okay, well, how was your afternoon? You stopped texting."

"It was...."

He glanced over to her just as all the things she held tightly sagged away. "Miserable," she said with a sigh. "Boring. Long."

Dawson reached over as his own heart softened toward her. He took the spoon from her and tucked it under his leg before sliding his hand around hers and settling his fingers between hers. Ah, yes. This was nice, and the sparks and flames that ignited when his skin touched hers warded off the chill of the night.

"Belle is not in a good place," she whispered. "We went to lunch, but she disappeared into her room when we got home, and she'd just come out when you rang the doorbell."

"Mm."

"Her husband doesn't want to be married anymore. It's—well, you know what? It's really hard to be told you're not wanted. That the family you'd been building with another person isn't wanted."

Dawson moved closer to her by sliding along the bench, and he released her hand so he could lift his arm over her shoulders. "I can't even imagine."

"She's about five weeks out from when Chuck came home and told her. She's in a lot of turmoil."

"I bet."

Caroline fell silent, and Dawson wondered where she was driving him with this backstory of her sister's. He figured if he waited, she might just come out and say it. When she didn't, he squeezed her shoulder and brought her closer to his side.

"And? You don't want to go out with me because of that?"

"It might be very difficult for her," she whispered. "I don't know how to tell her."

Dawson's heart wailed, but he couldn't

argue with the situation. He had no idea what he'd do if he found himself in a similar spot.

Be patient, he thought, and he groaned again as he got to his feet. "Well, you know where I am and how to get in touch with me," he said quietly.

"Dawson, wait," she said as she hurried to stand too. She inched in close to him, then closer still. He could probably count the light freckles across the bridge of her nose then, and he slid his hand along the bottom hem of that pretty sweater to anchor himself so he didn't fall back or away.

"I'm waiting," he murmured.

Caroline ducked her head, eliminating any opportunity to kiss her. The clean, soapy scent of her hair hit him, and Dawson dang near fell down. *This woman*, he thought.

"I just need a couple of days to figure out how to talk to her. See if she has a good day or a good hour where I can mention it."

"I stole you away from a community event yesterday," he said. "What did you tell her?"

"That the sight of those potatoes made me

see red, and I had to go up to your ranch for the owls anyway, and you made me—us—breakfast."

Dawson ducked his head, positioning his mouth close to her ear as he laughed almost under his breath. "I don't think things went in exactly that order."

"No," she said breathlessly. "But sort of. It's a tiny white lie so as not to hurt her." She curled one hand around the back of his head, and oh, Dawson had not been touched like that in a long time.

He didn't want to move away from her, but everything inside him told him he better. She wasn't ready to start a relationship, and he could never do what Lincoln had done a couple of summers ago and date someone casually.

No, Dawson played for keeps, and he was dead serious about the things—and people—he chose to spend his time on.

So he backed up and cleared his throat. "I should go. It's dark and late, and I get up early to run."

"Of course you do," she said with plenty of whip in her voice.

He gave her another head-nod without truly meeting her eyes and stepped past her. "It was great to see you, Caroline." It took all of his willpower to force himself to walk away from her, their lunch date tomorrow canceled and nothing on the calendar for when he might see her again.

He made it several steps before Caroline's soft, pretty voice said, "'Bye, Dawson."

He lifted his hand in a wave over his shoulder and kept on going. Otherwise, he'd go back and do something he'd probably regret, though he'd never regretted a kiss with a woman. The last several he'd tried relationships with had been like kissing his sister, but he knew without a doubt his first kiss with Caroline would call down all the stars in the heavens.

The rain abated and didn't pick up again, which meant no one flooded. Dawson didn't have to field dozens upon dozens of texts and arrange schedules to go help out other ranches. No one was going to have to come up to the Rhinehart Ranch.

He did have to work through some mud and muck in the morning that put him behind, but that didn't matter, because he didn't have to be back to the cabin at any particular time. He didn't even want to go by himself, so despite his growling stomach, he texted Brandon to say he had work to do in his office, and he'd eat some snacks there.

I'll bring you a sandwich, Brandon said. *Give me a half-hour.*

"Right," Dawson grumbled to himself. "A half-hour." In Brandon-time, that meant an hour, and he was probably texting the new woman he'd met through his dating app. He liked talking to lots of different people, and Brandon's biggest problem was having too many chances to take someone to dinner.

His mood worsened as he tromped through the mud, not having seen his crows, to the chicken coops. Ruffin worked with him today, and Dawson did calm when he saw his chickens. The big rooster, Rusty, strutted toward him, and Dawson found a smile touching his mouth.

He loved the low warbling of the chickens, as they always seemed to be making noise in the purest way possible. A squabble broke out, and Dawson looked on as Lulu scattered away from some of the other hens.

They had a pecking order, for sure, and Dawson could only deal with the aftermath, and while he loved Lulu, none of the other hens did. It looked like she'd lost a few more feathers, and he clucked at Peach, Pearl, and Ruby. "You guys leave 'er alone," he said.

The hens clucked and looked at him with their beady eyes that clearly told him they thought they were right. He fed them, his last task before he could escape to the barn-office, and his boots and the bottom of his jeans weighed ten pounds more by the time he'd tromped through the mud to make sure they had what they needed.

He cleaned his boots on the boot scrubber he kept outside his office, deciding to take off his shoes once he got inside. "Can't do nothin' about the jeans," he grumbled, his mood worsening again.

He just needed to get inside and go through his checklist, see his sticky notes lined up, grab a snack and a drink, and calm down. Once that happened, Dawson could finish the day on a high note.

He pushed open the door and stepped up into the office just as someone called his name. His grouchiness flew off the charts as he turned to find Alex Baxter jogging toward him.

"What are you doin' here?" he called.

Alex lifted a paper grocery sack and said, "I'm here for our lunch." As he came closer, his grin grew larger. "You forgot, didn't you?" He chuckled and shook his head. "I knew you'd forget."

Dawson's heart pounded in his chest, because he had forgotten. And now he had at least four men to try to figure out how to feed, like, right now.

Chapter Ten

Finley Ackerman pulled up to Dawson Rhinehart's cabin, and he found another truck parked there, as well as two horses. That meant he, Paul, Henry, and Libby had arrived last.

"You sure it's okay that we all came?" Paul asked, peering at the front door.

"Sure," Finn said. "I texted Dawson when we left." And it took just over an hour and a half to make the drive from Three Rivers Ranch to the Rhinehart Ranch. North to south, across the town of Three Rivers.

"I brought enough of Momma's potato

salad to feed a small army," Libby said. "So I'm going in." She opened the door and dropped from the back passenger seat of Finn's truck.

"I have three dozen chocolate chip cookies," Henry said, grabbing the bag of them and leaving Finn to look at Paul. They didn't have any food up front with them, and Finn grinned.

"We have to go in too, whether we have food or not."

"All right," Paul drawled, and he sounded a lot like Finn's Uncle Pete. Paul was his son, so that made sense. He lived and worked at Three Rivers with his daddy and Finn's, in agriculture.

Finn got out of the truck, with Paul following suit. They went up the steps to the cabin, where Libby had already gained entrance. Lincoln Glover had brought his younger brother, Smiles, and they stood near the back of the house, in the kitchen.

Brandon Rhinehart laughed, but Dawson couldn't be seen. Alex wasn't here either, and Finn watched as the cowboys at the back of the cabin cheered as Libby put down a big bowl and Henry added the cookies to it.

Finn went into the kitchen too and clapped Brandon on the shoulder. "Hey," he said. "How are you guys up here? Survived the rain?"

"Better than some where the rivers are lower," Brandon said. "Dawson said there's a lot of mud out there, but I've been helpin' my momma this morning."

He had a long row of bread slices on the counter, with plenty of sliced meat and cheese nearby. Sandwiches. Perfect. Finn loved a good sandwich.

"Nicki made homemade potato chips," Alex said from behind Finn, and he turned to face his brother-in-law. He loved him like a brother, because he'd taken good care of Finn's wife before she'd been his wife, before he'd even returned to town.

And he still did, though he was married now and had a pretty woman to take care of as well.

"Yes," Link said, going to meet him. He

took the brown paper bag from him and added, "I love these things."

"She made some with the barbecue seasoning just for you," Alex said. "I left them in my truck. Figured you could grab them on your way home." He grinned at Lincoln. "I know you don't like to share."

"Not Nicki's homemade barbecue potato chips," he said.

Finn noticed Smiles, who was probably sixteen or seventeen, standing there, almost out of the way, smiling of course. He moved over to him and said, "Hey, bud. When does school start again?"

"Tuesday," Smiles said. "We're not muddy at Shiloh Ridge."

"Yeah, we didn't get much at Legacy either," Finn said. "I think Alex is pretty wet, though."

"I'm what?" Alex asked as he arrived in the kitchen. He looked between Finn and Smiles.

"Wet," Smiles said. "From the rain."

"Oh, yeah." Alex rolled his neck as if

stretching it. "Since the flood a couple of summers ago, whenever it rains, it's like the water doesn't know where to go but all over the place at Coyote Pass."

"We're havin' sandwiches for lunch?" Dawson seemed to growl the words, and he cocked his eyebrows at Brandon. His younger brother muttered something to him, and then turned to Libby to talk to her, his expression brightening as he continued to spread mayo on what looked like homemade bread.

Something didn't seem quite right there, and Alex said, "Pretty sure they forgot we were coming." He flashed a rare smile, and these lunches were about the only time Finn saw Alex show that thing. Well, he sure did have a special smile for Nicki too.

Dawson looked over to Finn, who lifted his chin to him. As his friend came closer, Finn said, "You look tired, Daws." He wrapped him up in a man-hug and stepped back, grinning.

Dawson didn't smile, but he did relax. "Been busy the past few days."

"The owls?" Finn asked.

Dawson sighed as Link turned his attention from his phone to the conversation. "Yeah, the owls, though I guess now that they're here, we just can't bother them."

"It's not like you have to take feed and water out to them," Link said.

Dawson cut him a look. "Nope. And the crops keep growing, I guess. We set up the fence. It's done."

"And how's Caroline?" Link asked, and Finn was glad he had so Finn wouldn't have to. Because Dawson wore a tsunami in his expression. Link possessed some bravery to even ask; Finn thought he'd wait until Dawson had something to eat before he'd ask about Caroline Thompson.

"She's...we're not going out." Dawson ducked his head and reached up to remove his cowboy hat. He turned to the pegs along the wall beside the back door, and Finn met Link's eyes while their friend's back was turned.

"I asked outright," Link muttered. "Someone pick up the ball."

Dawson faced them again, and Alex asked, "Why aren't you goin' out with her? She cancel on you?" He'd never shied away from hard things, that was for sure.

"You said she seemed excited."

Dawson nodded, more of his grumpy exterior melting away. Finn's heart hurt for Dawson, because he recognized his own yearning and unrealized dreams in his friend's eyes. Finn had everything he could possibly want right now, but that hadn't always been the case. He'd spent nights alone, wondering what he'd done wrong.

He'd been stood up before, several times in foreign countries. He took the bag of potato chips as it got passed to him, and he wasn't going to leave those behind. Nicki had a green thumb and some skills in the kitchen, and Finn loved going to his brother- and sister-in-law's farmhouse for dinner any time they invited him and Edith.

"Not exactly," Dawson finally said. "Duke and I had some business last night, so I actually canceled on her."

"Oh, well, that's easy, then," Link said. "You just ask her out again."

Dawson gave him a dark look and took a couple of steps over to the counter to help his brother slice tomatoes. "I went down to get groceries for my mama, and I stopped by her place."

"Good move," Finn said. "And?"

"She...." Dawson focused all of his attention on his culinary tasks, which wasn't a good sign. Finn caught Alex's eye, and they had a quick conversation. "Her sister just moved in with her," Dawson said. "And she's only a few weeks into a divorce, so Caroline is a little worried about how she'll take her dating."

"How her sister will feel?" Link asked.

"Yeah." Dawson nodded. "Yep. That's right. So, I didn't ask her out again. We don't have a date set up."

"She was going to bring lunch today," Brandon said, and all eyes flew to him.

"Brandon," Dawson growled.

"What? She was." He stepped back from

the counter and surveyed it. A smile came to his face. "But I guess she decided not to." He looked over to Dawson. "Why'd you say?"

Dawson's jaw jumped, and he turned with the serrated knife to put it in the sink. With his back turned, he said, "She didn't want to lie to her sister. Not even a little one." He faced the group, his face cleared of frowns and concern. "Can we not talk this to death? I swear, y'all are worse than my mama."

He cracked a grin, and Brandon chuckled, which further splintered the ice. Finn smiled, and Link did too.

"God's told me to be patient," Dawson said. "So I'm gonna do that."

"Good plan, brother," Finn said, holding out his fist for Dawson to bump.

He did, and then he looked at the food. "So, we forgot y'all were comin', but we've got sand-wiches, potato salad, homemade potato chips, and chocolate chip cookies."

"It's a feast!" Finn called, and the other cowboys—and Libby—nodded.

"Henry's good with women," Paul said. "He might have some advice."

Dawson nodded and said, "I'll listen to whatever."

"I have an idea," Libby said. "We can talk about it while we eat."

"I've got a thought too," Smiles said, and that again brought all the eyes to a single person. Smiles was probably a decade younger than anyone there. "I mean, I'm young, but I go out with a lot of girls."

Link grinned at his younger brother and slung his arm around him. "He sure does. Real humble about it too."

Smiles just grinned and grinned. "It's just an idea."

"Let's eat," Dawson said. "And then we can keep talking about maybe some un-intrusive ways for me to keep in touch with her."

Henry moved to his side, and said, "You don't want to keep in touch with her, brother. She's not your elderly aunt." He grinned at Dawson. "We'll find a way that she can't *wait* to see you again, can't *wait* to come up here and check on those blasted burrowing owls." He picked up a paper plate and added, "I'll pray, yeah? And we'll eat."

Finn smiled, because he knew Henry hadn't eaten breakfast and was likely starving. Dawson nodded, and they all bowed their head while Henry squished his eyes closed.

"Lord," he said, his voice not as polished at prayer as others Finn had heard. He knew his cousin hadn't always walked on the straight and narrow path, and that he'd wanted to strike out into the world in a big way. In his own way.

He'd left his family and the ranch where they'd grown up together the week after his high school graduation, and he'd only ever come back to stay for short visits.

"We're really grateful to have friends we can rely on. Friends we can talk to openly about things that matter to us, to our families, and to our farms and ranches. We're all young here, Lord, and we need Thy help."

Henry paused, and Finn let his words really sink into his soul. He did need God's help —they all did—and he felt the overwhelming warmth and power and zing of pure love. Pure brotherhood. Pure belonging.

"Help direct our feet to the paths we should be on. Help those of us without a significant other to keep improving ourselves to be ready for when we'll finally meet our better half. Guide those of in relationships to say and do the right things, even if it's not the thing someone else wants to hear."

He cleared his throat, and Finn had the distinct thought that he needed to spend more time with his cousin. Henry was finishing up his farrier training, and he had his apprenticeship left, and Finn could hire him to come check his horses. Alex could too, and Finn could make sure he happened to be at Coyote Pass when Henry did the job.

"Help us with our daddies, to know how to talk to them, to make our mommas proud, and to be there for anyone who needs us. Oh." He took a breath. "We're real glad Dawson and Brandon overbuy on sandwich meat and cheese, and we're real grateful they're hosting us for lunch today. Bless them and their ranch and then bless the food, and anyone else here who needs something specific. Amen."

He cleared his throat again and immediately started making a sandwich, even while the other "Amens" that had been uttered lifted up to the ceiling. Henry wouldn't look up, but Paul watched him, his gaze switching to Finn a few moments later while Alex and Libby took paper plates and got in line behind Henry.

Finn lifted his eyebrows, and Paul nodded, which meant they'd both noticed something in Henry. Finn might be able to bring it up easier, and he'd text Paul about it later.

Right now, his stomach growled, and he wanted a turkey sandwich with cheese, bacon, lettuce, and tomato. They started to chat and chuckle as they got their food, and Finn happened to end up between Dawson and Henry, one of the last to make it to the table with his food.

"All right," Dawson drawled into a lull in the conversation. "Anything anyone wants to tell us all?" He looked at Finn, as if he might announce something like Edith was going to have twins in April.

Even Alex looked at him, and Finn's face grew hot. "Uh, sure, I guess I have something."

"You do," Alex said.

"Well, you could too," Finn shot back.

"But I don't." Alex lifted his sandwich to his mouth but didn't take a bite. "Nicki ain't pregnant."

Finn couldn't tell if Alex was upset about that or not, and he added it to the list of things he'd talk about with one of his best friends in a more private setting. Edith *was* pregnant, and they had learned the gender of the baby since the last time the group of them had met for lunch.

"Wedding plans are going well for us," Link said as he reached for a bottle of lemonade. "Misty's, uh, she's going to Dallas in a month or so to talk to her mom about coming." He nodded, and while Finn didn't know the whole story there, Link had told them all a little bit of his fiancée's past.

"And I appreciate you guys inviting Danny

to this." He nodded around, his expression somber and serious and full of gratitude. "I think I can get him to come to one of these if you keep at it."

Finn did love a good sandwich, and he took a big bite just to get something in his stomach besides a few potato chips before he said his news. His friends were incredibly patient, and they all knew his stalling tactics as they didn't say anything or start another line of conversation.

Finally, Finn couldn't put it off any longer, and he said, "Edith's gonna have a boy in April." A smile coated his face and filled his soul, because he still couldn't believe he was going to be a father. That a tiny baby would be entrusted to him to keep alive, to love, to teach, to care for. "We're making lists of names now, but she doesn't want anyone to know."

He shot a look at Alex, who wore that smile he so rarely gave the world.

"That's amazing," Dawson said. "Congrats to both of you." Other rounds of congratulations went around, and Finn took them all without too much embarrassment. He met Dawson's gaze again and switched his to Smiles'.

Dawson got the hint, and he said, "All right. Let's hear what the young bucks have to say about what I should do with Caroline."

Chapter Eleven

Lincoln Glover had silenced his phone, but it still nagged at him. Misty wasn't at work today, but she'd come up to the ranch to make jam with his momma and aunt Etta. They'd been nothing but kind to her in the past five or six weeks since he'd asked her to marry him—not that they hadn't been kind and accepting before that.

They had been, as Link had known they would.

But Misty hadn't spent much time with his family without him, and the pool of anxiety inside Link seemed to get pricked and poked over and over with every moment he spent in Dawson Rhinehart's cabin.

Smiles had no such cares. He grinned from ear to ear as he said, "Whenever I want to talk to a girl, but I don't have anything to talk about, or anything to say, or we're not in the same classes or whatever, I text her jokes about her favorite thing."

"Jokes?" Henry asked.

"I like it when I get those funny animal videos." Libby gave Smiles a kind smile.

"Dawson's a real joke-teller," Finn said sarcastically, and Link laughed. Even Dawson did, because they all knew him. He absolutely wasn't a joke-teller. Heck, it took a lot just to get the man to smile. And laughing? Link had heard him do it on occasion, but Dawson didn't go around cracking jokes and then tipping his head back and laughing about them.

Henry finished chuckling and said, "It's not bad, kid. Keeps your name on her phone, and it probably makes her smile."

"Women like that," Brandon said. "I'm always telling Daws to lighten up." He gave his brother a flashy smile that Dawson simply rolled his eyes at.

Link just watched his friend, because he knew some of the burdens Dawson carried that perhaps Smiles, Henry, and Brandon didn't. The oldest son, though he had a half-brother older than him in Duke.

His momma and daddy still relied on him for a lot, and Link had no idea what Dawson's afternoon would look like after this forgotten lunch. He'd have to redo his entire to-do list and move around several of his sticky notes, and all of that made him nervous and grouchy at the same time.

"You text me the jokes," Dawson said to Smiles, a brotherly smile on his face. "And I'll see if I can get myself to send them."

"You don't want to be someone via text who you're not in person," Libby said.

"She knows him just fine in person," Link said. He grinned at Dawson. "You know, Daws, a texting relationship might be in your favor."

Dawson rewarded him with a smile. "You're probably not wrong."

Link laughed, glad when Dawson joined him. "I know I'm not wrong."

"So texting," he said. "Jokes." He glanced at Libby and Henry, who sat across from him. "What else?"

"Anything about the owls," Henry said. "And then you casually branch that out to other things. Since they're owls, it's easy to go to animals from there. Dogs, Brandon's cat, your chickens, those crows who love you."

"She knows all about those," he said.

"Mm, nope." Henry gave him a smile and popped another potato chip in his mouth. "She's been here once, buddy. There's so much more to do. Take pictures of them. Send them to her. Make it seem like she wants to come to where you are." He flicked his gaze around the table. "And she eventually will."

"I can send her pictures of Ruffin," Dawson said thoughtfully, as if he'd never considered such a thing before. Truth be told, Link wouldn't have thought of that either.

"Mitch is great at dating too," he said. "I can

ask him for some tips too." He pulled out his phone to do that while Libby—the lone woman at today's lunch—started to talk about what women really wanted from their boyfriends.

Link got lost in his phone for a moment, because when he navigated to his text messages, he found Misty had sent five more messages since he'd silenced his phone and shoved it in his pocket.

Look! My first jar of jam! She'd included a picture of her holding up a beautiful Mason jar of red jam—strawberry. It make his heart sing, and he fell in love with his pretty strawberry-blonde fiancée all over again.

When will you be done? Holly Ann and Montana want to make bread to go with the jam, and your momma says a homemade piece of toast with lots of butter and jam will change my life.

So I want to stay and do that.

The last text was another picture of her, this time with one of his aunt's aprons around her waist and a whisk in her hand as she stirred something in a bowl. The sunshine hit her hair just right, and it shone like spun gold.

Ah, he loved her so much.

He smiled while the conversation went on around him. It didn't really matter when he finished here. He and Smiles had plenty of work to keep them busy until Misty finished her bread-making and toast-and-jam sampling.

His thumbs flew across the phone as those around him laughed at something he hadn't heard. *Remember when you brought me a freshly baked loaf of bread and my very own jar of jam so I could have toast too? That was an amazing evening.*

She didn't text back right away, and Link navigated over to his text chain with Mitch. *Looking for some good dating advice for Dawson. He's got a woman he likes, but it might be bad timing.*

Bad timing? Mitch sent back instantly. Then Link's phone lit up as Mitch called. "Mitch is calling, guys." He held up the phone. "Should I answer?"

Dawson wiped his mouth with a paper towel and nodded. "Yeah, answer it."

Link swiped on the video call, because he couldn't talk to his deaf cousin without being able to see him. He reached out and set the phone in front of him and Smiles, as both of them knew sign language and could communicate with Mitch. Dawson sat next to him, and he could talk to Mitch a little bit, but not nearly as easily as Link and Smiles.

A deep missing filled Link, though God Himself had confirmed to Link that Mitch was where he needed to be. Honestly, if he hadn't gotten that confirmation straight from heaven, Link would've loaded up in his truck, driven to Virginia, and brought Mitch back to Three Rivers. Back to Shiloh Ridge.

"Hey," he said, making the sign as he said it. He glanced over to Dawson.

"Just tell him the situation quickly."

Link did, making the signs and summarizing things as succinctly as he could. "And now, Dawson's trying to see her or stay in her life without having a formal date on his calendar." He looked over to Dawson and raised his eyebrows as if to ask, *Did I get that right?*

Dawson nodded, and Smiles said, "He goes too fast for me, Link, but he said 'This is an easy one.'"

Link hurried to focus on Mitch again, because he could keep up with Mitch most of the time. Not when he got really animated and excited, but this wasn't about him. Still, he knew Dawson well, and he loved talking about dating.

"An easy one, huh?" Dawson chuckled. "Maybe for Mitch."

Link watched his hands and tried to translate at the same time. Since Mitch had moved over the summer, Link's skills had gotten rusty at having to interpret, as he talked to Mitch all the time, but he didn't have to take what his cousin said and relay it to someone else.

"Uh, he says that he's a pro at flirting via texting, and he can send you some stuff, Dawson." He didn't dare look away. "He says it's the little things that will win her over until you can have your first real date."

"Little things?"

Link signed the question from Smiles, and Mitch's hands flew into motion again. "Yeah," he translated. "You can have her favorite food delivered to her house. You don't have to be there. Flowers, if she likes those. If she works a job where she might like a massage or a pedicure, you get a gift certificate and send it to her. Mail her a card for Valentine's Day right now. And then another one next week."

Link almost wanted to be taking notes for what he could do to make sure Misty didn't fall out of love with him. At the same time, he knew Misty wouldn't do that. She loved him, and he'd felt that deeply in his soul too.

"Maybe not every week," he amended. "But something else next week, and not the same thing as other men."

"What kinds of things?" Henry asked, and Link glanced across the table to him.

He signed the question, but Mitch hadn't finished answering yet. He fluidly moved into the next answer anyway, and it took a moment for Link to catch up. "Uh, like where some guys send flowers, you don't do that. You have to stand out. So you send an edible arrangement. Or you show up while she's at work and you leave her favorite treat on the doorstep. Then she'll know you were there, and she missed you. She *misses* you."

"This is really good," Henry said. "Same concept as I said."

"Then, you make sure the first date is really special," Link said. "Because if you show her you're listening to her texts and that you miss her too, then you have to follow that up with all the things you promised she'd miss."

"As if a first date doesn't already carry enough pressure," Dawson grumbled. "But this is great." He leaned into Link's side and made a sign. "Thank you, Mitch."

Mitch grinned at him, and Link could admit he looked better than last time he'd seen him. Link wanted to ask him why, or find out if he was nervous for the new semester to start, but he didn't want to do it in mixed company. Mitch signed with Smiles for a few seconds, and then Link said, "I'll call you again tomorrow, brother," and Mitch ended the video call.

"Libby?" Dawson asked. "Am I on the right track?"

"I'd say so," she said as she stood up. She collected Paul's empty plate, then Henry's and added, "Heck if a man actually listened to me, he'd be ahead of my last three boyfriends."

She moved into the kitchen with all of them watching her, and then Paul, who sat on the end, turned to look at all of them. Link felt the same bewilderment running through him that Paul wore on his face, and then Finn burst out laughing.

That set them all off, and Link sure did love his friends. He laughed with them, and he could tell them anything. He counted himself lucky to be included in this group, and he thanked the Lord Above for Finn and Edith, who'd started having game nights and parties at their house. These cowboys-only lunches had stemmed from that, where they could talk about the concerns on their own ranches and farms, with men their own age, with similar experience levels.

Sometimes Link didn't want to take his problems or concerns to Uncle Ward or Uncle Preacher, and especially not Daddy. He didn't want them to know of his insecurities and his lack of knowledge when it came to things they did as naturally as breathing.

So these lunches, though they'd only met a few times now, meant a lot to him.

Then Dawson lifted one hand, and the laughter started to die. "Guys," he said, his eyes glued to his phone. "Caroline just texted me."

He looked up, and it sure felt like all the air had just been swept out of the room. He sucked in a breath. "It says, 'I need some help. Like now. Could you come to my house right away?'"

Dawson looked around, his eyes round like full moons. Dinner plates. They held wonder and fear, and it was Finn who barked, "What are you still doing here, cowboy? Go."

"Yeah, go," Henry said, jumping to his feet. "Go, go, go!"

Dawson stood too, looked around wildly, and then streaked out of the kitchen and down the hall, muttering, "Shoes, I need some shoes that aren't caked in mud."

Link grinned at his back, then got up to help clear the table and put the sandwich fixings away. He took three cookies and looked at Smiles. "Come on, bro. We've got to get back and move those turkeys over to the east yard."

"Yes, sir," Smiles said, and he took three cookies too.

Dawson came bustling down the hallway wearing sneakers, and he grabbed his leather jacket from the back of the couch. "You guys okay here?"

"Yes," a whole chorus came back to him. "Go," Link added.

"Good luck," Libby called as Dawson jogged toward the front door, trying to put his arms through the sleeves of his jacket. Unsuccessfully, but still trying.

Link could only grin at him as he pounded through the door, and then he looked over to

Finn. He shook his head, smiling, and they all started laughing again.

"Go get 'er, Daws," Alex said, and Link could've echoed that sentiment. As he left the Rhinehart Ranch and took the private dirt road that led north to Shiloh Ridge, he prayed that Dawson would one, drive safely, and two, get exactly what he wanted when it came to Caroline.

If anyone deserved happiness, it was Dawson, and Link wanted that for his friend.

Chapter Twelve

Caroline looked away from the ground and instead focused her gaze on the horizon beyond her front yard. The panic she'd breathed through reared up again, and she fought against it until her heartbeat started to settle again.

"I'll call Belle," she said, and she pulled her phone from her pocket. She felt like she'd done this once already, but she didn't think she'd called or texted her sister. Sure enough, one glance at the phone showed her she hadn't.

She'd texted Dawson instead.

And he'd said, *On the way, Caroline.*

"Caroline," she said softly, imagining Dawson saying it in his throaty, husky, kind voice. Not the growly one, though she wouldn't mind that either. He didn't say her name much, but he had called her *darlin'* or *sweetheart* a time or two.

She looked at when she'd texted him, and she couldn't believe twenty minutes had passed. Now that she'd calmed and her rational thought had returned, having Dawson come from his ranch in the Southern foothills made no sense.

Caroline could call a neighbor to come right the ladder that had fallen and stranded her on the roof of her own home. She tapped to call Dawson, unsurprised when he picked up after the first ring.

"Hey, sweetheart," he said. "Wanna tell me what I'm walking into?"

"Oh, I, uh, well, the swamp cooler was having trouble, so I got up on the roof to take a look." She took a moment, so she could pretend she existed on low, level ground.

In that pause, he said, "Wait. What? You're on the roof?"

"Yes," she clipped out. "I'm capable of fixing everything around my house, Mister Rhinehart, believe it or not."

"I—"

"And Belle left with Judy to go to the petting zoo, so I'm here alone, and I must not have set the ladder right, because after I fixed the swamp cooler, I went to where I'd left it, and it had slid sideways."

He said nothing, and Caroline couldn't blame him. She'd barreled her voice right over the top of his.

"I tried to get it up," she said. "But it's an odd angle, and well, I may not be strong enough to do it."

"I'm fifteen minutes out," he said.

"I can just call my neighbor," she said.

"Then why did you text me?"

Caroline really only had one answer, but she didn't want to say it. She fought against the words surging up her throat, but so many of them flowed out. "I panicked," she said. "I'm not exactly the best of friends with heights, and well, the ground started to swim, and I had to scamper backward, and I—I gotta be honest. I don't even remember texting you."

"Just what every man wants to hear," he said dryly, and Caroline blinked.

"Did you—did you just make a joke?"

"I can hear you're okay," he said. "So I'm going to hang up, and I'll be there in a few minutes to help with the ladder."

"Dawson."

"See you soon, Caroline." He ended the call, and that ignited the fire in her chest.

"He hung up." She looked at the screen, where his name faded to black. "I said his name, clearly with something more to say, and he hung up anyway."

Caroline looked up, emotions circling through her, throwing oddly colored images into her vision, the way a kaleidoscope did. Everything felt too hot up here on the roof, but she simultaneously felt cold. Clammy.

She'd just been thrown back into her marriage, and Caroline would not put up with being treated like that again. She absolutely would not be spoken over, or belittled, or made to feel like her words and opinion did not matter.

And Joe had made her constantly question her worth. He'd said things to her that made her doubt everything, doubt herself, doubt reality, even. He'd hung up on her before, and Caroline's fingers tightened around the plastic case on her phone.

Before she knew it, Dawson pulled into her driveway, and he waved to her from the ground. "Around back?"

She didn't answer, and the handsome cowboy moved with confidence into her backyard. Her throat felt like she'd severed her vocal cords and then tried to iron them back into place. She could barely get air down into her lungs, and she startled and pressed her eyes closed as a metallic clattering noise rent the air.

Dawson climbed onto the roof a few seconds later, and he had a bright-as-the-noonday-sun smile on his face that felt like he'd put it there just for her. "Hey." He reached out his hand for her, but Caroline didn't reciprocate the gesture.

His expression changed, but he came the several feet to her and sat beside her with a groan. "It's hot up here."

"Mm." Caroline had so much to say, and it all tasted like poison inside her.

"Pretty view up here though," he said. "I like the perspective on the neighborhood."

Tall trees surrounded them, and in the spring and summer, they'd leaf up and make things green in Three Rivers. Right now, she could see further than she'd be able to when the trees had leaves, and it did offer a different perspective.

It showed her how her house existed among many neat rows of other houses, when it was so easy to feel isolated.

"You better tell me what I did wrong," he said quietly.

Caroline sat up straight and drew her

shoulders back. "When I filed for divorce from my ex-husband, I vowed I would never allow myself to get in a situation like that again."

Dawson looked at her, and the weight of his gaze on the side of her face landed like a load of bricks. "You've been married?"

"Yes," she said with a single nod. "For a few years. I've been divorced for five."

"How old are you?" He cleared his throat. "Wait, let me back up a little. Soften my tone." His hand slid across her knee and took hers into the safety of his. "I'm real sorry about your first marriage. Sorry that it obviously hurt you and brought you pain. Not sorry it led you here, to me, but sorry I did something to make you feel like you did then."

Caroline swallowed, because Joe would've never apologized. He always thought he was right, and he'd argue it and argue it, sometimes without even any facts. She squeezed his hand and summoned up the courage to look at him.

Dawson wore resignation and defeat on his face, and he ducked his head the moment she looked his way. His cowboy hat concealed his face, and Caroline sure did like his humility.

"You hung up on me," she whispered. "Without letting me say what I wanted to say." She drew in a breath and raised her voice. "My ex-husband did that constantly. Even when I found a way to say something, he'd twist it around until I was the one asking him to forgive me and questioning why I was so weak, so stupid, and so obviously not worthy of him."

Dawson kept her hand tightly in his, but he didn't look at her. "I'm real sorry about that," he said. "I didn't realize. I thought you were teasing me about making a joke is all."

Caroline gazed over the neighborhood again, an extreme calm moving through her. "Joe would've never apologized."

"I won't hang up on you again. It wasn't my intent to silence you or anything. I guess I just didn't feel like being teased about making a joke."

She leaned her head against his shoulder, glad when it felt good. Right. Easy. "I'm sorry too," she said. "This is a non-negotiable point for me, and it makes me a little hard-headed. A little harsh sometimes."

"I like a little harsh sometimes," he said, and Caroline could've melted into him. "*I'm* a little harsh sometimes."

She nudged him with her shoulder. "Just sometimes?"

"Hey, I came running when you texted, and I'll have you know that my house was full of my friends."

Shock zinged through her, first that he'd left his friends, and second, that he'd had friends over to his cabin for lunch. "It was? Why?"

"And now they've all seen me run—literally —to your aid. So I have no pride left, sweetheart."

"Was I going to eat with all of your friends?"

"I forgot we'd moved our lunch from yesterday to today," he said. "So it's a good thing you didn't come." He nudged her back. "You never said how old you are."

"Thirty," she said. "You?"

"Thirty-two," he said. "Never married, though I have dated quite a bit in recent years."

"Define 'quite a bit.'"

"Oh, I don't know," he said with a sigh. "Four or five women in the past year. That many the year before." He blew out his breath. "Nothing ever takes."

"What does that mean?"

He didn't answer right away, and Caroline liked that he seemed to think about what he might say before he said it. "I think my last attempt at a girlfriend sums it up," he said. "We went out a few times. She's nice. It's fun. I go to kiss her, and it's like...nothing. Bland. If I had a sister, it would be like kissing her."

"And you do that four or five times a year?"

He chuckled and nodded. "Seems that way for a while, at least."

She turned into him, and Caroline honestly had no idea where this fizzy, flirty feeling inside her stemmed from. But she liked it. "Do you think when you kiss me it'll be like that?"

"By all the stars in heaven, I hope not," Dawson whispered. "But I reckon we need to go out a few times before that'll happen anyway."

"You never know," Caroline said, teasing openly now. "Some people kiss before the first date."

Dawson chuckled again. "Yeah, a friend of mine—Link—kissed his fiancée before their second first date."

"Second first date," Caroline repeated.

"Yeah, they, uh, had to try twice, but they're real happy now. Gonna get married this summer."

"That's great," she said, her own throat closing up slightly. She'd never imagined she'd date someone again, and certainly she'd never get married again. Dawson had her rethinking a lot of things, and they hadn't even gone out on a date yet.

"You got something more to say?" he prompted gently.

"Did I sound like I did?"

"Yes," he said. "You sure did."

She lifted her head and slowly peeled her fingers away from his. "Maybe I do, but I think I'd like to hold it for another time."

"All right," he drawled. "Now, can I help you get off this roof? It really is hot up here."

"It's January."

"On a clear, muggy day," he said. He got to his feet first, and when he reached for her this time, Caroline took his hand and let him help her to her feet. With the pitch of the roof, she stood above him, taller, and looked down into his eyes.

"Thank you for coming, Dawson."

His eyes lingered on her mouth, and he pulled them up to meet hers. "I'll always come when you need me, Caroline." With that, he led the way to the ladder and went down first. He held it for her while she made painstaking progress down it, and then he took it down and put it away in her shed.

A new tension had accompanied them to the ground, and Caroline didn't know the steps to this dance. She could barely look at Dawson, and it sure seemed like all she could think about was kissing him.

"Belle and Judy will be home soon," she said.

"Ah, that's my cue to leave," he said with another quick flash of a smile she caught though she wasn't looking directly at him. "I won't ask you out, but I am going to hug you."

He drew her into his arms, and oh, Caroline had not known such a tender male touch in her life. Tears touched her eyes, and she clung to Dawson in a way surely he could feel. She stayed too long in his arms, and when he finally released her, she pulled in a deep breath and tried to stabilize her emotions.

She flashed a smile at him and said, "I'll call you, okay?"

"Can't wait." He got behind the wheel of his truck, tipped his hat at her, and backed out of her driveway. Caroline watched him go, wondering if the ground she stood on would crack and allow the earth to swallow her whole.

That was how her life felt right now. Like she had no idea what might happen next, and the thrill of that kept prodding her to make another almost irrational decision. Like....

"I am talking to Belle tonight," she vowed to the empty driveway. Then she added, "Dust and shadows," and spun to go back into the house, praying that the swamp cooler had been cooling the house since she'd gone up onto the roof to fix it and she could get the flaming in her face to go down a couple of notches.

Chapter Thirteen

Dawson crouched down to get the pictures Link needed. "He's not going to be happy about this."

Heck, Dawson wasn't happy about it. "Blasted owls," he muttered as he moved his phone to get a different angle. The resulting picture showed the bright yellow orbs of owl eyes in the den, and Dawson got to his feet.

Cawing sounded overhead, and Dawson looked up to find his two inky friends circling. He straightened, feeling a bit lightheaded for being crouched down and looking up, and he took a moment to get his bearings.

As he moved away from the property line between Shiloh Ridge and Hidden Hills, he whistled through his teeth, though he didn't believe for a moment that Nugget and Rocks couldn't see him.

Nugget tried to imitate him, but he didn't whistle well. They did descend toward him, but Dawson had started walking back down the fence line. They could fly alongside him the way Ruffin trotted at his side, or they could hop along the fence posts if they wanted.

Rocks, of course, had something gripped in one of his claws, and that only made Dawson smile. As much as anything these days, though he'd definitely taken his flirting game to a new level with Caroline.

"Yeah," he huffed out as his boots caught on a clod of dirt and he nearly face-planted. "You still haven't been out with her."

She sure seemed interested in him. She called him when she needed help. She responded to all of his texts, with funny memes and videos of her own. She laughed and flirted right back. So maybe the ball was in his court, and he hadn't even known it.

"No," he muttered. "You asked her three nights ago if she'd talked to Belle, and she gave you the thumbs-down." Dawson wasn't going to ask her out again until he felt certain she could say yes.

And then actually go on the date.

It cost him too much emotionally and mentally, and frankly, he was running out of pink sticky notes, as he used one every time he needed to remind himself to text Caroline. He wondered if she realized most of his texts came after three o'clock or in the evening, and he vowed to keep his barn-office locked so she'd never see his to-do list.... After all, she wouldn't want to know he had to *plan* to text her.

Nugget cawed again, calling him back to the present, and Dawson slowed his step to smile at the crow who'd just landed on the fence post a few feet from him. "Hey, you." He smiled at the bird, wondering if he could give him a stroke the way he did his dog.

Rocks swooped in, nearly flapping Dawson

in the face with his wings, and he dropped the object in his foot. Dawson didn't have the reflexes of a ninja, unfortunately, and the item thudded into the dirt at his feet.

That seemed heavy, and he bent to pick it up. Confusion puckered through him. He couldn't make sense of the bends of metal, but as he straightened, he realized what he had.

"A belt buckle," he said, his smile growing wider. Silver and shiny, it glinted in all the right ways to attract Rocks's attention. "Clever thing." He pocketed the belt buckle and nodded down the fence. "C'mon, guys. We've got to get back in service to call Link."

Nugget cawed and took off, but Rocks hopped from post to post as Dawson made the trek back to where the burrowing owls lived on his ranch. He'd parked near there, as the road didn't go much further.

"Uncle Dawson," someone called as he got closer, and he found April waving her hand above her head as if he might miss her.

Something heavy settled in his stomach, because it wasn't even lunchtime yet, on a school day. "Hey, you," he said as he went past his truck and toward her. He realized he'd just spoken with the same level of care and concern to his niece as he had a crow, but no one else needed to know that.

April stood at the enclosure marking the owls, and Dawson moved to her side. "What are you doin' here?"

She cut him a look out of the corner of her eye. Oh, so nothing good. "I couldn't go to school today."

"You *couldn't*? Or...why couldn't you go to school today?"

"It's not my fault, and as soon as Momma and Daddy meet with my history teacher, they'll know that."

Dawson sighed internally, but if he wanted April to keep coming around and telling him things, he couldn't let it out of his mouth.

"Still got the owls," she said.

"Yeah." He sighed now. "Still got the owls." He gazed at the dens, no birds in sight.

"Heya, Nugget." April grinned at the big crow as he came down again. "Can't you chase off these pesky owls for Uncle Dawson?"

That would be sublime, but Nugget simply put his beady crow eye on April and cawed right in her face.

"I'm going to take that as a no," she said calmly.

Dawson chuckled, and he turned toward his truck. "I have to take some measurements of the dens. You can hold one end."

"Yes, sir," she said, scampering to come after him. She didn't say anything, but her mind moved all the time, and if Dawson waited long enough, she'd talk. Sure enough, they'd barely reached the tailgate of his truck before she added, "It's really not my fault that Morgan can't be in my group. I've been keepin' track, and she never helps in a group project. Literally, never. Tami and Bri didn't want her in the group either; I'm just the one who'll say something."

"Mm hm." Dawson pulled a tape measure from the toolbox in the back of his truck. "So your momma and daddy are down in town right now?"

"Yes." She sighed. "And you should see my mom. She stomps around like she's never done anything wrong." She blew out her breath. "And I know she has. It's not like she's perfect."

Dawson looked over to her. "No, missy, she ain't, but that doesn't mean she doesn't want you to be better."

April looked at him, storms in her eyes, and so much confusion among the trust. "I...." She exhaled again and reached to slam the box closed. "I know. She says I have to learn to tame my tongue. Not to let everything I think—even if it's right—come out of my mouth."

Dawson thought of Caroline, and how tongue-tied she'd been in her first marriage. She'd told him a bit more about it since last week's roof rescue, and he didn't know the right thing to say here. God did, so Dawson turned to buy himself a quick moment to pray.

"Hm," he said. "She might be right, but you don't have to make yourself smaller to make someone else feel good about themselves."

"I—" April cut off as she came to his side. "Really, Uncle Dawson?"

He gave her a grin. "Okay, so here's how I see it, little miss. You've got two things working against you all the time, so you're gonna have to work *harder* than others to be nice."

"Two things working against me?"

Dawson nodded. "Your momma's red hair—that so gives you a fiery temper, and you just haven't learned how to let it burn out before you speak. But you will." He gave her a grin she seemed to need desperately. "And your daddy's grumpy-cat attitude about literally everything."

He spoke the last sentence with plenty of dryness in his tone. April laughed right out loud, and that made Dawson so happy. *Thank you, Lord*, he thought. Because God had given him the right thing to say, and all Dawson had had to do was open his mouth and let the words come out.

Maybe he needed to do the same thing with Caroline.

"You're pretty grumpy too, Uncle Dawson," she said.

"Yeah, well, you've met Grandpa."

She giggled again, sobering quickly this time. "Uncle Brandon's not like that."

"He's the youngest. Never got treated like me and your daddy." He glanced over to her. "So don't lie to me and tell me Shiloh has nothing to do with this."

April made a scowly face and looked away, which answered Dawson just fine. "I wish she'd gotten some of momma's fiery temper," she muttered. "But no. Oh, *no*. Shiloh has perfect grades, and Shiloh is perfectly beautiful, and Shiloh is kind to everyone."

Shiloh was all of those things, and it wasn't bad. It simply made April stand out when she wasn't, well, Shiloh.

"And the boys get away with murder, because Momma and Daddy are too tired to make them do anything."

Dawson chuckled as they neared the owl dens. "Now you know why Uncle Brandon isn't as salty as me and your daddy." He paused, the tape measure in his hand. "And hey, April?"

He rarely used her name, so when he did, she perked up and looked at him. She shone with so much radiance, and Dawson could see it. "Two things, okay? Can you listen to me on these two things?"

She scuffed her toe in the dirt and looked down at her cowgirl boots while she did. "I'll try," she murmured.

"Can't ask for more than that." Dawson took a breath, trying to decide how to start. "One, you know your daddy left Three Rivers for a long time, right?"

Her eyes flew back to his. "Yes, sir."

"Have your parents talked about this with you?"

"A little," she admitted. "They haven't told any of the other kids, but I think—well, honestly, Uncle Dawson, I think they think I'm going to be this rebellious heathen, and they're trying anything they can to show me that's not the path I want to go down."

He gave her a genuine smile and pulled her into his chest. "I love you, April Rivers. Don't you ever forget that."

Her arms came around him and gripped him tightly, telling him how much she needed to hear that. "Is that the second thing?" she asked, her voice high and tinny.

"Not quite." He hugged her tight too. "It's just a universal truth you have to remember, no matter where you are or what you're doing. Deal?"

She nodded and stepped back, her hand coming up to wipe her eyes. She focused on the owls and wouldn't look away. Her waiting game.

"Okay," he said. "I wasn't close to your daddy when everything happened, but I could see he wasn't happy. He never was, no matter where he went or what he did. Not until he came back and set things right here in town. With Grandpa, with everyone involved."

He didn't want to say too much, as this wasn't his story to tell. "And I can tell you this, missy, I've never seen him more broken, and then I've never seen a man change more powerfully than your daddy. He knows the bad and the ugly, and he is trying to save you from it."

She nodded and sniffled again. Dawson had felt the power of his own words, and he figured he didn't need to say any more.

"Second thing." He pulled out the end of the tape measure and handed it to her. "Get on down on the other end. We gotta see if this is expanding."

She moved that way without a word, but April wore everything out for everyone to see. They moved into position, but Dawson didn't bend to put the tape measure on the ground. He stood there, the long, yellow, metal tape measuring the distance between them and looked her right in the eye.

"You do not need to be Shiloh, ever. I see you, missy, and you are exactly who you're meant to be."

Her face crumpled, and she started to cry right in front of him. And April did not cry, hardly ever. He'd seen her take a hammer to the thumb and only yell out and then whimper when he put ice on it.

"God knows who you are," he said. "He gave you all this fire and all this passion, and

He's expecting you to figure out how to mold it, and tame it, and turn it into something that can be used for something amazing."

She nodded and wiped her face with her free hand.

"God gave you exactly *your* momma and *your* daddy. Not someone else's. They know how to be Shiloh's parents, but they're still learning how to be yours. The Lord wants that for them, and He figured because you're so amazing and so strong and so perfectly you, that you could bear with them while *they* learn and grow and change and learn how to be your momma and daddy."

Dawson couldn't remember when he'd spoken so many words out loud, and he bent down and put the tape on the ground. April did the same, and he snapped a picture of the measurement with his phone in his free hand.

As he straightened, she did too, and they lifted the tape over the fence as she walked toward him. She gave it back to him and moved in to hug him again. "I just feel so...wired all the time."

"Yeah," he whispered as he stroked her hair. "That's because you've got some ADHD in your blood, baby. I know, because I do too."

She pulled back and searched his face. "Momma said the doctor said—"

"Yeah, I know," Dawson said quietly. "And I'm not ADHD, but OCD. It's a lot of the same nervous energy, but it manifests itself in different ways. And I'm no doctor—I don't know exactly what your momma has taken you in for."

He took a big breath and faced the western sky. Rocks and Nugget had flown off at some point, and Ruffin waited in the shade of the truck, back several paces. "Mine's diagnosed, missy. I cope with some meds and a long run in the morning, a meticulous calendar, and sticky notes."

"I love your sticky notes," she said. "That's how I knew you'd be out here this morning."

Horror washed through his embarrassment as he sliced a look at her. "You went in my office this morning?"

"For like, two seconds."

Which meant yes, and that she'd seen the copious number of pink sticky notes.

April faced the western sky too, and asked, "Would you listen to me on one thing?"

Dawson's heartbeat hadn't settled back to its normal rhythm yet, but he said, "Yeah, I'll try."

"I saw all your pink notes about Caroline."

"Mm hm."

"You know what I think you should do?"

"Oh, I can't wait to hear this," he said dryly. "And if you see Smiles, you just tell him that all his jokes and memes have done nothing."

"Smiles told you to...do what, exactly?"

"Text her a lot," he said. "Funny stuff and... I don't know." He had the sudden urge to pat down his pockets for his phone, just to make sure it wasn't lying around somewhere April might be able to see it and be a witness to his pathetic attempt to be top-of-mind for Caroline.

"Well, he would know," she said. "Smiles is super popular. *All* the girls like him."

"Yeah, but."

"Okay, just listen." April turned toward him and grinned. "This will work, I'm sure of it."

When she didn't go on, Dawson growled. "Daylight's burning, missy, and Grandma said she'd feed me lunch today. So spit it out."

"Next time you see her, you just kiss her."

Dawson blinked, sure he hadn't just gotten kissing advice from his fourteen-year-old niece. Nope. Not happening. "Kiss her?" he blurted back to her.

"She'll like it," April said, her smile so, so wide. "And then you tell her you just couldn't wait another minute to do that, and you're real sorry, but she's just so beautiful and you haven't been able to stop thinking about her."

All true, but Dawson wasn't sure he'd be sorry when he kissed Caroline. He also wasn't sure without any dates at all that it wouldn't totally kill their still budding relationship. After all, no woman he'd kissed in the past couple of years had lit a fire in him at all.

"Girls like that," April said.

"She's not a girl," Dawson said. "She's a woman."

"She'll still like it." April looked at her smart watch as it beeped. "Ugh, Daddy says they're fifteen minutes away, and I better be at the house when they get there." She looked up, gave him a fierce look, and dove into his arms again. "I love you, Uncle Dawson."

"And I love you, April Rivers." He released her and gave her a slight push. "Go on, now. You'll have to pedal fast to get back in fifteen minutes."

She nodded and jogged toward the mountain bike she'd thrown to the ground upon her arrival. "Bye, Uncle Dawson!"

"Come for dinner," he said after her. "To tell me everything."

She waved, picked up the bike, and off she went, leaving Dawson with the burrowing owls, the blustering sky, and his own thoughts.

"Next time you see her, kiss her." He scoffed. What a terrible idea. Of course he wasn't going to do that. With a woman like

Caroline, he'd probably end up with a broken nose or a fat lip if he even tried.

He pulled out his phone and texted Link. *You're going to hate me. You've got owls on the property line. I've got pictures.*

Link had found a den further north, and he'd asked Dawson to check the line, because it was quite hilly and filled with trees on their side of the fence.

You're right, Link sent back. *I hate you.* He sent a laughing emoji after that.

Then, *siiiigh. Don't send the pictures. I don't want to see them and be more depressed. I'll get up there this afternoon myself. Can I come over to your side?*

Anytime, Dawson said, and he glanced up at the sound of tires crunching over gravel. Why was everyone coming out here this afternoon? How many more people had been in his office, snooping through his schedule?

The very idea had his blood running cold.

Or maybe that came from the gorgeous sight of Caroline, who currently stopped her

SUV right in front of him, her smile sitting prettily on those lips April had told him to "just kiss."

Chapter Fourteen

Caroline's heart pounded up into her throat as she faced Dawson. Flirting and texting with him via cellphone was completely different than being in his presence. And she hadn't even gotten out of the car yet.

Ruffin ducked his head and came toward her, making her smile and giving her courage enough to get out. She smoothed her hands down her ugly work shorts and prayed for the best as she stepped out to close her door.

"Hey, Ruffin." She crouched down to greet the dog, giving herself a few more minutes of peace before she had to talk to Dawson. She told herself she'd driven up here specifically to talk to him. "Yeah, you're the best, aren't you? Yes, you are."

She didn't see the crows today, but she had passed a teenage girl pedaling furiously on her bicycle. Caroline couldn't hide behind a canine forever, so she rose to her feet and took a deep breath.

"Hey, darlin'," he drawled, and oh, that made Caroline smile. His voice sounded so much better than the chime on her phone, indicating he'd messaged.

"Hey." She moved closer to him, noting that he did not come to her, and opened her arms to him. In an easy, oh-so-natural way, he received her, pressing one kiss almost on the corner of her mouth, then another higher on her cheek, and a third right below her ear.

Three kisses.

Caroline's eyes drifted closed and she breathed in the salty, musky, sexy scent of Dawson's skin. Part shampoo, and part cologne, and all cowboy, and she thanked heaven above she had him to hold onto, so she didn't fall to the ground.

"Mm, you're here." His voice rumbled in her ear, his arms warm and welcome around her. "What are you doing here?"

She held onto him for another few moments, just long enough to make sure she could stand on her own, and then moved back. Dawson didn't let her go too far, as he took her hand in his and squeezed.

"I had to check something down in Ritchfield today," she said. "So I was on my way back." She'd planned to stop at his ranch today, but she didn't say so. She honestly wasn't sure how much to say. He'd kissed her three times, so maybe he'd said a whole bunch already.

"And I just got a text from Lincoln about owls between your two ranches."

"So you were just driving by?"

"Sort of," she said, deciding she could be brave. Use her words. She turned toward him. "I haven't seen you for a few days. I...wanted to see you."

He smiled at her, and oh, she probably

shouldn't have asked him to do that. At the same time, so much light entered his soul when he did, and she didn't think Dawson could fake feelings even if he wanted to.

"It's great to see you," he said. He leaned toward her, and panic filled Caroline. Was he going to kiss her properly this time? He didn't, but nuzzled into her neck, crowding close and making her giggle.

And oh, how she felt cherished. Like he couldn't get enough of her with just his eyes and his hands, he had to smell her and taste her too.

He swept another series of tiny, barely-there kisses up the column of her throat and then lifted his head. "Mm, yeah. It's great to see you." He looked at the fence he and Link had erected around the owls. "I checked the fence for Link, because it's way easier to see from this side. I've got some pictures if you want to see them."

"I'm going to come out tomorrow with him," she said. "He said he got permission from you to approach from this side."

"Yeah," Dawson said. "We farm up there, so if you want to build something like this, I can help in the morning."

She nodded. "I'll keep you informed."

Everything sounded so clinical, and Caroline didn't know how to move past this. At least it was civilized now—more than civilized. His stomach growled as if he'd caged an angry pair of tigers in there, and he looked down at it.

"It's lunchtime," he said, raising his gaze to meet hers. "My momma is feeding me today. Would you—? You could come." His eyes searched hers, so much boyish hope living there.

Her first reaction was to decline. Lunch with him and his mom? They hadn't even been out on one date yet. They weren't dating. He wasn't her boyfriend.

All of the skin above her collarbone sizzled, seemingly to testify that she had indeed been doing things she'd only do with a boyfriend. Holding hands. Giggling. Accepting kisses.

So she opened her mouth, and "All right," came out.

He grinned even wider. "All right." He nodded to her car. "You want to drive in together? Bring me back out here? Or I can follow you in."

She glanced over to his truck. "How about you just follow me in? Maybe we could go for a walk or something after lunch."

His phone dinged, and he said, "That's my momma now. Just a sec." He pulled out his phone and typed something short and fast into it. "I'll follow you in." He nodded at her and stepped away, saying, "Come on, Ruff. Jump up."

The dog trotted over to the truck and got in the back while Dawson arrived in his cowboy speed. Caroline spun when she realized she'd been watching him and hurried to her car too. On the way back to the epicenter of the ranch, she gripped the steering wheel and talked herself into leaving without dining with the Rhineharts.

"His daddy is retired too," she muttered. "Of course he'll be there."

So she couldn't stay. Absolutely not. She and Dawson were *not* dating.

Desperation clogged her throat. She'd tried talking to Belle about Dawson, but it hadn't gone well, nor very far. Belle had seized upon something she'd said and ranted about her ex-husband for thirty minutes. Then she'd dissolved into tears and gone down the hall to the bedroom.

So definitely not a good chat, and certainly Caroline had not said everything she needed to in order to start a real relationship with Dawson. They texted constantly, usually in the afternoon or evening, and Caroline sure did like him.

He hadn't asked her out again, and she wished she could tell him she'd driven to the ranch today because she'd finally talked to Belle, and they could go to dinner.

She found herself rounding the corner of the barn, the exit road right in front of her. But she kept turning to the right and that put her in front of the farmhouse. It was clearly much older than the house a few hundred yards away, but someone took care of it.

The lawn had been winterized, and all the flowerbeds cleared for springtime blooming. The shutters had been painted a dark red, and a navy blue star sat up near the pinnacle of the roof. Everything else was white, and it screamed old-school Texas from the very foundations.

She got out of her car at the same time Dawson parked, and she smiled at the clucking and warbling of chickens somewhere nearby. Everything felt slower, more peaceful, here, and Caroline craved this small-town quaintness with her whole soul.

"Should be good," he said as he came around the front of the truck. "My momma is a good cook."

"What did she make?"

He took her hand at the same time the sound of another vehicle filled the air. They both looked toward it, and Dawson's frown deepened. "Looks like Duke and Zona are coming too." His expression turned to one of anxiety, and his hand in hers tightened. "Is that okay? You want to meet them all?"

"All of them?"

"Well, we all work here," he muttered. "I'm sure Brandon's inside. He's more of a momma's-boy than I am."

Caroline had no idea how to get out of this. She wasn't even sure she wanted to. She stood there while Duke pulled in, her mind buzzing and fuzzing. Finally, about the time the tall, darker-haired man dropped from the truck and slammed his door, she blinked. Focused. Knew what she wanted.

"I've already met Duke," she said. "And I want to meet them all." She slid her hand up his arm and moved her other one to clutch his. "Okay?"

He met her eyes, something dark and dangerous and enticing swimming in his gaze. Desire. "We're a barrel of fun," he deadpanned. "But this might be good. Meet us now, so you can get out early if you need to."

"You haven't even asked me out," she whispered.

"Didn't know it was an option," he whispered back. In a louder tone, he said, "Hey, guys," and started toward his family.

Duke and his wife Arizona had come, and the same teenager Caroline had seen riding her bike got out of the back too. She looked like she'd been crying, and Caroline instantly wanted to shield her, protect her, and also leave so this family could talk without a stranger present.

But Dawson had a hold of her hand again, and he said, "You guys haven't met Caroline, I don't think." He beamed stars and light and all shiny things at her for a brief moment. "This is Caroline Thompson. She's the Wildlife Officer assigned to our ranch for the burrowing owls, and...." He swallowed and cleared his throat. "And she's this really amazing woman I keep trying to go out with."

Duke smiled too, and the gesture totally transformed his face. "Sure, Caroline." He stuck out his hand, and she had to release Dawson's to shake his brother's. "It's great to see you again."

"You remember Duke," Dawson said. "He runs the ranch. His wife, Arizona. We all call her Zona." He smiled at her, and while tension radiated from the woman, she too had a friendly, bright smile and firm handshake for Caroline.

"And my favorite niece," Dawson said. "April." The way they held each other's gazes said something, but Caroline couldn't decipher it fast enough.

"It's my pleasure to meet you," April said diplomatically. "I'm gonna go see what Grandma made for lunch, okay?" She waited until both of her parents nodded at her, and then she left.

Dawson watched her, a frown furrowing his brow. Duke sighed, and Zona linked her arm through his. "She's a good girl," she murmured.

"The best," Dawson confirmed, turning his attention to them. "She came out to see me this morning."

They both looked at him with extreme interest in their eyes, but they didn't ask any questions. At least not verbally. Dawson shifted his feet and started toward the house. "She's gonna be okay," he said. "How'd the meeting go at the school?"

"Fine," Duke said. "The teacher is going to put Morgan in another group, and April...well, she wasn't wrong."

"She's just like...." Zona didn't finish, and Caroline certainly wasn't going to fill in any adjectives.

"Abrasive?" Dawson suggested. "Fiery, like you? Grumpy, like you?" He looked from Zona to Duke, clear challenge in his lifted eyebrows. Then everything about him softened, and one corner of his mouth kicked up. "Seems to me, y'all created this problem yourselves."

Duke looked like he'd just had ice water thrown in his face. Zona blinked a couple of times and looked at her husband. "He's not wrong. We're like vinegar and baking soda combined. No wonder she's this way."

"She's no *way*," Dawson said. "She's your daughter. Your smart, free-thinking, beautiful, talented,   a-little-on-the-brusque-side, daughter."

"A little?" Duke asked.

"Have you met yourself when you haven't eaten?" Dawson asked, opening the front door to the farmhouse. "She's fourteen. You're forty-five. Give her some time to grow into herself."

The scent of something spicy hit Caroline's nose, and her stomach growled in the most embarrassing way possible. Both Duke and Dawson chuckled, and the latter drew her closer as he took her into the house. "Hungry, huh?"

"I guess so," she said.

"Smells like chili," Zona said, and Caroline completely agreed, though she hadn't been able to place the scent before.

"I hope you're ready for something amazing," Dawson said as the front of the house opened up to the back. While it looked old on the outside, the interior of the farmhouse had been completely updated at some point in the recent past.

The living room she walked through held

beautiful furniture in a deep, dark brown leather. A hutch of trinkets stood beside the window to her left, and then a large dining room table took over the initial space in the kitchen. It pushed back through the house, with glinting silver appliances, and an island that held a feast fit for a king.

Or maybe just sons. Cowboys.

"We're here, Momma," Dawson said. "Duke and Zona pulled up at the same time."

His mother turned from the kitchen sink, where she stood with another younger man—clearly Dawson's brother. Besides April, she didn't see anyone else.

"Oh." His mother stopped completely, and Caroline's face heated slightly. She glanced at Dawson, who everyone seemed to be looking at, and April stepped over to the sink.

"I've got the rest of these, Grams."

The teenager's words seemed to thaw Dawson's mother. "Thank you, dear." She quickly wiped her hands on her apron, her smile blooming to life.

"Momma," Dawson said, a growly undertone to his voice. "This is Caroline Thompson. She's the woman I told you about." He held absolutely still, not a swallow or a blink in sight. "Where's Daddy?"

"He's finishing up with the well out back," his mom said.

Dawson nodded, his gaze flitting toward the back windows. "Caroline, this is my mother, Abby. My daddy is Wade. He'll be in soon, I reckon."

Caroline smiled with all she had as she stepped away from Dawson to greet his mother. "It's so wonderful to meet you," she said. "I hope there's enough for me. Dawson just invited me randomly." She laughed lightly, though what she'd said was true. "I mean, I guess—" She glanced over to him and tucked her hair behind her ear. "I surprised him by showing up on the ranch, and I don't think he could stand to have me delay his lunch."

"Now *that* sounds about right," Duke said as he eased to kiss and hug his mother hello. Then Caroline remembered that this was not his biological mother. He'd come from Wade's first wife, and Caroline was impressed with the love and care coming from Duke.

"My brother Brandon," Dawson said, nodding to the man standing at the sink, now drying his hands on a tea towel with a brightly colored chicken embroidered on it.

He nodded to her, his smile bright and so unlike Duke's or Dawson's. She even looked between the three of them, and nope. Brandon did not fit. He was lighter in every way, from his hair color to his eyes to his personality. At the same time, he fit with them, what with the shape of his jaw and the slope of his nose.

"Hello, Abby," Zona said quietly as she too hugged the other woman. "Thank you for making lunch."

"It seemed like a chili kind of week," she said, turning to survey the countertop. "Now, we don't need to wait for Daddy. He said not to, and you know how he is."

Caroline didn't, but murmurs of assent ran through the rest of them. She took in the quartered quesadillas, expecting to find a pot of chili to match the smell wafting through the house. But she couldn't find it.

She saw bowls of shredded cheese, sour cream, diced tomatoes, guacamole, and as she watched, April turned from the sink with one of freshly washed shredded lettuce.

"April," Abby said. "Will you pray?"

The girl froze, her eyes wide like twin full moons.

Caroline's heart skipped and shrunk, then pounded forward like she'd been holding her breath underwater for a long time. "I will," she blurted out.

Dawson looked at her. Abby looked at her. Brandon, Zona, and Duke looked at her.

"If it's okay with April," she said, trying for a fun, friendly smile for the girl who still hadn't moved. Silence rained in the house, and Caroline wanted to walk out of this tension.

"It's fine with April," Dawson said quietly, giving the girl a nod. "Go ahead, darlin'."

"Darlin'?" Duke muttered as Caroline lowered her chin and folded her arms.

And just like that, words failed her. She'd

prayed hundreds of times. Thousands proba-bly. At least, especially since she'd prayed dozens of times each day as she went through her separation and divorce. She honestly didn't know how she'd have made it out alive otherwise.

Something slid along the floor, and someone coughed, and then Caroline practi-cally yelled, "Dear God," into the stunted, soul-sucking silence.

The back door opened with a man saying, "That blasted well is going—oh."

Caroline looked over to Dawson's daddy, who quickly swiped his cowboy hat from his head, his eyes squeezing closed as he held it over his heart.

"We're grateful to be in Three Rivers," she said, not even sure where the words came from. They sounded so stupid, as the Rhineharts lived here. And had for years and years. At the same time, she wondered if they even knew how special their small town was. If they even knew how good their lives here were.

"We're grateful for Abby for making this

food. If it tastes half as good as it smells, we're going to eat like royalty today."

Dawson's hand slid along her waist, and Caroline melted into the touch. "Bless the food that it'll keep our bodies healthy and strong, and our minds clear and able to make decisions. Bless our hands that we can do good, and bless our eyes to see those around us who need help. Then, bless us to get out of our minds and offer our assistance, as each of us has so much to offer to those around us."

She honestly had no idea what else to say. She wasn't even sure what she'd already said, but she had uttered some gratitude and something about a blessing on the food, and she figured she might as well wrap up this massacre.

"Amen." The two-syllable word scraped her throat, and Caroline dropped her hands back to her sides, opened her eyes, and leaned into Dawson.

No one moved or said anything. They didn't even seem to be breathing. They all stared at her, and as she looked from April to

Abby to Brandon to Wade, it seemed to be for a different reason for each of them.

April seemed shocked. Abby grinned like a mother hen who'd welcomed home a long-lost chick. Brandon mirrored April, and Wade wrinkled his eyebrows in confusion.

"Well," Duke said. "I think that was about perfect." He smiled at Caroline as he reached to pick up a plate. They so weren't eating chili for lunch, but the scent in the air.... "It's sure nice to have a different voice say a prayer."

"What does that mean?" Dawson asked, plenty of bite in his tone.

"It means," Duke said as he picked up four quarters of a quesadilla to make a whole one on his plate. "That Caroline." His eyes switched to hold hers. "Said some real nice things. Good reminders, that weren't the same rote stuff we say at our house." He glanced at his wife. "Right, Zona?"

She cleared her throat and said, "Yeah. Yep." She too picked up a plate, but Caroline watched as Duke mounded shredded cheese onto each quesadilla. "I've forgotten to be grateful for where I live. It was a nice reminder."

"I liked the part about our hands needing to be blessed to do good," Brandon said.

Duke turned and put his quesadillas in the microwave, but Zona added cheese, dolloped on sour cream, then piled on lettuce, tomatoes, and guac before she took her plate to the table.

"What is happening here?" she murmured to Dawson, who hadn't moved to get in line. His father now washed at the sink, and April had gotten in line behind Brandon.

"It's a chili quesadilla," he said. "You just have to imagine a bowl of chili—with all the stuff. Cheese, green onions, sour cream—inside a tortilla." He indicated she should go in front of him, and Caroline knew his mother wouldn't get food until every one of her chicks had it and was eating.

"It's like a taco almost," April said. "I love 'em, and my grandma knew I was in big trouble today, so I'm pretty sure she made them just for me."

"That's not true," Abby said quickly. "I

started the chili last night, sweetheart, and no one knew you were in trouble then."

Caroline glanced at the girl as she loaded hers the same way her daddy did. She passed him the plate, and he swapped his for hers. She started loading it with the other toppings, and about the time she finished, she and her daddy were able to switch plates again.

She wanted to ask what kind of trouble the teenager had gotten into, but she held her tongue. "I'll tell you later," Dawson whispered, nudging her down the line. "You can eat them straight up," he added in a louder voice. "Like a legit quesadilla. I like to dip some of mine in ranch dressing." He leaned over and picked up the bottle on the edge of the counter. "And I like to make others into tacos, like April said."

"So it's chili," Caroline said, seeing all the pieces in front of her. Close family. Lots of good food. Warm house. "But it's a quesadilla-taco-type of situation."

Dawson grinned at her. "You got it, darlin'."

"You want your cheese melted?" Duke

asked, though his plate was done and he could join his wife at the table.

Caroline looked at the two quesadillas she'd put on her plate. "Just one," she said, quickly removing the other. She put a healthy handful of cheese on it and gave the plate to Duke.

"I'll get it for her," Dawson said.

"Thanks, brother." Duke said the word easily, but Caroline wondered how it landed in Dawson's ears. He didn't seem to think much of it, and he made all but one of his quesadillas into triangular tacos.

He did get her plate out, and she dressed up her second quesadilla the way he had. "Can I share your ranch dressing?" she asked.

"Absolutely," he said, taking his plate and the bowl of dressing toward the table. He sat next to Duke, leaving a place for Caroline on the end. Across from April, with a chair still at the head of the table.

For his daddy.

"Daddy," Dawson said when his father arrived with four quesadillas with only melted cheese on them. It was like a chili pizza at this point. "This is Caroline Thompson. Be nice to her please. I'm tryin' to get her to come 'round more often, and I don't need you scaring her away."

"He'll do that just fine on his own," Brandon teased.

Caroline smiled at him, then looked at Wade. "It's great to meet you."

"You too," he said in a perfectly pleasant voice. She'd just taken a bite of her chili-taco-dilla when he asked, "How long have you and Dawson been dating?"

Shredded lettuce flew down her throat she sucked in so hard. She immediately began to cough and choke, while around her, Duke started to laugh, Abby chastised her husband for asking, Wade grumped about being able to ask "perfectly normal" questions, and Dawson patted her on the back, handed her a napkin, and as she recovered, sat there with a positively murderous look on his face.

Finally, it was April who said in a very loud mock whisper, "Grandpa, this is *Car-o-line.*

The woman Dawson's in love with but can't get to go out with him."

"Dust and shadows," Dawson muttered, his eyes suddenly dark and filled with venom. "You can't come out to the owls with me anymore. In fact, you can't ever come out onto the ranch with me ever again. Also, don't come by my house. It's the end for you."

April simply grinned at him and said, "You should've done what I said."

Caroline finally got control of herself, though her lungs felt like they'd have shredded lettuce in them for the rest of her life. Shredded lettuce dipped in bleach. They burned, but she managed to breathe through the raging thoughts that everyone in his family knew about her.

They seemed to know how he felt about her, even the fourteen-year-old girl. This man... he didn't keep things secret—at least not from his family.

She looked at Dawson. "What did April tell you to do?"

"Nothing," Zona yelled from at the other

end of the table. "Everyone knock it off. *This* is why she's not going to come back." She gestured around with her hand, her arms long and reaching far. "And we don't even have all our kids here." She shook her head. "My word, you're as bad as my family."

"That is so not true," April protested immediately while Duke scoffed.

"As bad as your family?" He's the one who shook his head now. "Baby, you have eleven brothers and cousins. That's more than my whole family combined."

Zona said nothing as she bit into her next chili-taco-dilla. Duke looked past Dawson to Caroline. "And then they're all married. And we all have kids. You get together with the Glovers, it's like a hundred people—and that's if some of them are sick or out of town."

"Please," Dawson said. "None of them are ever sick or out of town."

That brought a beat of silence to the kitchen, and then all of the Rhineharts— Dawson included—burst out laughing. Even Arizona.

"He's right," she said as she giggled. "We're a circus." She looked lovingly at her husband. "But it's a good circus, right, hon?"

Duke nodded, a long string of cheese coming from his chili-pizza-taco. "Yeah, baby. It's a good circus." He smiled at her and then Caroline, and then went back to eating.

Everyone did, but Caroline had not gotten her question answered. So she ate her taco and then leaned into Dawson as she wiped her mouth. He bent his head closer in a beautiful, personal way, so he could hear her better.

Oh, she loved that. Always had.

"I still want to know what April advised you to do," she murmured.

To which he said, "I'll tell you later," with a delicious, ruddy flush crawling into his face.

Chapter Fifteen

Dawson breathed in the cool wind as he escaped the hot house through the front door. He looked up into the cloudy sky, feeling as gray and whipped and strung out as the atmosphere appeared to be. "Dear Lord," he breathed.

If he'd known would be an hour-long ordeal with everyone poking fun at him about his non-relationship with Caroline, he'd have herded her off the ranch himself. Ruffin looked up from the corner of the yard, where he'd been sleeping in the shade, and Dawson motioned him to come forward.

"Come on, bud. Let's get out of here." He turned back to open the door for Caroline, who had two plastic containers filled with food. *Of course* Momma couldn't let her go home empty-handed. *Of course* Caroline wanted some chili quesadillas for her sister and niece. *Of course* Dawson was being silly.

But he had work to do, and *lunch with girl-friend* had not been on his schedule for today. Neither had *counsel April.* Or *deal with Duke.* Or *be super social during a meal.*

In short, he was exhausted, running behind, and irritated.

Never a good combination for him.

Caroline spilled out of the house behind him, still exchanging pleasantries and promising to tell Momma how the chili quesadillas were received at her house. She finally made it outside, and the door closed, sealing everyone else in. Thankfully.

She grinned from ear to ear and said, "They're so great."

"Yeah?"

"Yeah." She looked over to him, pure sunshine pouring from her. "Thanks for inviting me."

Dawson nodded and walked with her to her SUV. "Listen," he said, the word vomit about to come up. Perhaps all he'd eaten for lunch would too. "I do want to go out with you." He gestured wildly behind him with one arm. "In case I'm the *only* one who hasn't said so today. So...what do you think? Dinner this weekend?"

Then she wouldn't randomly show up on the ranch and blow up his schedule. He didn't say that out loud, because he had more practice than April in schooling his tongue.

Caroline put the food containers in the back seat of her SUV, really torturing him by not answering right away. She faced him, her smile soft and bright at the same time. "I'd like that," she said.

"Yeah? You're not going to cancel last-minute?" He wasn't sure why he didn't believe her. "I mean, it would just be easier if you said you couldn't go. I get it."

"I didn't say I'd go," she said coolly. "I said I'd like to go to dinner with you this weekend."

He glared at her. "You know what? I've had enough games for one day." Enough teasing. Enough swoops of his stomach from embarrassment or frustration. "I have to get to work." He turned away from her to find Ruffin waiting like the trusty pal he was. And dogs never made fun of him, which suddenly became the biggest plus for them.

"Dawson," she said, latching onto his arm quickly. "I'm sorry. I didn't mean to make fun of you."

He turned back to her, finding worry in her eyes. "Really," she said. "I'd like to go out with you this weekend, and yes, we're going to make that happen." She swallowed hard, looked at her hand, and yanked it back as if just now realizing she touched him. "I am going to talk to Belle."

"I've heard that before," he said quietly, and in the softest tone he could muster in his current mood. "So it really would be easier if you just said no. Then, if the time is ever right and you do ever talk to Belle, we can go out."

"I'm going to talk to her tonight." She lifted her chin. "I've tried a couple of times, but I'm really going to do it this time."

"Okay," he said.

"It took me four attempts at a conversation with my ex-husband before I was able to tell him I was leaving."

Dawson froze, his gaze suddenly searching all over Caroline's face for answers. She looked past him, though, her way of protecting herself. He reached out and took her hand in his. "Okay, sweetheart. It's okay."

That got her to step into his arms. Dawson could hold her for hours and hours. He loved the shape of her in his life, and despite his irritation of only moments ago, he simply knew she belonged with him.

So he could be patient.

He pressed his lips to her lower earlobe, and then moved down a couple of inches to her neck. She smelled like fresh cotton and dirt and a little bit of chili, and he was instantly drunk on the scent of her skin.

He pushed her hair back and kissed her neck right above the collar of her shirt. "Okay," he said, sliding lower to her collarbone. "Whenever you're ready. Whenever Belle's ready."

She tilted her head back, and Dawson swept a kiss up to her chin, getting dangerously close to her mouth. But he couldn't do it. He couldn't kiss her in front of his parents' house, with likely everyone in his family watching.

Especially April.

So with blood burning like fresh lava, he straightened and looked at her. Her gaze had heated considerably too, and he simply nodded at her and pushed his cowboy hat lower over his eyes.

"Dinner," she said. "Friday night. Six?"

"I can make six work," he said in a strangled tone.

"So can I."

He reached past her and opened the driver's door. "I'll text you later."

She got in her SUV, backed out, and left

the ranch, dust lifting into the air behind her tires. Dawson stood there in the gravel parking area, and watched.

He hadn't even realized anyone else had come outside until Zona said, "April will do your small animal chores, Daws," as she went by. "And Brandon said he'd make dinner tonight. That should give you back the time you lost during lunch today."

She got in the truck as Duke and April went by, both of them wearing somewhat sheepish looks on their faces. So they at least recognized how they'd embarrassed him today. They left, and still Dawson stood there.

He had no idea where Daddy and Brandon went, but they didn't come out front. No, it was his momma who came and linked her arm through his. She stared down the road that led to Duke's and off the ranch. "She's a lovely woman, Dawson," she said fondly. "I do hope it works out for you two."

"Me too, Momma," he whispered.

"You been praying over her?"

"Yes," he admitted. "Her sister is having a

hard time right now, and Caroline thinks us dating with cause a lot of problems and pain for Belle."

"Ah, I see." Momma leaned her head against Dawson's arm, the way she so often did to Daddy. "So two more to add to my prayers. All right. I can do it." She turned and headed back to the house while Dawson marveled over the strength of his mother's faith.

And all at once, he realized he should've been praying for Belle too. Not just his own selfish needs and wants to have Caroline in his life. Not just for strength and clarity of mind for her to talk to Belle.

But for Belle herself to be healed enough for her to understand her sister. For her to support her sister. "For Belle," he murmured.

And then, because he had lost a lot of time already today, he turned away from the road, away from his thoughts, away from his family, and headed for the safety and the perfect organization of his barn-office.

Once inside, he locked the door and leaned his back against it. "Lord," he said, almost panting for how fast he'd walked here. "Calm my troubled soul." He took a deep breath, trying to fight off the panic, trying to ward off the rising desperation.

If he could just go through his routine, he'd be fine. He opened his eyes and caught sight of his whiteboard. "First," he said, stepping over to it and plucking off a blue note. "The owls got measured."

He put that note on the corner of his desk. "I moved the sprinklers in field four." The green note—an agricultural one—joined the blue one. Blue, for physical facilities tasks. "I ran five miles this morning."

The yellow note—personal goals—got added to the *completed* pile. He meticulously went through what had been done, and he made new notes for Link coming to the ranch to see the owls on the fence line, for a phone call he needed to make in the morning, and for a meeting he'd found out about via email just before April had shown up.

Then, he stared at the pink pad of sticky notes, his fingers twitching toward it. He'd written on so many of these, but only once had he used the word "date."

Now, he quickly peeled off a note and picked up his pen. *Date with Caroline*, he scrawled, and then he stood and added the pink note to Friday's column on his board.

"Dear Lord," he prayed. "Bless Belle that she can have ears to hear and a heart open to her sister's words."

And blast it all, Duke had been right. It *had* been real nice to have a different voice utter a prayer in the Rhinehart family.

Now, if only God could make this prayer come true soon. "Tonight," he whispered, totally begging for himself now. "Please, God, help them both to make it through this tonight."

Chapter Sixteen

Caroline paced on the back deck, still wearing her putrid half-yellow, half-forest-green shirt and her work shorts. She'd gone straight to the cupboard to get the Biscoff when she'd gotten home and found Belle's car gone.

"Where is she?" Displeasure streamed through Caroline. Why couldn't anything be easy? Why couldn't she have met Dawson a year ago, when Belle was whole and there were no owls between them?

"The owls are not an issue," she told herself as she dug into the jar of Biscoff for another spoonful of comfort. "His daddy didn't even blink when Dawson introduced you." Nothing about their relationship was scandalous. People met through their jobs all the time.

She scoffed as the deliciously sweet cookie butter hit her tongue. *You don't even have a relationship to label.* Something couldn't be scandalous if it didn't exist.

She'd just licked the spoon clean when Judy yelled, "Aunt Caroline! We're he-ere!"

Caroline spun from the back railing of the deck, caught with her stress treat in her hand. Before she could move, Judy came running outside with all her six-year-old enthusiasm. "Guess where we went?"

Caroline stabbed the spoon in the Biscoff jar and set it on the railing behind her as she asked, "Where?"

"To this really cool buffaloes museum." She wore the look of someone who'd just been told that unicorns exist—and she'd seen one.

"Buffaloes." Caroline laughed as she shook her head. "That's not how you say it."

"What's the plural of buffalo?" Belle asked, and Caroline lifted her gaze to find her sister standing in the doorway, a kind smile on her face.

Judy turned toward her, her smile slipping. "Buffaloes."

"It's just buffalo," Belle said. "Like deer, remember?"

"Sure," Judy said, though she clearly didn't remember. She skipped past Caroline and into the back yard. "Then Momma bought us cheeseburgers on the way back!" She started singing about cheeseburgers and French fries as she went through her exploration of the yard.

That left Caroline to face Belle, and as she did, something welled up in her throat. The choking sensation filled her whole mouth and ballooned up into her brain. These feelings couldn't stay here, and with everything feeling too hot and like it might explode at any moment, she said, "I have to talk to you about Dawson."

Belle's expression changed from one of ease, and plural buffaloes, and a fun afternoon with her daughter, cheeseburgers, and French fries to one of surprise.

Caroline almost scoffed. Surely Belle knew Caroline had been texting him. She flipped her phone over whenever they were together, and she silenced it whenever his sound came in.

"He's asked me out," she said. "And I'd like to go out with him." Those few words—how many had she spoken?—freed everything else inside her. "I know you're going through a really hard time with Chuck and being here and wondering what your life is going to be." Caroline held up one hand as Belle opened her mouth to say something.

Probably to deny everything Caroline had just said. But they both knew Belle had been a complete mess since she'd arrived in Three Rivers. Caroline had been praying and praying for ways to help her sister, and she'd only ever gotten one answer.

Be there.

If she dated Dawson, she wouldn't be there for Belle.

A tear ran right down the middle of her soul, and a mighty wail came rising from it.

"I'm still going to be here," she said. "I am.

Even if I could see him once a week, I think we'd both take that. But I won't go out with him if it's just too much for you." Caroline meant every word, though she immediately started praying.

Please don't let her say it'll be too much for her, she thought. *Please, please, please. One date a week isn't that much.*

"I can go to his cabin for lunch," she said, seizing onto the silence and injecting something into it. "You won't even know I'm dating him."

Belle's surprise had melted into something else, but Caroline wasn't entirely sure what emotion she wore now. She'd gotten good at masking how she really felt, but the moment she spoke, Caroline would know the truth. Belle could hide things on the surface, but voices came from deep within a person, and she was a terrible liar.

"How can I keep you from dating him?" Belle asked, a fair bit of anguish in her voice. "I can't do that." She moved closer and right into Caroline's arms. "If anyone deserves the kind of happiness we both dream about, it's you."

"It's just a first date with a cowboy," Caroline whispered, though her afternoon, evening, and late-night texting sessions with Dawson could probably be counted as several dates. She shivered in her sister's arms at the thought of the way he'd kissed her today.

All around her lips, but never landing on them.

"Which one's Dawson?" Belle asked as she stepped back. She wiped her eyes as she moved past Caroline to the edge of the deck. She folded her arms, protecting herself as she watched Judy play in the yard. "Isn't he the one you griped about for months?"

"Yes," Caroline clipped out. "But he's really sweet in real life, and I don't know. I at least want to try."

"We sat by his parents at the New Year's fundraiser," Belle said.

Caroline moved to her side and nodded. "Yep."

"You disappeared with him." Belle sounded

accusatory, and Caroline's defenses rose straight up. "You said it was a 'lame breakfast' though he did know how to make the hash browns you like."

"Maybe I was trying to protect both of us." Caroline crossed her arms too, trying to hold everything together. "I've never thought I'd date again. Or get married." She didn't need to explain more to Belle.

A new, horrible, agonizing thought filled her, drowning out what Belle said next. *You don't have to tell Belle, but you will have to tell Dawson.*

He knew she'd been married, and she'd stood up to him when he'd hung up on her, but he didn't know the whole iceberg, the knobbled, craggly ledges of ice that existed beneath the surface of a divorce.

"...go out with him?" Belle asked.

Caroline blinked. "Sorry, what?"

"When are you going to go out with him?"

"I don't know. Friday night," she said, her mind splitting and coming back together quickly. "It's really okay? I mean, it might be terrible."

Belle scoffed, doing what Caroline had wanted to do a few minutes ago. "Please. You should've seen your face when you said you wanted to go out with him."

"Oh? What did I look like?"

"Like you're dying to see him right now. Like you won't make it through dinner if he doesn't show up and give you a reason to keep living."

Caroline finally turned to look at her sister. Their eyes met, and she saw so much of herself inside Belle. The strong parts of her that she'd developed over the past few years of heartache, trauma, and healing. Belle's were babies, while Caroline had definitely had time to build up her wells of strength. She had strategies for when she started to backslide, doubt herself, or long for something she didn't truly want.

Belle would get there, but as Caroline looked at her, she knew she wasn't there yet.

"I do not need him to show up before dinner so I can keep living," she said dryly.

Belle burst out laughing, a drastically different sound than Caroline had heard her make recently. It lifted her heart and calmed her soul, and she allowed herself a small smile. Maybe she'd *like* to see Dawson, but she didn't *need* to in order to keep breathing.

Belle's fingers found Caroline's and held on. "Really, sissy. Go out with him. Maybe it'll be wonderful and you'll finally find a man who'll cherish the ground you walk on."

"Maybe," Caroline murmured. "It's not like we'll go fast," she said. "My rule is—"

"All four seasons and a road trip," Belle said together with Caroline. "I know."

"And Thanksgiving, Christmas, and both birthdays," she said. "I'm not *ever* going to have my birthday ignored again."

"Does this Dawson know when it is?"

"Not yet," Caroline said. "And I'm not going to tell him that what he does for me is a deal-breaker."

"Hmm," Belle said. "That seems unfair. Seems like you're setting him up to fail."

"No," Caroline said. "That's why you date

for at least a year to get all the experiences. I want to know how he celebrates things. Him. Not me influencing him."

"Okay," Belle said, a heavy dose of doubt in her voice. "You know what you want, Caroline, I know that."

"Yes," she said as she squeezed her sister's hand. "And it's not Biscoff for dinner, so since you and Judy already ate, I guess I'm on my own."

"I called you," she said. "You didn't pick up."

"I was maybe in the office," she said. "I swear, that place is a black hole."

"Order that Chinese food you like."

"Ooh, good idea."

"And go text Dawson." Belle gave her a shaky smile that strengthened after only a minute. "I promise I won't ruin things for you, okay?"

"It's not going to be easy for you." Caroline's worry tripled, but she had a coping mechanism for this. "I know it's not my job to make sure you're okay," she said quietly. "You have to make sure you're okay. I can help by doing certain things or not doing them, for sure. But...."

"I am going to be okay if you start dating," Belle said. "Okay? I promise I am."

"I'm just worried." Caroline released her sister's hand and put her arm around her. "I know what this feels like for you, and I want to be here for you."

"You are," she said as she leaned into her. Belle had lost about twenty pounds in the past couple of months, and she seemed like such a shell of the person Caroline had once known and loved. Of course she still loved her, but she felt like she was getting to know her all over again.

A new, different version of her.

She took a deep breath, becoming a new, different version of herself. A woman who'd finally told her sister about a handsome cowboy who would surely kiss her properly on their first date on Friday night.

"Okay." She exhaled. "I'm going to go call for Chinese and let Dawson know that we're on for this weekend."

"Okay," Belle said, and Caroline took her Biscoff and went back toward the house. She capped the jar and put the spoon in the sink to load into the dishwasher later. She looked out the window to find Belle sitting on the top step of the deck, her knees drawn to her chest. In the fetal position almost.

Her heartbeat crunched and shrieked, and Caroline didn't see how she could possibly go out with Dawson, no matter what Belle said.

"You're not responsible for fixing her," she told herself, something she'd said hundreds of times in therapy about her ex-husband. "You're only responsible for fixing yourself. For how you feel."

She couldn't control Joe or what he said or felt. How he acted. That belonged to him.

Caroline could control what she said or felt, as well as how she acted. And she didn't have to be small or less than she was so anyone could feel better about themselves or their life.

"I just didn't think that should include Belle," she murmured. Her phone vibrated in her pocket, and Caroline took it out, her fingers brushing the gross fabric of her work uniform. She needed a shower, dinner, and to call Dawson.

But he'd texted. *Thinking about you and praying for you and Belle. Did they like the chili-taco-dillas?*

In the wake of her stress, Caroline had forgotten about the chili quesadillas. She quickly tapped out a message to Dawson, hoping it would spur him into a good mood the way it had her.

Talked to her, Dawson, and we're....
ON FOR FRIDAY!

Chapter Seventeen

Dawson walked out into the main living room of the cabin and spread his arms wide. "Well? Trying too hard?"

Brandon looked up from his phone, his smile appearing before he'd even taken in Dawson's clothes. April got to her feet while Link and Misty studied him too. He'd invited them all to help him make sure he didn't humiliate himself on this very important first date with Caroline.

"The jeans are great." She circled him, looking from high to low and back, and he dropped his arms back to his sides. "Cowboy boots. Sexy. Caroline will like those. The belt buckle too."

He growled and gave his niece a side-eyed look before returning his attention to Link. "Link?"

"You look great," Link said. "Right, baby?"

Misty beamed at Dawson, and she got up, leaving her fiancé on the couch. She joined April, and they both studied his shirt. He felt naked in front of them, and he looked over to Link. He'd known the cowboy just fine before he was made the junior foreman at Shiloh Ridge, but when that had happened, their friendship had grown and strengthened.

Link had moved to a house closer to the Rhinehart Ranch, and he oversaw a lot for his family's ranch that brought him south more often, and what he needed was what Dawson did for his family's ranch. They'd been going to game nights at Finn and Edith's, and Dawson had been the seventh wheel with them, Link and Misty, and Alex and Nicki for far too long.

Fine, only about six months. But still. It felt

like a long time. Or like he and Brandon were a couple when they went out with their dating or married friends.

"It's a shirt," he said to Link. "What are they looking at?"

Link chuckled and shook his head. "Don't ask me, cowboy."

"It's kind of dark," April finally said, and Misty snapped her fingers as if she hadn't been able to think of a word to describe his shirt.

"Yes," she said. "It's dark, Dawson. Don't you have something a little more...festive?"

"Festive?" Dawson glared at her. "We're going to dinner at a place that only serves potatoes."

"Not true," Brandon said from the couch. "They have tons of meat to go with the potatoes."

"It's not a steakhouse," Dawson said. "Or anything fancy. I just don't want to be embarrassed when I show up." He held out the fabric of his navy blue shirt and looked at it. "This one's clean."

"Honey, this woman you've been pining for

deserves more than 'this one's clean.'" Misty smiled at him. "Can we see the choices?"

"I have not been *pining*."

"I know which bedroom is his." April started down the hall without permission from Dawson, and he decided a simple cowboy like him couldn't lasso a tornado and rein it in.

"Shadow lands," he said to Link. "Do you go through this every time you go out?"

Link looked up from his phone. "No, but Mitch helped me for a bit." He raised his phone. "He wants to see the shirt."

"Sure," Dawson said darkly. "What's one more opinion on a shirt I'm pretty sure I'm not going to be wearing tonight?" He turned in a full circle for Mitch and made the sign as he asked, "Well?"

Mitch started signing, but Dawson couldn't understand him. He held up both hands and said, "Link, help me out."

Link looked at his phone and laughed, signed back, and looked at Dawson. "He said it's kind of boring. Bland." His eyes glittered with mischief. "And too dark."

"This one, Uncle Dawson," April said from behind him, and he turned to see her holding up a bright orange plaid shirt. *Orange.*

"I didn't even know I owned that shirt," Dawson said dumbly.

"It's not as bright as you think," Misty said. "It's got blue and black stripes too. Tons of white." She gave him a pretty grin. "She's going to love it."

He pulled off his blue polo and put on the plaid shirt, buttoning it up to the throat. "One or two buttons undone?"

"Oh, two," Misty said, swatting away his hand and pulling open the button he'd just fastened. "Let me see." She stepped back and April joined her, wearing an impish look on her face. "Yes, this is it." She looked at April. "Don't you think?"

"Totally," she said. "You're hot, Uncle Dawson."

"Ew," he said, which made April giggle. "Don't ever tell me that again."

Someone knocked on the door, and they all turned toward it. Dawson was already up and he lived here, so he figured he could get it. "Seems strange someone's knocking," he said. Duke and anyone in his family would just walk in.

"Oh, I bet it's my brother," Misty said. "He was going to come here after he showered, so we could go grab dinner."

Dawson pulled open the door, expecting to find Danny Granger standing there—and he did. "Howdy, Danny." Dawson grinned and stuck out his hand for the other man to shake.

He did; he smiled; he said, "Howdy, Dawson."

"C'mon in. Seems like we're all leaving." He stepped back and then went into the kitchen to get his truck keys. "Miss April, you're coming with me. I'll drop you at home."

"No, I got permission to go hang out with Pearl Jo and Chaz tonight," she said. "Aunt Willa is going to pick me up here."

"So you're just going to hang out here alone?" He cocked his eyebrows at her. "When is she coming? They're goin' to dinner, and I've got to get too."

"Let me text her."

"I can drive you down there," he said. "Are you at Ace's or Cactus's?"

"I don't know." Her fingers flew over her phone, and she looked up a moment later. "What? You don't trust me in your house?"

"You just dug through my closet and found a shirt I didn't know I owned," he said. "So, no, not really." He grinned at her, because they both knew he trusted her to stay in his cabin just fine.

Her phone chimed, and a moment later, she said, "She just passed the Top Cottage. She'll be here in two minutes."

Dawson nodded and took in the others around him. He would die in a family as big as the Glovers, but he did love the camaraderie coming from everyone in his house right now. Link sat signing to Mitch, while Misty chatted easily with Danny and Brandon.

April simply looked at him, and he moved over to her and gave her a quick hug. "You be good now, ya'hear?"

"Yes, sir," she said.

"All right." He stepped back and lifted his hand. "I'm headed out. Pray for me and wish me luck."

"You got it, brother," Brandon said while Misty yelled, "You don't need luck. She's going to love you!"

Link waved, and April said, "Just do what I said, Uncle Dawson. You'll be fine." She grinned at him wickedly, and while Dawson was dying to kiss Caroline, he wasn't sure how or when that was going to happen. He'd figure it out as the night progressed, he supposed, but not if he didn't get going.

The drive to her house happened during a single country music song, he swore. He couldn't even remember making the turn or if the light had been green when he had. But he now drove down her street, his mind kicking at him to focus and be present.

He pulled into her driveway, every muscle in his body tense and screaming. Probably because of the orange shirt, which also had a lot of white in it. It wasn't really orange at all, at least not a solid color. "It's fine," he said. He didn't have a back-up shirt, so it would have to be fine.

The trek up her sidewalk to the porch took at least as long as it had for him to drive here, and he listened to her doorbell ding and dong through her house. Dawson tucked his hands into his pockets, praying with all he had that he hadn't missed a text.

He'd left his phone in the truck, so he couldn't even check.

The door didn't open, and he checked to make sure her car sat in the driveway. It sure did, which meant she was home. Belle had her own car, and it wasn't here. That only made Dawson's pulse accelerate, and when the door started to swing open, something grabbed him by the throat and held on tight.

Caroline appeared, a beautiful smile on her face and a gorgeous flowered dress falling to her ankles. It spilled pink, blue, purple, and peachy blooms from top to bottom, and Dawson couldn't help smiling at such a fun pattern. Her bare shoulders teased him, as did the V in the neck that stopped just short of showing too much. "Hey," she said easily. "I just need my sweater."

She turned slightly away from him to collect that, and Dawson somehow knew to move into the house to help her put it on. It came in the same color of blue as the flowers, a perfect match, and he said, "You are stunningly beautiful, Caroline," in a voice he himself hardly recognized.

He held the sweater while she put her arm through it, and he smoothed down the sleeve as she settled it in place over her chest. "Thank you." She looked up at him, and Dawson didn't even think.

He simply took the woman he'd definitely been pining over into his arms, lowered his head, and kissed her where he'd wanted to days ago.

Yes, her lips tasted just as amazing as he'd imagined. Better. Softer. She didn't protest in the slightest, and the way she kissed him back told him she'd been pining after him too. Every woman he'd been out with in the past couple of years had been stale. Dry toast. No spark when he kissed them.

But Caroline...oh, Dawson had caught fire and was burning, and he didn't even care. As long as he got to keep kissing Caroline, and kissing Caroline, and kissing Caroline.

Chapter Eighteen

Caroline did her best to keep up with Dawson. He knew how to kiss a woman to make her feel adored and cherished, like he'd do anything just to make sure he could kiss her again later.

She hadn't been kissed like this before. Not ever. Not even with her husband. Never, ever, ever. The level of care he could broadcast, the way he seemed to want her but also respect her was a whole new thing for her.

When he finally pulled back, Caroline's chest heaved. She kept her eyes closed, and she had no idea where the words came from as she asked, "Well? Was that like kissing your sister?"

"Absolutely not," he said huskily. "In fact, I'm going to do it again." He claimed her lips again, but only for a couple strokes. Then he moved that magical mouth of his to her cheek, her ear, and down her neck. "There's a whole lot of something here, darlin'."

"Yes," she said, her voice mostly made of air. "I think so too."

He pulled back and straightened. Caroline managed to open her eyes and look at him. No shyness or embarrassment pulled through her, and Dawson gazed back at her just as seriously. "Sorry, I suppose I should've waited until after the date. You just...I've wanted to go out with you for a while is all."

"It's absolutely fine," she said, straightening her sweater and shouldering her purse again. She ran her fingers up the buttons on his shirt, a cute orange, white, and blue checkered pattern. "I really like this shirt."

One of his hands tightened on her waist. "Are you just sayin' that?"

"Why would I just say that?" She flipped up one corner of his collar and then smoothed it flat again. "You look amazing. It goes with your hair, and sort of...brightens your personality." She smiled at him, but his lips didn't tip at all.

"I need my personality brightened?"

"No," she said. "That's not what I meant."

"Well, what did you mean?"

"I just meant that you look good in it," she said. "You wear it well. It fits you."

"It is my size," he said dryly. He put pressure on her lower back, just enough to get her to exit the house.

"That's not what I meant either," she said. "It fits *you*, like who you are."

"How so?"

She watched her step as she went down the stairs, because she wore a long dress and a pair of sandals she didn't normally strap her feet into. "Because you have all these different facets of yourself, you know? You're the favorite uncle, and you've got crows for pets, and you make lists, but you're also sort of this rough-and-tumble,   not-afraid-to-get-his-hands-dirty kind of cowboy too. So the shirt isn't something I'd pick for you, but it fits, because you have a lot of different parts of yourself that make you, you."

Dawson started to laugh, and Caroline smiled at the throaty sound of it, almost like it was rusty and he didn't do such a thing very often. "That was a lot of words, sweetheart."

He opened her door, and she paused and turned to look at him. "I like the shirt, Dawson," she said. "I like that you kissed me without even saying hello. I like—"

"I said hello."

She grinned at him and leaned her palm into his chest. "You did not. You said I was beautiful, and then you kissed me."

"Well, hello then," he said, grinning.

And there was that smile. She'd asked him for it, but this wasn't a forced gesture. He really did seem happy to see her. "Hello," she murmured back, her gaze dropping to his mouth, almost as if she'd miss her mark if she wasn't looking right at it.

She kissed him, so glad that physical barrier

had been broken. But he didn't let her carry on too long. "I have something real special for you," he said, his lips barely brushing hers. "So get in, okay? I don't want to be late."

"You do not like being late," she said, safe and warm within the radius of his body heat.

"I do not."

"Are you gonna tell me more about why that is?" She backed up and caught the hint of surprise in his eyes before she turned to get in the truck. He said nothing as she smoothed her skirt under her legs, and he closed the door.

Caroline's heart pounded, but she wasn't entirely sure why. Maybe from the way Dawson muttered to himself as he rounded the hood, or maybe from the way he glared at the sky like it had done him a personal wrong as he turned toward his door.

"You don't have to," she said the moment he opened his door. "It's—you mentioned that there's a reason why you like lists so much and don't like being late, and that you'd tell me about it sometime. But it doesn't have to be tonight."

"Okay," he said.

"Okay." She breathed easier and looked straight ahead as he adjusted the air. "So what's this special thing?"

"It's not a *what*," he said as he backed out of her driveway. "It's a *where*, and it's a surprise." He looked left and then right, his gaze holding on her before making the turn off her street. "If you don't know about it, which would be kind of wild."

"What is it?"

"How can I tell you if it's a surprise?" He made the turn, and he sounded a tad disgruntled. "I think you'll like it, and if you've been there before, fine. If you haven't, then I think you'll like their menu."

"So it's a restaurant."

"I just told you it was a place," he said.

"You said it was a where," she said. "Not a restaurant."

"Okay, fine," he said. "It's a restaurant, and I'm pretty sure I have the menu memorized at this point." He sounded like he'd rather swallow broken glass than keep talking to her, and Caroline pressed her palms together.

Dawson gripped the steering wheel tightly—so tightly his knuckles had started to turn pale. Her pulse felt just as stretched, taut, and she wanted to snap at him. Revert to her default and demand he take her home if he couldn't be in a good mood.

At the same time, she'd just told him about all these different facets of himself and how she liked them, and his grouchy persona was one of those.

"Hey." Caroline reached over and curled her hand around his closest one. It took a moment for him to relinquish his hold on the wheel, and she ran her fingers over his. She moved her other hand to do the same, and he finally relaxed under her touch. "I didn't mean to upset you."

"I'm so dang nervous," he growled. "It's not you." He took a breath that expanded his wide chest, and Caroline smiled to herself.

"Why are you nervous?"

"Because I'm always nervous when I do things outside my routine."

So he was routine, didn't like to be late, and made extensive to-do lists. Caroline took a peek at him, this gentle giant of a cowboy driving her somewhere he'd obsessed over. Had the menu memorized.

"What's inside your routine?" she asked. "What do you like to do?"

"I like running," he said.

She giggled, which drew his attention from the road. Finally. "No one really likes running, do they?"

"Don't they?" He finally dropped his left hand to the bottom of the steering wheel instead of strangling it. "I do. It helps me pound out my frustrations and align my head for the day."

"So you get up early to do this."

"Yes," he said. "Five o'clock."

"It's almost past your bedtime now," she teased. "This place we're going better be fast." She smiled at him, relieved and a bit proud of herself when she got his grin in return.

"I don't care how late we are," he said. "It's our first date, so time doesn't matter."

As if Caroline hadn't already been swooning over Dawson. *Time doesn't matter.*

She knew it did, as she'd wasted so much time on Joe. So much time trying to make things work between them. So much time trying to get herself back again.

But with Dawson, time didn't matter right now. The night was young, and he'd sacrifice whatever he had to in order to be with her. That was what he was really saying, and Caroline turned to her window to check and see if the heat she felt in her cheeks had turned them red.

She couldn't really tell, and a minute later, he said, "Here we are."

Caroline looked out the windshield and caught sight of a sign that read Spudalicious. Pure happiness burst through her in pops and sparks. "Spudalicious?"

"They have more than potatoes," he said. "But I thought you'd find something here you like." He gave her another smile, this one a little hesitant, and then got out to come get her door. She stared at the sign as he came around, noting it wasn't only for Spudalicious. At least a dozen names sat on it, not all of them restaurants.

The building in front of them stretched up for at least a dozen stories, and Caroline peered up to the top of it as Dawson opened her door.

"It's on the roof," he said. "But they have heaters for outdoor seating, or we can request a table inside." The sun had started to settle into dusk, and Caroline shivered in her sweater. Maybe that was from the flesh memory of Dawson's warm hands skimming her skin as he helped her into the garment.

Or the idea of a restaurant with only potatoes on the menu. Or the fact that Dawson had arranged their first date at a rooftop, potatoes-only restaurant, because *she'd* like it.

He'd thought about her ahead of time. So far, this man ticked every box Caroline had, and she tucked her hand in his and went with him down the sidewalks and up to the building.

Heat blew inside, and they crowded onto

the elevator with several others going up to the rooftop restaurants. "How did you know this place existed?" she asked as they all got spit out into the lobby and had to face their dining choices.

Six different restaurants took up the top floor, from Spudalicious to a pizzeria, to a smoothie shop that wasn't open right now. Dawson led her toward the bright brown façade of the potato place, and she expected bright, spuddy music to come pouring out.

Caroline wasn't far off, but the song wasn't as beachy and festive as she'd imagined. This place definitely boasted a bright atmosphere, with white lights and cartoon potatoes in a variety of shapes, sizes, and ages decorating the welcome wall.

Dawson moved past the others sitting or standing to give his name to a hostess, and she consulted the tablet in front of her. Caroline felt like a movie star on his arm, every cell in her body glowing with an unnamed energy.

The hostess picked up two menus with

leather covers, handed them to someone, and said, "Diamond, two-twelve."

The other woman took the menus and smiled heartily at Dawson. "This way, sir."

"Thank you," he said diplomatically, and he nodded to the hostess before he went with the other woman. Caroline almost stumbled after him, as she'd been expecting to be told they'd have to wait a half-hour before they could be seated. After all, there were at least a dozen people waiting for tables, and everywhere she looked, she saw patrons already eating.

Baked potatoes. Potato chowder. French fries. Latkes. Hash browns—and Caroline's heart tumbled to her toes and rocketed back into its rightful place in her chest.

"Those look amazing," she said, her eyes glued to someone's crispy, browned, hash browns on their plate. Her mouth watered, and she'd never been so glad to be hungry in her life. "Dawson, did you see those?"

"I see 'em, darlin'," he said, still tugging her along through the maze of tables and chairs.

The woman in front of him led him to a snort flight of three steps, and up they went. She opened a glass door and led them past one, two, three empty tables.

"Would you like the window open and the heater on?" she asked as she indicated the last table on this narrow strip that was elevated above the rest. "It's the best atmosphere, and we can always close the window if you're too cold." She smiled at Caroline, who looked at Dawson.

"Window down or up?" he asked.

"Down," Caroline said. "Please." She turned to see the floor-to-ceiling windows did have a pane that could be lowered to let in fresh air. Her heartbeat settled like a deep bass drum in her soul when she saw the view. "Dawson," she breathed out. "Look at this."

"Menus here," the woman said. "I'll get your window down and your heater on, and Candice will be your waitress tonight." She left while Dawson came to Caroline's side, the two of them admiring the gorgeous view of Three Rivers and then the wilderness beyond.

"See that street lamp at almost eleven o'clock?" he asked. "A bit out there. Past that strip of lights on the right."

Caroline searched in the near distance, finding the strip of lights and then moving further south. "Yeah," she said when she found it.

"That's the turn to Seven Sons Ranch," he said. "Hidden Hills is another twenty minutes past that."

"Can we see my house from here?" she asked, suddenly scanning the pricks of light in the town. "I need a picture of this. It's incredible." She whipped out her phone and took a few shots of the town while Dawson told her that her house sat to the west, and no, they couldn't see it.

"If we eat at Cagney's," he said. "The Teppanyaki place next door, we probably can." He took his seat at the table, and Caroline joined him on the adjacent side. The square table had been situated so that the point of it reached the wall, with a slanted seat along each side. No chairs waited for a party of four, as this was obviously a booth for two people to sit side-by-side and enjoy the view of Three Rivers.

"Dawson," she gushed as she joined him. "This is so amazing. I love this so much." She'd never felt so sparkly and full of light.

"Wait'll you see the menu," he said as he lifted up the slim volume and handed it to her. Anticipation and excitement threaded through her, mirroring the way she'd felt during the drive up to his house a few weeks ago for their proper New Year's Day breakfast together.

She flipped open the menu, hardly daring to hope for all the potatoey things she loved best. The first word at the top of the menu had cartoon potatoes dancing all over it, with the two As made entirely out of a potato with a carved oval in it for the hole in the letter.

BREAKFAST.

The best word in the English language.

Caroline looked over to Dawson, who'd buried himself in the menu he claimed to have memorized. "This is the best date I've ever been on," she blurted out, causing Dawson to lower his menu.

"Yeah?" he asked. "We haven't even ordered yet. Maybe it'll be gross."

Caroline almost felt like crying she was so excited. She set down her menu and held his gaze. "Thank you for brining me here. Will you order for me?"

He swallowed but said, "Yeah, of course," as if he'd been planning to order her food for her tonight all along. Glad she didn't have to decide, Caroline sighed happily and looked out the window again. It had been lowered, and a distinct hint of heat came in from an appliance she couldn't see.

Yes, this was the best date ever, and she decided it didn't matter if the food was good or not. Dawson had *thought of her* and planned something *for her*, and that was worth more than the taste of a really great plate of perfectly crispy hash browns.

Oh, yes, it absolutely was.

Chapter Nineteen

Mitchell Glover laughed as Link told him about Dawson's "potato date" from the night before. He'd feel bad if Dawson wasn't right there on the screen, also laughing about it.

So it went well, he signed, not really asking. Dawson had a glow Mitch could probably get a tan from though he lived a thousand miles away from the Texas Panhandle.

Went great, Dawson said, as he knew a little sign language. Sometimes he had to have Link interpret for him, especially if Mitch signed too fast. Now that he lived around and with so many other deaf people, he sometimes forgot that he couldn't speed through the signs with his family.

I only ordered breakfast for her, Dawson said. *It's her favorite meal, and then I got her a plate of French fries and an extra-bacon-loaded baked potato.*

Wow, Mitch said. *So you're to kissing level after a date like that.*

Dawson looked at Link, who translated for him, and Dawson simply nodded. Mitch laughed again, so glad for his friend. He honestly was. But he knew this video call would end, and he'd be trapped back in his silent bubble.

You're being unfair, he told himself. He'd been really trying to call out his negative thought patterns when he had them. Mostly at the advice of his therapist, who asked at every appointment if he'd been able to start rewiring his mind.

Mitch reached for the notebook he kept on the table with his laptop, as he'd also identified that a lot of his self-depreciating thoughts came when he spoke with his family via video. Guilt had riddled him about that realization for the first few weeks, and with the help of his counselor, he'd been able to let that go.

The Glovers were simply a very hard family to live in. Amazing, but hard. *So much to live up to*, Mitch thought as he wrote the thought out.

He looked up again just as Link said ...*not listening*.

No, Mitch wasn't listening, which he couldn't do anyway. Not in the way other people could. He hadn't been *watching*, and that was different than Link. He could write down a thought, even if his handwriting looked like chicken scratch, and hear the person on the other end of the call at the same time.

Mitch couldn't.

Focusing on what you can't do instead of what you can, he thought, and he held up his hand for Link, so he could write that down too.

Sorry, he finally said. *Writing stuff down for my therapist*.

Link immediately sobered, though he'd

been grinning about something with Dawson. *What's she having you do?*

Write down negative thoughts, he said. *It's working too. I can recognize them all the time now, and she's helping me switch them around.*

Negative thoughts? Link looked over to Dawson. *About what we were talking about?*

Mitch didn't want to get into it right now. Link, though he lived far away, had been nothing but, well, Link. Kind and supportive, any way he could. He'd sent Mitch dinner on his birthday, as well as a ten-pound package of all of his favorite chocolate treats, with a card signed by every person in the Glover family—even the babies.

He felt loved and missed on every side, and he simply needed his mind to stop telling his heart that he wasn't.

He waved his hands like, *No big deal,* and Link nodded. He wouldn't drop it, but he'd leave it for now. No, Mitch had not started attending the deaf church at Whispering Paws, though he'd heard the pastor was a deaf man himself and said amazing things with his hands.

A friend of his had said he could practically hear Pastor Darvy's passion and bellowing voice, though he was a non-vocal deaf person, like Mitch.

For now, Mitch relied on Link's testimony that God loved him, and when he was ready, he felt certain he'd be able to return to his faith. He hadn't spoken about any of it with his momma, as she was a pastor in Three Rivers. Not only that, but a pastor everyone loved. Absolutely adored.

Mitch couldn't even count how many people had told him how much they loved his momma's sermons—how much they loved her.

And Mitch did too, but he had a hard time separating her sermons from her as his mother, and he simply needed...time.

He knew church attendance was important. At least he supposed it was, but he knew people who didn't believe at all but went to church every week. Cactus, who Mitch called Dad, didn't attend church very often to this day, though the man had more faith in and love for God than anyone else Mitch knew.

So he needed time, and with Link's encouragement, Mitch had prayed to know what to do. God had answered him in the most maddening way in the world—*what would you like to do, Mitch?*

He didn't want to decide. *How about that?* he'd asked God. *Just tell me what to do.*

He'd not gotten another answer after that, and the Lord had left it in his hands. Every day, Mitch got up in silence and went about his day in silence, the question blazing through his mind.

What would you like to do, Mitch?

Hey, he said next. *I'm going for my cochlear implant consultation next week.*

Link stayed sober as he nodded. *When is it?*

Mitch smiled and shook his head. *I'm not telling you. Then you won't be able to show up unannounced.*

Link glared at him, his blue eyes filled with challenge. *Mitch,* was all he said.

And you can't tell my parents, Mitch said, though Link had already sworn he wouldn't. Some of the best doctors in the world lived here in Virginia, and with the deaf school and college nearby, they had plenty of business for cochlear implants.

But such a device wasn't for everyone. Mitch had never been verbal, and he'd already learned that even with implants, he likely wouldn't be able to speak English with men like Link and Dawson for at least a decade after his surgery.

Ten years.

Of constant study and language input from TV shows, movies, podcasts, anything he could practice hearing with and see captions at the same time. That way, he could learn how the vowels sounded in words he already knew but only with the shape of his fingers.

I want a full update the moment you walk out of there, Link said.

It probably won't be something I can do, Mitch admitted, though he'd been far more downtrodden after the initial interest meeting. He was almost twenty-eight years old, and all he wanted in the whole world was to have a regular conversation with someone on the phone. Not a video call.

He wanted to hear his phone ring and know it was Link before he saw the screen. He wanted to hear his best friend's voice. He wanted to use his own. Everything inside him felt like he had so much to shout about, and yet, Mitch never used a perfectly good part of his body—a piece that worked.

His vocal cords.

He had not grown up in a sign-language-rich environment. He'd learned to get along in the world by reading lips, through invented signs, and through learning exact English. When he'd finally gone to live with his mother and Cactus in Three Rivers, he'd been nine years old—and his mom had worked tirelessly to teach him true American Sign Language then.

She'd been working on it during their time apart, and Cactus had started learning as well. They'd taught all of their kids and anyone who wanted to learn at Shiloh Ridge. Link had studied it on his own as well, and he'd acted as Mitch's interpreter through all of high school.

Thankfully, as it was embarrassing for Mitch to have to call his mommy so he could understand what a teacher wanted from him. Or another student. Or anyone, as hardly anyone at his high school knew and could use ASL.

When he'd come to Whispering Paws the first time, he'd realized how far behind he was, in literally every way. He'd been taking classes for the past several months, and he taught at the college level, for students interested in agriculture, ranching, and farming, as he had a lot of experience and knowledge with signs in those areas.

Still, sign language was regional and varied even from state to state, so plenty of living, of experiences, were also necessary for a good interpreter—and to be able to live outside of the culture he'd grown up in.

Anyone giving you flack for it? Link asked, his mouth moving too. Probably so Dawson knew what they were talking about.

Mitch shook his head. *Not so far. Things are pretty open here, though there are definitely people who think an implant is going against our culture. Others who don't really care. And others who are pro-implants for various reasons. It's just a consultation.*

Yes, he'd added that last sentence for himself. To keep his own hopes and expectations in check. Link relayed the message to Dawson, and then he said, *Want to see our tuxes for the wedding?*

You have them already?

He and Misty were getting married in June, right before her assignment in Three Rivers ended. She'd then quit her job and move to Shiloh Ridge Ranch with Link. As far as Mitch knew, she wasn't sure what she'd do from there, but Three Rivers had grown to about twenty thousand people now, and there were jobs to be had.

I tried mine on over the weekend, Link said. He tapped on his phone and brought up a picture. He turned it toward the camera, his mouth moving but not his hands. *Not sure if you can see that.*

It took a few seconds and some tilting of the phone, and then Mitch could see the midnight black tuxedo. Link had gripped the lapels with both hands, struck a pose, and wore a very serious, very dapper expression.

He laughed again, because Smiles had probably told him to stand like that. Link pulled the phone back and grinned too. *All the boys are wearing them,* he said.

Who's all the boys? Mitch asked.

Everyone younger than you, Link said. *Finn, Alex, Dawson, Danny. The groomsmen and the male cousins.*

What about your daddy?

Regular suit, Link said. He grinned again. *And you should see the stink your daddy is throwing over that.*

Mitch could see it all, and he grinned. *I should probably come visit before then.*

Link sobered again and he only said one word: *Yes.*

Mitch nodded too, and then he said goodbye to Link and Dawson and let them end the call. He had some videos to grade for his class, and then his alarm would sound—a buzzy, vibrating thing that told him to walk Honor.

Then, he had to get over to the hearing dog academy and continue the training with the two dogs he currently worked with: Amaretto and Liberty.

Thankfully, Link hadn't asked about Gillian, a woman Mitch had been out with a couple of times. She was hearing, but she knew sign language, and Mitch had settled into trying to figure out what and who he wanted in a partner. A spouse. Someone he could take home to Three Rivers and Shiloh Ridge Ranch, to the enormous family he belonged to.

In his heart of hearts, he saw himself with a hearing person, but it hadn't worked out with Gillian. Mitch had another date set up with someone else—a deaf woman named Brindie from the college.

That wasn't until the weekend, and Mitch had a lot to look forward to in the next several days. He reached for the pencil and jotted that down too. His therapist would be thrilled to find a positive thing among the negative this month, and Mitch smiled to himself as he put down the pencil and opened his university work.

He wasn't as far along as Link and Dawson, nor Finn and Alex, but he didn't need to be. He'd been assured and reassured by his own feelings and plenty of people around him that he was right where he needed to be. He loved his job here, and he was learning so much.

Maybe Brindie would be a fit for him, and maybe she wouldn't.

Maybe the cochlear implants would work out for him, and maybe they wouldn't.

The point was, Mitch had options, and for the first time in over a year, he felt like he wasn't drowning with every breath. He felt like he'd find exactly what—and who—he was looking for, as long as he didn't quit searching.

So he wasn't going to quit, plain and simple.

Chapter Twenty

Henry Marshall felt thrown back in time. Walking into the same huge classroom with stadium seating for the luck-of-the-draw moment when he may or may not be chosen for a position at Lone Star, the biggest and best boarding stable in the Texas Panhandle.

If Henry had any hope of doing his farrier apprenticeship somewhere besides Three Rivers, he had to be here. Had to jump through these hoops. Had to play this game.

He was tired of the rigmarole, that was for dang sure. Still, he'd put in his number, because Lone Star and his farrier academy had started a lottery system for how they chose cowboys to come work at their facility.

Henry had gotten a partial placement last summer, during which he'd learned a ton. He needed more practical experience, with the best farriers out there, and Lone Star had two veteran farriers who'd been doing hoof and horse care for thirty-plus years each.

Bard White himself was a force to be reckoned with, as he'd started in horse husbandry with his daddy at Lone Star, and he'd complete his farrier training at an elite academy in Tennessee before coming home to run the family business.

The old man had aged quickly, and he simply couldn't keep up anymore. His daughter, Angel, had started taking on more administrative roles, but she herself wasn't a farrier. She had one brother who'd suffered a fall several years ago and had recovered as much as possible. He wasn't quite right in the head, and he walked with a cane on good days and two crutches on others.

Henry had helped the man into the saddle

more than once last summer, and he liked Trevor a whole lot. He could still ride like no one's business, and he trained cutting horses with the best of them. Somehow, his brain could still do that, but there was no way Trevor could handle the complicated schedules of two dozen farriers, the financial strain of the stable, the billing, or anything like that.

Angel White did that, and Henry wasn't surprised at all to find the gorgeous blonde standing inside the classroom, at the long counter that ran across the front of the huge room. Henry joined the throngs of cowboy hopefuls, wishing there was some way of getting this job other than having good fortune.

He'd been praying for it, and he'd even gone so far as to ask his family to pray for him to get an apprenticeship at Lone Star too. If he did, it wouldn't be a summer-only position like last year. It would be at least a year, with the option to discuss further training once he officially graduated from his program.

"Howdy, Angel," he said, tipping his hat at the woman as he approached. She was exactly his type on the surface, but she'd bitten off the top of a volcano as a baby, because she could spew some serious fire when provoked.

Not that Henry had provoked her last summer. Or ever.

She simply ran a tight ship at Lone Star, and her expectations were so high, he could blast off to the moon and not reach them.

"Henry, hey." She actually gave him a smile this afternoon, and Henry's heart did a backflip. He needed to rein himself in, because Angel had a boyfriend she'd been seeing for at least six months.

He'd learned of the man last October, after his summer internship had ended, and as February had just dawned, and given the way Angel had squealed in the grocery store when Henry had seen her with her boyfriend, he was estimating the six months. Could've been five or even seven. But not longer than that.

She didn't wear a diamond ring, and Henry found himself wondering what it would take to lasso her, pull her closer, and get her to wear his diamond.

Such thoughts startled Henry. He'd not given much thought to dating for marriage. He dated for fun. To have a social life. To get out of the dorm room at night, away from the other cowboys, to find relief from his own thoughts.

But now that he was almost done, his thoughts had started to shift. The last few women he'd been out with he'd found insipid, and the loud laughter and quick fun he'd so enjoyed in the past had dulled considerably.

He hadn't imposed another female fast on himself; he simply hadn't found anyone interesting to go out with.

But Angel....

He ducked his head and headed up the steps to a row with a couple of his friends. Jake would be done with his program in a few months too, and Henry knew he wanted an apprenticeship with Lone Star too. Everyone in the room did. Cedric wouldn't be done for another year, and he was here for the internship announcements.

"Take your seats, please," a man announced, and anyone who hadn't found a place quickly did so. The chatter and conversation died, and Henry couldn't help watching Angel. She seemed tense and on-edge too, but he wasn't sure why.

Her place in life was secure. It was his—and everyone else's in this room—who'd thrown their life into the air the way jugglers tossed up balls, and they were all praying they'd get caught on the way down.

"Welcome to our apprenticesehip and internship assignment meeting," the man said. "We have representatives from three facilities here this year." He beamed down the row at them. "We have Davey Castle from Castleton Breeds."

A tall man in an even taller cowboy hat stepped out from the other end of the counter. "He's looking for four apprentices this year, and if you filled out the application packet completely, including the three essays, he considered you."

Henry had done the whole packet, figuring it could only expand his opportunities. He didn't want Castleton, though. He'd take it if he had to, but it was over in Lubbock, a town Henry didn't particularly enjoy.

Smaller population, drier conditions, too far to go home and do his laundry on the weekends. Or just escape back to his momma's comfort and good cooking when he needed to.

"We've got Angel White representing Lone Star," the man continued. "She's only doing internships this year, guys. I know that's a—"

"Wait," someone called out. "I thought there were apprenticeships there too."

Angel steadfastly kept her eyes on the man up front, one of their instructors, a man named Calvin. Henry's heart beat faster and faster, trying to claw its way between his ribs. No apprenticeships at Lone Star? Why was he even here?

"Lone Star only has room for one full-time apprentice," the man said raising the hand not holding the mic. "The Whites have selected that person and requested a meeting with them; they will not be announcing any apprenticeships at this meeting."

Murmurs of dissent ran through the crowd,

and Jake elbowed Henry. "Did you get notified? Was it you?"

Henry's jaw tightened as he folded his arms, a lame attempt at keeping his simmering anger inside. He couldn't even trust himself to speak, so he just shook his head.

"Me either." Jake sighed. "Maybe they'll take me as an intern again this year."

Lone Star was known for doing that, and Henry decided to stay for that reason alone. No sense in marching out when his number could be pulled for the internship. It wasn't what he needed to graduate, but it would be better than nothing.

Calvin announced the next facility looking for apprentices—a huge horse ranch up in Oklahoma. His cousin Libby seemed to like living there, but Henry wasn't as willing to branch out as she was.

He suffered through the internship announcements, the apprenticeship announcements, at Castleton. He didn't get anything.

He leaned forward as Angel announced their full-time internships at Lone Star. His number didn't shine on the screen, but Jake jumped to his feet, both fists in the air. "Yes!" he shouted.

He wasn't the only one celebrating. Cedric had gotten a full-time internship too, as had several others.

Henry's anger started to bloom, and he'd need to call his momma as he started the drive back to Three Rivers. It would take the whole hour to vent out all the negativity inside him.

Especially when he didn't even get a part-time internship from Lone Star, and nothing from Oklahoma.

The auditorium started to empty, and Henry sat there, feeling hollow and completely abandoned. How was it possible that he'd gotten nothing?

He had top marks in his classes. An excellent recommendation from Bard himself at Lone Star. And not one other facility wanted him? He had all the required hours to move into being an apprentice. He'd had to scrape and call random ranches to get those hours too.

He'd worked incredibly hard to get this far. And now what?

He was supposed to sit here and accept defeat?

Henry hung his head, but he had more dignity than to cry in front of everyone. Well, almost no one now, as most people had left the classroom.

Dear God, he prayed. *This hurts too much.*

His fingers tingled with it, and his chest felt so, so small. Not big enough for his lungs to expand properly, and air became the wrong thing to breathe anyway.

He had to get out of here before someone saw him wallowing. He got to his feet, but they too had turned numb inside his cowboy boots. Somehow, he made it down the steps without falling, and as he approached Calvin, a horrible, bitter desperation spewed from him.

"Did I mess up my application packet, sir?" Henry swiped his cowboy hat from his head, his pulse one big pounding of a bass drum now. "I wasn't—I mean, I'm not the best or anything, but I didn't get anything."

Calvin looked up from his tablet, surprise in his expression. "Yes, yes, your paperwork is in the office," he said.

Henry blinked, sure Calvin hadn't heard him right. The man went back to his tablet, clearly distracted—and disgruntled—and Henry looked out the double-wide doors. "Okay," he said. "Thank you, sir."

"Congratulations, Henry," he said "Everyone was impressed with your application."

Henry turned back to him, so many questions firing through him, but Calvin's phone rang, and he answered it with, "I'm coming right now," before he brushed by Henry and left the room.

Henry followed him, more confused than ever. "If my application was so great, why didn't I get anything?" he wondered.

The office teemed with people, and Henry really didn't want to be among the celebrators. He didn't wish them any ill will, but he didn't want to exist among their smiling faces, the high-fives, and the inflated egos.

If you'd gotten something, he thought. *Yours would be the biggest one.*

And it would be. And Henry knew he needed to pull on the reins on his ego, humble himself, and figure out what to do next. His momma had told him never to apologize for his big personality. She said it came from Daddy, and that was one of the things she loved most about them both.

He'd find the right thing for him, she'd promised. The right career. The right place to be. The right woman for him.

He hovered out of the way, trying to get his bearings. One by one, the victors got their paperwork and settled in to fill it out. Henry finally stepped forward to the girl there—Mandi.

He sucked in a breath. "Oh, hey," he said.

"Henry Marshall," she said back. He'd dated her best friend last fall, and well, that had not gone well. Mandi clearly didn't like him, and she simply sat there without giving him any further directions.

He had no idea what to say. "I...."

"He's with me," a woman said, and Henry's attention flew up and behind Mandi.

Angel stood there, and to his complete surprise, she motioned him forward. "Come on, cowboy," she said. "I don't like to be kept waiting."

Henry practically fell down in his haste to step past the table Mandi manned and toward the little room where Angel filled the doorway. After all, he had a few choice words for her, and his big personality would absolutely allow him to say them all.

Chapter Twenty-One

Angel White took a big breath as she closed the door, which was totally the wrong thing to do. Henry smelled like leather, dirt, and cologne—all of her favorite things. She'd seen the man work with horses too, and he possessed a calm, gentle spirit and a crafts-man's touch underneath all of his bluster.

Yes, he had a loud laugh, and she'd smiled at the sound of it before.

Yes, he could be brash and over-the-top, but Angel suspected that was more for show than it was who Henry Marshall was, at least deep down.

She'd seen the tall, dark-haired, bearded man rush to her brother's aid, and he'd brought her family dinner more than once last summer. *Yeah*, she thought. *Because he wanted an apprenticeship at the stable.*

Which was true, yes.

He also happened to be an excellent candidate.

She turned to face him, wondering if he'd say something first. Perhaps a "Thank you so much," or "I'm not going to let you down." Something.

He stood over by the window, his bulky arms folded and making himself look bigger. Angel absolutely could not be so attracted to him. Number one, she had a boyfriend. Yep. Mm hm. She really liked Calder, and she'd never been a cheater. Maybe things between them had grown stale, or maybe Angel had simply gotten too busy for a serious relationship as more of the farm's responsibilities fell to her.

Daddy was finally moving into semi-retirement. Her momma wasn't well most days, and

Angel spent a great deal of time, energy, and worry on Trevor as well. Though he lived alone, Angel still went by his place each morning and each evening to make sure he had what he needed.

Most nights, she fell asleep on the couch, and she'd reached a new low last week while pouring over the apprentice applications by falling asleep at the dining room table.

So she did not need Henry's gorgeous eyes sizing her up, nor the scent of his cologne in her nose, and she prayed with all she had that she hadn't made the biggest mistake of her life by calling him in here.

"You—" she started, but he cut her off with, "You have some nerve."

Angel blinked, trying to keep up. "I have some nerve?" He was the one who hadn't even responded to her message.

"Yeah," he said. "You told me that if I applied for your stupid apprenticeship program, I had—and I quote—a very good chance of getting something." He settled his weight onto one leg. "I got nothing out there."

Angel blinked again, not sure they were speaking the same language anymore.

"Not even at *Browning House*," he sneered out, the name of the farm in Oklahoma dripping with disdain. Almost like it was a swear word. "I'm sunk, Angel. I have nowhere to work this summer, and that means I'm gonna have to go crawling back to my daddy like a kicked dog."

He scoffed and spun away from her, the window in front of him so he wasn't just facing the wall. Angel had no idea what to say or do. They seemed to exist on two different planets.

Which is probably a good thing, she thought. After all, Daddy had instituted a strict no-fraternizing policy between colleagues at the stable, as he couldn't stand the drama. Therefore, Henry—and all other cowboys and farriers who worked for Lone Star—were outside of Angel's dating pool.

She couldn't even believe she was thinking about dating. She. Had. A. Boyfriend.

Her memory blipped at her, taking her back to a summer day last year, when Lone Star had fed everyone their thank you and farewell dinner. Henry had come, though he hadn't been taken on as a boarded farrier last year. He'd made the commute six days a week. He'd risen right to the top of the crop of men they'd brought.

It hadn't taken her father long to make him a shift lead, and then a group head. Henry had taken on the leadership roles as easily as breathing, and when Angel had put the top three applicants in front of her father last week, he'd barely looked at the other two before tapping Henry's folder.

"I want him."

And if her daddy wanted him, then Daddy got him. Not only that, if Daddy wanted him, that only made him more off-limits for Angel. And it hadn't been easy for Angel to get Henry, and he certainly wasn't making it any easier.

At the farewell shindig, Henry had sat a few seats from her, and she'd heard him telling another farrier that he didn't want to "run home with his tail tucked between his legs" because he couldn't cut it somewhere besides his family's equine therapy unit.

"I have something to prove, you know?"

Boy, Angel knew, and his words had stuck with her for months now. She had something to prove too—to her brother, to her daddy, to every single farrier at Lone Star, and to herself.

Angel did a terrible thing—she moved closer to him. "Can you not do an apprenticeship this summer?" As she rounded the oval table in the middle of the room with enough seating for six, Henry cut a glare at her.

"What?"

"Why won't you have anywhere to work?" She frowned at him. "I'm so confused."

"Join the club." He turned and faced her fully. "I hate the lottery system. I know you guys are overloaded and all that. The academy here has grown, and there aren't many big operations to take on the farriers coming out of the program. I get it."

"Yeah," she said slowly, because all of that was true.

"But I don't get why you can't weed us out

by grades or something. Then look at applications after that. I'm good, Angel." He released his breath and quickly took another, almost like he couldn't quite get enough oxygen. "And I don't say that out loud very often. When my momma calls and asks me how I'm doing, I tell her everything I'm learning. I never brag about how I was the only one—the *only one* out of all your guys—to get Whiplash in the cross ties last year. Not even Flint could do that."

His chest heaved, and she wanted him to look away. Anywhere but at her. He simply exuded male magnetism, and Angel couldn't stand under the weight of it. She gripped the back of a swiveling conference chair just to steady herself.

"Yeah," she said. "That's why we consider applications for apprenticeships. It's only the internships that are done on a lottery—and." She pointed one manicured fingernail at him. "We weed those out too, I'll have you know. I look at so many applications from October through January, it's a miracle I even have time to celebrate the holidays like a normal person."

Her chest heaved too, because this man rubbed her all wrong. He acted like she could work more hours than God had given them in a day. She reminded herself she didn't have to defend any of her decisions to him. Daddy wouldn't have.

"So are you saying you don't want the apprenticeship we've offered you?"

"I'm saying—" He clamped his mouth shut as his eyes widened. "I—what? What apprenticeship?" His mouth dropped open now, and oh, Angel didn't need to see those perfect straight white teeth gleaming at her.

Still, she smiled. "Now I know what to do to get the mighty Henry Marshall to slow down and stop talking," she said.

Henry's glare came right back, and his mouth snapped closed. He had full lips that Angel tore her gaze from quickly. Dots started to connect, and a complete picture came into view.

"I'm going to assume you did not receive

my email," she said, turning back to the table. She'd laid his paperwork there, and she ran her finger along the top of the folder. "I sent it twenty-four hours ago, and I did ask you to confirm that you A, wanted the apprenticeship and could complete it as outlined in the email, and B, to schedule a time with me to go over everything."

She picked up the folder and hugged it to her chest. "You have not responded, but when I saw you outside, I figured maybe you'd just checked your email after the announcement inside."

Henry stood there, the perfect living, breathing human male specimen of a statue.

Angel mimicked him, but she raised her eyebrows after a couple of seconds. When he still didn't say anything or move, she asked, "Would you like a moment to check your email now? I'm quite certain I typed it in correctly. It's the one you put on your application."

That got him to fumble for his phone in his back pocket, and he swiped and tapped quickly, sputtering, "I never check my email. I'm so sorry," as he did.

Angel liked this more vulnerable, less imposing version of Henry Marshall, and she turned away from him. She'd seen him like this over the summer too. Nothing special about him.

There can't be, she told herself as she balanced herself at the head of the table now, a professional, appropriate distance between them that prevented the scent of his cologne from infecting her female judgment too strongly.

"This is unbelievable," he said, his voice full of awe. "You had one spot, and you picked...me?"

"You were the best candidate," Angel said with as much matter-of-factness as she could muster. "And let me tell you, Mister Marshall, I had to fight off Brownstone and Castleton for three full days before they'd relinquish you. Davey said he'd double my proposed salary for you just to get you, and boy, did that make me mad." She *tsk*'ed a time or two and smiled at him. "You do *not* want to see me upset."

She also didn't want to lose Henry. She couldn't even imagine returning to the stables this evening and telling her father that someone had stolen him away with the promise of more money or better working conditions.

"No, ma'am," he murmured, lifting his eyes to meet hers. They held a boyish sense of wonder now. "I want this job."

"You haven't had time to read that." She nodded to his phone. "I worked for two hours typing up the requirements of the apprenticeship, as well as what would be provided."

He grinned at her, and oh, that lopsided smile should be illegal when used on women. "I'm sure you've used this exact language in the past."

"Actually," she said. "I started with Daddy's template, but it's been dissected and torn apart quite a bit. I'm in charge of apprentices now, you see, and that goes from start to finish."

"I do see," he said, clearly flirting with her. He absolutely could not do that, and Angel flipped open his folder and set it on the table. She turned toward it, her eyes glued to it. They had to be, or they'd be stuck to him.

"I'm glad you're accepting the apprenticeship," she said. "We can schedule another time to meet, if you'd like. Perhaps you'd like to go over the contract, which I attached to your email, with your parents first. A lawyer. Someone." She tilted her head and looked over to him.

"Do people do that?" he asked.

"Smart people definitely have someone else look over any contracts they sign before they sign them," she said, lifting her head fully and smiling at him. "And Henry, you're one of the smartest cowboys I know."

He grinned fully then, and dang if the temperature in the room didn't shoot up ten degrees. Everything about him, from his grumpiness to his happiness, influenced everyone around her—she'd seen this personally last summer—and he whooped.

A loud, rodeo cowboy type of whoop. He tossed his cowboy hat into the air and laughed.

"Yes," he said through his chuckles. "Yes, I want this apprenticeship. Thank you so much, Angel."

And before she could even comprehend what was happening, Henry took the two strides to her and lifted her right up off her feet. "Oh," she squeaked as he laughed over her.

"This is so great. My momma is gonna be so happy." He beamed down at her, and then, before she even knew her feet had touched the ground again, Henry Marshall kissed her.

And oh, Angel couldn't help herself—she kissed him right on back.

Chapter Twenty-Two

Dawson took Caroline's pint of ice cream from her and set it on the conveyor belt at Wilde & Organic. He moved down to pay, his phone vibrating in his back pocket. When it rang out loud, he knew whoever was calling had done so three times within five minutes.

He took out his phone and wallet and handed the money to Caroline. "I have to get this," he said. He'd explained to her that he put his phone on sleep mode during their dates, but that if someone needed to get ahold of him for emergencies, it would ring.

Her eyes broadcasted concern, but she turned to the clerk as he looked at his screen. His eyebrows puckered, and he almost let the call go.

Because it was his niece, Shiloh. Something told him to answer, and Dawson's thick thumb barely got the call open before it went to voicemail. "Hey, Shiloh," he said. "What's going on?"

"I need you to come over to Ollie's," she said. She panted through the line, indicating running or fear. Something.

"Ollie's?" he asked. "Oliver Walker's place?'

"Yes," she said, a baby starting to wail in the background. Ollie and Aurora had three children, and their first had been born really, really small. Like, teeny tiny small, as she'd stopped growing in the womb. Rory had lived in the hospital for months while the baby continued to develop, and Jewel was still a tiny little girl, though she had to be six or seven years old now.

"JJ's here babysitting, and it's...a mess. Lara fell outside and she's bleeding all over. JJ's panicking, but he won't call his parents or Ollie, and I can see you're at Wilde and Organic."

"I'll be there in a few minutes," Dawson said, turning back to the check stand. Caroline held his wallet in one hand, took a step and picked up the now-bagged ice cream with the other, and faced him. "Do you need to call an ambulance?"

"No," Shiloh said. "We just need someone who can think."

Dawson took the ice cream and headed for the exit. "Do you need me to stay on the line?"

"No," Shiloh said. "I'm going to try to get the other kids out of the way. Lara isn't letting either of us anywhere near her, so we can't really tell what's wrong."

"She's a stubborn little thing," Dawson said. He, Rory, and Oliver were all the same age. They'd been married for twelve or thirteen years now, and they had three kids. That was what happened when two people got married at nineteen and started building their life together.

Dawson really liked Ollie, but he wasn't a

farmer or a rancher. He'd been friends with Finn too, but since Finn had gone into the Army and Ollie had moved back East for school, they didn't stay in touch.

He'd been back in town for a while now, but he worked in one of the downtown buildings, lived closer to town, and Dawson didn't often think of him when getting together with the other cowboys—like Finn, Alex, Brandon, Link, and Mitch.

It was simply life; it didn't mean he didn't like and wouldn't help Ollie. In fact, he hung up and said, "My niece needs us at a friend's house to help with a small bleeding issue."

"My goodness," Caroline said as she picked up the pace. "All right, then. The end of this date just got exciting."

He chuckled, though he didn't like the idea that the beginning and middle of the date had been boring. He'd been trying to figure out how to tell her about his OCD and anxiety, and every time he tried, he couldn't do it.

He'd written it on a pink sticky note, so he could easily check it off any time, but he kept moving the note from one day to the next without actually doing it.

Ollie and Aurora only lived a few blocks from Wilde & Organic, and Dawson jogged up the front sidewalk to the porch while Caroline and the ice cream brought up the rear.

"Hey, hey, hey," he said as he entered. Chaos existed around him, and Dawson paused in the doorway. A little boy of probably two sat on the loveseat in a diaper, a partially eaten and totally soggy graham cracker in his hand. He looked at Dawson with wide moon eyes while another child cried from further within.

Jewel sat at the dining room table, singing to herself and coloring, like the happenings in the house this evening were completely normal.

To Dawson, they weren't. It wasn't like the house was dirty or falling down, but shoes lay by the front door in a heap, unpacked plastic grocery sacks sat on the kitchen counter, and both JJ and Shiloh stared at him from the other side of the long couch.

"Praise the heavens," Shiloh said. "Lara's in the kitchen, and she still won't let us help her."

"What happened?" Dawson asked as he moved forward.

"I don't really know," JJ said. "She was playing out in the back yard, and Shiloh came over with dinner. So I was getting the door. Next thing we know, she's screaming and blood's pouring from her mouth. Or nose." He glanced at Dawson as he hurried by. "Somewhere. She usually likes me, but she's freaking out."

So was he, and Dawson didn't blame him. The young man was probably only twenty years old. Maybe twenty-one at this point. He wasn't married and had no children. Of course, Dawson didn't either, but the Walkers were kind of like the Glovers in that they had a plethora of offspring.

JJ was one of the oldest, so he'd grown up with a lot of younger siblings and cousins. No wonder this household of a singing child, one about to smear soggy cracker on the couch, and one bleeding, wailing child wasn't all that abnormal for him. At Duke's and Zona's, this was about par for the course too.

For Dawson, his anxiety had just hit the roof and broken through. He took a breath as he rounded the island and found a little girl sitting on the floor, her back pressed to the cabinet behind her. Blood had been smeared on the floor, and it now fell in a dripping pattern as she held her head over her knees as she sobbed.

"Hey, there." Dawson got down on his knees too, deciding the blood didn't bother him. "Lara, baby, look at me, okay?"

To his great relief, the girl looked up. She had some sort of liquid coming from every hole in her face, but Dawson smiled at her. "Tell me how you got hurt."

"Swallow," she said between her sobs. "Tripp-ed...and my shoe...toof went...boom." Tears ran down her face, and no wonder JJ needed help. Dawson wasn't even sure everything Lara had said was in English.

And he didn't know what to do. Then, like God providing manna from heaven for those wandering in the wilderness, light and ideas flowed into Dawson's mind.

"JJ, can you get Lara a popsicle?"

Thankfully, he didn't question Dawson. He just moved to the freezer drawer and opened it. Caroline put their ice cream in there and said, "Come on, you guys. Let's go get these other kids dressed and ready for dinner."

"Okay, yes," Shiloh said, and they left to do that.

JJ handed Dawson the red popsicle, and he started to unwrap it. "Hey, Lara, have you ever gotten a little cut on your finger?"

The girl looked at him with teary eyes but said nothing.

"See, cold things slow things down. Like ice in the river."

She babbled something about a river, and Dawson smiled at her. "Right," he said, though he had no clue what she meant. "I want you to suck on this, okay? Can you put it right against what hurts?"

He kept his grin in place as he tapped her nose with the popsicle. "Are you gonna put it right here?" She had blood on her nose, but as far as he could tell, it wasn't actively bleeding.

"No," she chirped out.

"Okay," he said. "I want you to put it on right where it hurts." He held out the red treat. "Can you show me where?"

She opened her mouth and said, "Toofs."

Her whole mouth seemed to be bleeding, and JJ handed him a washcloth. "Okay," Dawson said. "I'm just gonna wipe some of this away, and then you can have the popsicle. Remember." He started swiping as quickly as he could, without putting too much pressure on the girl's face. "You're going to put it right on the tooth that hurts."

"All hurt," she whimpered, and Dawson took one last swipe at her chin.

"Okay, then," he said. "I want you to put the whole thing in your mouth, yeah?" He gave her the popsicle, and to Lara's credit, she did just that. The whole thing went in her mouth, and he expected her to rip it right back out and start crying about the cold.

She didn't, and he picked up the little girl and set her on the edge of the counter next to the sink. JJ had another washcloth ready, and he cooed at her, "I'm gonna wash your hands, sweetie. Just keep the popsicle in your mouth."

Together, he and Dawson got Lara mostly cleaned up, and JJ turned to tackle the floor. Dawson lifted the girl into his arms and said, "Okay, take it out for a minute. I want you to spit everything in your mouth into the sink."

She did and it was just all red. Dawson wiped her face again and gave her a quick glass of water. "I want you to swish it like you're brushing your teeth," he said. "Like your momma taught you, okay?"

"She teach-ed me to brush swish-swish-swish." The girl mimed brushing her teeth and then Dawson held the glass for her while she took a drink of water...and swallowed it.

"Spit this one out, baby," he said. "I want to see if you're still red inside."

She did what he said, and he saw only a trace of red. He rinsed the popsicle and handed it back to her. "Popsicle back in."

Lara sucked on that as Shiloh returned. "Oh, she's cleaned up." She hooked her thumb over her shoulder. "We have Jewel and Mason ready for bed. Jay-J, should I get dinner out?" She looked over to him, and Dawson took a moment to study his niece.

Jay-J? Like, rhymes with Gage?

JJ wasn't in high school anymore, Dawson knew that. And Shiloh had just gotten her driver's license.

"Yeah, if you could get it out, that would be great." JJ straightened to toss away the antibacterial wipes he was using to clean the floor. He pulled out a few more and added, "Jewel, Mason, time for dinner."

"I eat," Lara said. "I hungry."

"Just a minute, sweetie," JJ said. "I want you to finish your popsicle first." He met Dawson's eyes, who nodded.

"How long since you graduated?" he asked, shooting a look over to Caroline, who'd come to help Shiloh get out dinner.

"A year or so," JJ said.

"It's almost two years now," Shiloh said. JJ shot her a glare, but she simply kept working. "What? It's true. You'll have been graduated for two years in just a few months."

"But it's not two years yet," he growled.

No matter what, that put him at least four or five years older than Shiloh. And she wasn't even the one Dawson worried about. "What are you doing?" he asked. "College? Trade school? Working your ranch?"

"Just working the ranch right now, sir," he muttered.

"And babysitting for your cousin," Dawson said.

"Yeah," JJ said. "I'm the manny so Ollie and Rory can go out once a week. They pay good, and I'm trying to earn enough to go to the Dominican Republic on that mission tour this summer."

"Oh, sure," Dawson said, as he'd heard the pastor talk about that. He also knew the Walkers had plenty of money. Like billions of dollars plenty. JJ would never need to work another day in his life, and he'd be fine. "What about after that?" he asked as Lara finished up her popsicle.

"I don't know." JJ took the red-stained stick and tossed it in the trash with the last of the wipes. "Did you know exactly what to do with your life, Dawson?"

He looked at the young man, and JJ reminded Dawson so much of himself. "I mean, I always knew I wanted to work the ranch. So I suppose."

He handed Lara to JJ and said, "Baby, tell us what happened."

"I be running so fast," she said, and now that she wasn't all nasally from the crying and her mouth wasn't filled with blood, Dawson could understand her. "Like, zoom! Zoom! Zoom! And I fell-led, my shoe just pop-ped off, and I go flying down. Bang and boom!"

JJ grinned at her. "Bang and boom aren't good."

She looked at him with wide, earnest eyes. "I lost-ed my toof, JJ. See? It gone." She lifted up her lip, and at least her gums had stopped bleeding. Dawson couldn't see any other damage either. "I ha- a toof 'ere t'day." She dropped her lip. "Now, no toof."

Her eyes filled with tears. "I swallow it. Now I sad." The saddest tears in the world slid down her face, but Dawson had to turn away to hide his smile. He caught Caroline watching him, and she had the warmest smile on her face too.

"Why are you sad?" JJ asked. "It's just a tooth. They'll all come out, sweetie."

"But I get no prize from Toof Fairy."

Ah. All the things came together, and Dawson turned his grin on JJ. The young man looked stumped, though, and Dawson couldn't believe he hadn't lived through little children believing in fantastical creatures.

"Well, I happen to know that the Tooth Fairy doesn't need the tooth," Caroline said, surprising both him and JJ. They turned toward her with eyebrows raised, and she plucked Lara from JJ's arms. "My brother lost a tooth at school once, and his teacher put it in one of those plastic containers that snaps closed. He wore it on a string around his neck *all* through the day. But when he got home, he realized it had popped open while he was playing, and the tooth was gone."

She set Lara in the booster seat at the table,

and she held everyone's attention now, Dawson's included.

"And you know what?" She put a bowl of macaroni and cheese in front of Lara. No chicken nuggets like the other kids had. "The next morning, he had a dollar bill under his pillow. The Tooth Fairy *knew*."

"I got a five-dollar bill for my last tooth," Jewel said.

"Yes, mm hm," Caroline said without missing a beat. "The Tooth Fairy has to account for inflation, I guess."

Dawson burst out laughing then, because it was just too funny to think of the Tooth Fairy having to deal with inflation. Caroline grinned back at him, and he swore he felt the house shift a little. Or maybe that was just his position in time and space, and that he'd fallen slightly.

Fallen in love with the stunning woman now serving a two-year-old she didn't know another dinosaur-shaped chicken nugget.

"Shiloh," Dawson said as he breathed in, trying to distract himself. "What were you doin' here?" He cut a look at JJ, who'd just dished himself some food too.

"I'd just finished up work," she said nonchalantly. "Clara Jean asked me to bring JJ the food for the kids." She took a bite of dinner too, which told Dawson something—like she'd planned to come here and eat dinner with JJ and the kids maybe.

"Did you call your momma?"

Her face paled and she coughed. "Shoot, no." She pulled her phone out of her back pocket, and she *was* wearing her work polo for Wilde & Organic. Clara Jean *was* JJ's sister. Shiloh and Clara Jean *were* good friends.

Her story sounded plausible, but JJ was still four years older than her.

"No." Shiloh moaned. "She's already called twice."

"Then go call her," Dawson said, and Shiloh retreated from the house to do that. The moment the front door snicked closed, he turned to JJ. "So, you're what? Twenty-one?"

"Will be this summer, yep," he said.

"You know she's sixteen, right?" Dawson

asked, his meaning ultra clear. So clear, JJ's hand froze with his fork halfway to his mouth. He stared at Dawson, pure shock pouring from him.

"All right," Shiloh said, bustling back into the house. "She knows I'm not dead."

Dawson looked at her and said, "All right. Great. Do you two need us here still?" He reached for Caroline. "If not, I'd like to finish my date." He nodded to JJ. "Do I need to call Ollie and let him know what's gone on here?"

"No," JJ said, becoming mobile again. "I'll tell them."

Caroline ran her hand along JJ's broad shoulders. "And son, she'll need some painkiller for her teeth."

"Oh, shoot. Sure." JJ practically toppled the table he got up so fast, and he moved over to a cabinet that held various bottles of medicines. "Let's see...."

"Go help him, darlin'," Dawson said. "I want to say something to Shiloh."

"Be nice," she whispered before she went to help JJ find the children's painkiller.

"Shiloh," Dawson said, because he didn't have much time. "You tell me straight. You seein' this boy who's going to be twenty-one soon? Do I need to worry about this or not?"

Shiloh blinked, her daddy's dark eyelashes fluttering a mile a second. "What? No, Uncle Dawson, I swear." But her face took on the color of a pink sunset. "Clara Jean said he was babysitting tonight, and he'd ordered food for the kids. But something got messed up with the flower delivery for tomorrow, so she couldn't leave the store when she was supposed to. So she asked me to bring it by on my way home."

He nodded to the bowl of macaroni and cheese she'd eaten from. "And you thought you'd stay and hang out with him."

She looked at the bowl too, clearly horrified. "No," she said flatly. "No, I didn't—" She cut off and pressed her lips together. "I wasn't going to stay at all. I swear, Uncle Dawson."

"So I don't need to tell your momma and daddy anything," he said as Caroline went, "Oh, whoops!" and a clattering of pill containers hit the counter.

"No," Shiloh muttered. "Nothing going on here. Momma's already watching April like a hawk because she flirts with Rusty like he's the only boy alive." She rolled her eyes. "I don't like JJ."

"All right," Dawson said as the young man came over to the table with the right medicine for his niece.

"We gotta have this, sweetie," he said, giving Lara the medicine. She took it just fine too, and JJ's gaze caught on Dawson's. "Thank you for coming, sir."

"I'm barely older than you," Dawson said. "You don't need to call me sir."

"You went to college, right?" he asked.

Dawson nodded. "Yeah. I got a degree in ranch management, but you know, lots of ranchers and farmers don't do that. They just stay and work their family land. There's no shame in that." He studied JJ as his head dipped. "Or you can go to the trade programs or one of those vocational things. They do things with finance or machine repair all the time. It's useful to have those skills, and they don't take long. You can work the ranch while you do them."

"Yeah," he muttered. "I know."

"Have you talked to your daddy about taking over the ranch for him?" Dawson didn't want to pry, but JJ had asked. He seemed open to talking to Dawson about this. "He's gotta be what? Close to sixty, because Duke's in his early fifties."

"Sixty-one now, sir," JJ said.

Dawson nodded. "When my brother came back to Three Rivers, we suddenly had a whole slew of conversations to have. See, my daddy had changed his will, thinking Duke would never come home. So he'd named me as the sole successor of the ranch."

Caroline watched him, keen interest in her eyes. He shifted, a tiny current of discomfort running through him, what with Shiloh listening too. "So we started having a lot of conversations," he said. "I hated them, because I don't want to talk everything to death."

"Talking is real hard for me," JJ said.

"The best part of communication," Caroline said. "Is that it can be learned—with practice." She moved to stand in front of JJ too. "So you just have to practice doing it, and you'll find you'll get better and better at it every time you need to do it."

"I don't even know what to say," JJ said.

Dawson exchanged a look with Caroline, and she clearly wanted him to give the advice. He didn't know how to counsel twenty-year-olds any better than four-year-olds. But God gave him the words as he opened his mouth and said, "Do you check in with your parents when you get home late at night?"

"Yes, sir," JJ said.

"So you will tonight?"

"Yes."

"Is your momma the only one awake, or is your daddy up too?"

"They're both up," JJ said.

Dawson nodded, expecting no less from Jeremiah Walker. "So tonight, when you get home, you walk into their bedroom and you say, 'I have to talk to you about something.' And you sit down on the end of the bed, and in the dark

—it's so much easier to talk in the dark when you're first starting out—you tell them, 'I want to take over the ranch, and I need help knowing what to do next.'"

"*If* you want to take over the ranch," Caroline said.

"Right," Dawson agreed. "Or you say, 'I want to go to that vet technician class I told you about a few weeks ago,' or 'Hey, I heard of this vet technician class I want to do, and I need your help in knowing how to enroll.' Or 'I want to run away to the circus, and I'm packing tonight. Don't worry. I *don't* need your help with it.'"

He grinned at JJ, who finally smiled back. "Okay," he said. "I get it."

"They'll turn on the light," Dawson said. "And then it gets harder. But son, if I know one thing about your momma and daddy, it's that they just want to help you. They want you to be happy. They probably have a dozen ideas for what's best for you, and they're just waiting for *you* to open the door with the one you think you want to hear about."

"Right," he said. "Okay."

"You only have to be brave for as long as it takes to get the first sentence out," Caroline said. "Trust me on that. Once that first sentence is out, the rest will follow." She nodded, her expression kind but also filled with intensity. Dawson wanted to hear more about how she'd practiced her hard conversations, because she was so good at saying just what she wanted.

"Thanks again," JJ said, and he quickly hugged them both. "Thanks for dropping the food by, Shiloh."

"What? Oh, sure." She took her bowl over to the sink and rinsed it out. "I have to get going. My momma needs me at home."

Dawson doubted that very much, but he didn't argue. JJ didn't either, and the three of them left, still calling good-byes as the door closed.

They'd left the street and the neighborhood and started back toward Caroline's where they'd been planning to climb up on the roof and eat ice cream, whispering and laughing into the night until they were too tired to continue, when Dawson remembered the ice cream.

"Doesn't matter," Caroline said, her fingers in his tightening. "I've got Biscoff."

"I'm gonna need the story of the Biscoff," he told her.

"Yeah, well, get in line, Mister. You have a million stories to tell me still."

He chuckled. "Fair enough." He pulled into her driveway but didn't immediately get out. "Would you go out with me on Valentine's Day?"

She turned to face him, surprise etched in every line of her face. "You're asking me out? It's not implied?"

"Are we to implied dates?"

"I mean...I guess—I don't know."

"I'm asking you to be my Valentine," he said with a smile. "Yes or no?"

"Dawson, of course." She leaned toward him, cradled his face in her hand, and kissed him.

He suddenly didn't need ice cream—he had something sweet in Caroline. "Okay," he whispered against her lips. "And *now* we're on implied dates for everything. Birthdays, weekends, lunches, Fridays, Tuesdays, your mom's birthday, anniversaries, breakfasts, all of it." He smiled against her curved lips, and kissed her, once again feeling the earth move just a little... tiny...bit.

Chapter Twenty-Three

Caroline looked up to the corner of the mirror when she caught movement there.

"Aunt Caroline," Judy said in her cute little-girl voice. "Can I help you with your makeup?"

Caroline nodded instantly. "Come sit by me here." She scooted over a little on the bench where she sat at her vanity, and Judy climbed up.

"Your hair is so pretty," her niece said.

"Your momma did it." Caroline smiled warmly at the girl in the mirror. "When I'm finished with my makeup, we'll take out the net, and the curls will fall down."

Judy picked up the eyeshadow case and popped it open. "Ooh, this one is blue."

Caroline smiled at her and said, "You can put on a little bit. It just goes right here on your eye." She dabbed on a little more of the creamy eyeshadow she'd been putting on. "Not all over your face."

Judy did that, extending the blue too far up and too far out, but Caroline didn't correct her. Belle let her put makeup on any way she wanted, and Caroline simply wanted to enjoy the innocence of a six-year-old.

"How do I look, Auntie-C?" Judy got up on her knees and blinked her eyelashes, probably the way she'd seen countless princesses do in animated movies.

"You're always beautiful," Caroline said. "With or without the makeup." She rubbed her nose against Judy's. "Okay? Remember that, honey. You don't need the makeup to be beautiful."

"Why do you wear it then?" Judy put both

hands on the sides of Caroline's face. "I wear my blue dress to be pretty."

"No," Caroline said gently. "You wear your blue dress to *feel* pretty. You *are* pretty whether you wear a blue dress or a red pair of jeans or a big brown potato sack."

Judy giggled. "No one wears potato sacks, Auntie-C." She sat down flat again and picked up the eyeshadow applicator again. She hummed to herself as she brushed on more color, and Caroline looked at herself in the mirror.

After her divorce, she'd examined every single thing in her life. Did she make her eggs over-easy because Joe had told her to, or did she like them that way? Did she even like any of the clothes in her closet, or had she bought them and worn them to please Joe?

Who *was* she? What did *she* like? What made *her* feel good about herself?

She'd had to answer all those painful questions, because she felt like she'd bent herself completely to his whims. They never ate breakfast for dinner, because he wouldn't allow it.

She couldn't wear jeans more than two days in a row, or she wasn't taking care of herself according to his terms. In fact, Caroline now wore more makeup than her ex-husband would've preferred, and he'd made her wash her face before he'd go out with her on his birthday.

Her birthday?

Ignored. They didn't go out. He never said a word to her about it.

She blinked, and that past version of herself disappeared. She looked at Judy, and she hoped and prayed with everything inside her that she'd never have to go through what Caroline had.

"Or Belle," Caroline murmured, but Judy didn't hear her.

The doorbell rang, and Caroline startled, her adrenaline spiking and shooting to the top of her head. "What time is it?"

"I've got it," Belle called, and Caroline wouldn't be running down the hall in her netted hair and slip anyway.

She got up from the vanity and stepped into her dress, a pretty white background with watercolored flowers on it in a variety of reds and pinks. Very fitting for Valentine's Day.

She needed heels, a chunky necklace, and her hair let out, so when Belle appeared in the doorway—a bit flushed—Caroline gestured her closer. "Is it Dawson?"

"He said he was too nervous to wait at home." Belle closed the door behind her. "Seriously, Caroline, he is the sweetest man alive."

Caroline smiled as she turned her back on her sister. "Get the net, would you?"

"I mean, you've been dating for what? A month? But he's nervous to come pick you up on Valentine's Day?" Belle sighed, and she got the bobby pins out of the net keeping Caroline's curls bouncy and contained.

Her hair now flowed over her shoulders, and she turned to face Belle. "He's...he's definitely got some anxiety. He hasn't shared a whole lot more with me, but he's meticulous with things. Loves lists. Keeps track of different things on the ranch with colored sticky notes. Sets a schedule and sticks to it religiously. That kind of thing."

"You like routines too," Belle said.

Caroline draped a string of red beads around her neck. "Yes, but this is different. He hasn't told me yet. We're in month one."

"Going on two." Belle smiled at her and added, "You're the most beautiful woman in the world."

"What about me, Momma?" Judy stood on the bench at the vanity now, and her whole face bore color. Caroline sucked in a breath, but Belle only laughed. She went to swoop Judy into her arms, and Caroline turned to step into her heels—also bright red.

With every piece making her feel as beautiful on the outside as she was on the inside, Caroline drew in a deep breath of her own. She could only imagine what Dawson might be wearing tonight for their Valentine's Day evening together.

She left her sister and niece giggling in the bedroom to go meet her cowboy. Dawson stood in the living room, holding an enormous bouquet of roses—all in shades of red and white. He had the deep burgundy ones, the bright red ones, a smattering of pink ones, all accented by white.

He wore a black-as-midnight cowboy hat on his head, pure light in his eyes, and black slacks that hung over black cowboy boots. She couldn't quite see his shirt past the flowers, and she wanted to pause time and take as many pictures of him standing there with those blooms, from as many different angles, as possible.

"Howdy, ma'am." He somehow reached up and tipped his hat a millimeter.

"My goodness, Dawson." She rushed at him and straight into the flowers. "These are gorgeous."

"I've heard women like roses, but I wasn't sure with you."

She looked up, only the bouquet separating them. "You think I wouldn't like roses?"

"You seem to like things a certain way, and well, I forgot to ask about your favorite flower." He smiled at her, unleashing the full power of Dawson Rhinehart. Caroline had vowed to never let the special occasions of her life dictate major decisions. Not again.

But her heart swooped, and her pulse fluttered, and since she'd once fallen very far, very fast, she knew what such a thing felt like.

That had been her downfall, and the aftermath had not been pleasant.

This falling felt a little different. Exhilarating, and freeing, and like she was in only helpless for Dawson for a moment. Then she regained control, smiled back at him, and said, "I'm going to need five vases for these."

"Wow-wee," Judy chirped as she entered the living room. "Look at all those pretty flowers."

"Wow-wee," Dawson said right back to her, not making fun of her at all. He didn't pitch his voice up to talk to little children, something she'd learned when they'd gone to help Shiloh and JJ last week. "Look at your makeup. Did your momma do that?" He grinned at her. "Or did Auntie-C?"

"I did it!" Judy spread her arms wide and turned in a circle.

"Come on, Judes," Belle called from down the hall. "Leave Auntie-C be."

Judy turned and went down the hall, and Caroline gathered as many of the roses as she could. "I think we can put them in the mixing bowl."

"The mixing bowl?"

"I'm not a big baker anyway," she said as she bent to get out the metal bowl. It tapered at the bottom to fit into the stand, and she put her roses in and held them to the side so Dawson could cram in the rest. She beamed at them. "They're really kind of pretty with the metal."

She held another stem out of the way as she filled it with as much water as she could hold, and then she turned and set the bowl in the middle of her dining room table. Dawson moved to her side, and she leaned into him easily.

"I love these," she said, melting into his warmth. "I love roses." She turned toward him. "Thank you, baby."

"Happy Valentine's Day," he murmured just before he kissed her. He'd texted her early this morning too, the same words but the thought meaning so much to her.

"I love your hair," he said as he moved his mouth to her jaw. "I love those shoes." He kissed his way down her neck. "I love this dress, and I *adore* the way you smell."

Caroline hung onto his shoulders as he lifted his head. She grinned at him, loving the way she fit in his arms and the way he knew how to hold her close while still letting her have space.

"I love that you're wearing a pink shirt," she whispered as she pressed her cheek to his. His beard tickled as it brushed against her skin. "I love that your tie has birds in the shape of hearts on it. I love that you were early, and I *adore* every minute I get to spend with you."

He pulled away, something akin to lightning in his eyes. "I was early, Caroline, because I can't stand being ready and waiting around."

"Mm hm." She fiddled with his tie, the heart-birds making her so happy.

"I'm early." He cleared his throat. "Because this date is the last thing on my list, and I just wanted it to get started. Then I could stop obsessing about it."

Caroline realized he was telling her something important here, and she slid her hands down his chest and around to his back. "Okay." She tilted her head back and looked at him, waiting.

"I have OCD," he finally said. Just like that. "Diagnosed. I manage it pretty well, though I do take a mild medication to help with that. I've seen a counselor for years to develop coping strategies. I...I know who I am, I guess, and I'm okay with how I do things. I'm hoping you will be too."

Caroline gazed at this beautiful man, and she couldn't believe he was the same grump she'd come home fuming about only a few short months ago. My, how things could change when she got to see the layers beneath a person's façade.

"I will be," she said.

"It's a lot to take in," he said. "I know that. It's...I manage it really well."

"I've never seen you not manage it really well."

"Well, we're still new," he said.

"Yeah," she agreed. "I might have a rule for us."

"You might? Or you do?" He took her hand and led her out of the kitchen. "We need to get going. It's going to be busy tonight."

"I want a picture," Caroline said. "Do we have time for that?"

"Sure," he said.

"Belle," she called, and her sister came out of the guest bath halfway down the hall. "Will you take our picture?"

Belle shone like a new penny, and she kept her smile hitched in place as she took Caroline's phone and snapped the pictures. Then Dawson hustled them outside and into his truck, and when they'd both belted themselves in for safety, he looked at her. "I didn't realize we had any rules at all."

Caroline clasped her hands together as an internal debate kicked off. "I have some," she finally admitted. "I made them for myself as I was coming out of my divorce fog. As I started rebuilding myself into who I am now."

"Okay," he said quietly. "What's the rule?"

She looked out the window, where dusk had started to claim the light of day. He'd been right about one thing—it was easier to talk in the dark. "I require twelve months of dating," she said slowly. "I want to see how you and your family do things for every holiday, every month of the year. I want you to see how I do those things. I want to see how you celebrate my birthday, and I want to celebrate yours with you. I want time to talk about everything that's important to us, and everything that's not, and everything in between."

Dawson said nothing, but Caroline had to breathe. She did that, only semi-calmed that he hadn't slammed on the brakes, declared their relationship over, and taken her home. Of course he wouldn't, but anytime she'd said something Joe hadn't liked, something that dramatic would've happened.

"And a road trip," she said. "That's the rule. Twelve months of dating, all the holidays and birthdays and traditions, and a road trip. I need to see how you act when we're running late, or when we get lost, or when we show up to a hotel and they've lost our reservation."

"I see," he said.

"And you need to see me in all of those situations too," she said, so this wasn't a critique on him. This was about *them*. This was about truly being able to determine if they were a good fit for one another or not.

She drew in a deep breath. "So that's the rule."

Dawson made a turn and then switched his blinker to make another one. "I think I can live with this rule. I have a couple of follow-up questions, though, if you don't mind."

"I suppose I don't." She turned to look at him, glad when he met her eye.

"Does the twelve-month period start from the first date? Or when we met? Like, what are you counting as Day One?" He drove nonchalantly, like he usually did, and Caroline worried she may have given him one more thing to obsess over.

"I don't know," she admitted. "That's a great question."

"Because we shared breakfast together at the diner, oh, when was that? October?"

"It was October, yes," Caroline said.

"Or maybe it was when you crashed into my office," he said, grinning. "And thought I was Duke—which was totally insulting, by the way. Duke's like, almost twenty years older than me."

"It's not from the moment we met," she said. "I'm going to consider the diner, though. I didn't like you then, so I'm not sure it'll count."

"When did you start liking me?"

"You know what? I'm not sure."

Dawson ground his voice through his throat. "I'd like to go on the official record and say I've always liked you."

"You have got to be kidding me." She clapped her hands on her lap. "That is not true. You didn't even speak a word to me during that diner breakfast." She gave a mirthless laugh. "That is so not counting as our first date. We didn't even speak to one another."

"You seemed like you didn't want to talk," he said.

"I didn't."

"So I was respecting your wishes." He threw her a grin, but she sat there open-mouthed, staring at him.

"You did not like me when we met."

"I thought you were beautiful," he said.

"So not the same."

"You badgered me about bogus paperwork."

She couldn't even argue, and Dawson was enough of a gentleman not to throw it in her face. "The moment those owls appeared, I filled out your paperwork. I complied with the law."

"I know you did," Caroline said quietly. "Maybe that's when I started liking you."

"Mm, I think sooner," he said, his tone thoughtful, making her wonder what he was really thinking. "You didn't badger Link or Finn about their paperwork. Or Brit Bellamore. No one but me."

He looked over to her, those sexy eyes devouring her like so much aquamarine water. She couldn't argue this point either, because she hadn't cared if anyone else filed their paper-work. Only him.

She shrugged one shoulder, hoping to play this down a little. "Okay, maybe I liked you a little bit at some point before New Year's."

"You sure didn't act like it."

"I was never going to date again."

"Ah, another rule."

"One I broke, I'll have you know."

"Obviously." Dawson chuckled and reached for her hand. She loved the tingle his touch gave her, especially when he brushed his thumb over the back of her hand a couple of times. "So tell me, Miss Thompson. What other rules of yours do I need to start thinking about breaking?"

Oh, Caroline had opened a can of worms now, and she blinked and breathed, trying to find an answer that wouldn't blow open every-thing she'd been trying to contain...at least for now.

Chapter Twenty-Four

Dawson hadn't realized how loaded his question had been until Caroline didn't answer it with one of her snappy comebacks. "Let's start with something easier," he said, making the last turn that would get him to their dinner reservation. "When's your birthday?"

The woman wanted special, Dawson knew. She hadn't come out and said so, but the need for it pulsed in his heartstrings. He had a feeling she had spent most of her first marriage as an invisible identity, and she simply wanted to be seen, acknowledged, cherished, and loved.

"May tenth," she said.

"Brandon's birthday is in May," Dawson said. "Twenty-third." He gave her a smile. "Mine's in October, so we've got a ways to go to get to that one."

"What day?" She picked up her phone, like perhaps she'd type in the date. Like they'd still be together in eight months' time.

"The second," he said. "I'm glad it's at the beginning of the month, though the stores do bring out Halloween about mid-August these days."

Caroline grinned, agreed with him, tapped and tapped, then looked up. "I like to decorate for the holidays."

"Do you?" he asked. "I didn't see anything for Valentine's Day. No wreath or anything on the door."

She paused, and Dawson wished he could get inside her head and see all the layers there. He couldn't, so he waited for her to say something as the big barn he'd booked reservations with tonight came into view.

"You're right," she said. "Traditionally, I've hated Valentine's Day. Nothing good for me to celebrate." She wrapped her arms around herself in a crossed-arm hug. Pure vulnerability streamed from her, and Dawson wanted to wash it all away. Make everything better.

"You don't have to tell me right now," he said. "But your ex-husband...did he abuse you?"

"In so many ways, yes," she said. "Physically, no. But it's the mental and emotional wounds that take the longest to heal." She drew in a deep breath through her nose. "And no one sees those."

"Don't they?"

She swung her attention to him, those gorgeous curls bobbing a little with the moment. "They do?"

"We see how people act," he said quietly. "And if there's anything I learned in therapy, it's that nearly all decisions we make and the subsequent actions we take stem from our experiences." He made the turn into the big parking lot and followed the directions of the man with the light-up sticks, motioning for him to come forward and turn down an aisle on the right.

"So we see the wounds; we just don't categorize them that way. We think a person likes to make lists, or they enjoy getting up at five a.m. to run, or they like having rules for their life. But those, darlin', are the scars of our emotional and mental wounds. They're visible, if you know how to look."

"I—" She clamped her mouth shut, and Dawson pulled into the appointed space. He quickly turned off the ignition and grabbed his wallet before vaulting from the truck to go help her down in that sexy, vibrant, red-flower dress.

When he opened the door, he found her brushing at her eyes, and panic like Dawson had never felt before flooded him. "Dust and shadows," he swore as he crowded into her personal space. "I said something stupid, didn't I? I'm sorry."

She shook her head and sniffled. "No, you said something perfect." She gave him a kind, if a little watery, grin. "I've never thought of my emotional wounds being so visible."

"You follow the rules to a T," he said gently. "It's not a bad thing, but it also tells me that, at some point, you've been punished for coloring outside the lines." He put one hand on her knee and reached up with the other to cradle her face. "You can color anywhere you want with me, darlin'."

Her eyes drifted closed as she pressed into his touch. "Thank you, Dawson."

"Have I mentioned how gorgeous you are tonight? Did I say hello? Or did I go straight to kissing again?"

She grinned at him, bringing back the vibrancy that fueled his spirit. "You said hello, baby. Howdy, actually." She dropped to the ground and pulled her skirt with her.

Dawson linked his arm through hers. "Okay, now this just looks like a regular barn, but I'll have you know it's one of the biggest reasons I love Texas."

"You do love Texas," she said with a giggle.

"Don't act like you don't," he said.

"I'm still getting used to the Panhandle, though."

"Fair enough," he said. "Now, if you don't like this place, I'd appreciate it if you kept it to yourself until after the date. Then you can tell me never to bring you here again, and I'll have to decide if that's a deal-breaker for us."

The sidewalks leading to the big barn door—which was painted a bright white with a huge red heart in the middle of it—were lit by soft-glow lanterns hovering a foot or so off the ground. Everything had been cast in the color of romance, and Dawson felt it starting to hum through his veins.

"So you have deal-breakers for relationships," she said.

"Sure," he said. "The first one was that kissing my girlfriend can't be like kissing my sister, and you passed that one just fine." He cleared his throat. "Still do."

The door loomed closer, and Caroline's heels clicked with every step she took. He reached the door and opened it, letting out a wave of heat, but not much noise. It would get loud later, once the band started playing, but for now, Dawson's anxiety over tonight's festivities stayed dormant.

"Rhinehart," he said to the woman

standing behind a podium that had been made from reclaimed barn wood. It too bore the romantic lights, and flowers existed everywhere. Wreaths, and vases, and more horizontal displays, like the kind Dawson's momma put out on the table for Thanksgiving.

"Dawson," Caroline gushed. "Look at these flowers."

"All of our floral arrangements are for sale tonight," the hostess said. "Your table is number thirty-one, Mister Rhinehart, and you can go back any time you want."

"Thank you." He took the ticket from her and went with Caroline to look at all the arrangements.

"Did you ever think to buy yourself some flowers for Valentine's Day?" he asked. "Or another special occasion?"

She looked over to him, part alarm and part relief in her expression. The two warring emotions didn't go together, and Dawson feared he'd messed up again.

"No," she whispered. "But I should."

"Pick one of these," he said. "I'll get it for you."

"Baby, you already got me the biggest bouquet of roses in the world." She took his arm again and leaned into him. "Honestly, I don't think any other woman in Three Rivers got roses, because you bought them all."

He laughed, and it felt so good to do that. He loved being with this woman, and he loved making her smile, and he absolutely adored the way she made him feel.

She turned away from the rest of the room, not even looking at the rest of the arrangements. "Come show me why you love Texas."

Dawson led her to the entrance of the main room in the barn. Sometimes they had shows out here, with Chuckwagon dinners and fiddles and real barn-raising music. Sometimes they had a display of Christmas trees that Three Rivers residents could buy, and all the money got donated to the Food Bank for the holidays.

And on special occasions like tonight, the big space had been transformed into a lover's paradise, with tables that weren't too close to each other, a big area in the middle for dancing, and huge, splashy urns full of...more flowers. Several had silver, white, pink, or red heart-shaped balloons rising from them, while still others had the cardboard variety poking out of greenery and blooms.

Bare light bulbs hung from the ceiling over every table, providing a rustic atmosphere while also providing that pale, yellow, romantic light. The dance floor stood empty and waiting, and a man moved over to Dawson.

"What number, sir?"

"Thirty-one," he said, showing the man his ticket. All the waiters wore tuxedos, with the waitresses in black dresses.

"This way." The man led them out of the doorway and into paradise, getting them to the right table far faster than Dawson could've. He pulled out Caroline's chair for her, and as she sank into it, he leaned over and whispered, "I love Texas even more now that you're here."

He went to his seat and sat down, taking the menu from the man who'd escorted them to the table. Once he'd gone, Caroline said, "I've lived in Texas for a while, actually."

"Then in Three Rivers," he said without missing a beat.

The menu only held three choices for an appetizer, three for the soup and salad course, three main dishes, and three desserts. "It's one price," he said, noting there were no listings on the menu. "I've paid for two, and you get one thing from each section."

"Okay," she murmured.

"Do you like seafood?"

"Not this far from the ocean," she said.

He grinned at her, catching her eye for only moment as she glanced up while he looked down. "I love seafood," he said. "Even this far from the ocean."

"Noted," she said coolly as she lay down her menu. "I know what I want."

That she did, and Dawson needed to start praying that she'd continue to want him in her life. If he had a pad of sticky notes, he'd make himself a note to remember to pray for such a thing—on a white note.

Dawson had the menu memorized, so he set his aside too. "So do I."

"Can I guess?"

He gestured for her to go right ahead, feeling playful and alive, because she wore such a playful and vibrant look on her face.

"Well, knowing the seafood thing now, I think you'll get the scallops for an appetizer. You only eat green things when your momma makes you, so I'm going to go with the French onion soup for the second course. Surf and turf for your main, and the dessert...that's tricky." She folded her arms on the table and tilted her head in the cutest way.

"I'm going to go with chocolate," she said. "You seemed nuts about it in ice cream last week."

"It is the best kind of ice cream," he acknowledged.

"So the chocolate mousse cake," she said. "With ice cream, but I bet that's vanilla."

He grinned at her. "My turn."

"I want to know if I'm right."

"We'll do a tally at the end." He raised his

eyebrows, clearly asking her if that was okay, and when she nodded, Dawson forced his shoulders down. He needed to relax. This was a fun date, not a job interview.

"So for your appetizer, discounting the seafood, you're going to get the Caprese salad. Your salad course is also going to be soup, but not French onion. Mushroom, which I've had here before, and it was excellent, so good choice. Your main...." He took a sideways glance at the menu. "I'm going to go with chicken cordon bleu. Feels like you. Dessert is one thousand percent going to be the butter-scotch cheesecake."

He watched her lips twitch with every menu item he said, and he knew he'd nailed it. "So? How'd I do?"

"Rate me first."

Their game paused as a waiter appeared alongside another man. "I'm Omar," he said. "I'll be your server tonight, assisted by Gregory. He's got our signature wine tonight, but we have other drinks if you'd like something else." He beamed at Caroline and then Dawson.

"I'm driving," he said. "But I'd take a virgin mojito if you can do that."

"Of course," Gregory said, looking to Caroline.

"I'll take that wine," she said. He poured her a glass, and they all watched as the pink liquid flowed into the goblet prettily. "Thank you." She lifted it and swirled it, and Dawson had never found anything as attractive as her smelling it, brightening, and then taking a sip. "Mm, that's good."

"We'll give you a couple of minutes with the menu," Omar said. "You know how things go here?"

"Yes, sir," Dawson said. "Thank you."

They left, and he looked at Caroline again. "You got three out of four."

Her eyes widened, and then her face fell in a pout. "What did I miss?"

"I'm not going to get the scallops for the appetizer," he said. "I love a good steak tartar."

"Oh, my word," she said, a note of horror in her voice. "You like all the things I don't."

"Not all of them." He reached across the

table and took both of her hands in both of his. "I like you, and you like you."

"Funny."

"We both like ice cream," he said. "And over-easy eggs. And potatoes. And breakfast for dinner. I'm *wild* about breakfast for dinner." He grinned and grinned until she finally cracked a tiny smile for him. "I got all of yours, didn't I?"

"Yes," she clipped out. "And quite annoyingly, too." She didn't pull her hands away, but she looked toward the dance floor. "I mean, who gets labeled as *feels like chicken cordon bleu?*"

He laughed then, because he had said that about her. But he hadn't been wrong.

Everything inside the barn felt touched by magic, or maybe by the hand of God. He wasn't sure which.

He knew the food came out hot—or cold—and amazing, and he knew he was about to pop by the time the band started setting up. And he knew with one look at Caroline that she liked live music and dancing. Or at least one of those things.

She watched the band for a few minutes, and then she trained her pretty gaze on him. "Do you dance, cowboy?"

"Yes," he said simply. "It's a requirement of all true Texas cowboys that we know how to spin a lady around the floor."

"Spinning?" She lifted her eyebrows in a clear tease. "I just ate so much."

"Hm, seems like a you-problem."

Caroline blinked once and then threw her head back and laughed. Her curls had loosened as their dinner had progressed, and Dawson couldn't wait to run his fingers through them. Maybe fist his hand there while he kissed her good-night.

That was something to be considered too, as she'd mentioned that she didn't like kissing him on the doorstep. She felt like Belle might be watching, as they had a camera system, or she might realize how long they stood out there, ending their date.

And tonight, Dawson wanted a red-hot,

fiery, Valentine's Day kiss good-night. He wanted one of those every time he kissed Caroline, but especially tonight.

The first strains of music met his ears, and he perked up. He pulled his napkin off his lap and tossed it on the table. "Will you dance with me?" He stood and offered her his hand. When she didn't immediately slide hers into it, he added, "I won't spin you."

"In that case." She put her hand in his and let him steady her while she got to her feet. They moved out onto the dance floor as plenty of other people did, and Dawson's private bubble burst. Of course he wasn't here with Caroline alone. Of course he couldn't kiss her the way he wanted to on the dance floor. Of course he'd have to mind his manners.

Especially when he saw Link and Misty step onto the floor ahead of them. Dawson hadn't been out with his friends and Caroline yet, though he, Finn, Alex, and Link had talked about it.

He reminded himself that Caroline knew

the cowboys in this town, and she'd chosen to go out with him. It helped that all of his closest friends were married or engaged, but he pushed that thought away as he took her into his arms.

They moved effortlessly, and being with her even in the silence was so easy. Dawson had labored to talk to other women in the past, but not Caroline. She was the one who broke the silence between them with, "So what are your nieces doing tonight? Shiloh really didn't have anything going on with JJ? April is keeping her nose clean?"

"I think they had a party," he said. "At someone's house in town. I guess they decided going to the school dance was lame. Shiloh was driving them, and Zona lectured her for a solid twenty minutes about driving home late at night, in the dark." He smiled just thinking about his sister-in-law. "And, um, Zona and Duke would like to get together with us again, on a more, uh, *formal* I think was the word Zona used, basis. Dinner together or something."

"Sure," Caroline said easily. "I liked your family, Dawson."

"Miracles do still happen," he joked.

Caroline giggled into his shoulder, and he took the opportunity to knead her closer. "My friends and I go out sometimes too," he said. "Finn's married, and he and Edith have a baby on the way. Alex and Nicki are married too, and Link and Misty are engaged. Since we're to implied dates and all that, I'm wondering if group dates count."

"Yes," she said simply.

"So you'll go to Link's wedding with me?"

"Yes, I love weddings."

"Do you?" Dawson pulled back enough to look at her. "Seems like they'd be on the same level as Valentine's Day."

"My wedding was the one thing I liked about my marriage," she said. "They're such happy occasions. They hold so much hope. They're like a window to the future. I like that."

"All right," he drawled. The song ended, and another started. This one was definitely a twirling, spinning dance, and he stepped back again.

"I can do this," Caroline said. "It's been a while since I've danced this way, though, so consider yourself warned."

"I've been warned," he said, grinning. "My little nephew says, 'I have to beware you, Uncle Dawson.'" He chuckled. "That reminded me of him."

Caroline smiled too, shooting joy out into the barn. "All right, then, baby. *I have to beware you* that I haven't danced this way in a while. I could fall down or kick you or step all over your feet."

"All risks I'm willing to take," he said, taking both of her hands in his. He waited for the next beat, and then he started the first steps of the swinging dance. They laughed, and he spun her away in a slow cadence, bringing her back after only one twirl instead of the two or three other women did.

And when that song melted back into something slow and beautiful, he tucked her against his chest and let himself fall and fall and fall toward being in love with Caroline.

It was a scary thing, falling, and Dawson had never done it with a woman before. He loved other things, of course. Ruffin, Rocks, and Nugget. All of his hens and roosters. His parents. His brothers. Duke's family.

He loved the wide Texas sky, and the town of Three Rivers, and being a cowboy.

And he loved dancing with Caroline, in the perfect place, on the perfect night—and he couldn't help but wonder: was she the perfect woman for him?

And if so, would it really take her twelve months and a road trip to realize it?

"I have another follow-up question about your twelve-month rule," he murmured. "But I can ask it another time. Will you just remind me to ask you?"

"Sure, baby," she said almost sleepily, and then she let him cradle her in his arms exactly the way he wanted to.

Chapter Twenty-Five

Caroline shuffled paperwork around her desk, the day still two hours from being over and her headache throbbing behind her eyes. She'd been reading about a new law for the Wildlife Division that would go into effect on July first, and she then had to prepare materials for all the surrounding farms, ranches, and anyone who had honeybees in a four-hundred mile radius.

Everyone in Amarillo, all the way to the Oklahoma border, throughout Three Rivers, of course, and throughout dozens of other small towns in her region. She'd done projects like this before, and they started out messy.

She'd gotten a new yellow legal pad to take notes, and she had a blue pen—her preferred writing utensil when absorbing a lot of information she needed to distill down into bullet points—words and lines all over several pages.

When she caught herself staring at a black screen on her computer, with no idea how much time had gone by since she'd last been aware, she stood up. Her screen saver took fifteen minutes to come on, and she wondered who in the office had seen her staring at literally nothing.

She glanced over to Ivy's desk, and thankfully, she had her head bent over something probably labeled "super important" that wasn't. Caroline moved over to her desk, and said, "I'm dying here. It's so boring and slow. Do you want to go to the bakery and work the last couple hours of today?"

Ivy blinked like she'd just come out of a dark room and hadn't seen sunlight for a few years. "Yes," she breathed in the next moment.

"That sounds like heaven." She slapped her folder closed and stood faster than Caroline had ever seen a human woman stand.

"Great," she said. "Let me get my stuff too. I'll meet you there in fifteen minutes?" The bakery sat only a couple of blocks from their office, and it boasted great air conditioning, big tables, and in the afternoon, it wouldn't be busy.

Caroline had learned that one of Three Rivers' great matrons—Heidi Ackerman— owned the bakery, and she was Finn's grandma. Finn, of course, was one of Dawson's good friends, and he had a one-man operation that had almost escaped the burrowing owls. Then he'd called to say he'd found a single nest on his south fence, and Caroline had accepted his paperwork and taken him the conservation supplies.

The owl sightings had slowed considerably in the past month or so, and she just had to do regular check-ins with the ranches who had them. She wasn't sure what the owls would do. They tended to be transitory birds, but not until they had their chicks and raised them.

Fifteen minutes later, she had the work items she needed to finish that day, a fresh cup of coffee and a chocolate croissant, and a renewed sense of energy and purpose. She'd arrived at the bakery before Ivy, and when her friend and co-worker got there, Caroline took a sip of her coffee and asked, "How are things going with Colt?"

Ivy grinned like she'd entered Wonderland and had taken on the form of the Cheshire Cat. "He's wonderful," she said with a sigh. "We're talking about getting married now." She looked up, a measure of fear in her eyes.

"Why do you look like you have burrowing owls in your bed?" Caroline gave her a smile and reached for another sugar packet for her coffee.

"My daddy thinks I'm too young to get married." Ivy looked out the window, an expression telling Caroline that her thoughts lingered far away. "And Colt is quite a bit older than me. He's set here, ready to take over the apple orchards when his mom retires."

"And when will that be?"

"Oh, gosh." Ivy inhaled and breathed the air all back out. "She keeps saying this year, but Colt said she did that last year too." She smiled. "These generational places. They're hard for people to let go of, you know?"

Caroline thought of Dawson and Duke. Link and his family at Shiloh Ridge. The conversation with JJ Walker about what he should do with his life—take over the ranch his daddy ran? Or do something else?

"Yeah," she said. "I'm learning that about this part of Texas."

"There are real deep roots here," Ivy said. "It's what makes the community so great, but it also makes it hard for the second generation to take over and assure their older parents that they're not going to burn everything to the ground." She grinned and dipped her spoon into strawberry pistachio tart. "And maybe in Colt's case, he will." She trilled out a laugh and said, "That man loves fire."

Caroline wasn't sure if she should laugh or not, but she did smile as Ivy took a bite of her tart. "Oh, this is good."

She didn't normally bring her personal life to work, but Caroline had seen how open Dawson was with his friends and family. Belle knew about her relationship, of course, but Caroline was ready to shout it from the rooftops.

"I started seeing a cowboy like that," she said.

Ivy nearly choked on her whipped cream. "Who?" She wore wide eyes like Caroline dating someone was akin to a small town scandal. Or impossible. She supposed she had not been all that open to dating for a long time now, and other women had a way of picking up on that.

"Dawson Rhinehart," she said, noting how soft her muscles became as she said his name. "It's going pretty well."

"Yeah, I can see that." Ivy grinned at her. "Good for you, Caroline. The Rhineharts are a great family."

"Yeah," Caroline said, parroting her

friend's word back to her. "It's new—only a couple of months in—but yeah." She still hadn't decided when she could start the twelve-month period for her and Dawson, and she remembered he'd asked her to remind him of another follow-up question he had about her rule.

So, while she should be working, she quickly sent him a text instead. *You were going to ask me something else about the twelve-month rule.* Then she flipped her phone over and sternly told herself to work for a half-hour before checking her phone.

The man texted her most afternoons once he made it to his office-barn, and all through the evening if they weren't going out. But truth be told, at this point, they saw each other almost every night.

They had a surprise birthday party for Link coming up, and then a double-date with Duke and Zona on the calendar as well. Sometimes he stopped by with a brown bag of fast food and they ate it from the tailgate of his truck, parked right there in her driveway.

Sometimes she brought lunch to his cabin

for him, Brandon, and Ruffin. She may or may not have been tossing shiny quarters from the window of her SUV in the hopes that Rocks would have something to find on the ranch that he could then take to his friend.

Just the thought of those crows made her so happy, for a reason she couldn't name. There was something pure and simple—and so good—about Dawson and his life that Caroline really needed in her life.

Every minute passed painfully slow, and then she checked her phone to see if Dawson had replied.

Yeah, he'd said. *A couple actually. Let's start with this one: Does the rule mean that you can't get engaged before the twelve months are up and the road trip has happened? Or you just can't say I-do before then?*

Her heart hammered out of nowhere. Caroline's vision blurred, and she blinked, trying desperately to hold onto reality.

You're not marrying Joe, she told herself. *Joe's gone. He's not Joe.*

She hadn't had to revert to this level of reassurance for a long, long time, and if she were being completely honest, she wasn't sure why she'd spiraled so quickly.

"Caroline?"

She opened her eyes, not sure where she was. Then the familiar scent of yeast and sugar met her nose, and she remembered.

The bakery. Coffee and croissant. Working on a slow afternoon.

A good friend with pure concern in her eyes. "Are you okay?"

"I...think so."

"You kind of moaned." Ivy glanced down at her hands. "You're gripping your phone really hard. I thought maybe you were having a seizure."

Caroline shook her head, trying to find a logical explanation that didn't make her sound crazy. Then she remembered that her actions testified of her emotional and mental scars— and Ivy had just seen one burst wide open and start bleeding again.

Her phone buzzed, drawing her attention again.

Dawson: *Like, let's say we fall in love. Go somewhere amazing this summer—that's my next question—and we want to get married. Can I propose before the twelve months and we get married after it? Or is it a strict no-diamond policy until all twelve months have passed?*

Dawson again: *Follow-up to the follow-up: If you could go anywhere on a road trip, where would you go?*

With that last text, her vision cleared. Her mind centered, and Caroline saw the sweet, caring, gentle side of Dawson that truly epitomized him. Sure, he was gruff on the outside. No, he didn't want anyone in his barn space. True, he kept things close to the vest until he was ready to share them.

All those things made him, him, though, and Caroline liked all the pieces of him he'd shown her so far. And she knew without a doubt that if she said she wanted to go on a road trip to Hawaii, he'd find a way to pave the Pacific Ocean.

I'll have to think about the road trip, she sent him quickly. *And we need to talk about what just happened when I read your other texts, but I don't want to do it with letters.*

I'm meeting with Ward tonight, Dawson reminded her. *I can swing by and get you about eight, and we can grab doughnuts from that place next to the fountain. A quick dessert date. Yeah?*

Yeah, she sent back. *I still want the walking tour of Three Rivers one day.*

You're so demanding, he sent back, complete with several smiling emojis. She mimicked them, and Ivy said, "Oh, so you're falling for him already."

Caroline put down her phone, her date set up. "Maybe," she acknowledged. "And I need help with this."

"You do?" Ivy set down her pen, and they were apparently going to have a chatty-working afternoon. "Do tell."

Caroline took a deep breath. "Okay, you know how I was married before?" She waited for Ivy to nod. "Well, I actually made a pact with myself that I'd never date and get married again. So, this is obviously all blowing up in my face, and well, I think I just had a little panic attack when Dawson texted me with the words, *marriage, proposal*, and *engagement*."

She put her head in her hands, a wail starting in her stomach and easing its way up her throat, where it would have to come out. "That's bad, right?" She looked at Ivy, hoping her friend would reassure her that it was normal to panic about these types of things.

Ivy looked like a scared jackrabbit herself, a feeling currently stomping across Caroline's lungs. "I mean, I feel like I'm about to pass out at the thought of getting married," she said. "And I've been dating Colt for ten months. So I'm the wrong person to ask."

Caroline had already broken her no-dating rule. Marriage was way down the line. Way down. Twelve months, at least.

Perhaps only ten, a tiny voice whispered, and Caroline squashed it quickly. "I just need to talk to Dawson," she said. "That's all."

"I'm sorry," Ivy said, wearing her concern in her voice. "I'm of no help to you on this." She covered Caroline's hand with hers. "I'm sorry your first marriage was so bad you don't want to try again."

"Try again," Caroline murmured. That was all she needed to do. Try again, this time in a different place, at a different time, with a different man. Heck, she was a different person.

Instant calmness came over her, and Caroline pressed her eyes closed and said, "Thank you, Lord, for this reassurance." It felt like the Savior himself had draped her in a blanket straight from the warmest source of heavenly light. She opened her eyes and looked at Ivy. "I just need to be brave for long enough to get the first sentence out."

She'd done it before, with a far harsher man and far worse consequences. *This is Dawson,* she told herself again. *And he's not Joe.*

She didn't want to lose her cowboy in shining armor, not without giving herself the time and space she needed—*they* needed—to come together. And if there was one thing she'd learned as she'd been reborn from the ashes of her marriage, it was that some rules *should* be broken.

Caroline just hadn't realized she'd made any of that kind for herself.

Chapter Twenty-Six

Dawson's impatience began to bleed through his carefully crafted defenses. But holy tar and feathers, were all meetings this painful? This boring? This long?

He flipped his phone over again and saw that he was now late to leave to pick up Caroline by eight. *You told her you'd swing by*, he told himself. *She's not expecting you right at the top of the hour, with flowers.*

Heck, he hadn't even been home to shower yet.

He wanted to cancel, but something told him not to. He forced himself to listen as Ward

Glover went over their upcoming cattle drive into the hills, something the Rhinehart Ranch participated in with Shiloh Ridge every year. If they didn't, the work would take three times as long and be an awful ordeal.

But every single Glover—and all their cowboys—pitched in during the drive, and Duke piggybacked off it. Now, Dawson was learning how this worked, and he reminded himself he needed this information.

"Preliminary information and schedules will be out by next week," Ward said from the comfort of a conference room on the second floor of the homestead at Shiloh Ridge Ranch. "Look it over, and get me and Preacher—you have to reply-all." He paused, his eyes glued to Bear, specifically. "Any changes you need by the end of next week."

"I'm not going to look at this," Bear griped. "Send it to Link."

Lincoln was in attendance, and he lifted his hand in a half-wave to indicate to Ward that yes, he should simply send him the email.

"You could still learn how to email, Bear."

"I know how to send an email."

"Yes, but do you know how to *reply-all* to one?" Ward cocked his eyebrows, and oh, the gauntlet had been thrown down.

"Don't teach him how to do that," Preacher teased. "Then we'll all be getting his private emails, meant only for him and Sammy or something."

Bear folded his arms, his glare positively predatory. Ward and Preacher, along with several others, chuckled, and Ward flipped off the projector. "Thanks for comin' in, everyone. Dot and Holly Ann made brownie bars."

And Dawson saw his opportunity to still get his dessert date with Caroline—and they wouldn't even have to leave her driveway if he brought dessert with him.

Everyone started chit-chatting, and Dawson couldn't grab a pan of brownies and race out. He talked with Preacher for a few minutes about making sure his horses were shod before the drive, and he got the name of a great farrier Shiloh Ridge had been using.

That meant Chris Palms probably wouldn't

have time for the horses at his ranch, but he took down the info anyway. The farrier world wasn't that big, and if Chris couldn't come do it, he'd have another recommendation.

He chatted with Link about how Valentine's Day had been for him and Misty, then something about the wedding, and then he finally picked up a paper plate and put four brownies on it. No one said a word to him about the number of them, and he almost felt like a criminal sneaking out the door and hurrying to his truck.

After sending a quick text to Caroline, so she'd know he was just-now leaving, he did just that. Sometimes he hated the long drive into town, but most of the time it brought him a sense of comfort and relief. He could calm down in this quiet time, instead of having to move immediately from one thing to the next.

So by the time he showed up at Caroline's house, his pulse had returned to normal and his irritation with the evening had fled. Thankfully.

Caroline sat on her front steps, already

waiting for him, and Dawson picked up the treats and headed toward her. "Hey, you," he said, feeling bright and bubbly all of a sudden.

She looked up at him, something soft in her eyes. Something guarded too. "Hey, baby."

He handed her the plate of brownies and settled beside her. "I love it when you call me baby," he said to the dark sky. Her porch light blazed into the night, but it was above and behind them, and it didn't pierce the darkness for very long or very far.

"I love seeing you after a long day at work," he said. "And I *adore* getting off the ranch and seeing you on these steps."

She reached over and took his hand, but she didn't start her list of things she loved and adored. Dawson shifted and picked up a brownie. He wasn't sure what to say next, because he wasn't the one who needed to say it.

"I freaked out at your follow-up questions this afternoon," she said, her fingers oh-so-tight in his.

"Is that right?"

"You used words like *proposal* and *marriage*

and *fall in love,* and I don't know. I wasn't ready for them."

Dawson took a bite of his brownie so he wouldn't take a leaf out of Bear Glover's book and growl. Or say something he'd regret the moment it left his mouth. Caroline leaned her head against his shoulder and cradled his hand in both of hers now.

That was definitely something he could say he loved and adored. But he said nothing.

"It's stupid, I know," she whispered. "I want to fall in love again."

"Do you?" he asked.

"Yes," she said.

"So what is it that scared you?"

"I didn't say I was scared."

"But you were," he said, not really in the mood for games or semantics. "*Freaked out* is the same as *scared.*"

Caroline lifted her head and looked at him, her eyes cool and full of fire at the same time. He didn't normally challenge her, but Dawson wasn't going to be railroaded either. He was one-half of this relationship, and he wanted to be a full fifty percent.

"It's okay if you were scared," he said. "I'm terrified. I've never been in love. Never even thought about marriage. I don't have a house to live in with a wife. Nothing." He sighed and picked up another brownie. "It's a good thing you have this rule, so I can get my ducks in a row. You know, if I need to do that."

Caroline leaned against him again. "My grandma had this saying about ducks. She said hers were never in a row, that they didn't even know what rows were."

Dawson smiled, because that sounded like the opposite of Caroline.

"And she'd say, 'But it doesn't matter, Caroline, because if you can't get your ducks in a row, then maybe you only have one, and he's always right where he needs to be.'" She laughed lightly for a moment. "Then, she started saying she only had geese, and geese were mean, so she just tried to stay out of their way."

Dawson chuckled with her. "Geese *are* mean," he said.

They both sobered, and Caroline said, "I was scared by the texts. You have valid questions I don't know the answers to, but it made me realize that this thing between us is leading somewhere."

"Mm."

"And it's either like you said—proposals and marriage—or it's not. There's only two ways it ends."

"Oh, I don't know," he said. "We could end up friends."

"Yeah, right," she said. "If you break up with me, you'll never speak to me again."

"Who says I'm going to break up with you?" He bent his head to look at her, but she kept staring out toward the darkened lawn.

"Baby, if we break up, I can guarantee it'll be because of me," she whispered. "And my insane rules, and my inability to let go of even a little bit of control, because I had so little before, you know?" She sniffled, and oh, Dawson couldn't have that.

He lifted his arm and drew her into his side, "Hey, you can't cry over this. It was just a couple of follow-up questions, mostly for myself. For the house thing, and maybe for my obsessive side to start thinking of road trip ideas. That's all. It's not a big deal."

"I can feel myself morphing all over again," she whispered. "And it's not very pleasant, Dawson. It's good. I can feel that it's good, but it's not easy for me."

"Okay," he said. "What can I do to make it easier? Not ask questions?"

"I don't know if it's something you can make easier," she said. "This is the reason I have the rule. So that I have the time I need to make adjustments, and sometimes those are just within me."

"Okay," he said. Silence poured between them now, and he wasn't sure if they were okay or not. Feeling brave, he asked, "So...road trip destinations?"

"You know what I've always wanted to do?"

"Do tell."

"A Mississippi Riverboat cruise."

"That sounds like a boat trip, not a road trip."

"A road trip first, and then a boat trip," she said. "Can you stand boats?"

"I don't rightly know," he said. "I don't think I've ever been on one."

She moved to wrap her arm across his stomach. "Will you look into it, baby?"

"Yes," he whispered. He pressed a kiss to her forehead, needing just a little bit more from her. "Caroline, tell me where we are."

"We're sitting on my front porch, talking about a road-boat trip."

"Come on," he said, perhaps a bit grumpily.

"I think I'm coming out the other side of a personal crisis," she said. "This is one of those emotional wounds you talked about. You get to see that scar, and I'm trying to patch it all back up, so it doesn't define me."

"It's just a little piece of you," he said.

"Right," she said. "I'll get there, and I'm sorry I freaked out."

"Hey, I dang near took a whole pan of brownies and fled the meeting earlier," he said. "Everything is just so *slow*."

She laughed and finally picked up a brownie and took a bite. "Mm, these are good."

Dawson had already eaten two, so he didn't take a third. "So we're good?"

"Yes." She wiped brownie crumbs from her lips as she nodded. "We're good. I'm working on things, just like you are."

He studied her, those light eyes he liked so, so much. "I hope we can end up in the same place, at the same time," he murmured. "Because I sure do like you, Caroline."

She grinned and touched her lips to his. Kissing her was the absolute best thing in the world.

"I sure do like you too, Dawson."

Okay, fine, hearing her say that and *then* kissing her was the absolute best thing in the world. Now, all Dawson had to do was figure out the rest of his life—his role on the ranch, where he'd live with his own wife and family when those things came along, and literally everything else—so he could keep this woman with him.

Chapter Twenty-Seven

Link never wanted to see another cow as long as he lived. He'd spent the last four days working with Uncle Cactus and his veterinary crew to get all the cattle checked and ready to go out into the hills for their summer grazing.

He'd go out on the cattle drive this year, the way he had been for the past fifteen. His momma hadn't let him go with Daddy until he was twelve, and that was still the rule for kids at Shiloh Ridge Ranch.

But they didn't leave for four more days, and that meant a metric ton of preparation was going on around the ranch. Horses who needed shoeing, and saddlebags that needed packing. Food and water for twenty men, and this year, Uncle Bishop was bringing his son Robbie to help run the chuckwagon. They'd make sure they all ate well, and Uncle Cactus was also sending up two new dogs to stay with the cattle.

Uncle Cactus himself wasn't going. In fact, none of the older uncles were going.

Uncle Ranger, nope. Uncle Cactus, nada.

And Daddy...Daddy was staying home from the cattle drive for the first time since he was twelve years old.

Link knew it would be astronomically hard for his father to stay home. Everyone knew it was time, but that didn't make change any easier.

Daddy had been just as involved in the preparations to go on the drive this year, and Link hoped that helped him adjust to the fact that he wouldn't be saddling up and riding out with them in a few days.

And tonight, Link had to get showered up,

changed, and ready for his birthday party. Momma did one every year, but this one he got to share with the love of his life.

Misty would be here in a half-hour, and despite her being his fiancée and their wedding coming up in only three more months, Link kept thinking she'd pull up to True Blue, see the number of trucks there, and rush right back to her house in town.

He kept thinking she'd do that with every new family thing Link introduced her to, and Link hadn't been able to curb in his mother. Even Daddy hadn't been able to stop Momma from throwing the "biggest, bestest party this family has ever seen."

Momma's words. Link's nightmare.

She wanted Misty to have the best birthday ever, as she'd grown up without much in the way of parties, family traditions, or even food in the fridge. That did not sit well with Momma, and Link had decided to let her have her party for the two of them.

Misty's birthday wasn't until the end of the month, but Link had already bought her present, and he'd give it to her tonight. He had something for her for later in the month too, something a little more personal and private.

Tonight, he'd barely buttoned up his shirt when someone knocked on his door, and Misty's beautiful voice called, "It's me, Link."

"Come on back," he said as he moved through his master bathroom to the doorway of his bedroom. Misty would not come back, as she didn't ever come back into his bedroom.

He found her in the living room, loving on the dogs who liked to follow Link around the ranch.

"You ready for this?" he asked.

"I'm ready." Misty straightened and looked at him. She wore pure nerves in her face, and Link reached for her.

"Hey, if it's too much, we just go out the back door for a few minutes," he said. "There are so many people there, they won't even notice."

"It's a birthday party for *us*," she said. "They're going to notice if we're not there."

"Maybe," Link said, to which Misty simply

cocked her head. "If it's awful, I'll give my momma a look, and she'll rein it in."

"It was your momma we couldn't stop before."

Link leaned down and touched his lips to hers. "I know, baby. It's going to be amazing, okay? Low key. Good food. Birthday cake. The end. It's not like we can stay out late. We're cowboys, and we'll all be dead by seven-thirty." He grinned at her, so warm inside when she grinned back.

"I love you," he whispered, his lips catching on hers.

"I love you too," she said.

"Happy birthday month."

"To you too."

Link could stay in his cabin and kiss Misty for a long time, but he didn't want to incur Momma's wrath, and she had spent considerable time and effort to plan this party. "Let's go party."

The road from the Top Cottage, where Link lived, to True Blue, the family's recreational barn where they had all their big celebrations—and where Link and Misty would be married in another three months—only took five minutes.

Yes, plenty of trucks had already parked along the road in front of the barn. The front doors stood open, and Link wouldn't be surprised to hear a pumping beat coming from the barn once he parked and got out of the truck.

He grinned at the stall that had been saved with bright blue streamers. A banner strung from the top corners that said "Birthday Couple," and he enjoyed the way Misty giggled at it too.

"Your mother is an amazing person," she said.

"That she is," Link murmured as he pulled into the marked spot only a few feet from the door. He couldn't hear or feel a bass beat, but the strumming of guitars met his ears as he got out to go get Misty's door.

As she slipped from the truck, he took her hand in his, and they faced the entrance together. He hoped he could face every single thing in his life moving forward with her at his side. With her hand in his, he could do anything. Conquer anything. Face any fear or any unknown, or endure any difficult time.

"It feels like we're late," Misty said as they entered the small foyer off the front doors. Link turned to his left, the big room of True Blue opening up before him. Tables and chairs stood dressed and ready to feed a lot of people dinner, but Link didn't see a single person.

That alone got him to come to a stop, confusion furrowing his brow. "Maybe we're early."

The kitchen window had been lifted, and Link definitely detected the scent of hot food in the building. The evidence of people was everywhere, and Link took another couple of steps into the room before someone exited the hallway that led back to the kitchen.

Link's heartbeat came to a complete standstill, which also froze his feet to the ground. His eyes were surely betraying him.

Because Mitch currently strode toward him, wearing a fantastically large grin and waving his hello.

"Mitch." Link automatically moved into using his hands to accompany his voice as he spoke. "What in the world is happening? What are you doing here?"

Mitch had gotten a lot faster and better at sign language since he'd been at his deaf school, and that alone testified to Link that his cousin and best friend was in the right place for him.

It's your birthday, Mitch said. *And I never miss your birthday*. He arrived in front of Link and drew him into a brilliant, brotherly hug. Link wrapped him up in his arms too, laughing right out loud as the surprise continued to stream through him.

Link stepped back and let Misty say hello. She knew a little bit of sign language, and that made Link's heart happy. Then he asked, "Where's everyone else?"

Mitch turned and looked toward that hallway as aunts, uncles, and cousins started to pour out of it. They came from the back hallway too, which branched to the left and led outside and to the right back to a couple of bathrooms and other rooms they used for staging before weddings, parties, and other events.

Cheering started, with the clapping of hands, congratulations, and shouts of "Happy birthday!" and yeehaws.

Link's smile popped onto his face, and he reached for Misty so she wouldn't get swept away in the tide of Glovers. He hugged his family members, as did Misty, and things got loud for the next several minutes.

He finally made it to one of the back tables, where he found Finn and Edith, Alex and Nicki, Caroline, Dawson, and Brandon. Ollie stood nearby, talking to Uncle Mister, but Aurora sat at the table, her little boy on her lap as she talked to Nicki about something. Janie sat with Ralf, and they brightened when they saw Link and Misty.

"Hey, you guys." Link grinned at his friends, glad his mother had included them too. They were important to Link, as Finn, Alex, and Dawson were all in his same stage of life. Starting or running their own ranches, or moving into more leadership roles as their daddies aged and retired.

He went around and hugged all of them, a keen sense of satisfaction moving through him that Misty fit with this table of people. She didn't just stick with Janey and Ralf, though they were definitely her comfortable place.

She laughed with Edith, put her hand on her bulging pregnant belly, and then took Rory's little boy from her. She cooed at Mason, and Link swore God had just given him a vision of his future.

True Blue. Another Glover family party. Misty holding a little boy that she passed to someone else, because they wanted to see her son and give her a mini-break from being a full-time caregiver.

She looked over to him, and Link already had his smile in place. He wasn't sure what she saw, but she ducked her head, so many unspoken things between them that he understood. She wanted kids too, though she'd told him she wanted some time with just the two of them.

In truth, she'd confessed that she wanted to take some parenting classes before she became a mother. She wanted to study up on what she claimed she didn't know, and Link would support her any way he could.

"Oh, hey, the party's arrived," Ollie said, and all eyes moved to Mitch. He carried a huge platter of buffalo wings, which he put on the table.

He laughed and went around hugging everyone too. And with the food out, that meant the party had started. Link was a little surprised that Momma hadn't made him and Misty sit up on a raised stage in the front, but he hadn't even seen her yet.

So he took a seat at the table with his friends and faced Mitch. "So tell me about your cochlear implant appointment. You've been intentionally vague."

Mitch's smile slipped a little, but because not very many people could speak his language, he started signing. Link had a hard time with technical words, and he had to ask Mitch to slow down almost immediately.

I don't think it's going to be for me, unfortunately, Mitch said. *As much as I want it to be, I wasn't brought up in a language-rich environment.*

"I'm not sure I know what that means."

It means I haven't had the opportunity to use my voice. He actually touched his throat, as if indicating his vocal cords. *Some deaf people learn to speak from childhood. They learn the sounds the vowels make, and they're vocal even though they can't hear. That wasn't my life.*

"So that means you can't have implants?" Link wasn't sure why it mattered. Speaking and hearing were definitely linked, but he wasn't sure how intimately.

They say it could take ten years before I could actually speak. Ten years after I get the implants, and that's with me doing constant input of hearing and practicing with my voice.

Mitch glanced around, and Link sensed he was done explaining. Or close to it.

It takes a long time to learn to talk, Mitch said. *Even when you can hear, and I'm almost thirty years old. Maybe if I were younger....* He stopped signing there and shook his head. *I don't feel good about it, so I don't think I'm going to explore the implants anymore.*

Link put his hand over Mitch's, feeling his cousin's sadness through his skin. "I'm so sorry," he said, looking right into his cousin's eyes. "I know how badly you want to talk on the phone."

That had been the thing Mitch talked about the most. He was tired of texting and video calls. He wanted to hear the phone ring, and he wanted to pick it up and answer it with his voice. Hear another voice on the other end of the line.

He wanted to communicate with his ears and mouth, not his eyes.

Mitch looked away, his eyes filling with tears. He sniffed and wiped the back of his hand across his face. The tears were instantly gone, and his smile came back for a brief moment. *It's okay*, he signed. *I mean, it's not okay, but God is helping me shift my focus.*

That made Link's heart skip a beat. "God is, huh?"

Mitch rolled his eyes. *Slowly. I get God is this eternal being, but I think He forgets we're not, and that some of us would like things to move a little faster.*

Link laughed, because that was so Mitch. He had patience in some things, but not with religion. Not with God. He wanted to change quickly and get it over with, and God was more of a master sculptor, pinching out a detail here and smoothing out something rough on that side, slowly, over time.

"Lincoln."

He turned toward the sound of his mother's voice, and Link jumped to his feet. "Momma." He stepped into her arms, as there was nothing as good as a hug from his mom.

"Oh, you're my favorite boy," she said as she hugged him tightly. He grinned, because Momma had lots of boys and girls to love, but when she told him he was her favorite, he believed her. "I love you."

"Love you too, Momma." He stepped back and swept a kiss along her cheek. "Thank you for doing this."

"Hey, Misty-girl." Momma took Misty into her arms, and Link's whole world slowed as he watched his fiancée sink into that warm embrace, her eyes drifting closed in bliss. "Happy birthday, sweetie."

"Thank you, Sammy," Misty murmured, and when she stepped back, Link was right there at her side.

"Well, there's tons of food," Momma said as she cleared her throat. "Daddy's got the uncles singing some songs in a little bit, and Smiles organized all the younger cousins for a dance number." She grinned widely, and Link started laughing again.

"A dance number, wow," he said, sliding his arm around Misty and keeping her close. "Never had one of those before."

"It's Smiles, and a bunch of children under the age of fourteen," Momma said. "I expect the applause to raise the roof."

"Yes, ma'am," Link said with a chuckle. "I'm sure it will."

"Okay, well, make sure you find Daddy before you and Misty sneak out." She smiled between them and then turned to go find her place for dinner.

Link hadn't even turned back to his table of friends before Uncle Preacher's miked voice filled the barn. "I need the birthday couple up here, please."

"Here we go," Link said as music filled the barn. Everyone turned to look at him and Misty, and Link had gotten used to it over the years. He moved through the crowd to where Preacher stood—thankfully, not on a platform, but just in front of a microphone.

Uncle Ward, Uncle Mister, Uncle Judge, and Daddy played guitars, and Preacher beamed at Link and Misty as he said, "It's time to sing Happy Birthday to Link and Misty, and then we have a short program before we're going to pray. Then there's a bunch of birthday cake and food, and the night is yours."

So maybe ten minutes, Link thought. He could endure this spotlight for ten more min-utes, and then he'd be able to retreat to the back table to enjoy the delicious food surely Uncle

Bishop and Aunt Etta had been in charge of making.

The song started, and Link did his best to smile through the whole thing. He'd always thought *Happy Birthday* was a long song when it was being sung to him, and with Misty beside him, it seemed to drag on and on until Aunt Dot's high-pitched voice sang that last note completely off-tune on purpose, the way she always did.

The last word cut off into applause, whistling, and laughter, and Link added his own to it. Then Smiles appeared in front of him and said, "All right, you gotta go stand in the crowd."

Link grinned at his younger brother and did what he said, taking Misty with him. They stood at the front of the crowd as Smiles called all the littles up front for their "performance."

Besides Ollie and Rory, Uncle Mister and Aunt Libby had the youngest child—a little boy named Brantley, who was five years old and would start kindergarten this fall.

When Smiles had them all gathered

around him, he held up a bright blue ball that filled his palm and could easily be seen. "All right, you guys. This is for cousin Link and cousin Misty, okay? Remember what we did?"

Link doubted very much that this would go off without a hitch, but he couldn't stop grinning. Smiles looked up and called, "Hit it!" in the direction of the kitchen. Link didn't dare look away from the kids, and when the first popping beat hit the sound system, he was glad he didn't.

For Smiles had gathered the kids around him strategically, and the outer circle of them jumped up and faced the crowd upon that first beat. "Everybody clap your hands," Smiles yelled, bringing his hands up over his head to start the beat.

The kids around him did the same thing, and it only took one more clap to get the crowd involved. Link laughed as he brought his hands together, glad to see Misty doing the same thing.

The kids in the second circle in jumped up and turned around to face the crowd, and then the final circle of them did too. Smiles was the tallest of them all, but Shiloh, Gunn, Rock, Wilder, and Robbie were all fourteen or fifteen years old too. They took up the back row, spaced out to help the younger kids.

They grapevined to the left, which made Link whoop to watch little Dallas—Zona and Duke's youngest son—nearly trip over his feet. Whoever had choreographed the dance had kept it simple, having everyone move left or right to the beat, and as the dance number came to a close, all the kids reached behind them and pulled something from their pockets.

Popsicle sticks with colorful, curly ribbons on them, which they shook as the music ended. Before Link could take in the rattling of the streamers and the amazingness of the people in front of him, they all shouted, "Happy birthday Link and Misty!" in a perfect chant.

And that was when the barn positively erupted, just the way Momma wanted it to. Link added his voice and applause to the deafening noise, and then all the kids ran at him and Misty and surrounded them as they cheered for them.

He and Misty got separated, but she didn't seem to mind. This was pure chaos, but pure chaos built from pure love. And in the midst of all that, Link knew he'd just experienced the best birthday of his life.

And one look at Misty told him she had too.

Chapter Twenty-Eight

Finn took the bowl of white chocolate popcorn that Edith handed him and took it over to the tables they'd set up in their living room. Two six foot tables for game night, and Finn sighed happily as he put the popcorn next to a bowl of pretzels that he'd poured peanut butter M&Ms into a few minutes ago.

"Do you think we made the right decision in assigning food tonight?" Edith came to his side and looked at the few bowls of snacks, one hand resting protectively on her baby belly. Finn loved her endlessly in that moment, because she was soft and maternal and oh-so-beautiful.

"I think Alex and Nicki are more than capable of bringing drinks for ten people," Finn said.

"But we gave the main dish to Dawson and Caroline," she said.

"And they're both adults who've managed to keep themselves alive for three decades," Finn told her, pressing a kiss to her cheekbone. "It's going to be fine."

Link and Misty were bringing desserts, and Ollie and Aurora had been assigned side dishes to go with whatever main dishes Dawson and Caroline brought. Finn had no idea if they'd communicated with each other or not, and he didn't really care. No one would starve tonight, he knew that.

If anything, Edith would make sure of that. Before she could worry over it further, the front door opened and her brother walked in. "We're here," he said needlessly, holding the door for his wife, who carried a couple of cases of soda pop. Alex had some in his arms as well, and Finn went to relieve them of their burden.

The door didn't close, because Link and Misty had arrived too, and they'd apparently carpooled with Rory and Ollie. The island counter continued to fill with food, and Edith laughed at something Nicki said as she arranged the items where she wanted them.

Finn could count on cowboys to show up somewhere on time, so he wasn't surprised to find Dawson knocking on the door the moment the clock struck six-thirty, their agreed-upon time for dinner. He'd previously been part of a twosome with his brother, so having a pretty woman enter the farmhouse behind him was something new for all of them there.

Finn had met Caroline before, briefly, at Link's birthday party last month, but he hadn't spent much time of consequence with her. She was personable and bright, and she eased right into the group of ten as if she'd been there for years.

After several minutes of socializing and catching up, Edith clapped her hands and said,

"Let's eat, because we have a murder mystery to solve tonight, and just because it's Friday doesn't mean you cowboys are gonna last all night." She grinned around at everyone, and since she was a night owl, she loved to tease about how early Finn and his friends went to bed.

The food started going around, and Finn settled into dinner beside his wife. They'd hosted several get-togethers over the last year since they'd been married, but tonight's was a bit different.

One, Mitch Glover wasn't here, and Finn took a moment to type a note into his phone to text Mitch in the next few days. Two, they'd started hanging out with Oliver and Aurora Walker more and more since Edith had found out she was pregnant.

Ollie and Rory had three kids, and Finn found he wanted to just sit in their house and watch how they did things. Edith was due in another week, which iwas why they'd chosen to have their game night dinner party tonight, and

Finn wasn't sure how he could be trusted to keep a tiny, helpless infant alive.

He told himself that they had a bed for the little boy joining their family. Thanks to a huge baby shower at his family ranch a couple of weeks ago, they had diapers, and clothes, and bottles. If there was something physical he and Edith could prep, they'd done it.

What he couldn't prepare himself for was how to literally be responsible for raising a child. Edith had been reading a book here and there, but she didn't seem nearly as concerned about it as Finn. She'd assured him and reassured him that as soon as their baby was born, he'd know exactly how to hold the little boy, and everything else, they could learn.

Dinner finished up, and Finn got up to make a pot of coffee while Edith lingered with their friends. Alex joined him, and Finn tossed a smile in his brother-in-law's direction. "Nicki wants to know if you have hot chocolate powder."

"In the cupboard by the stove there." Finn

nodded to it and opened the fridge to get out cream. "She liked that, huh?"

"She sure did," Alex said with a chuckle. "Now she's mixing and matching flavors all over the place." He didn't sound overly enthused about that, and Finn couldn't help grinning at the grumpy undertone in Alex's voice.

He worked his ranch hard, and he never said more than what needed to be said. Ever. He'd liked Nicki for months before he asked her out, and their romance had been very fast and very hot since that very first date. She was quite a bit older than Alex, and Finn had expected them to start a family as quickly as he and Edith had, but no announcements had been made yet.

Finn eyed Alex as the scent of coffee dripped into the house, but he seemed just fine. Nicki chatted with Caroline and Rory, a brightness about her she'd always possessed. Finn really liked her, and she'd brought out a lot of Alex's sunnier qualities too.

Others started getting up and bringing over their plates, as well as the main dishes. The snacks and desserts remained on the table, and Finn passed out coffee mugs while someone took the cream and sugar over to the table.

"Murder mystery," Nicki sang as she found the bulging box on the credenza where Edith had set it earlier. "Hurry up, you guys. We can't open it until we're all ready." She gripped the box like it contained a live hedgehog and it vibrated in its attempt to escape. Or maybe that was just her extra energy and excitement for the murder mystery.

Finn had never actually played one before, and he was unconvinced the ten of them would be able to complete the game in a single evening. In less than two hours.

He stifled a yawn as the coffee finished and he took the pot off the burner. He went around and filled mugs as others returned to their seats. Edith put a stack of clear plastic cups on the table, the way she liked to dole out snacks, and then she sat in her seat with a groan.

Finn watched her for a moment, and when she met his eye, he reached for her hand. "Okay?"

She nodded, her smile flashing back to her face. It only stayed for a moment, then it disappeared completely.

"Edith?"

"I'm okay." She pressed one hand to her belly, which also caused a flash of alarm to reverberate through Finn.

Then Link laughed, breaking into the bubble he'd put around himself and Edith. She relaxed at his side, and Nicki held up both hands. "Okay, okay," she said. "Let's get this murder mystery started."

She waited while they quieted down, though Link and Dawson continued to chuckle about something. Finn sometimes wished he'd found a ranch on the south side of town, where Link and Dawson worked. But if that had happened, Finn wouldn't be adjacent to his daddy's land, and he would've had to drive his own cattle out onto the range, without the help of his father's two dozen cowboys. Without the help of his mother's cooking.

Nicki read the instructions and started dealing out characters for each person. Finn picked up his character case study and flipped open the folder. "I have to be the balding guy?" His voice got lost among the others poking fun at their characters or showing them to the people next to them.

He looked over to see who Edith had gotten and found her staring open-mouthed at her portfolio. "Who'd you get?" he asked.

She blinked and tilted the folder toward him. "How could an old lady be the murderer? There's no way I could've done it."

The picture fake-clipped to the top of the folder showed a woman of at least sixty-five, her white bob, glasses, and straight-faced mug shot so unlike Edith. And a murderer.

"You never know," he said, showing her his photo. "This guy's not even thirty and he's lost almost all his hair."

She glanced at his, her giggle cutting off after only a second or two in favor of a gasp. Finn looked at her and found her dropping her folder so she could put both hands on her belly this time.

And not the top of it. The bottom, as it she

needed to hold their baby up and inside her. "Ohhh," she groaned.

Around them, Nicki kept reading directions and handing out different items to people. The board would come together in pieces, but Finn's heartbeat drowned out everything. And he instinctively knew he would not be playing his first murder mystery tonight.

"Finn," Edith moaned next, and he found her looking down at the ground. "My water just broke."

His vision fuzzed. The whole world came to a complete stop, despite the activity around them.

Edith looked at him, her eyes wide, and that brought Finn back to reality. He jumped to his feet and said, "We have to get to the hospital."

That got everyone to stop talking as effectively as Nicki had earlier by saying she was going to open the box. His thoughts raced around his neural pathways, and he couldn't find the right thing to say into the resulting silence.

It took forty minutes to get to the hospital. Edith's water had broken already. Did they have time to get there? Could she get outside to the truck? What about their game night?

Edith groaned, and that seemed to open a dam of activity. Chairs scraped against the floor as Nicki and Rory both jumped to their feet and swarmed toward Edith. Alex said something, and before Finn knew it, someone had shoved his car keys into one hand and their packed-and-ready baby bag into his other.

"You know the way to the hospital," Oliver said. "Edith's a few steps ahead of you. We'll get everything cleaned up here."

Finn walked out his front door, still so unsure of anything that had happened in the past sixty seconds. Alex and Nicki flanked Edith as she took laborious step after laborious step, and Finn tossed the bag in the back seat and got behind the wheel while they helped Edith into the passenger seat.

When the door slammed, sealing just the two of them in the cab, he looked at her. Everything became clear in that moment, though his beautiful wife had gone pale and sweaty.

"We're having a baby," he said.

"If it happens in this truck, I'll never forgive you," she quipped right back.

Glad he'd found his wits again, Finn laughed as he started the truck and got them on their way. Edith groaned over the bumps in the dirt road on the way to the highway, where her next contraction hit.

Finn drove like he'd never driven before, his level of anxiety worse than it had been when he'd worked in Army Intelligence. Finally, he pulled up to the labor and delivery emergency entrance and hurried around the truck to help Edith down.

He helped her inside, where a nurse met them with a wheelchair. She took all the information she needed, and Finn once again felt his world start to spiral.

He needed to call his parents. Then Edith's. Had he even brought his phone? Or his wallet?

Everything seemed to be moving so fast—

until they got into the hospital room. Edith changed into a gown with the help of two nurses while Finn, feeling helpless and insignificant, stayed out of the way.

He got a text from Dawson that said, *Good luck, brother. We all want pictures when he's born, with all the stats.*

He got a similar message from Alex, and Lincoln, and Oliver. His heart swelled with love for his friends, and he quickly tapped out messages to all of them, as well as his parents and Edith's family text string.

Then everyone left, and only the two of them remained. He took a seat next to her and took her hand in his. "We're having a baby," he whispered, lifting her wrist to his lips. "And we have the best friends and family in the world."

Edith smiled softly at him, her face only relaxed for a moment. Then another contraction came over her, and she cried out as she leaned forward over her belly. Finn wanted nothing more than to take this pain from her, ease this burden. It seemed to go on and on, and without any doctors or nurses in the room, Finn started to panic a little.

Then, just as the contraction started to fade, a man entered the room. Relief punched through Finn's whole body, making it easier to breathe. "Doctor Rougeman," he said, jumping to his feet. "She's contracting a lot."

"That's great news," the doctor boomed as he plucked a pair of rubber gloves from a box. "Because that's how babies are born, and it's time for this little guy to meet his momma and daddy."

Chapter Twenty-Nine

Caroline smiled down at her phone as Belle drove them all to church. "Oh, he's the sweetest baby in the whole world," she murmured to herself. She still marveled that Dawson's friends had accepted her into their group so readily. But they had, as this text had come from Finn Ackerman himself.

He hadn't only texted it to Dawson and expected him to forward it along. No, she'd become part of their group simply because she was with Dawson.

And as she gazed at the beautiful fair baby

boy on the screen, Caroline's heart squeezed at her.

She wanted children. She'd always known she wanted to be a mother someday, but she'd spent a great deal of time thanking God that she had not had any children with Joe. She'd have been tied to him forever that way, and God had been merciful by not giving her children in her first marriage.

"They named him Theodore Baxter Ackerman," she said, reading aloud from the text. "I guess Baxter is Edith's maiden name." She looked up and away from the precious infant. "They were fun. I hope we get to hang out with them again."

Belle said nothing, and Caroline looked over to her to find her fingers gripping the wheel tightly. She quickly put her phone in her purse. "Sorry," she said, as Belle had been able to get pregnant with Judy fairly quickly into her marriage, but she'd never been able to have a second child.

She'd just started to explore possible reasons why when she'd discovered her husband's infidelity.

The rest of the ride to the little white church building with the big stained glass window happened accompanied by tension and silence. It wasn't until Caroline opened her door that the mood broke, and all the difficult things that had accumulated in the car simply got whisked away by the wind.

Judy didn't seem to notice the way Caroline's lungs clenched around the oxygen, and she skipped ahead of her and toward the steps of the church.

"I'm sorry," Caroline said again as she joined Belle at the front of the car.

"It's not your fault," Belle said with a sigh. "I should be happy for people who get to have babies."

"You have a beautiful daughter," Caroline said, smiling ahead to Judy. She didn't say it was more than she had, because they both knew it to be true.

"Howdy, ladies," a cowboy drawled, and everything inside Caroline lit up. She turned toward her handsome boyfriend, hoping Dawson's appearance wouldn't further upset Belle.

"Hey," she said as she moved to the right toward him. He took her easily under one arm, quickly swiping his lips along her cheek. She did the same to him, feeling the weight of his hand on her hip and the zing of pleasure from his touch. "Did you get the picture of Theodore?"

"Sure did."

"Isn't he the cutest?" She deliberately held back while Belle went ahead, collected Judy from where she'd crouched to look at something, and started up the stairs. Only then did Caroline link her arm through Dawson's and take the first step to follow her sister.

"Do you want children, Dawson?"

"Yes, ma'am," he said. "I think that would be real nice."

"You're good with kids," she said.

"So are you."

They started up the steps too. "For a while there, I didn't think I had the patience for children," she said. "But I've learned a lot, and I've really enjoyed having Judy living with me."

Dawson simply switched his hand to her lower back as she preceded him into the church, and he leaned in close to ask, "Can I sit with you and Belle today?"

Caroline's heartbeat bumped erratically through her veins. "I think maybe just you and I should sit together."

"Is Belle okay?"

"She's...." Caroline searched for the right word. "Grieving."

Dawson's jaw jumped, but Caroline had chosen the right word. It was hard to believe she had one life, only to find out she didn't. Had never had what she thought she'd had.

"Let's just sit over here." She led the way into the chapel and to one of the shorter pews on the left. Dawson filed in dutifully behind her, and she sat down. He didn't get too close, so Caroline closed the distance between them, really snuggling into his chest as he lifted his arm and put it around her.

"I love your hair clipped back like that," he

whispered. "I love your shoes and how white they are, and I *adore* that we get to sit together at church today."

She smiled at the charge in his voice, and she took his hand in both of hers. "It's the first time."

"Is it significant for you?" he asked.

"A little," she admitted.

"Me too." He shifted slightly, but services hadn't started yet, so she didn't expect him to stand quite yet. "I looked into the river boat cruise like you asked. They've got one at the end of June that would work real nice with my schedule on the ranch."

"No branding or breeding in June?"

He chuckled huskily in her ear. "A lot of agriculture, which means my brothers can spare me for a few days."

"It'll be humid and hot in June."

"Sure will, but I don't think we're ready to go right now," he said. "And I can't be gone too much in the fall. There's so much with bringing the cattle back, market day, the harvest...."

"So in a couple of months," she said.

"Two and a half," he said. "You'll have had your birthday by then, and you'll know if you can stand me for a road trip and then a boat trip."

"A road-boat trip," she murmured as the band started to play. They couldn't talk much more about this right now, so Caroline put it in her pocket for later. She did want to go on a road trip with Dawson, and six months into their relationship sounded about like the perfect time to do it.

After the rousing opening number, Pastor Glover stood up and headed for her place behind the microphone. Caroline liked the woman's sermons, and she liked her brother's too. She always felt safe and like she was with friends when she attended church, and she settled into a restful state in Dawson's arms as the pastor started to speak.

"When I was a child, my father was training for a marathon. He'd get up before work and run. He'd run after work sometimes. When he got faster, he did something I didn't understand as a little girl." She smiled out into the crowd, and she had such a way with story-telling. Caroline loved listening to her, and she tried to piece together where Pastor Glover was going in the story before she got there.

"He put books in a backpack and started to run with the backpack. Every week, he'd add another book. He let my brother and I pick them, and I tried to pick the thickest, heaviest one, thinking it would be too hard for him to carry."

Pastor Glover gave a light laugh. "Of course, he could run with the books, and the extra weight helped him get stronger. When the day of the race came, and he wasn't wearing the backpack of books, he practically *flew*. It was incredible to watch, almost like he'd grown wings on his feet and wasn't burdened by any-thing anymore."

Caroline suddenly knew where the pastor was headed.

"When we carry unnecessary burdens, we may start to feel like we're strong enough to walk alone. That we don't need the help of the Lord. That we don't need Him in our lives at all. But my friends and neighbors, when we discard our burdens at the feet of the Lord, He makes it so we can fly. He makes it so the things troubling us—whether those be sins or mental turmoil, or physical ailments—are like shedding that backpack. You see, when we rely on God, we're stronger than when we carry the backpack of books. Because we're lighter, we can fly."

Caroline very much liked this idea of flying, of not carrying the weights life had placed upon her.

"It sounds so easy to lay your burdens at the feet of God," Pastor Glover said next. "But it's not as easy as it sounds. None of us likes to feel like we can't handle the things in our lives, and it takes true humility to shed who you were before and become someone new through the blood of Jesus Christ."

Caroline had done a lot of changing in her life, this proverbial "shedding" the pastor was talking about. But as she sat there, she realized she'd given nothing to God. She'd carried it all herself. She'd *wanted* to carry it all herself.

Doing so had made her stronger, but now Caroline wondered if she could fly—if she could figure out how to set down the burdens of her old self and become someone new.

The pastor continued to talk about the ways God had given them to find their way to Him, including the scriptures, the rest of the Sabbath Day, sermons like this, prayer, and more.

Caroline found herself sinking into a prayer, her eyes falling closed and everything. *Lord*, she thought. *I want to be the person You'd like me to be. I want to trust You explicitly and lay down the things I'm carrying that I don't need in my backpack. Will You...Will You help me know what those things are and how to set them down?*

She didn't get an immediate answer, and her eyes fluttered open again as Dawson lowered his head and whispered, "You okay, sweetheart?"

Caroline drew in a breath that made her emotions shake. She nodded, though, because she was okay, and she had confidence that while God hadn't answered her prayer right this moment, He would.

She turned her head toward Dawson and whispered, "Will you come to lunch at the house today?"

"Today? Like, in an hour?"

"Yes."

"With you, Belle, and Judy?"

"Yes," she whispered.

He hesitated for a moment before he straightened and looked back toward the front. He hadn't answered, and Caroline sure didn't like the buzz of anxiety in her chest. She could admit that she hadn't brought Dawson around the house much, but they'd been dating for a few months now, and Belle would have to figure out how to have him around.

Because Caroline wanted him around.

The sermon ended, and Caroline stood to sing the closing hymn. Dawson did the same, and once the meeting had ended, he turned right into her. "I'll come to lunch."

Caroline beamed at him, wishing she wouldn't feel guilty if she kissed him right there in the chapel. "Great." She leaned into his chest. "Now, go on. My thoughts are so big, and I need to get outside so they can get out of my head."

"Big thoughts, huh?" He gave her a grin before turning to step into the aisle. "I want to hear about those."

Caroline would like to tell him—once she sorted through everything herself.

Chapter Thirty

Dawson hadn't picked up Caroline, so he drove the streets from the church to her house, arriving only a few seconds after her sister pulled into the driveway. Judy burst from the backseat, and she launched into a skip as she headed for the backyard.

He eased up to the curb and watched as Caroline and Belle both rose from the car. Caroline looked toward him, her smile warm and wide and welcoming. Belle called something after her daughter, and she only threw a cursory glance toward Dawson.

"Lord," he said without moving his lips.

"Help me through this afternoon." He wasn't sure why those words came from him, but they did. Caroline had not invited him to her house for lunch after church before, and Dawson felt like he was becoming a new person and they would be a different couple as he dropped from the truck.

"Hey," she said. "Belle and I were trying to decide what to make for lunch." She reached him as he stepped up onto the sidewalk. "And we need your vote."

He so didn't want to vote, especially if it was to break a tie between Caroline and her sister. But he simply said, "All right," as he took her hand in his.

"We've got some leftover King Ranch casserole," she said, and Dawson knew immediately that wasn't her idea. Caroline liked leftovers well enough, but she liked something special on Sunday. Then she'd eat that throughout the week if she had to. "Or I got out some hamburgers this afternoon, and we can grill those up."

Dawson took a few steps as they went up

the driveway, giving himself a moment though he knew exactly what to vote for. Even if he hated hamburgers with a passion, he'd vote for them. "I think hamburgers," he said. "It's a nice day to be out on the deck grilling."

Caroline grinned up at him. "It is, right?"

"I can help put together all the toppings," he said. "Slice tomatoes, fry eggs, that kind of thing."

"Eggs?" Caroline led him to the side door that went into the kitchen, instead of going down the sidewalk to the front door. "You put eggs on your hamburgers?"

"Oh, yeah," he said. "My granddad did it, and I turned up my nose at it for a long time." He smiled and even laughed a little. "I can still remember the first time I let him put an egg on my burger." He smacked his lips. "One of the best things I've ever eaten."

"Well, then," Caroline said. "I'll let you fry the eggs." She opened the door and walked inside just as something started beeping. It took Dawson a moment to place the sound, and then he put the pieces together.

Belle had just opened the microwave, after it had beeped at her that it had finished reheating something. Caroline dropped his hand and said, "You're going with the casserole," in a dark, dangerous voice.

"I'm hungry right now," Belle said. "I don't want to cook." She barely looked at either Caroline or Dawson before she moved over to the sliding glass door that led out onto the back deck. She opened it and stepped out, obviously done talking.

Tension rode in the air, and Dawson took a look at Caroline. She wore a frown on her face, and it went way deeper than just the lines between her eyes. He wanted to put his arm around her and soothe her, but he wasn't sure she'd appreciate that.

"We could just go out," he suggested.

Caroline's attention flew to him. "What?"

"They don't want to eat," he said as gently as he could. "She doesn't want me here. Why go through the chore of cooking and cleaning up when we can just go out? Enjoy each other's company this afternoon."

Caroline softened right in front of him, and Dawson eased her into his arms. It took her a moment to melt into him, but when she did, he closed his eyes and took a deep breath of her hair. "After lunch, we can take a drive, get a drink, find a place to watch the wind."

"Watch the wind?" She lifted her head, her gorgeous smile aimed in his direction.

"It paints a pretty picture sometimes," he said. "I like a slow Sabbath Day afternoon."

"You'll have to get back and do your evening chores."

"Mm, yep," he said.

"Maybe I could come meet the chickens, finally."

Dawson leaned down and touched his lips to hers. "You've met them."

"Not your favorite ones," she murmured back, kissing him back a moment later.

True, his hens had been scattered the day Caroline had tried to meet them, as Dawson let them roam freely. "How does Marshland sound?"

"Sounds like a lot for a Sunday lunch."

"Does it? They have a great brunch buffet on the weekends."

"Yes, and it's expensive." She stepped out of his arms, and Dawson suddenly got what she meant by "a lot."

"Good thing I'm rich then," he said evenly.

Caroline had started to unpin her hair, and she froze, only her eyes moving over to him. "You are?"

He burst out laughing as he shook his head. "No, but that got you to stop, didn't it?"

Caroline gave him a dry look and continued removing the barrettes from her hair. "Marshland is too much." She walked away from him. "I'm going to go change."

"So I have to go in my church shirt and tie, but you don't?"

She simply threw a grin over her shoulder and kept going, leaving Dawson standing in her kitchen alone. He moved over to the glass doors that showed the outside, and he found Belle sitting on the top step, looking out into the yard. He couldn't see Judy anywhere, and his pulse sped as anxiety bled through him.

He didn't want to cause tension between Caroline and her sister. He didn't want them talking about him later, which he knew Caroline would do. She had a strong mind of her own, which he normally enjoyed just fine, and she wouldn't let Belle walk all over her.

Feeling a little outside of himself, Dawson slid open the door and stepped outside. Belle twisted to look over her shoulder, and she'd clearly been expecting Caroline. Surprise shot across her face, and she got to her feet, something he felt certain she wouldn't have done if her sister had come out to check on her.

"Hey." Belle set down her empty container and hugged herself.

Dawson slowed and stopped a good distance from her. "Hey, I just wanted to let you know that we're gonna go out for lunch."

"Oh." Belle looked past him, her gaze coming straight back. "Okay."

"You won't have to hide out here." He gave her a smile. "I'm sorry I make it uncomfortable for you."

"You...don't."

Dawson gave her the kindest smile he could. "I know I do, and it's okay. I know me and Caroline just aren't something good for you right now." He stuck his hands in his pockets, his voice about to give out on him. He wasn't even sure why he'd come out here. He didn't know Belle; he only knew what Caroline had told him.

He cleared his throat. "I just wanted you to know we'll be going in a couple of minutes." He took one step forward and then rocked back again. "And I just want you to know I sure do like your sister." He ducked his head, his feelings too heavy for his neck to stay straight. He nodded a couple more times, his eyes glued to the wooden decking. "All right. That's all."

Dawson turned and did his best not to flee as fast as possible. Back in the air conditioning, he took a deep breath and blew it out as he continued through the house to the living room. Thankfully, Belle didn't follow him inside, and Caroline came down the hall only a minute later.

"Ready?" she asked brightly.

He got to his feet. "Yep. Ready."

"Let me just tell Belle we're going," she said, turning toward the back door.

"I told her," Dawson said.

Caroline spun back to him. "You did? What did you say?"

"I told her we were going out to lunch." He silently begged her not to go talk to Belle right now. She didn't need the mental load, and he just wanted to go.

Her gaze wouldn't leave his face, and Dawson once again ducked his head. "She said it was okay."

Caroline took a breath, and he looked up as she came toward him. She'd arranged her face into one of determination. "Okay," she said. "Then let's go." She unlocked the front door and went out first, leaving Dawson to follow her.

And follow her, he did—with a tiny smile on his face. He had a feeling he'd follow her anywhere, and he could only hope and pray that he could take some of her burdens every now and then, just as he had by telling Belle they were going to lunch.

Once they'd gotten in the truck, and Dawson had pulled away from the house, Caroline tapped on her phone and said, "I think I found the perfect dress for Link and Misty's wedding."

"That's great," he said. "Do I get to see it?"

"It's not my wedding dress," she said, turning her phone toward him. "So of course you can see it."

Dawson did his best to look at the dress while driving, and he managed to get the gist of it. "Pretty," he said. "You're always stunning in flowers."

Caroline smiled and looked at her phone. "I do like floral patterns."

Dawson liked them on her, that was for certain. She sighed and tucked her phone away, but she didn't say anything. Dawson let the silence permeate the space between them, because sometimes it said more than words could. Plus, he liked that they could ride along in silence and not have it choke them.

He thought of another meal they'd shared in near-silence, and it hadn't been nearly this relaxed. This calm. This peaceful. Their breakfast in the diner from months and months ago now made him smile, and it also painted a picture for how far they'd come in their relationship.

Dawson reached over and took her hand in his, once again maintaining the silence. Caroline squeezed his fingers, and Dawson squeezed back, hoping to let her know that he was okay with where they were.

After all, it wasn't even May yet, and they still had a long way to go to get through a full year—and a road trip.

Dawson watched Caroline walk toward him as he tightened the buckle on his saddle. April came from the other way, leading her saddled and ready horse. "Uncle Dawson, Grandma wants me to go get the food."

He tore his eyes from his girlfriend. "Okay, just throw the reins over the post there."

She did, and then April started toward the house. She saw Caroline too, though, and she detoured toward her. Dawson once again couldn't tear his eyes from the woman who'd crowded into his waking hours, infused herself into his morning running, and followed him into his dreams too.

She smiled at April, said something to her, and listened as Dawson's niece spoke back to her. Dawson liked watching them, as Caroline had a way with kids and teenagers too, whether she could see it in herself or not.

When Caroline looked over to him, he busied himself with the saddle that was already ready.

"Hey, baby." Caroline took a couple last steps to him, running her hand down Architect's nose before switching her attention to him. "You're going to be gone for three days."

He grinned at her, a chuckle coming from his throat as something really warm settled in every nook and cranny of his body. "Are you saying you miss me already?"

Caroline's head bobbled, like she might be saying yes and no at the same time. Dawson laughed, and he moved closer to her. "I miss you like crazy," he whispered. "So kiss me while we're alone out here, because my brother and niece are going to be back any minute."

He snaked his hand up her arm to the back of her head as he guided her mouth to his. He sank into kissing Caroline, as it felt so natural and so good and so right. He sure hoped she felt like this kissing him, and he hated that he'd be gone checking the herd for the next three days.

The warbling of chickens entered his awareness, and Dawson broke the kiss. He stayed close to Caroline, existing inside the comfortable bubble they'd managed to create.

"What's this one's name?" Caroline asked, her voice soft, almost muted.

Dawson turned toward his beloved hens. He found Rusty, his big rooster with them, and they made him so happy. "Well, here we've got

Lulu, Peach, Pearl, and Ruby." He looked back to her. "My favorites, finally."

"With Rusty."

"Seems they're palling around together."

"I can't believe you just let them run around like this."

"They're free range," he said.

"But you don't eat them."

Dawson chuckled, as they'd had this conversation before. "They like it, baby." He pressed another kiss to her forehead. "You'll babysit the owls for me while I'm gone?"

She leaned into him as she wrapped her arms around him. "Yep."

"Okay," he said. "Duke's kids are going to feed my chickens. I suppose I can survive away from this place for a few days."

"You'll be fine."

He wanted to protest that he wouldn't be, that he craved routine and disrupting it bothered him more than he'd told her, but he stuffed the words back down his throat.

"I've got the food," April thankfully called, and Dawson stepped away from

Caroline. Brandon brought his horse around from the side of the stable too, and the three of them would stay together for the next few days while they journeyed out into the hills to check on their cattle and dogs.

"Load us up, missy," Dawson said. He whistled for Ruffin, and the dog perked up from where he lay in the shade. "Let's go, buddy."

Brandon swung into the saddle, and April collected her reins after putting the food in Dawson's saddlebags. He'd made himself several sticky notes for what needed to be done when he returned, and he'd done all of the required items before this trip.

"All right," he said. "We're headed out." He turned back to his horse only to find Caroline pulling her hand back from his saddlebags. His eyebrows went up, his curiosity off the charts. "What's goin' on here?"

"Nothing," she said airily.

"Did you put something in or take something out?" He peered at her hands, but she'd folded her arms. "I need all the stuff I put in there."

"I didn't take anything." She watched him with that familiar fire in her eyes.

Dawson grinned at her, because those eyes mesmerized him more than anything. "Caroline—"

"Just look when you get there," she said. "Okay? Please? I don't want you to see it right now."

"All right," he drawled. "Is this something I should try to open when I'm alone?"

"Not necessarily."

"My niece is fourteen," he teased. "You sure?"

Caroline huffed out her breath and then finally smiled. "Maybe the note."

"Oh, there's a note?"

"Are you going to flirt all day?" April asked from atop her horse as she shuffled it closer. "Or are we going?"

He looked up at her, catching her impish grin before she flattened it. "We're going," Dawson growled. He took a quick step to Caroline and swept his arm around her as he kissed her cheek. "I'll call you later, okay?"

"Have fun," she said. She raised her hand to April. "You keep him in line, okay?"

April grinned at her. "Yes, ma'am."

Dawson worked hard not to roll his eyes as he swung into his saddle. "All right," he said. "Lead us out, you."

April threw him a grin and swung her mount around to do just that. Dawson couldn't wait to get out into the wilderness and bask in the Texas sunshine. He couldn't wait to let the wide sky above Three Rivers cleanse his thoughts and remind him of who he was.

And he absolutely couldn't wait to see what Caroline had snuck into his saddlebag.

Chapter Thirty-One

Caroline woke slowly on the morning of her birthday, Dawson's last text from last night running through her mind.

You're my favorite person, and I can't wait to celebrate your birthday with you.

She could hear him saying those words in his deep, cowboy rumble, and his voice always made her warm from the inside out. She wasn't sure she'd ever been anyone's favorite person, and it sure felt nice that she could be that for a man like Dawson.

The sun had started to rise, as summer was getting nearer and nearer, and she finally opened her eyes to check the time. Her alarm hadn't gone off yet, so it couldn't quite be seven a.m., and since Dawson couldn't really take a whole day off from his ranch duties, Caroline wouldn't see him until lunchtime.

She had plans to sleep late—seemed like that wasn't quite working out, though—and spend the morning out in the cool shade of her garden, then shower, and get ready to take Dawson lunch in his office.

They'd spend the afternoon together, and then Dawson had plans for dinner too. He hadn't told her much of what he'd put together for them, and that was just fine with Caroline. She liked a good surprise, and as she sat up and stretched her arms above her head, she exhaled out the past three decades of her life.

"Dear Lord," she prayed. "Thank You for the first thirty years of my life. Thank You for helping me become this woman that I am, and help me to know how to set down the things that need to be put aside so I can continue to become who You want me to be."

She paused, something not quite right with

what she'd said. "Who You *need* me to become."

She usually went from her bed to the shower, but this morning, she padded down the hall to the kitchen in her pajamas.

"Happy birthday, Aunt Caroline!" Judy yelled, as she was already standing on the chair at the dining table.

Caroline grinned and grinned at her. "Thank you, sweetie." She stroked her hand down Judy's hair, which hadn't been brushed for school yet. "Where's your momma?"

"She went outside," Judy said. "We got you this brownie." She had a German chocolate brownie in front of her, and Caroline knew where that had come from. Heidi Ackerman's bakery.

"She's been up early," Caroline said.

"Okay, thanks!" Belle came in the back door as she called to whoever she'd been talking to outside. She turned to face the kitchen, and she strode forward before coming to a complete stop when she saw Caroline. "You're up."

"Yep."

Belle didn't seem happy about that, and she carried a brown box very similar to what they'd get a dozen doughnuts in. "What's that?" Caroline asked.

Belle looked at the box, her eyes coming back to Caroline's wider than before. She hesitated for a couple of seconds, and then she rolled her whole head with her eyes. "Fine. It's not like you wouldn't have found out. I was just hoping—*we* were just hoping to surprise you."

"I'm surprised," Caroline said. "You've been to the bakery already this morning."

Her sister came over to the table and put the box down. Something that smelled salty and savory lifted from it. "I didn't go to the bakery."

Caroline's surprise grew, but she wasn't sure she should open the box. "Well, someone did. I would've sniffed this out last night when I was looking for something sweet before bed." She offered her sister a smile, hoping Belle's displeasure with Caroline's earlier rising time would disappear.

Belle started to lift the top of the box. "Judy, honey, get Auntie a fork."

Judy jumped down to do that. "Okay, Mama."

Caroline had many questions, but she simply watched as the lid came off the box. Right in front of her, a gourmet breakfast appeared. Clearly homemade, with perfectly cooked over-easy eggs, toast with crunchy Biscoff spread, several strips of bacon, and the crispiest, brownest, most perfect hash browns in the world.

This breakfast had Dawson written all over it. Caroline's insides felt like melting gelatin—warm and ooey and soft and oh-so-comfortable.

"He brought the brownie too," Belle said as she set aside the box top and then sat down. Judy arrived with a fork and Caroline had no choice but to take it.

"Happy birthday, Auntie," Judy chirped.

"Thank you, sweetie," Caroline murmured. She looked over to Belle. It had been a couple of weeks since Caroline had brought Dawson home after church. That hadn't gone over well with Belle, and she and Dawson had ended up going out for lunch.

"He coordinated this with you?"

Belle nodded, her expression turning to one of something softer. More appreciative. "Yes, he did."

"And you—?"

"He's a very sweet man," Belle said. "Are we going to talk about this to death?"

Caroline looked at the breakfast in front of her. "No," she said. "We're not. I'm going to eat, and then I'm going to go check on my peas and carrots."

And she did exactly that, thoughts of Dawson and how "very sweet" he was foaming through her in every minute.

By the time she knocked on his barn-office door, he'd texted her several times—something he didn't normally do—and a bouquet of flowers and one of balloons had shown up at the house.

The lunch she carried felt extremely inadequate, and Caroline actually questioned whether Dawson would be able to do this every year for every birthday. Or for every anniversary. Or if she'd influenced him to do all these things.

"Of course you did," she muttered, not sure if she was happy about that or not.

Then the door swung inward, and Dawson stood there. "Hey, you." He grinned at her and took the bag of food she'd brought. "C'mon in. I brought in another chair for you."

"How thoughtful," she said as she stepped up and into his small office. She'd been here a few times in the past, but not for a while. Dawson was pretty protective of his space, and Caroline had tried to be respectful of that.

His whiteboard with his sticky notes hung from the wall on her right, and she couldn't stop herself from looking at it. She found blue, yellow, green, tan, white, and pink notes there, and he'd told her he used specific colors for specific things.

His writing was cramped and small, and

she didn't linger there, trying to read any of his reminders.

"You brought the pizza pasta," he said, pulling things from the bag. "This is great." He smiled at her, and Caroline quickly closed the door behind her, as Dawson didn't like to lose his air conditioning.

"Dawson," she said, really stretching out his name.

He looked up, clearly sensing something. "What's wrong?"

Caroline realized then that her eyes had filled with tears. "It's just—there's no way you'll ever be able to do this again next year, and I'm just freaking out a little that you've gone way overboard for my birthday, and we haven't even done the afternoon or evening stuff yet."

She sniffled, pure embarrassment running through her. Dawson straightened and simply looked at her. She shook her head. "This is so silly, I know. I told you birthdays and stuff were a big deal to me, and now I'm upset that you've made it a big deal?"

"Did I?" he asked. "It was the texts in the morning, right? I never do that."

She wiped her eyes, and her brain finally recognized the teasing quality of his voice.

"Or it was that breakfast. I knew it would be cold by the time it got to you, but God told me it would be okay. I'll have a word with Him about it."

Caroline burst out laughing, glad when Dawson allowed a smile to come to his face too. He took her into a hug, and Caroline wanted to stand in his arms forever and ever. Within the strength of his chest, he could protect her from the negative things in the world. With him so close, she didn't have to worry about what plagued her.

"Happy birthday, darlin'," he drawled, his mouth right at her ear. "I didn't think I'd gone over-the-top, but if you think I have, I apologize. I just want you to feel important today, because you're really important to me."

You're really important to me.

Caroline didn't think better words could be

spoken, and her eyes burned with unshed tears again. She clung to him until she felt certain she wouldn't break down into sobs when she stepped back. "You hungry?" She couldn't quite look at him, and he gave her the time she wanted to put herself back together.

"Yes, ma'am," he murmured.

They settled down to eat, and Caroline's heartbeat didn't quite calm back into its normal rhythm. Dawson finished before her, and finally, when she only had a couple of bites left, he said, "Talk to me, sweetheart."

"I guess I...what are we doing this afternoon?"

He ducked his head, which didn't exactly comfort Caroline. "You said you wanted to see *The Bridge on the River Kwai*, and it's playing this afternoon at the Maven. I got us tickets to that."

"Mm."

"The deluxe package," he said. "With the candy and the soda pop and the popcorn, so I should've warned you before you started eating lunch."

Caroline had eaten a lot, but she'd always have room for movie theater popcorn. "And tonight?"

"Dinner," he said. "Miggliano's. If I'd have known you'd bring Italian for lunch, I'd have chosen somewhere else for dinner." He finally looked up at her. "Too much?"

Caroline wasn't sure. She honestly wasn't sure why her thoughts and feelings zipped left and right inside her. "What if I said I wanted to cancel it all, and we could, I don't know, go back to your cabin and just lie on the couch together, talking? Could we do that?"

Dawson didn't answer right away, which somehow made her appreciate him more. "We could," he said. "If that's what you want." He took both of her hands in his. "But I'm confused. You wanted a big deal. I sent breakfast and flowers. That's normal boyfriend stuff, isn't it? And dinner and a movie? It's nothing special."

"I don't know," she said.

"It feels kind of boring to me," he said. "But

Miggliano's is a nice place. Very romantic. But a cold breakfast and some flowers? Snooze fest."

"And the brownie," she said. "And the balloons. And I'm in your office, where you never let me come." She raised her eyebrows at him, but Dawson simply gazed evenly back at her.

"My mother wanted a couple loaves of bread from the bakery," he said. "Your brownie was an afterthought. The balloons came with the flowers. And I needed to work, thus, I needed you to come to me for lunch. That's even *more* unromantic."

"Dawson."

"Caroline."

She looked at him, and she wasn't sure why she'd started to dig this hole. *Lord*, she thought, and God performed a miracle for her. He opened her mind and heart, and Dawson Rhinehart waltzed right into both.

"I love that you brought breakfast," she said. "Even if it was a little on the cold side." She squeezed his hands. "I love that you talked to my sister about my birthday and that you coordinated things with her this morning, and I *adore* the idea of dinner and a movie."

She leaned toward him, adding to their game. "I adore you, Dawson."

"Good," he whispered as she neared, obviously about to kiss him. "Because I adore you too."

He kissed her and kissed her, and when he finally pulled away, Caroline couldn't catch her breath. "So, it's a yes to dinner and a movie, or you want to lie on my couch and talk this afternoon?"

Caroline giggled and buried her face in his chest. "I want to do what you planned for us, baby."

"Okay," he said. "Then we only have a few more minutes for kissing. That movie is almost three hours long, you know."

"Mm, I think it's okay if we miss the first few minutes," she said just before she kissed him again. And she decided in that moment that all the physical tokens—the flowers, the brownie, the breakfast—didn't matter.

Kissing Dawson on her birthday was the best thing he could do for her, because it ironed flat all the jagged edges inside her.

Caroline knew she'd have to do something about those on her own, but for now, kissing Dawson was enough.

Chapter Thirty-Two

Dawson ignored his phone while he finished up the last of his work for the day. If he could just get this last order submitted, he could be done for tonight. Done for the weekend—except his small animal chores every morning and evening. Just done.

But his phone was blowing up, and when it chimed five times right on top of each other, he growled and reached for it. Duke, Zona, April, and Shiloh had all texted, and Dawson's first thought was, "Daddy."

His father had passed away. Or he'd fallen

while trying to do something around the house that Duke, Dawson, and Brandon had all told him to stop doing.

He got to his feet, his heart pounding in his chest and neck and throat. Duke had just texted, so Dawson tapped there. His brother had messaged several times, each one about... Caroline.

Dawson quickly put the pieces together, and his brow furrowed. "She's at the house already?" He checked the time, and she was a whole hour early.

Zona had texted about her early arrival, as had April and Shiloh. It was a little odd, because Caroline didn't miss details like this. And Dawson hurried to leave his barn-office, despite the fact that he hadn't put in the last order for the fertilizer he needed.

By the time he arrived at his brother's, he realized he hadn't gone home to shower. He hadn't changed. He wasn't ready for dinner with his girlfriend and his brother's family.

He got out of the truck frustrated and irritated, and he went right up to the front door and inside, calling, "I'm here."

No one responded to him, and Dawson's boots practically echoed in the empty house. "Hello?" He hadn't texted anyone back, because he'd run out of his office so fast and come straight here. It had to have been maybe five minutes since the flurry of texts had come in.

"Where the devil are they?" Evidence of dinner prep sat on the counter, but Zona didn't stand there at the cutting board. He looked toward the back door, and sure enough, his sister-in-law came inside.

"There you are," Zona said, pure relief in her voice. She quickly brought the door closed behind her. "Caroline's here."

"I gathered as much from the five thousand texts," he said dryly.

"The kids are entertaining her now. April's got her feeding the rabbits, and Duke's got the grill going a little early."

"I don't know why she's early," Dawson said. "I told her six-thirty, and she's always got her details together."

"She said she wanted to meet us." Zona picked up her knife and kept cutting up the zucchini.

"Meet you?"

The door opened again, and Shiloh came inside with April and Caroline. "Momma, it's too hot outside. We're coming in."

"Fine," Zona said, clearly stressed.

"Caroline," Dawson said, and she seemed to see him finally.

"Oh, hey." She beamed at him, but something stormed inside him. She scanned him down to his dirty work boots and back to his face. "You didn't go home and change."

"You're super early," he said, unable to keep the irritation out of his voice. Everyone heard it, and the smile slipped from Caroline's face. She glanced over to April and then Zona.

Dawson didn't want to be here right now. "Can we talk outside?" He turned and headed for the front door without waiting for her to answer. Mercifully, she came with him, and another miracle occurred that Duke and Zona's house faced east, so the western sun blazed in the back while the front porch was bathed in shade.

He sat down on the bench, though he felt like pacing like a caged tiger. Caroline perched beside him, and he wasn't even sure why he was annoyed.

"I got the dress for the wedding," she said.

"Great." He took a breath, held it, and let it all go. "Why did you come so early?"

"I was just pacing at home," she said. "I figured I'd just come up and meet them. I mean, I've met them before, but yeah."

He nodded, but a sting burned through him. "Did it occur to you that I'd maybe like to introduce you around to everyone?"

"I—no."

"No." Of course not. Dawson looked out across Duke's front lawn, past the dirt road that ran in front of it, and into the pretty, growing fields he'd put in himself. "Why did you come so early?" he asked again, because he thought he knew the real answer—and he didn't like it.

"I—I—well, I thought it would be nice to meet them—I mean, I've met them—get to know them by...myself."

And there it was. Dawson's insides felt like someone had injected some substance into his gut that was rapidly turning everything to liquid. So many things entered his mind, but Dawson didn't know if he should say any of them.

Caroline would, he thought, and that got him to look over to the woman he'd been steadily falling for.

"Not everything is about you," he said.

"I know that."

"I wasn't finished with my work for today." He flipped his gross, sweaty shirt. "I didn't have a chance to go home and shower. Zona and Duke aren't ready for us to be here."

Caroline nodded in a tight, controlled way, and that meant Dawson didn't have to say more. "I just thought they might like to get to know me...outside of you."

"And that's what I don't understand," he said, his frustration rising like steam from a boiling pot of water. "I'm okay being me, and I love how you're you. Have I ever asked you to be someone different than who you are right now? This minute?"

She shook her head and swiped at her eyes. *Be gentle.*

The words came into his head, and Dawson took a breath, trying to find the voice that could be gentle. He didn't know how to conjure that, but he'd had plenty of conversations with April that hadn't driven her away.

"Caroline, sweetheart, I'd like to be *me with you*, because I think *we* would be amazing."

She laced her fingers through his. "We are."

"See, I don't think there's a 'we' for you. I'm starting to think you can't be part of *us*. Part of a 'we' at all." He wasn't sure if he was making sense. There were so many small words in his head, making big thoughts and big sentences.

"Which I'm not really sure I understand, and my heart hurts so much at the thought of not having you and not being us. But you seem to have an idea of what you want, and I love that you absolutely know who you are."

He exhaled, because he hadn't planned to have this conversation. There was no way a man could ever plan to have a talk like this. No sticky note could prepare him for it. Caroline didn't jump right in and defend herself or refute anything he'd said, which only made his heart wail even more.

"I guess I've been foolishly hoping you'd make room for me in your life," he said.

"Dawson, baby, I have."

"Room for you to be you, of course," he kept going. "But I guess a version of you... with me. An *us*. A *we*. Something. I don't know, and I'm going to stop talking now." He did just that, and again, Caroline didn't jump to fill the silence with any explanations.

A couple of minutes passed, and Dawson detected the scent of something cooking inside. He groaned as he got to his feet, and pure humiliation filled him. "I'm going to go shower," he said in a near whisper. "I'm sure Ruffin would love it if you'd come sit on the couch with him."

She sniffed and got to her feet, nodded, and went ahead of him down the steps. Dawson didn't know what to do next, but he did need to shower, and he really only needed five more minutes in his barn-office.

So he let Caroline get in her car and pull out of Duke's driveway ahead of him. She turned to go down the road toward the rest of ranch, and he assumed she'd go to his house as he'd suggested. He returned to his office and finished the order that needed placing, and then he approached his cabin.

Brandon's truck wasn't there, and Dawson's brain was so buzzy that he couldn't quite remember where his brother had gone tonight. Inside, he found Dumpling and Ruffin both on the couch with Caroline, and his girlfriend studying something on her phone.

She didn't look like she'd been crying, but she barely looked up when he entered. "Hey," she said, and oh, that tone reminded him of their first meal together at the diner. The one where he'd attached himself to her just to get a table, and they'd barely spoken three sentences to each other.

Dawson sighed, regretting the words he'd spoken in the past half-hour. He walked over to the couch and collapsed onto it, and then twisted so he could lay his head in her lap. "I love seeing you when I come in from the ranch," he whispered. "I love that my pets love you, and I *adore* that you're willing to come up here and have dinner with my nosy brother and sister-in-law and all their kids."

Caroline breathed out, and it seemed like all the tension in her body went with it. She set his cowboy hat aside and ran her fingers through his hair. He closed his eyes and simply basked in the zinging, tingling touch of her.

"I love coming up to this ranch," she whispered back. "I love your dog and even this cat that won't touch grass, and I *adore* that you weren't afraid to speak your mind with me."

"I'm afraid I broke us," he said.

"No," she said. "I needed to hear it."

"I'm sorry."

She covered his mouth, and he opened his eyes and looked up at her. "Don't you dare apologize to me," she hissed. "You did nothing wrong. I'm the one who, well, everything you said was right. I'm the one who hasn't made room for us."

"You have six more months," he said, a smile lifting his heart and his lips.

Caroline blinked at him. "Six more months?"

"Our first date was absolutely on New Year's Day," he said.

Her mouth flickered into a smile that only lasted for a heartbeat. "Then I have *seven* more months to figure things out."

Dawson laughed and sat up, the blood rushing to his head in a way that made it swim. He sobered though Caroline giggled and smiled with him. She did the same, and the moment between them felt powerful and meaningful, and Dawson simply opened his mouth and said, "I'm going to be in love with you way before those seven months are up, my sweet Caroline."

Her eyes filled with tears, and she closed them and shook her head. "No darling?"

Dawson slid closer to her and touched his mouth to hers. He didn't correct his pet name for her, because his kiss hopefully said it all. She was his sweet Caroline and his darling, and Dawson may or may not already be in love with her.

Chapter Thirty-Three

Misty Granger came out of her bedroom and moved down the hall, the fabric of the skirt swishing around her legs. "What about this one?"

Janey, her best friend, and Ralf, her other best friend, looked away from the cheese and crackers Ralf had brought.

"I think it's too blue," Misty said. "I don't look good in blue."

"It's fantastic," Ralf said at the same time Janey said, "The purple one is better."

Misty looked down at the dark blue fabric, which had shimmering flowers woven through it in a lighter blue. She'd tried on several dresses so far, everything from beige to tangerine to blue to purple.

"Go put the purple one back on," Janey said. "And let's go. You're going to be late to your own wedding dinner."

"It's a rehearsal dinner," Misty said over her shoulder as she turned to go change yet again.

"It is not!" Janey called after her. "To rehearse something suggests you'll be doing it again as a real thing!"

Misty giggled as she ducked back into her bedroom and started the process of getting undressed and redressed all over again. It was true that she and Lincoln Glover were getting married tomorrow.

It was also true that they were having a "rehearsal dinner" tonight that wouldn't be replicated the following day. Misty had said she didn't mind having a big shin-dig with all of his aunts and uncles, of which there were dozens.

But Link had put his boot down and said

no. He wanted something simple, and Misty knew that was for her.

Finally ready, Misty returned to the common areas of the house, where her friends waited. "Ready," she said.

Janey came immediately to her side. "This is going to be great," she said.

"Don't leave my side for a second," Misty said, her stomach one of total chaos in that moment.

"Honey, I can't stay at your side all night," Janey said. "There will be cowboys I'm not related to there." She grinned at Misty, though she'd be moving back to Dallas next weekend, when their project officially ended.

Misty had finished her portion of the project, so she could get married and go on her honeymoon without having to lose any time from work. From a job she wasn't returning to. Tears filled her eyes, because her life was about to change so, so much.

So much she couldn't even think of all the ways things would be different tomorrow.

"I just don't want my mom clinging to me

all night," Misty said, using the words to strengthen her voice.

"Danny will be there," Janey promised. "And Link, of course. And you two have so many friends, Ralf and I don't even get invited to game night."

Misty sobbed then, part of it a laugh that made no sense. "When Link and I have game night, you two are going to be at the top of the list."

"I'd rather die than play a game with other couples," Ralf said in a deadpan. "So leave me out of that."

Misty threw him a smile and together, the three of them moved to leave the house. The drive to Shiloh Ridge Ranch took forty minutes from their subdivision, and Janey made it for them tonight.

Without Janie, Misty wasn't sure how she'd have survived the past month. Dealing with her mother's travel, where she'd stay while she was in Three Rivers, and all the finalizing of the wedding details. Misty felt like she needed forty hours in every day, and she still only got twenty-four.

They pulled up to True Blue, the family barn at Shiloh Ridge where they had a lot of big functions. Weddings, parties, birthday and anniversary celebrations, or even just Sunday meals. Misty had attended all of those things in the past year since she and Link had rekindled their romance, and she'd always felt more than welcome every time she walked through the door.

Tonight, she expected nothing less than that, and since it was partly her party, the spotlight would definitely be on her. Ralf and Janey flanked her as they entered, the barrels shining and overflowing with fresh flowers.

Danny was bringing their mother, and Misty immediately looked around for them. Her eyes caught on Bear and Cactus Glover, who both grinned at her like she'd figured out how to peel back layers of heaven and let the divine light into all of their lives.

"Howdy, Misty," Bear drawled, his big personality matching his smiling cowboy hat. He drew her into a hug and added, "Link just ran into the kitchen for a minute. He'll be right back."

She nodded as she stepped back. "Okay. Have you—have you seen my mom?"

Loretta had been in town for two days, and Misty's nerves and patience seemed to renew by the hour. A gift from God, she was sure, and she'd wept on her knees last night for all of His many blessings. Bear was one of those, as was Cactus, who hugged her next.

"How's Danny doing?" she whispered in his ear. Her brother had taken a shine to animal care after he'd come to Shiloh Ridge, and Cactus had simply taken him in, as if he wasn't an ex-con and hadn't come to the ranch by way of prison.

"He's amazing, Misty," Cactus murmured back. "Don't worry about him so much."

"I can't help it," she said as she stepped back.

"Well, you're movin' on now," Cactus said. "It's time you let him do the same."

Misty wanted to argue, tell him she'd let

Danny move on, but the truth was, maybe she hadn't. Maybe she did expect him to mess up again at any moment, though he'd given her no reason to think that. So with tears in her eyes for yet another reason, she nodded and went back to looking for her mother.

"Your mom went with Sammy to look at the dress," Bear said. "They're in the bridal room."

Misty looked toward the back corner of the barn, but her feet didn't take her that way, for her gorgeous almost-husband had just come back into the main room. Her gaze immediately went back to his, and Link spotted her in the next moment.

Love like she'd never known filled her, and Misty's wavering emotions solidified as he came her way. She went to meet him too, nodding and smiling to his aunts and uncles and cousins. But when Link was in the room, there was only Link.

"Hey, you're here," he said as he swept her into his arms. She laughed and grabbed onto him, because he made her feel like her life wasn't about to implode. He had everything under control, and he would take care of anything that Misty couldn't handle herself—which in this moment, felt like everything.

"What was going on in the kitchen?" she asked when he set her back on her heeled feet.

"Oh, that?" He waved his hand in a way that meant he was about to lie. "Nothing. It was nothing." He grinned at her. "Now, come on. We're about to start, and we're supposed to be up front."

"I haven't seen my mom yet," Misty said.

"My momma has her," Link said. "She's okay, and she's at our table anyway." He didn't seem nervous on the outside, but the way he gripped her fingers and strode like he was fleeing a zombie apocalypse told her otherwise.

Someone started to clap as they neared the front, and Misty's face burned. She wasn't used to being scrutinized, and she told herself over and over that wasn't what the Glovers were doing. They were *celebrating* her and Link, and that was totally different than having eyes on her for a negative reason.

Janey had already found her seat at the front table, and Misty found two spots between her and her best friend. One had been labeled with Danny's name and the other her mother's, and Link stood behind her chair, that look of adoration on his face that Misty loved.

Because it meant he loved her.

"Do they need to look again, my love?" he whispered as he drew her closer. "Turn away from everyone, okay?"

Misty did, pressing her cheek to the lapel of his jacket. He wore black from head to toe, with a light purple shirt, and her fingers found the end of his silk tie and fiddled with it while she took in a breath.

"It's just us," Link said in her ear. "They love us; they're not thinking anything of us."

"Other than I'm a mess," Misty muttered.

"A beautiful mess," Link said. "Come on, now, sweetheart. This is something special for two special people."

Him and her.

Misty took in as much air as her lungs would hold, she held it there, and then slowly let it leak away. The tension in her shoulders melted away, and Misty put a smile on her face. "Okay," she said. "I'm ready to have them look again."

"Okay," Link said. "And you look at them too, Misty, okay? You look at them." He stepped back and pulled her chair out for her.

Misty looked down at it, then turned and lifted her eyes to the crowd. All of them had started to take their seats too, and Misty copied them. Link sat next to her, moved his chair closer, and draped his arm around her. "See them?"

She gazed out into the vastness of the barn. Tables had been set up, with matching chairs. But it didn't matter if the chairs matched, because Sammy and her army of sisters-in-law had put lavender covers over the backs of the chairs and tied them with white ribbons.

Tall vases of flowers went straight up from the middle of each table, the blooms spilling overhead without blocking the view of the guests sitting across from one another.

The table closest to them had Etta and August corralling their children into their seats while Bear came forward to sit at the front table with her, Link, and a few other significant others in the wedding party.

Misty had Ralf, Janey, Danny, and her mom. Link had his parents and his grandmother—who had helped Misty and Sammy plan a lot of the wedding.

She caught sight of her mom and Sammy, and they both wore a smile. So things couldn't be too bad, right? Misty's pulse skipped over itself, but she forced herself to stay in her seat as Danny and Ralf came to take their seats too.

Link's grandmother leaned over him and gave him a hug and kiss, and he murmured, "Love you, Grandmother," before Lois moved to Misty.

"Thank you so much for this," Misty said to Lois as she hugged her too.

Lois beamed at her with all the love Misty could imagine from a grandmother. Her heart warmed at the look on Lois's face, and she struggled to believe she was worthy of so much attention, so much adoration, so much goodness from the Glovers.

"I'm so thrilled for you and Link," she said, her voice shaking. She moved to sit at the end of the table with her husband, and finally, Sammy arrived with her mom.

"Mom." Misty stood up and embraced her mother. She clung to her tightly, noticing the scratchiness of her mom's dress. She seized onto that so her emotions wouldn't spiral out of control.

She pulled back and smiled at her mother. "I love your dress, Mom." She was working on forgiving her mother for all of the things that had happened over the years. But that didn't happen overnight, and Misty needed more time and experiences with her mom to replace the images and opinions she'd lived with for so long.

Every minute created a new version of the relationship Misty had with her mom, and she'd been praying for weeks and weeks that tonight and tomorrow would go off without a hitch. That her and her mom would have a chance to build new and different bonds with one another.

"Thanks," Loretta said, but she said nothing of Misty's purple dress. She swallowed back the bitterness suddenly on her tongue and turned toward Sammy.

The woman pulled her straight into a hug. "How beautiful are you?" she asked. "This dress is *perfect* for you." She smiled and smiled at Misty. "You and Link will take fifteen minutes with the photographer after dinner, won't you?"

She glanced over to Link. "With your shirt and tie matching Misty's dress so perfectly, you have to."

"We will, Momma," Link said, looking up to her. "Can you sit down, please? Uncle Bishop has steam rising from his head, and we're five minutes late."

"Glovers are never late," Sammy said, and she cradled his face for a couple moments before she moved to sit beside him. The moment she did, the lights popped and went out, and plenty of people yelped or cried out, Misty included.

"Link," she said over the brand new noise.

"It's part of the night, baby," he said.

"Part of the night—what?"

The lights—rather, a single light—illuminated a single person at the back of the hall, and he held a guitar but kept his head down, his cowboy hat hiding his face. Misty's adrenaline pounded through her, but she couldn't look away from the man directly in front of her.

Then the man lifted his face, and Misty saw it was Link's uncle Ward. He started to play, his fingers moving deftly over the strings to create a beautiful sound.

"He used to play in a band," Link said, his mouth right at her ear so she could hear. "Uncle Mister too."

That explained the second sound that came in—another guitar—and the man who joined Ward. Mister wore a grin the size of Texas itself, which was the opposite of Ward, who looked about the same as he always did: halfway to irritation.

Then he looked over to Mister, and his face dissolved into a smile too. That somehow made Misty relax, and she only jumped slightly when someone started crooning into the microphone.

The Glover family whooped and cheered, and Misty found herself getting swept along in the wave of their joy and celebrating. She clapped along to the beat, and she found herself yelling when another uncle and then another joined Ward and Mister as they advanced toward the front table.

And when they started begging Bear to get out there and dance with them.... Misty leaned forward and looked at the grumpy grizzly bear sitting beside his wife, his arms folded.

"Go on!" she yelled at him, and he cut his eyes over to her.

Link laughed, and Misty did too, because they both knew Bear was going to get out there and dance with his brothers and cousins. When he finally did, the roof on the barn practically vibrated with the screams and applause.

His grumpy mask broke, and out came the

panda bear that Misty had grown to know and love. He laughed with his brothers, and on the next step, he easily moved into the line of men performing a dance.

A legit line dance, while two of them played and Ace sang. They all danced a grapevine move to the left, clapped in unison, and started cowboy-stepping it back to the right. Misty could not stop laughing, because this was the stuff of legends. The family party she'd dreamed of.

The family she'd dreamed of, period.

The song ended, and she cheered and clapped along with everyone else in the room. Then Bishop took the mic from Ace and told everyone to take their seats. He moved to stand in front of the long table where Misty and Link sat with their families.

"All right, all right!" Bishop yelled into the mic. "That was an amazing intro to tonight's dinner, and no finer beginning to a wedding celebration has ever been seen."

The last chatter and laughter finally subsided as Bishop finished speaking, but he kept on going with, "Link has asked me to pray over dinner, and then we're going to eat. There will be music and dancing after that, and I've been tasked to remind everyone that the wedding is at ten-thirty sharp tomorrow morning, right here in True Blue."

He nodded and waited several seconds while cowboy hats got removed and arms folded, and then Bishop bowed his head and prayed. "Lord, we thank Thee for a reason to get together in this barn, which we love. There's nothing as amazing as a wedding, and we're so grateful that Misty has somehow been blinded to all of Link's flaws and agreed to marry him anyway."

He laughed lightly, and Misty found herself giggling too. She glanced over to Link, who wore a smile while keeping his eyes closed. She reached for his hand and took it easily, and she squeezed his fingers in hers.

"Kidding aside, we're grateful for Link and Misty, and for each other. We're grateful for families, and we're grateful for our Lord and Savior Jesus Christ." He paused, and Misty had learned that all of Link's aunts and uncles had emotional triggers, and if they got pressed, the Holy Spirit could flow effortlessly throughout the whole room.

Exactly as it was now.

Misty found herself tensing up with emotion again, and she fought against her tears for the umpteenth time this week.

"Bless those in our company who need Thy special care, and bless the ranch while Link is gone, and we pray a special blessing on this young couple as they travel for their honeymoon. And now." He took a big breath, the sound of it actually going through the microphone. "We ask Thee to bless this food, which was made by masterful hands, and we're real grateful for the bounty You have always poured onto us here at Shiloh Ridge. Amen."

"Amen," got bellowed through the barn, but Misty murmured her seal of approval on Bishop's prayer.

She assumed there'd be a buffet, but she didn't stand up to go get food. Only a few seconds later, Smiles, Link's younger brother, appeared with two plates, one in each hand. He served Link first and then Misty, his smile wide and warm.

"Thank you," Link said, and Misty tried to echo him, but Smiles was already gone. She watched as all the teens in Link's family served the others still seated at the tables, marveling at how amazing this family was that she would be part of tomorrow morning at ten-thirty sharp.

Chapter Thirty-Four

Link tugged at his shirtsleeves, his legs starting to get that jittery feeling in them again. He had to move, and he needed to do it now. He got to his feet despite his uncle's protest, and he shook both hands to try to get the nerves to dissipate.

"What time is it?" he asked, though he knew he still had at least a half-hour before he'd be leaving this room and heading for the altar. If his wedding were any closer, his momma would've come in to let him know.

She hadn't appeared yet, which meant she was still in the room down the hall with Misty.

He focused on the beautiful woman he couldn't wait to marry and focused on the person who'd come to stand in front of him. Uncle Cactus. "Why am I so nervous?"

"Because this is an important thing." His uncle reached out and straightened Link's bowtie. He smiled at him. "You're going to be making covenants with God to love and cherish and take care of a good woman, and she's going to expect you to uphold that."

Link swallowed, not sure this was quite the pep talk he needed.

"And you're going to make covenants with her, and she's going to do the same for you, and then, there's no going back."

"I don't want to go back," Link said. "I'm worried she'll want to go back."

Uncle Cactus nodded, always so sober—until he could smile and laugh and joke. "Son, I've seen her with you, and there's no way—absolutely none—that she's backing out of this. She adores you."

"You think so?" Link's throat felt as wide as a straw, and he couldn't swallow or breathe.

"And she's the luckiest woman in the world to have you," Cactus said, finally lowering his hands and leaving Link's collar and tie and lapels alone. "Don't forget that and don't ever doubt it."

"Do you sometimes doubt it with Aunt Willa?"

Uncle Cactus gave him one of those rare smiles and said, "Well, Willa is a unicorn, son, and I thank God every day that He gave her to me."

Link felt the same way about Misty, and he exhaled as he prayed God would make him into the man she deserved, needed, and could love for a lifetime.

"Link," a woman said, and he spun toward the door. Momma stood there, wearing a gorgeous, glittering dress in a deep purple. "You've got twenty minutes."

"I'm setting the timer," Daddy said as he approached Momma. He kissed her quickly, and they spoke for a moment before Momma looked over to Link again. She grinned at him, and Link moved toward her.

"Momma," he whispered as he arrived in her arms. "I'm so scared."

"There's nothing to be afraid of, my sweet boy," she said as she gripped him tightly around the shoulders. "You've been waiting for this day for a long time. So has she, and you two are just perfect for each other."

"I wish we could've just eloped." He stepped back. "There are so many of us, and everyone stares."

Momma laughed, but she kept it short. "Link, baby, you're literally supposed to watch two people when they get married."

"I know." He rolled his shoulders, trying to get the tension to dissipate. "I can't wait until we're on the ship, and no one knows us, and we can just have our own adventures."

"Getting to Spain is going to be an adventure all its own," Momma said with a grin. "Now, you're down to sixteen minutes, and we may have been a little late last night starting dinner, but we will not hold this wedding for anyone—not even the groom." With that, she left the room, and Link faced the closed door for a moment.

Then he turned to face all the men in his family, and as he looked at them—truly looked, the way he'd advised Misty to do, all he could see was love.

Exactly fifteen minutes later, Link stood at the back of the barn, the aisle stretching in front of him. The music filtering through the barn changed, and that made everyone turn and start to stand when they saw him.

He resisted the urge to fiddle with his cufflinks again, and thankfully, Daddy stood only five feet from him, ready to lead everyone down the aisle to their seats. His wedding party consisted of his friends, not his family, and they waited to Link's right.

He'd lead them down the aisle, and while he walked, Misty would get into position with her brother, who was walking her down the aisle and giving her away.

His legs wanted to run, but Link held very, very still. Momma came to Daddy's side, and the Glover family procession started in the next breath. One by one, couple by couple, they walked toward Link, pressed their fists to their hearts, and moved past him.

He kept his fist pressed to his heart too in the Glover salute of love and support, and once his family had gone, he looked over to where Finn Ackerman stood with his wife, Edith. Link didn't know who had their son, but he was real glad to see them waiting there, both smiling and shining with rainbows and sunshine.

He nodded to them, and then he faced the crowd, which was suddenly so much larger. Then he took the first step and led his friends down the aisle to the altar. He kept his head held high, his hands loose at his sides as he walked in the slow cadence his mother had taught him.

He arrived at the altar and he hugged Finn and Edith, then Mitch, who'd walked alone in the wedding party, Alex and Nicki, Dawson and Caroline, Brandon and Janey, Ollie and Rory, and then Henry Marshall and his date, though Link had only met her that morning.

They moved to stand in an arc around the

altar, and his aunt joined him at the saddle that Misty had spent considerable time painting in her own special way. He studied the shape of his name and how it flowed into hers, and he found the word GLOVER done in what looked like old western letters along the bottom.

He reached out to touch it, marveling that Misty had managed to capture everything about their two individual lives in one piece of art.

"There she is," Aunt Willa whispered, and Link tore his eyes from the saddle altar to look down the aisle.

Misty stood there, her dress a bright white in the lights in the barn. She had her arm linked through Danny's, who wore a midnight black tuxedo, a cowboy hat, and a healthy smile on his face.

Her sleeves puffed and bulged away from her arms, giving the top of the dress such an interesting shape. The bodice clung to her chest and ribs and flared over her hips, and when she finally started to move, it looked like her legs and feet didn't even touch the skirt.

She glided like a princess, and Link absolutely could not stop smiling. She was here, and she was his, and they were going to have the most amazing life together.

They arrived, and Misty leaned into Danny and kissed his cheek. He whispered something to her, and then transferred her arm from his to Link's. "Love you, brother," Link said, and Danny repeated it back to him before he went to stand next to Henry.

Link gazed at Misty, with her lined eyes and ruby red lips. "You are absolutely gorgeous," he murmured. "I've just fallen in love with you all over again." He slid his hand along her waist, pulling her closer.

Every moment where she looked at him made him into a new version of himself. The Link who loved her in that second, and then the next, and then even more in the third. He'd had no idea that love would be able to affect a person so much, but it did. Its power could change hearts and minds, open the door to forgiveness, and inspire kindness, conversations, and bind families together.

He leaned down and kissed her, which got a rise from the crowd gathered in the family barn. Embarrassment funneled through Link, and he pulled away when Aunt Willa cleared her throat loudly.

"Sorry," he murmured, but Misty still stood there with her head tipped back and her eyes closed.

"I'm not," Misty murmured, and she slid her hand behind his neck and pulled him back to her for another kiss. "I love you, Lincoln."

"Gotta say I-do at some point," Daddy called, and that got Misty to pull away, giggling.

Link chuckled too, and he tucked her against his side as they faced Willa. "Okay," he said. "We're ready."

"Mm, yes, I can see you are." She nodded over to Misty, inhaled, and said in a loud voice, "I get more joy from marrying two people in love than from anything else I get to do as a pastor." She signed as she spoke, so Mitch could participate fully.

She pressed one hand to her heart, fisting her fingers. "And the fact that it's one of my very favorite nephews only makes today probably the best day I've had in years. I'm not going to delay this for too much longer, because today is a fabulous day to get married."

Link held onto Misty while his aunt spoke about compromise and communication, and to her eternal credit, she didn't go on for too long before she said, "Remember that love is not simply an emotion, but a choice you make every day. You must choose each other. Love is patient and kind. It bears all things, believes all things, hopes all things, and endures through all things. So be patient and kind and loving with each other, every day of your lives."

She reached out and set her Bible on the saddle. "It's time, you two. Join hands and face one another."

Link shifted to do that, catching sight of his parents out of the corner of his eye. Misty's mom sat next to Momma, and she wiped at her eyes.

"Misty Jeanine Granger, do you take Lincoln Wyatt Josephs Glover to be your lawfully wedded husband, to have and to hold, from this day forward, to love, cherish, and support?"

"I do," Misty said, and her voice seemed to fill the whole barn. Link's throat felt like someone had scrubbed it with sandpaper, and he hoped he could speak when it was his turn.

Aunt Willa repeated the question to him, and he swallowed, looked Misty right in the eye, and said, "I do." Thankfully, his voice sounded normal and came out loud enough.

Aunt Willa then picked up the rings she had on her side of the altar, and she placed them on the Bible. "These rings are a symbol of an unbroken circle of love, signifying to all the union of this couple in holy matrimony."

She nodded to them, and Link had been told that was his cue to pick up the diamond he'd bought for Misty. He did, and she reached out and picked up his band too. She slid his ring on his finger, her smile so beautiful, and Link did the same for her, fitting the two pieces of her ring together into the final piece.

"By the power vested in me by the state of Texas and the Almighty God, I now pronounce you husband and wife. You may kiss your bride."

Link tore his gaze from the glittering diamond on his wife's finger and looked into her eyes. "You're mine now, but I don't want you to think you're special or anything."

She giggled and said, "Oh, stop it. I already know I'm the special-est."

Link laughed and pressed his lips to hers in a sloppy marriage kiss. The crowd behind them did what they always did best—they made a lot of joyful noise as Link kissed his wife.

Only when someone said into a microphone, "Ladies and gentlemen, I give you Mister and Missus Lincoln Glover!" did Link pull away and lace his fingers through Misty's.

Then he led his new wife down the aisle as those they loved applauded, whistled, and cheered.

Chapter Thirty-Five

Caroline found herself sitting at her desk in the middle of a summer afternoon, staring at paperwork she didn't care about. And she never thought she'd think that. Paperwork usually made her happy, and she filed it away with a great deal of satisfaction.

But today marked the eighth day she hadn't seen Dawson in the flesh. They'd attended Link and Misty's wedding, and while they'd danced and laughed, chatted with their friends, and he'd kissed her when he'd dropped her off, there was something new between them.

Caroline knew it was her inability to scoot

over and make room for Dawson in her life. At the same time, the cowboy had rooted himself solidly in her life. So she wasn't sure what she needed to do to become "us" with him, but she knew she hadn't done it yet.

She flipped her phone over, almost desperate to call him. He'd been busy with a couple of meetings immediately following the wedding, and then he and Duke had gone up into the hills to check on their dogs and cattle.

Then, he'd moved into a round of planting, and he'd told her this busy season would be upon them. Once it finished, though, he claimed that a large part of the work around the ranch was watching things grow. That was when they planned to take their road-boat trip —something Caroline wasn't sure they should be doing.

"What are you saying?" she muttered to herself. "That you want to break-up with him?"

She absolutely didn't want to break up with Dawson, but she couldn't help wondering if he'd like to end things with her.

She knew where the man lived, and she

knew his favorites for breakfast, lunch, and dinner. She could see him if she wanted to, and her fingers itched to do just that. Her left leg started to bounce with the pent-up energy pulling through her.

Heck, she could use the burrowing owls as an excuse to go up to the Rhinehart Ranch and get paid to see her boyfriend. She ran her hands through her hair, because she wasn't going to use the owls to get up to Dawson's ranch.

She needed to figure out how to be herself while being part of a couple. She hadn't been able to do it in her first marriage, and now she wondered if the person she'd been back then had been the problem. She'd been so weak that she'd just allowed Joe to take over her every thought. Dictate to her how every moment of her day would go. How long her showers could be. Everything.

And now, she was still a problem, because she'd gone too far the other way. She'd closed the door on anyone who might want to come into her life, because she was so strong and so capable and so sure of who she was.

Her chest shook with pent-up emotion, and she lay her head in her hands, dangerously close to tears. "Dear God," she whispered. "I don't want to go on like this. I don't want to lose Dawson. And I absolutely don't want to lose myself."

She'd been resisting laying down the pieces of herself she'd fought so hard to develop, because she wasn't sure who she'd be without them.

Her thoughts scattered, and then they came back together. She sat up straight, the words in her head ones she wasn't sure she could say. But if she did...and God answered her prayer... would she be obligated to do what He said?

"Help me to find a new way to be Caroline," she said, her lower lip shaking. "One who can be herself *and* be with Dawson Rhinehart. And if You can do that—show me the way— then I'll do it."

And of course she believed God could show her the way. He'd given her the way out of her first marriage. He'd led her to Three Rivers. He'd given her the resources to help

Belle and Judy. Every step of Caroline's life had been touched by the hand of God, and the moment she uttered her desperate plea for help, she knew the Lord would answer her.

And probably not how she wanted Him to.

After all, she'd known she needed to find a way to lay down her burdens, shed who she was, and become a new creature through Christ. If only that wasn't quite so painful and didn't take quite so long.

She stayed at work; she went home and stood on the back deck with a jar of crunchy Biscoff and an overly large spoon; she put a smile on her face when Belle got home from swimming lessons with Judy.

She ate dinner with her sister and her niece; they all went shopping for new Fourth of July clothes—something festive in red, white, and blue. Caroline could admit she'd found the cutest navy blue sweater with stars and stripes on it, and bonus, it was short-sleeved, so she felt like she could wear it even in the sweltering Texas heat.

"I'll wear it with a pair of white shorts,"

she'd told Belle, and they'd gone home happy. But for Caroline, that happiness only existed on the outside. She retreated to her bedroom early, her phone silent.

Dawson usually texted and called starting about the time he made it to his barn-office, but he'd been silent today. She searched her memory, trying to remember his schedule and where he'd told her he'd be today.

Everything had scattered again, and she paced in her bedroom where Belle and Judy couldn't see her. "Maybe we've broken up," she said. "And I'm just the last to know."

But that didn't sit right with Caroline. Dawson had not argued with her much in the past six months, but he didn't hold back when there was something important to say. He spoke his mind, and if he didn't want to be with her, she couldn't imagine him wasting his time for even a single day.

"No," she told herself with a firm shake of her head. "He'd say something."

He did have a lot going on, and Caroline's default was to let him take care of what he needed to. His sticky notes were probably out of control, and he was probably stressed trying to make them, move them from one column to the next, keep them all organized.

Keep himself organized.

Go talk to him.

The words streamed through her mind, but Caroline bucked against them the same way she'd been pressing back against the pastor's advice to give up herself to God.

"It's late," she said to her empty master suite. Cowboys went to bed early, and Dawson followed that rule, due to his five a.m. running habit.

The words came again—*Go talk to him*—and Caroline noticed they were louder. More intense. She grabbed her phone from where she'd set it on the dresser and dialed Dawson instead. His line rang and rang, and he didn't pick up. When his voicemail picked up, Caroline's frustration fired through her.

His inability to do what she wanted irritated her as much now as it had when he wouldn't file the blasted owl paperwork. She had to squash down the feelings, because Dawson might be at dinner with his parents, and he silenced his phone during such an activity. He might be out on the ranch where they didn't have service. He might be in the shower, mere minutes away from going to bed.

She hung up without leaving a message, and the prompting came again, almost a shout in her head.

Go talk to him!

Caroline headed for the door, and she called, "I'm going to see Dawson," as she swiped her keys from the kitchen counter. It was forty-five minutes to the ranch, and it would be dusk-bordering-on-dark by the time she arrived.

"Dust and shadows," she fake swore as she exited the house. Dusk had already started to settle over Three Rivers, which meant she'd be showing up at Dawson's cabin at full dark.

She hesitated, and God practically bellowed at her: *Go talk to him.*

Caroline made the drive, barely glancing at Duke and Zona's house when she went by. She couldn't believe she'd thought it would be a good idea to show up there an hour early, simply so she could relieve her own anxieties over becoming part of the Rhinehart family.

"That's what it was," she whispered to herself, the words rising slowly and serenely, the way the dust did under her tires as she drove down the dirt road.

She'd been anxious about the steps she and Dawson were taking, because they led to her becoming a Rhinehart. Truly becoming part of his family.

She thought of Zona and how headstrong she was. Then April, who definitely had her own mind and spoke it, lived it. Caroline could maintain herself while giving up some of the control that had literally saved her in the past.

"But the past is the past," she told herself as the homestead came into view. Dawson lived a short jog around the corner, and Caroline made the drive easily, as she'd done it many times before.

Tonight felt different, because Caroline felt different. Both his and Brandon's trucks sat in front of the cabin they shared, and she found Ruffin lying in the shade of one of the big trees in the front yard.

"Odd," she murmured. Ruffin usually stuck close to Dawson, and if he was outside, then....

Caroline slammed on the brakes when she saw Dawson rise from a chair on the front porch. He held something in his hands, but she couldn't quite tell what. Her heartbeat boomed at her as if God Himself had picked up a mallet and hit a big, bass drum over and over again. The beats told her to keep moving; she'd come this far, and Dawson had now seen her. She couldn't just drive away.

She managed to get the car moving, and she parked it next to Brandon's truck. By the time she got out, Dawson had come down the front steps, his hands now empty. He looked at her and tucked his hands away in his front pockets.

"Hey," she said, and the slam from her car door closing made her flinch. "I'm a little surprised you're not in bed."

"And yet, here you are," he said, stopping a

healthy distance away. So there was definitely something wrong.

Caroline twisted her hands over and around one another. "Are we still together?"

Dawson opened his mouth, then quickly closed it. He looked away, his jaw jumping in a way Caroline had seen before and didn't like.

"Because I don't want us to *not* be together," she said, feeling her old strength come into her body. She pushed it down, because now wasn't the time for Caroline to be her old self.

Her chin shook as tears filled her eyes. "I hate that you didn't text or call me today, and I hate that you're thinking of breaking up with me, and I really, really *loathe* that you believe I won't make room for you."

He ducked his head in that adorable way he had, the sweetness just pouring off him. He didn't refute anything she'd said, which meant he hadn't texted or called on purpose. He absolutely was thinking of breaking up with her. And he one-hundred percent believed she couldn't change and make room for him.

"I'll just sit with you," she said. "Is that

okay? We don't have to talk, the way we didn't at the diner that one time."

He lifted his head and nodded at her, then turned and went back toward the porch. She followed him, and he retook his seat, picked up a knife and a hunk of wood, and started whittling again.

Caroline took the only other seat on the porch, the small, round table between them. "I didn't know you whittled," she said.

"From time to time," he said in his gruff voice. "When I need my hands busy."

She'd learned in the past six months that sometimes Dawson said only half of what he meant. And when he needed his hands busy, it was so he could work through the troubling thoughts in his mind.

Caroline pressed her lips together, because she'd told him they didn't have to talk. They'd never had to fill the silence with mindless chatter, and Caroline took a deep breath and clasped her hands together in her lap.

Lord, she thought. *Thank You for this beautiful night.*

Her prayer ended there, because she only wanted to thank God for the blessings in her life right now. She didn't want to ask Him for anything, because she'd already begged for what she wanted.

And He'd answered.

She was supposed to talk, but she didn't know what to say. She didn't want to push Dawson further away, but God had told her to come talk to him. Not sit here in silence.

Caroline decided that when the right words came, she'd say them.

Chapter Thirty-Six

Dawson hated the tension between him and Caroline, and he hated that he hadn't welcomed her with a smile and a kiss, and he absolutely *loathed* this silence between them.

"I can hear you not talkin'," he finally said.

"I just—" Caroline cut off, perpetuating the not-talking she was doing.

"Just say what you came here to say."

"I don't know what to say," she admitted. "I came because God told me to come, and He told me to talk to you, but I don't know what to say."

Dawson smiled to himself, his eyes trained on the movement of his knife and the shavings falling to his feet. "God's not giving you the words?"

"No." She huffed out her breath. "He's being very silent right now, and I'm—well, you know what? I'm trying to give myself to God, the way Pastor Glover said to do weeks ago, so I'm just going to sit here and wait until He gives me the right thing to say to keep you in my life."

Dawson looked up then, his hands coming to a stop. He glanced over to her, but Caroline had her eyes fixed on something out on the ranch.

"The silence between us has always been comfortable," he said. "Because I just liked being with you. But this is uncomfortable."

"Well, you're going to have to get comfortable with the uncomfortable," she said. "Because God told me to come talk to you, and I'm not leaving until I do." She threw him a semi-scathing look and then went back to gazing out into the darkness.

Dawson went back to his whittling, though he was literally just shaving the stick down to nothing, the curls of shavings falling to the porch for him to clean up later.

A minute went by, then another. Finally, Caroline said, "Every time I came to your ranch, I'd toss something shiny out the window for Rocks to find."

Dawson's heartbeat accelerated as his surprise flowed through him. One, he sure liked being with Caroline, even if they were sitting in uncomfortable silence. He sure liked the sound of her voice, and he sure liked that he wasn't out here alone, stewing in his own thoughts.

"No wonder he's been bringing me quarters and random bits of metal." He looked over to her. "Where did you even get those?"

She smiled at him, and there was his beautiful Caroline. "I never threw random metal onto the ranch," she said. "I value my life, thank you very much."

"What did you throw then?"

"Mostly coins," she said. "Half of an old pocket watch I found on another ranch. Once,

Judy made a shiny star out of some soda cans. I tossed one of those. Anything I thought would make you smile."

Dawson could only stare at her.

"I can hear you not talkin'," she teased.

Dawson finally cracked a smile and set aside his knife. His pulse ricocheted through his body, but he better tell her the truth. Dawson didn't know how to do otherwise. "I was considering breaking up with you," he said. "But every time I thought about it, my heart would start to scream, and I knew I couldn't do it."

Caroline wiped at her eyes, which made Dawson's heart crack. "Did you cancel the Mississippi River Cruise?"

"No, ma'am."

"I can feel the space between us," she said. "I hate it. I didn't think I'd like having someone so close, but it turns out, I do." She shrugged, her tears slipping from one eye now. "And not just someone, Dawson Rhinehart, but you. I like having *you* close to me."

He got up and went to kneel in front of her. "I'm sorry for the distance."

"If you need it, that's fine," she said. "I understand I'm a frustrating person from time to time, but I would really like a chance to give myself to God, and then you can decide if she's not the right person for you."

He took both of her hands in his. "Okay," he said. "I'm sorry the ranch is so busy right now."

"This is why we have the year," she said. "So I can see what life is like in the spring, the summer, the fall, the winter, on a ranch."

"The fall is hectic," he muttered, dropping his head again. Now his hands held still, holding hers, the mix of their skin tones and textures so different and yet fitting together so beautifully.

"You wanna come in and have an ice cream sandwich?" he asked.

"Yes," she said. "That is exactly what I want."

He got to his feet and offered Caroline his hand. Their eyes met, and Dawson pulled her closer. She sort of stumbled into his arms, and Dawson breathed in the scent of her hair, her skin, her very being.

"I love that you came up here tonight," he said. "I love that you came even though you didn't know what to say, and I *adore* that you made room for me tonight."

Caroline nodded, her eyes full of intensity that slowly faded.

"I don't need you to change completely for me," he whispered as he leaned forward and touched his cheek to hers. "That's the last thing I want, actually. If you feel like you need to change, then do it for you, darlin', okay? Not for me."

He pulled back and looked into her eyes again. "If you do it for me, you'll end up resenting me the way you do Joe. It has to be for you."

"It is for me," she said. "I heard the pastor, and her words penetrated right into my heart. I do need to rely on the Lord more, and I know that. I don't have to be the strong one all the time."

Dawson pushed her hair back off her face, and she sighed as her eyes drifted closed. He smiled at her, her softness infusing into his heart. And he knew in that moment that he loved her.

She opened her eyes and looked at him again. "I've never cried in front of a man," she said. "And tonight, I did, and you didn't scorn me or look at me in disgust, and I...feel like I gave some of my pride to God, and it felt real nice."

"I'm glad," Dawson said.

"I'm not changing for you, Dawson," she said. "I'm not." She shook her head. "I'm changing so I can be the woman who gets to be an 'us' with you." She smiled then, and she leaned into his chest in a way that made him feel strong and sexy and wanted and desirable. "Will you kiss me? I just want to know we're okay for now."

"I can do that, darlin'." And he could, and he did, because kissing Caroline was life-changing every single time. And in fact, this time, as Dawson kissed Caroline, he definitely sensed something different in her touch. In her. Between them.

It could've been a change inside him, because she reformed him with every breath he took. Or it could've been a change in her, but Dawson definitely felt the shift between them. He felt like they were together, and that they could absolutely become the "we" and the "us" he'd always wanted to be part of.

She pulled away first, and said, "All right, now I want ice cream and to see the plans for our river cruise."

Dawson took her face in his hands and gazed at her for just another couple of moments. He grinned, glad when she did too, and said, "Yes, ma'am."

Chapter Thirty-Seven

Henry re-entered his apartment at the farrier academy, thinking and hoping and praying it would be for the last time. "That's it," he said to his older brother, who turned from the window. They both scanned the bedroom that had been emptied of anything personal.

Paul smiled at him, and he seemed happier than Henry had seen him in a while. Probably because of his new girlfriend, who he hadn't brought along today but whom Henry would meet this weekend, when he came back to

Three Rivers to get a few things from the house where he'd grown up.

For he had a new home at Lone Star Ranch, and he had enough room to store more than he had here, in this tiny bedroom in a tiny apartment he'd shared with three other farrier students for the past couple of years.

"Ready?" Paul asked as he clapped a hand on Henry's shoulder.

Henry took a deep breath, his nerves marching like fire ants through his body. "I guess I have to be, right?"

Paul sobered slightly. "You're going to be amazing at Lone Star," he said. "Remember how they had to fight off the other stables and farms to get you? And they only chose one man —the best man—and that was you."

His brother had always been extraordinarily good at building him up, and that was only one reason Henry had to kneel down at night and beg God for forgiveness, because he sometimes had bitter and resentful feelings toward Paul.

Perfect Paul, who walked in their daddy's

footsteps and would take over Courage Reins when Daddy retired. Who never strayed too far from home, or from the straight and narrow path of his religion, or from doing and being just so...good.

Henry felt like the warped, deformed, discarded version of Paul, though his parents loved and believed in him. He intellectually knew they did, but sometimes his rebellious streak and his loud laughter told him that he didn't really belong with them. That they didn't really want him around.

"All right," Daddy drawled, and Henry turned toward him. "We've got everything, yeah? Let's hit the road." He never was one to waste much time, and Henry had inherited that from his father.

"Thanks for coming to help," he said, a wave of gratitude flowing over him, drowning him, until his emotions choked him. He swallowed, trying to find a way to breathe normally, but when his father looked at him with those piercing, all-seeing eyes, Henry actually coughed.

He'd wanted his daddy to be proud of him for so long, and he couldn't quite decipher the look in his father's eyes right now.

"We'll always come when you need us," Daddy said, and he pulled Henry into a hug. Henry gripped his daddy's wide shoulders and pressed his eyes closed, really sinking into the embrace, into the comfort of a good parent, into himself and his place in the Marshall family.

His two younger brothers, John and Rich, had come to help too, and with a family of four young men, Henry hadn't had to rely on any outside help. John had just turned twenty-two, and he would graduate from Baylor in December. He'd gone into Industrial Manufacturing, and he had an internship with a horse trailer company in San Antonio this summer.

He started next week, and Momma and Daddy would be helping him move then. Henry wouldn't go, but he assumed Paul and Rich would. Rich had just graduated from high school last year, and he and JJ Walker were going to the state college in Amarillo come fall. They'd both been working their family ranches for the past year, but Rich had said he finally felt "adult enough" to figure out what he wanted to do.

Henry had left home the very moment he could, not even waiting through the summer to move from small-town Three Rivers to the bigger city of Amarillo, and he hadn't cared at all that he didn't feel ready or didn't know what to do with his life.

Daddy pulled back, and Henry let go of his father. He still wore that concerned, penetrating gaze, but he simply said, "Let's not keep Momma waiting."

Henry followed his daddy and brother out of the apartment and downstairs to the parking lot, where his truck had been loaded with everything he owned here. Daddy had brought his horse, a pretty gray named Stormchaser, and they'd used the bed of his truck for the few boxes that hadn't fit in Henry's.

Paul got in the passenger seat of Henry's truck, while Daddy got behind the wheel of his. Momma and the other boys were already in the vehicle, and Henry suddenly felt the weight of all of them on his shoulders. Daddy could map his way to Lone Star, but he'd wait to follow Henry, so he put the truck in drive and pulled out of the parking space.

"You seem really nervous," Paul said as they left Amarillo in their rearview mirror.

"Yeah." Henry gripped the steering wheel. He bit back the confession that he'd made a total fool of himself with his new boss—for Angel White absolutely was his boss—and he'd seriously considered giving up this apprenticeship simply so he wouldn't have to see her again.

Ever.

At the same time, Henry desperately wanted to see her again in the flesh. He hadn't for a couple of months now, because paperwork and instructions and details could be done via email, texts, and more emails.

No in-person meetings necessary.

But he was going to come face-to-face with her in less than thirty minutes, and Henry swallowed so he wouldn't throw up.

"*Why* are you so nervous?" Paul asked.

"You worked at Lone Star last year. You're a fantastic farrier. You're not going to encounter anything there you can't handle."

"Thank you, Paul," Henry murmured. He looked out his side window, wishing his life had been as easy to understand as Paul's, wishing what his brother had said could actually be true.

Because no, he wasn't nervous about anything with the horses. He wasn't even nervous about dealing with Bard's grouchiness. He knew the cabin would be satisfactory, as Angel had sent him photos and even a video walk-through of the place. As their single new apprentice this year, she'd given him a choice between two cabins and two bedrooms, and he'd chosen the one he wanted.

Lone Star employed plenty of other cowboys and horsemen to work with their large boarding and breeding stable. Some other farriers too, all of whom had more experience than Henry.

"I'm the lowest man on the totem pole," he said, because that had contributed to his anxiety a tiny bit. "There are four other apprentices there, and of course, their master farriers." Lone Star had three of those, and Henry had worked with all of them last year.

He liked Clay, Ford, and Shad a lot. They worked with a lot of younger men with patience, kindness, but absolute no-nonsense. Henry had always enjoyed spending time with men older than him, as well as younger men his own age. He wouldn't hurt for people to hang out with at Lone Star, that was for sure. Of the male variety, at least.

"They know you," Paul said. "You'll fit in brilliantly. You always do." He turned away as he said the last sentence, and that drew Henry's attention.

He dry-swallowed again, wondering how many times a man could do that without causing damage to his throat. "You and I should double," he said. "I'll find someone to go out with, and you can introduce me to Brielle." He looked over to Paul, who didn't move at all.

"Maybe," he said.

Henry didn't push the issue, because he

and Paul had reverted back to their usual places. Of course his brother would come help him when he needed it. Henry would drop anything to be there for him too. For any of his brothers, for his parents, for his aunt and uncle and any of his cousins. He hadn't had a bad life at Three Rivers Ranch, Courage Reins, or any of it.

He simply felt like he might suffocate if he couldn't carve out his own path in the world—and the world was so much bigger than Three Rivers, Texas.

But Paul had always felt inferior to Henry, for it was Henry who'd been popular in high school. Henry who had all the girlfriends. Henry who lived with passion and excitement—Paul's words, not his.

Henry who'd fought the most voraciously with both Momma and Daddy. Henry who'd slammed the most doors as a teenager, who'd snuck out at night and hitchhiked into town, who'd initiated their family game nights and Turkey Bowl tradition on Thanksgiving.

Pure foolishness ran through him, because

he felt like a bulldozer in a newly planted and growing field. A big bull in a china shop, clomping around and causing problems for everyone he came in contact with.

He sighed, because he couldn't change who he was, not way down deep, anyway. He had learned to curb his temper in the past decade, and he'd figured out that not every thought that entered his mind had to come out of his mouth. He'd learned to work hard, be serious about things that mattered to him, and how to push through not-fun things to achieve the reward he wanted.

Before he knew it, he'd turned from the highway leading back to Three Rivers and onto the well-kept dirt road that led to Lone Star. It sat north of Stinnett, about thirty-five minutes from the town of Three Rivers. To get home to the ranch, though, would take Henry another forty-five, so he was still over an hour away.

Close, but not so close he couldn't breathe. Close enough to go home for the day and then sleep in his own bed. Not close enough for

Momma, but a good distance for Henry and his father.

And apparently Paul, he thought, wishing he could keep the resentment out of his head. He really didn't need it right now, faced with the arch of Lone Star as he was.

Henry rumbled along after passing under the arch, the buildings of the stable coming into view as he rounded a bend in the road. The trees standing guard on either side of the road thinned as the ranch expanded in front of him, a big, two-story house that looked like it had been recently repainted welcoming them to the facility.

Bard and his wife lived there, both of them aging and not in the best of health. Well, Bard was, but his wife had been ill for quite some time now. Angel and her brother lived on the ranch too, but not in the main homestead. They each had their own cabin around the corner to the right, but Henry went left to get to his assigned house.

He wasn't the only one moving in today, as Lone Star had selected six summer-only interns this year too. So he wasn't surprised to find other men moving into the cabins that lined the road on the south side. The line of them faced north, with the homestead kitty-corner to them, and the long rows of stable houses in front of them.

Henry had chosen to live in the very last one, so he drove by all the activity happening at the other five dwellings until he reached it. A single truck sat there, but the other man who lived here didn't have to move in or out today.

Levi Tanner had started his apprenticeship with Lone Star last year, and he'd just graduated from the program Henry had been doing. He'd chosen to stay on as a second-year apprentice, as many farriers did. Moving from farm to farm was an option, to get a variety of experience, and Henry wasn't sure what he'd do.

Some farriers simply worked their whole careers at places like Lone Star. Some started their own businesses and had to find work, operating from a central location and going to the ranches and farms that needed them on a daily basis. Some worked in academia, teaching the rising generation about horse care and shoeing and everything a farrier needed to know.

No matter what, Henry felt like he'd finally found something he could do for longer than a couple of months, and he sighed as he came to a stop in front of where he'd live for at least the next year. "We made it."

"You sure did," Paul said, and he got out of the truck as Daddy pulled in beside them. "I'll get Stormchaser out for you." His door slammed, and Henry pressed his eyes closed again.

"Lord," he prayed, the word barely slipping out from beneath his tongue. His mouth certainly didn't move, because he didn't want anyone to see him talking to himself. And he wasn't doing that anyway—he was talking to God.

"I know I made a mess of things with Angel, and I've tried to fix it. Please, please, please help me to have some dignity when I see her again, and bless her with a forgiving heart."

He had no idea if she was still seeing her boyfriend or not. It wasn't like they talked about personal things. He might've been able to do that if he hadn't disastrously kissed her when he'd discovered he'd gotten this apprenticeship.

But she'd shoved him away, those blue eyes like liquid lightning and told him to "Get in control of yourself."

He'd apologized profusely, right there in person and later in emails and texts. She'd finally told him it was over and done, and he didn't need to keep saying he was sorry. So he'd stopped that too.

Henry also knew that in the couple of seconds before Angel had pushed him away, with his mouth on hers, she'd kissed him back. Absolutely, definitely, for-sure had kissed him back.

His lips tingled just thinking about it, and he mentally commanded them to stop. He sighed again, this one filled with frustration.

"Help me to be in control of myself," he said, and then he opened his eyes. In the next moment, Momma opened his door, and he turned toward her.

"You ready, baby?"

"Yeah." Henry slid from the truck and into his mother's arms. She had a fiery streak too, and she'd often passed Henry to Daddy as he'd grown up, because she didn't know what to do with him. She'd told him once that God had told her to "simply love him," and she'd been doing that and leaving the disciplining and lectures to Daddy.

Henry hugged her and said, "I hope I make you proud, Momma."

"You do, Henry." She pulled away, her dark eyes filled with worry. "Of course you do."

"I know I'm not Paul." He looked down and scuffed his feet along the tufts of grass growing through the dirt. "But—"

"You do not need to be Paul," Momma said. "Look at me, Henry."

It took him a moment to look up, but he managed it. She wore a fierce look of determination on her face now, and Henry wasn't sure what to do with it. "I have never wished you were more like Paul," she said. "Never once. I have loved being your mother, even if you pushed me and stretched me, and I had no idea how to be that mother for you."

Part of him wanted to apologize, but he wasn't sure for what, so he stayed silent.

Momma put one hand on his shoulder and the other cradled his face. "You are an amazing young man, Henry. You work hard, and you're so smart, and you're fun." She smiled. "You have made me and Daddy so proud, baby. Okay?"

"Yeah, okay."

"Repeat it back to me."

"Momma." He scoffed and looked away. "I'm not gonna do that."

"Yes," she said. "Repeat it back to me."

He met her eyes again, his cells blazing in such a way that told him he wore a fierce look on his face too. "I'm not ten years old."

"You need to hear yourself say it," she said.

Henry took in a big breath as Daddy started taking boxes to the porch. He exhaled and looked at his mother again. "I know you and Daddy are proud of me."

"We love you."

"I know you and Daddy love me."

"You're going to be the best farrier Lone Star has ever seen." She smiled at him, her lips painted a perpetual red that Henry had grown up with.

He grinned back at her and chuckled, so glad she'd broken the tension inside him. "I'm going to be the best farrier Lone Star has ever seen."

Momma nodded, like what she wanted would absolutely come true. "Good. Now, let's go move you in and go to lunch. I'm starving." She turned and opened the back door while Henry moved around her to lower the tailgate.

He went up the steps first, and he knocked once before opening the door. "Levi?"

The person standing in the kitchen wasn't Levi, but a woman, and since Henry was already in motion, he couldn't stop himself as she turned.

Angel White stood there, holding a steaming mug of something, stirring it with a spoon. "He's out in the stables," she said coolly, those blue eyes sending fire right into Henry's lungs.

He came to a complete stop, for he hadn't anticipated finding her in his house.

"I've got everything you need, cowboy," she said, and oh, she shouldn't say things like that.

She doesn't mean it that way, he chastised himself. *Get control of yourself and your hormones.*

Henry forced himself to move forward, because he could hear someone's boots coming up the steps behind him. His father, and that only made Henry's pulse clatter through his body even more than it already was.

"The final contract?" he managed to croak out as he went past the dark brown couch in the cabin. He'd seen it in the video walkthrough, but it looked even more comfortable in person.

"Yes, sir," Angel said, her gaze switching to the doorway behind him. "I can wait until you're settled, but I've got it here." She moved over to the small round table in the corner of the kitchen and pulled out a chair. A manilla folder sat there—with his final contract, he assumed—and Angel sat in front of it and set down her coffee mug.

Henry carried a box he suddenly didn't know where to put, and he had to watch his father turn to go down the hall to the bedrooms. Of course. Most of Henry's stuff would go in his bedroom.

"Uh, yeah," he said, not sure where his brain had gone. "Let me put this down, and I'll come right on back." The box in his hands slipped, and Henry lunged to catch it. Embarrassment squirreled through him at his sweaty palms, and he hurried to follow his father once more.

"I just have to sign something," he said as he dumped the box on the floor. "You guys don't have to unpack without me."

"We got it," Daddy said in a chipper voice. "You go do what you need to do."

Henry nodded, turned, and as he walked down the hall toward Angel, he wiped his palms on his jeans, hoping when he shook her hand he wouldn't leave hers dripping wet.

Chapter Thirty-Eight

Angel pushed against the nervous masculine energy flowing toward her. Henry was a bundle of anxiety this morning, and she couldn't say she was surprised. She hadn't been able to sleep much last night, and she'd been telling herself it was because today was move-in day. And move-in day was stressful for her on a lot of levels.

But faced with the tall, broad-shoulders, handsomely hot Henry Marshall, Angel knew she'd been lying to herself. She'd known it last night too, but it had been easier to rationalize away.

Not anymore.

"I just need your signature for the rental agreement," she said, refusing to make eye contact as Henry neared the table. "It's separate from the apprenticeship." She shrugged one shoulder in an attempt to be nonchalant, but if he could see her pulse, he'd know how he affected her. At least she'd broken up with her boyfriend, so she didn't have the crushing guilt she'd had back in February. When she'd kissed Henry Marshall back.

"I mean, they're connected, but separate." She fake-glanced at him as he sat down right next to her. "So you need to sign this."

She flipped open the folder, her hand flying right into her coffee mug as if she'd released a spring and it had finally been let loose. The mug slipped and hot liquid splashed over the rim and onto the papers.

"Oh, good gravy," she muttered as she pulled her hand away. She hadn't gotten a paper towel, but Henry sprang right back to his feet to get her one.

"Here you go." He pressed the paper towel

onto the puddle on the page, and the dark liquid seeped into it.

Angel looked at him then, but he was settling back to his seat, the paper towel still there, the coffee stain still spreading through it. He looked at her, and the whole world froze.

Her heartbeat kept booming through her, and her breath going in tickled her nose. But she couldn't speak, couldn't think, couldn't even remember why she'd come to this cabin.

Through all her preparations to see Henry again, she had not anticipated this complete freezing of herself.

He had such nice eyes, and he'd recently gotten his dark hair cut. His beard sat neatly trimmed on his face, his sideburns melting up into the short sides of his hair. He wore his cowboy hat, and oh, that thing should be criminal on a man as good-looking as Henry.

He checked every physical-looks box for Angel, and she absolutely couldn't have that. *What are you going to do about it?* The thought emerged from all the other stuck things inside her, and she managed to blink.

"I can reprint this," she said.

Henry shifted, as if he didn't quite fit on the small kitchen chair. "If I can still sign it, it'll be fine." He pulled the folder toward him and used the edge of the paper towel to further dry the paper. "Oh, it's up at the top. I'm sure it's fine."

He balled up the paper towel and tossed it to the table, his eyes already scanning the page. It was a simple contract stating that his rent would be zero dollars from June first to May thirty-first, but that he'd be responsible for a flat-rate utility fee each month. Fifty dollars.

Lone Star fed the cowboys, horsemen, and farriers who worked on the ranch three times each week, did special holiday celebrations, and whatever else Angel could put together without losing her sanity or sleep.

"You got a pen, Angel?" The way he said her name in that sentence made it sound like an endearment, like a pet name, not her real name.

She held a pen in her hand, but she didn't quite realize it. "I...." She looked at him again, and this time, Henry cocked his head at her, tipping that cowboy hat smile sideways.

"Are you okay?" he murmured, his eyes darting over to his brother as he walked through the kitchen with a stack of two boxes. "I mean, I'm sure you're fine, but I don't want us working together to be awkward. I was kind of hoping it would only be weird for a minute."

Angel came to her senses, nodded, and lifted the pen. "It's not going to be awkward."

He took the pen with one eyebrow raised, didn't question her further, and signed his name to the contract with a flourish.

"And the final contract," she said, needing to get away from the cowboy-scented cologne, the piney goodness coming from him, and that smile. He wasn't even aiming it at her, but she felt it dive right into her heart and start to swim around. That so wasn't good.

She pointed to the part he'd protested about. "Daddy agreed to the change about working only with the master farriers."

"Thank you," Henry said. "I really can learn from anyone. Jake is an amazing farrier."

Angel merely nodded, and Henry flipped the page and signed his name for a second time. He sat back like he'd just finished a major project, a long sigh slipping from between his lips. He tossed the pen to the table, took off his cowboy hat, and scrubbed his free hand through his hair.

Sugar cubes, she swore in her head. The man had gorgeous hair—and a lot of it—and Angel needed to get out of this cabin, now. Stat. Immediately.

She reached for the pen and the semi-soaked folder. "Thank you, Henry," she said as diplomatically as she could. Did he hear that catch in her voice when she said his name? A man like Henry Marshall...of course he did.

He looked at her curiously, and Angel ducked her head, expecting her hair to fall down. Of course it didn't, because summer had come, and that meant Angel put her hair in a ponytail every day just to survive.

"Roll call tomorrow morning at seven," she said. "Welcome to Lone Star." With that, she headed for the door, nearly colliding with a beautiful, dark-haired woman as she did. "Oh, sorry, ma'am."

Her chest squeezed at the life in Henry's momma's face as she smiled. "You're fine." She quickly set down the bag in her hands. "You must be Angel White. Henry's told us so much about you."

"Has he?" Angel couldn't even imagine what Henry would've told his parents about her. It wasn't like they were friends, despite the amazing kiss he'd bestowed upon her a few months ago.

"He said you fought for him to be here," his momma said. "He's so thankful and real excited to be working here."

"Momma," Henry said, his voice carrying a warning tone. He pressed in close to Angel, and oh, she couldn't have that. Not when his body heat seeped into the skin along the back of her arm and her side, and not when his intoxicating scent tickled her nose—and kicked up her attraction to him—again. "What are you saying to her?"

"Nothing," his momma said, looking at her

son. Angel could see where he got his dark features and some of his sass, though his mother hadn't said anything bad at all.

Angel's pulse hammered at her to get out of there, for an entirely new reason this time. "Well, I'll leave y'all to get settled. We are having dinner tonight, Henry. In the barn dining room."

"Yes, ma'am," he said, and Angel slipped past his momma and out of the house. She held her head high as she went down the steps and past the trucks, her goal anywhere she could get where no one could see her.

The stable ahead was her best option, and Angel made her strides as long as possible without breaking into a run. When she entered the shadiness of the stable and darted around the corner, her breath came in quick pants.

She pressed the folder to her chest with both arms crossed over it, trying to breathe, and breathe, and *breathe*.

Her momma's illness didn't affect her too badly most days, but sometimes—like right now—Angel could feel how sick she was, and the hurt and grief and worry of that slapped at her until she couldn't ignore it.

Tears ran out of her closed eyes, and Angel couldn't stop them. She'd be horrified and humiliated if anyone saw her like this, and yet, she couldn't move away from the wall which only provided the barest of protections.

Lord, she thought, but her prayer couldn't continue. She simply didn't have the mental resources to put her plea to the Lord in words. It didn't matter. He knew what she was going through, and He already knew what she needed.

The soft huff of a horse's breath touched her neck and shoulder, and Angel opened her eyes. She hiccuped as she breathed in, everything that had gone rigid inside her starting to loosen as the equine dipped her head and pressed the long length of her nose against Angel's shoulder and upper arm.

She turned into the horse, one hand coming up to hold onto her mane. "Hey, girl," she whispered. "Yeah, I'm okay."

She wasn't, and both of them knew it, but if

she could just stand here for while, she could wipe her face of any teary evidence and get back to her house for a few minutes before she had to go give the paperwork to Daddy.

Then she wouldn't have to see Henry until that evening, and he'd be with a lot of other cowboys. Surely he wouldn't affect her as strongly as he had today every time she ran into him, and she took a long breath in as she reminded herself she hadn't completely broken down over Henry.

But his mother.... She sniffled again, wishing she didn't have such pinching unfairness streaming through her. Wishing she wasn't quite so angry at literally everyone and everything for her family situation. A sick, now almost absent mother. An aging, grumpy father who loved her dearly but sometimes didn't know how to show it. A disabled brother who she loved with her whole soul, but who required someone to look after him pretty much all the time.

Everything felt too heavy for her to carry alone—Lone Star itself housed over two hundred horses that required around-the-clock care. They—*She*—employed almost two dozen men to do that job, and they all reported to her.

Her.

"I'm too small to do this," she whispered to the horse, really trying to tell God she needed help.

At the same time, she was also pretty angry with God for putting her in this situation in the first place. Even as she called on Him, and believed in Him, and loved Him, she desperately wanted Him to make things right.

For He'd let them go wrong, and He expected her to pick up the pieces. It sure seemed wildly unfair to Angel, but she didn't know what to do about it.

Daddy had taught her to square her shoulders, lift her head, take a breath, employ her faith, and go to work.

So Angel stayed with the horse for several more long minutes, until she felt like she could breathe and talk and face anyone on the ranch, and then she did those things.

She squared her shoulders and scrubbed

her face clean. She lifted her head and tightened her ponytail, putting everything back together. She took in a breath until her lungs felt like they'd explode, held it, then let it all out. Let it all go.

"I love Thee, Lord," she said. "I love my momma and daddy and brother. I love this ranch. I love this life You have given me, and bless me to be grateful for it. Bless me to be able to shoulder all the burdens You have placed upon me, for I know Thou wouldn't give me anything I can't handle."

With her faith properly stitched in place, Angel faced the bright square of sunlight coming in through the open stable door.

And she went to work.

Chapter Thirty-Nine

Caroline put another swimming suit in her suitcase, then took it back out. "Do I even need one suit?"

She paced away from her bed, so many neurons firing through her. She hadn't taken a road trip in years, and certainly not with her boyfriend.

The thought of Dawson calmed her, and she looked in the mirror above her bureau. "Lord," she said. "This is make-or-break for me."

It had been three weeks since she'd made

her night-drive to Dawson's cabin, cried in front of him, confessed several things, and eaten ice cream until he was yawning every other second.

They'd been texting and talking as normal since then, but they both knew this trip would set a defining line for both of them. She wasn't sure what it was for him, and to be honest, Caroline had no idea what this road trip would do for her either.

She only knew it would do something.

So she finished packing just in the nick of time, as Dawson rang the doorbell just as she leaned heavily into her bag to get it to zip closed.

"Come in!" she called, though Belle was home and could surely answer the door. She somehow knew the front door had opened, and she hefted her bag off her bed and started to wheel it down the hall to the living room.

She paused when she heard Belle laugh in a way Caroline hadn't in a long time. Months. Judy did too, and Caroline inched past her bag to see the scene in the living room.

Dawson held Judy in his arms, the two of them smiling and giggling as he held out a doll for her.

She took it, and Caroline switched her attention to Belle. She glowed, positively *glowed*, as she pressed both hands to her heart.

"We'll miss you," she said to Dawson. "But Caroline is *so* excited, and you two are going to have the time of your lives."

Dawson chuckled and said, "I don't know about that, but I'm excited too." He set Judy down and turned toward the hallway, where he caught sight of Caroline. "Oh, hey, sweetheart."

Caroline wasn't sure of all the things running through her heart and mind. She only knew one thing—she loved Dawson Rhinehart.

So she rushed toward him and took his face in her hands and kissed him, the words, *I love you, I love you, I love you*, running through her head.

Caroline couldn't wait to get out of the truck, but she forced herself to stay belted until Dawson came to a complete stop. Then she groaned as she spilled from the truck in front of the hotel he'd chosen for their first night stay of their road-boat trip.

A hotel in Shreveport, Louisiana, as they had a fourteen-hour drive from Three Rivers, Texas to New Orleans, where their ship would disembark and head up the Mississippi River.

She put both hands on her lower back and bent backward, feeling the pull up and down her body. "Nine hours in the car is too long," she griped to Dawson as he came around the front of the truck.

He simply tossed her a smile and said, "Amen," as he hurried inside. "I'm going to hit the restroom, and then I'll get our rooms."

"Okay," Caroline called after him as the hotel entrance swallowed him. Dawson hadn't scared her once on the drive here, and they'd had bouts of silence mixed with plenty of conversation too.

Right now, Caroline's head ached, and she

was simply ready to be alone again. She wasn't sure what that meant about her, or Dawson, or the two of them. Perhaps she just needed to get out of the small space of the truck and let her thoughts roam for a few minutes.

Her stomach growled, as lunch had been hours ago. Dawson had stopped for drinks and snacks, but her belly wanted real food, and she turned back to the truck to get her purse. After such a long drive, she just wanted a bellhop to come collect her bags and lead her to the nicest room in the hotel.

Neither she nor Dawson were made of money, though, and they'd gotten regular rooms at discount rates. She'd pulled their bags from the truck bed by the time Dawson returned, and he said, "Hey, you don't need to do that." He took her backpack from her and shouldered it himself. "I was coming right back."

"I'm capable," she said.

"Mm, yes, you are." He kissed her quickly and then faced the hotel. "They weren't busy inside, so we should be ready for dinner soon." He glanced over to her, and she wasn't sure what her face looked like, but he paused. "You don't want to go to dinner."

"I'm tired," she admitted. "Who knew driving could be so tiring?"

He grinned at her and shook his head as he chuckled. "Maybe we're not cut out for road tripping," he said. "Because it's a lot of driving." He led the way into the hotel, and Caroline let him take the lead to get their room assignments and keys. The front desk clerk went over the Internet passwords and pointed out the way to the elevators, but Dawson leaned into the counter.

"We're tired, but hungry. Can we get room service here?"

"I'm sorry, sir," the woman said. "We don't have room service, but we have a restaurant in the corner of the first floor, and you can call and do a take-out order."

"Okay, thanks," he said.

She put a couple of pamphlets on the counter in front of him. "Or you can order from several places nearby. They deliver right to the room."

Dawson swiped the papers from the counter and said, "Thank you, ma'am," with the tip of his hat. The woman practically preened under his attention, and she glanced over to Caroline as if just seeing her for the first time.

Caroline gave her a smile, using up some of the dregs of her energy.

"You look tired," Dawson said. "What's up? We didn't leave until eight-thirty."

"I maybe didn't sleep well last night," she said as she turned to go with him to the elevators.

"Too excited?"

"Yes," she said simply.

He yawned, nodded, and pointed to himself. "Me too." They got on the elevator, and he pushed the eight for their floor. "I sure did like today," he said. "Just me and you, without any wind, or rain, or dogs, or crows."

"Oh, come on," she teased, bumping him with her hip. "You love the dogs and the crows."

He laughed, and Caroline's second wind

started to grow in her chest. "Yeah," he said. "But I literally never take a vacation from the ranch. It feels weird...and nice."

"Yeah," she said as she leaned into him. "I don't take many vacations either."

"When we're married, I'd like to take a vacation at least once a year."

Caroline's eyebrows went up. "When we're married?" They hadn't had this conversation at all in the past eight hours, though they had another five or six to go tomorrow. Then they had to get on their boat by three p.m., and off they'd be on the Mississippi River.

Dawson wouldn't look at her, and the bell on the elevator dinged, saving him. "This way," he said roughly. Caroline followed him off the elevator, her mind fuzzing a little with every step she took. The hallway snaked around, and she hoped she'd be able to get out if necessary.

He keyed open one door and dragged his suitcase inside. "You're right next door," he said, and he moved to that one and held the key to the electronic pad. It beeped and flashed green, then he pushed down on the handle, and the door opened.

He entered first and held the door for her, so she could wheel her suitcase past him and into the room. The air hadn't been circulating, and a certain stuffiness entered her nose and lungs. She scooted her bag against the wall and searched for the thermostat while Dawson lingered in the doorway.

"What do you want to do for dinner?" he asked.

She tapped on the down arrow to get the AC pumping. "You decide." Caroline ducked back around the corner and found him looking at her. "I really don't care. I don't want to go out, but if you order something, I'll come to your room, and we can have a picnic."

Grinning, she moved toward him. She ran her hands up his chest and leaned into him, her mouth nearly catching on his as she said, "This was a great first day of road tripping."

"Yeah?" His eyes had fallen closed, and he hadn't backed up an inch. "You're too tired to eat."

"Baby, I'm never too tired to eat." She pressed her lips to his. "I'm just too tired to go out. But give me a half-hour, and I'll come see if your room is nicer than mine."

He chuckled, his hands encircling her, drawing her closer. "They're exactly the same, baby." He released the door, which he'd been holding with his foot, and it slammed noisily closed.

Caroline wrapped her arms around him and let him hold her there in the narrow hallway of the hotel room.

"Caroline," he whispered. "I want to talk about marriage and family on this trip."

She stilled, grateful for a beating heart and breathing lungs that never stopped. She straightened and studied his face. He wore seriousness there, and she loved the flecks of darker blue in his aquamarine eyes. She didn't need to be afraid of any conversations she had with this man, because that was what they were—conversations.

Not demands. Not a dictatorship, with a

king telling her what to do, how to think, where to be and when.

"I do too," she said.

"Yeah?"

She smiled and traced her fingers down his sideburn and along the side of his jaw, his beard soft and prickly beneath her fingers. "Yeah, baby."

"Good," he said, his voice back to rough and husky, like he'd swallowed a nail or two and had a wound near his windpipe. "Because I'm in love with you, and we need to start making plans if we're really going to be serious."

Caroline pulled in a breath. "Dawson Rhinehart," she whispered. "Don't you say it if you don't mean it."

He gave her a soft smile. "I've already said it, darlin'." He kneaded her closer, until she had to shut her eyes she was so close.

Behind her eyelids, in the semi-darkness, everything was easier to see, to feel, to say. So she said, "I'm in love with you too."

Dawson pulled in a breath, but Caroline

didn't open her eyes to see him. She wanted to bask in this moment, this feeling of contentment, where she'd finally released the secrets of her heart, and a very good, very handsome cowboy had received them for safekeeping.

"Caroline Thompson," he murmured. "Don't you say it if you don't mean it."

She smiled, her muscles like melting frosting over hot cinnamon rolls. "I've already said it, baby."

He kissed her gently, the movement intensifying and increasing until he'd stolen her breath with the passion and love in his stroke. She hoped she was kissing him back in the same way, and when he broke the kiss and rested his forehead against hers, his breath came quickly.

"Can you answer my questions for me now?" he asked.

"Which ones?"

"The one about when our year started," he said. "And the one where I'd like to know if the wedding has to be after the twelve months, or the proposal has to wait until then." He did ease back then, but Caroline couldn't quite meet his gaze.

"If you can't answer—"

"I can." She settled her pulse and looked up at him. "I think New Year's Day was our first date. The breakfast at your cabin."

"Great," he said without missing a beat.

She swallowed, suddenly so unsure of herself. "And I don't think you'll like this, but I think the diamonds have to wait until the twelve months are up."

His jaw tightened, but he nodded. "Fair enough."

"Are you upset?"

He ducked his head and tracked his lips along her neck. "Only because I want to be with you," he whispered. He kissed up to her ear. "But otherwise, no, sweetheart. I can respect your rules, and besides."

Dawson lifted his head and stepped away from her as his stomach growled. "This gives me time to talk to Duke and my daddy about a place for us to live on the ranch."

"You think I'm just going to come live on the ranch with you?"

He opened the door that joined their rooms, but his door was locked. He had to face her and backtrack to the door, where she stood. He grinned at her and said, "Yeah, sweetheart. I think you're going to come live on the ranch with me, and my dog, and those crows, and we're going to have an amazing life."

After kissing her quickly, he said, "I'm going to go order dinner and take a shower. I'll unlock my door when I'm done, and you can just come over, okay?"

She nodded, and Dawson pulled open her door and left. The resulting slam made her flinch, and Caroline hugged herself as she walked through the room to the window.

"Lord," she whispered to the scene beyond her window—a courtyard with a swimming pool in it. "Did I do the right thing with my twelve-month rule?"

She didn't get a sick feeling in her gut, and she relaxed her arms. "I love him," she said next. "I know that, but I still want to see what life will be like during harvest, during the round-up, during the holidays, for his birthday. I want to be prepared, and that's not a bad thing, right?"

She once again didn't get any indication that it was, and she relaxed even more. "How am I doing?" she asked next, a dangerous question when talking to God. "I feel like I've been giving You more and more of my troubles to carry, and I'm real grateful for that. If there's something specific You want from me, please let me know."

God once again remained silent, but Caroline waited. She'd learned over the past couple of months that sometimes the Lord spoke softly, and she had to stand still to hear Him.

Her mind felt sharp despite her earlier exhaustion, and after several long, still, silent moments, she finally felt more than heard, *I am pleased with you, Caroline.*

She wept openly, basking in the warm love of God right there in a hotel in Shreveport. As she calmed and wiped her eyes, she closed her eyes and murmured, "Thank you."

For the assurance that she was on the right path.

For a second chance at a life she wanted to live.

For the love of a cowboy like Dawson Rhinehart.

Oh, and for this road-boat trip that had already changed her life.

Chapter Forty

Six Months Later:

Dawson ducked under the fence and strode toward the starter burrows he'd gotten permission to develop on the state land bordering the ranch. The burrowing owls had left the ranch in August, after their chicks had been born and taken flight.

But since they normally returned to their nests to lay their eggs during breeding season, Dawson expected them to return. Caroline did too, and while they hadn't been that big of a problem for the eight months they'd called the Rhinehart Ranch home, Dawson had petitioned the state to build "starter burrows" on the state land only twenty yards from the border of the ranch.

When Link had added his name to the petition, it had gone through, and Dawson expected his friend to show up at any time with his horse and a shovel. They needed to loosen the dry, baked dirt out here in order to make the ideal burrowing holes the owls liked.

Dawson had already installed the tree-like structure that would provide the perches for the owls, and it looked like a winter-time tree: leafless and barren, with craggly branches reaching up, left, and right in strange angles.

He'd taken the branches from his mother's contorted Filbert bush at the house, and he'd used wooden nails to attach them to a pole similar to what they used for their fences on the ranch.

The sun shone overhead despite the New Year's holiday. He'd skipped the firemen's fundraising breakfast in favor of working on the burrows this morning, and he planned to see Caroline at his cabin within the hour.

He looked up into the sky, searching for his crows. Thankfully, he didn't see them, and while he had his head tipped back, he prayed, "Lord, I've got a lot riding on Rocks. Can you please guide him to the beads I left out?"

Foolishness filled him, because Dawson realized in that moment that he'd literally planned a proposal around a *crow*. A flighty bird that he hadn't seen in at least a couple of days.

He put his head down and got to work on the burrows, glad when Link showed up only a few minutes later. He tethered his horse to the fence, then came over it and toward Dawson.

"Hey, brother." He clapped hands with Dawson, pumped his hand, and then pulled him into his chest for a quick bump-hug. Link radiated joy, and Dawson fed off of it. "How's it going?"

They both surveyed the man-made burrows, and Dawson thought it looked like the Taj Mahal for owls. The nearby scrub brush provided some shade and additional camouflage from predators, and if the owls would nest out here, neither Dawson nor Link would have to alter their ranching operations.

"It looks amazing," Link said.

"I'm just roughing up the land," Dawson said. "Because Caroline said if it's too hard, the owls can't dig their own burrows."

"You've got the pipe?"

"Yep, in the back of the truck."

Lincoln nodded, and they got back to work in softening the ground. Dawson then went to retrieve the four-inch drainage pipe he'd use to create the entrances to the future burrows. He gloved his hands and rejoined Link with the pipe.

They only had one, but Link helped Dawson get it in position, and then Dawson jammed it into the ground as far as he could. Then he pulled it out, and Link scraped the earth out, leaving a forty-five-degree angle entrance for the owls.

After a half-hour, Dawson wiped the sweat from his forehead and reseated his cowboy hat. "I think this is enough."

"It's amazing," Link said. "Better than where the owls were on the ranch, I think."

"I agree," Dawson said. "I'll bring Caroline out later today and get her opinion."

"Let me know if I need to come back." He turned and started back toward his horse, and Dawson turned away from the built burrows to go with him.

"Today's the day," he said to Link, who glanced over to him. "I'm going to ask Caroline to marry me." He couldn't keep the smile from his face, and he didn't have anything to hide from Link anyway.

"That's amazing, Dawson," Link said. He laughed and added, "You're going to love being married."

"Yeah?"

"Oh, yeah," Link said. "It's amazing to come home to your wife after a busy day on the ranch." They went over the fence, and Dawson put the pipe in the bed of his truck. "Where are you going to get married?"

"I'm not sure what Caroline has in mind," Dawson said. "I'm gonna leave it up to her."

"Smart. I can ask about using True Blue if you want."

"I mentioned that to her," Dawson said. "And I said we can just get married here, outside. I don't know what exactly she wants." Mostly, Caroline didn't know exactly what she wanted, so though they'd talked about it, Dawson couldn't say for sure where they'd get married.

"How are you askin' her?" Link asked.

Dawson sighed and ran his hand up the back of his neck, bumping his cowboy hat forward. "Well, I'm hoping this crow friend of mine will find the gold Mardi Gras beads I left on the side of the road near my cabin," he said. "I've attached a diamond ring to it, and she's coming for breakfast this morning." He shrugged, feeling stupider and stupider with every word he spoke.

"I don't know."

"She's gonna say yes," Link said as he came to a stop next to his horse. "I've seen the two of you, and she's totally in love with you."

"Yeah," Dawson said with a sigh. "I love

her too, but I'm worried this proposal is going to be a nightmare." He should've just put the diamond in his pocket, gotten down on both knees the moment Caroline pulled up to the cabin, and asked her to be his.

"Well, Uncle Bishop says the house is coming along real nice. I didn't ride up the road, but I'm gonna go back that way to look at it."

Another smile sprang to Dawson's face. "Yeah," he said. "The house is looking real good."

Link grinned at him and pulled him into another brotherly hug. "I'm really happy for you, Dawson."

"Thanks, Link."

Link pulled away, his grin as contagious as his happiness. "Stay in touch with the owls and the wedding venue."

"You'll be the first to know on both," Dawson said.

Link stepped up and swung himself into the saddle, pulled his horse around, and said, "Good luck, Dawson," as he rode away, his shovel balanced horizontally in front of him on the saddle.

"Thanks," he called after his friend, and he once again found himself looking up into the sky.

Still crow-less.

"This is so going to be a disaster," he muttered to himself as he moved to get behind the wheel of his truck. "But I'm doing this today, with or without the help of a silly crow."

And with that, Dawson headed back to the cabin where he'd only live for another couple of months. Then his house would be finished, and he'd move in there ahead of his marriage to Caroline.

"If she says yes," he growled as he drove. "She has to say yes first."

Chapter Forty-One

Caroline didn't see Dawson's truck when she arrived at his cabin. The absence didn't concern her, and she parked, reached over to the passenger seat, and picked up the sheet pan of cooked, crispy bacon. She'd made it this morning in preparation for her second annual New Year's Day breakfast with Dawson.

She'd been looking forward to this morning for weeks now, and she looked left as she got out of her SUV, expecting to see Dawson heading her way from out on the West End

Fence. He'd said he'd be working on the owl burrows this morning, but he'd meet her here at eight-thirty.

Maybe she'd shown up a few minutes early, but she went up the sidewalk to the front porch, then climbed the steps to the front door. She knocked, and when no one answered, she twisted the knob and entered the cabin.

"Dawson?" she called. "Brandon?"

No one answered, so Caroline continued to the counter at the back of the house and set down the pan of bacon. She turned to heat the oven, which would get the bacon slowly back to warm. She didn't need to cook it; she just wanted to warm it up a little.

Dawson had promised eggs, hash browns, and toast, and Caroline didn't really want to make more than she had. She would gladly sit with Dawson while he did, so she sat at the bar and pulled out her phone.

Are you almost here? she asked him. *I'm inside your house.*

She then tapped over to her maps app, where Dawson had shared his pin with her a few months ago. She smiled at the memory, because it had been a defining moment in time for her, for their relationship. It felt like such a spousal, ultra-significant-other thing to do, and while the ranch had been extremely busy during the harvest, then the round-up, then Market Day, she'd been able to find him any time she wanted to.

Then Dawson had slept for an entire weekend and gone right back to his regular day-to-day life. With her back in it, of course.

She'd partnered with Zona for food when the cowboys returned with the herd, and she'd come several times during the harvest simply to give Dawson and Brandon sandwiches out in the fields they were mowing, baling, turning, and then clearing.

No, she didn't super-love autumn on the ranch, other than the weather had cooled slightly, and the trees in the Panhandle had turned colors in the most glorious of ways.

She found Dawson out near the West End Fence, but his status had been updated six minutes ago. He certainly would've left by now or called her to say he'd be late. He hated running late, and Caroline slid from the barstool and moved toward the front door.

Outside, she found him literally pulling up to the cabin, and she tucked her phone in her pocket in favor of smiling at her handsome cowboy boyfriend. She leaned against the post of his porch as he parked and got out.

"Hey, sweetheart," he called. "Sorry I'm late."

"You're not," she assured him, though she didn't move. She loved it when he hurried to her, as he was now, and she giggled as he took the steps two at a time to get to her.

He drew her into his arms and whispered, "Hey," in a much softer, sexier voice.

"Happy New Year," she said.

"Oh, is it New Year's?" He stepped back and gave her a sly smile. "Let's go make breakfast." He took her hand in his and headed for the door.

"I put the bacon in the oven. Or I was going to."

"Okay," he said. "I was thinking we could eat outside today. It's so nice."

"Sunny but not overly hot yet," she said. "That's great."

"Great." Dawson got busy in the kitchen, and Caroline simply sighed with such supreme satisfaction that she was back here, in this cabin, with this man.

She slipped onto his couch and lay back, her feet up on the armrest, so incredibly comfortable here. "How's the house coming?"

"Great," he said over the sizzling of something, probably the potatoes he'd just shredded and was now going to crisp up. "We can go by after breakfast, and I want you to come look at the burrows too."

"Of course," she said, her heartbeat dancing a jig behind her ribs. Today marked a year of her official dating relationship with Dawson, and she'd be lying if this was the first time she'd considered him asking her to marry him today.

He'd been putting all the pieces in place for months now, starting with meeting with his brother and father about building a house for her and him right here on the ranch. It turned out, there was a small one-bedroom cabin that looked one stiff wind away from blowing away on the road that led north toward Shiloh Ridge Ranch.

That land had been deemed Dawson's, and he'd started working with Bishop and Montana Glover to knock down the older structure and build a brand-new house. One she and Dawson could raise their family in, right here on the ranch.

Bishop had drawn up plans, and Dawson had included her in every decision along the way.

Now, all she needed was the diamond ring.

"We're ready," Dawson said as he went by the couch. "You didn't fall asleep, did you?"

"No," she said as she sat up. "I'm coming."

He carried a big tray in his hands, and he'd already dished up two plates of breakfast, and Caroline sat on her side of the table and let him serve her. He set the tray aside and sat across from her. After taking her hand, he bowed his head and said, "Lord, we're grateful for this food, our friendship, this land, and the New Year. Bless us to be happy and healthy, kind and patient, and we're grateful to have time together today. Amen."

"Amen," Caroline murmured, and she beamed across the table to Dawson. He picked up his fork and nudged the bottle of ketchup closer to her with it.

When she didn't move to use it or eat, he asked, "What?"

"I love you," she said, wanting him to know in this moment.

He grinned at her, a hint of a flush crawling into his face. "I love you too, darlin'."

She did pick up the ketchup bottle then, and Dawson cleared his throat. Alarms and alerts sounded through her, but when she took a sneaky peek at him, he'd simply cut into his over-easy eggs and started eating them. He picked up the salt-shaker, used it, and then did the same with the pepper. Another bite of egg, and her adrenaline eased.

She'd taken one bite of her ketchupped hash browns before she heard the distinct cawing of Nugget. "The crows are coming," she said as she looked out into the front yard.

"Did you toss them something shiny?" he teased.

"Not today." She smiled at him, because he wasn't really upset about her tossing out nickels here and there.

Nugget landed on the porch railing, only a few feet from where she and Dawson dined, and cawed again.

"Not so loud," Dawson told the crow. "We're right here."

Rocks didn't land on the railing, but Caroline saw him down on the grass. She stood and moved over to the railing to see him better. "He's got something," she said, not really sure what her eyes were seeing. All at once, it clicked. "Beads."

She turned toward Dawson. "He's got a string of beads."

"Does he?" Dawson got up too, but Caroline squished past him to get to the steps.

"I'll check and see if he's caught or if he's just carrying them."

"Okay," Dawson said from behind her, his voice almost stuck down in his throat. He coughed, and Caroline thought he'd maybe swallowed too fast.

Down the steps, she approached the crow, but he was a wild bird, and Rocks hopped away from her. He wasn't as verbal as Nugget—in fact, she'd never heard him make a sound. Nugget cawed again, and Caroline crouched down.

"Come on, bud," she said. "Are those beads stuck, or can you drop them?"

He hopped toward her, and she held still, her hands loose and nonmoving. Rocks came closer, and he lifted up his foot. He clearly had the string of gold beads clenched there, and she grinned at him.

"Yeah, you've found something awesome," she said. "You're so smart."

He dropped them, took flight, and landed on the railing next to Nugget. Caroline reached out and picked up the string of gold beads before she straightened. Something heavier hung down, and she moved her fingers to lift it up, to see what it was.

She sucked in a breath and couldn't look away from the shiny gold ring with a great big diamond on top.

"Caroline," Dawson said, and she spun to face him. He knelt on the porch and gestured to her. "Come here, darlin'."

Her legs felt like logs as she moved, but she somehow climbed the stairs until she stood at the same height as him, though he was down on both knees.

"I'm in love with you," he said. "It's been a year now, and we had an amazing road trip over the summer. And it sure looks like someone put this ring out there for Rocks to find especially for you."

He gently took the string of beads from her and expertly removed the ring from it, as if he'd put it there.

Of course he put it there, she thought as he looked up at her again. "We're building a house to raise our family in together. I know I'm not perfect, but I think we're perfect together, and I think we will make the best 'we' and the best 'us' there could ever be."

He held up the diamond ring. "Will you marry me?"

Caroline started to nod, her neck feeling like she'd lost all her bones. "Yes," she said, her voice scratchy and low. She cleared her throat, her smile widening. "Yes," she said again. "Yes, I'll marry you."

She laughed, enjoying Dawson's giddy grin. He tried to straighten it but couldn't quite do it as he slid the diamond onto her ring finger. They both stared at it for several long seconds, and then Caroline lifted her eyes to his.

She had another powerful moment of love, the way she had when Dawson had come to pick her up for their road-boat trip. She took his face in her hands and said, "I love you so much. Thank you for being so patient with me."

"We made it a whole year," he said. "It's not like you've never had to be patient with me."

"Yeah, the harvest was pretty rough."

He grinned and leaned in a touch more to

kiss her. She would never get enough of Dawson, of kissing him, of being his best friend, of being his.

"I love you, Caroline." He smiled at her and then reached out to use the post to help himself stand up. "And let me tell you, I was really worried that Rocks wouldn't find those beads." He exhaled and turned back to their breakfast.

"You planted those beads."

Dawson laughed as he sat down, and he didn't let her go by him to her seat. Instead, he pulled her onto his lap and kissed her again. "Of course I planted those beads," he said right before he slid his lips along her neck. "I can't wait for you to be my wife."

Caroline let her fingers slink through his hair, enjoying the way he held her and loved her.

"When can we get married?" he asked.

"I've talked to my mom and sister about it," she said. "I don't think we need anything extravagant."

He lifted his head and looked at her. "No?"

She shook her head. "How do you feel about maybe...March?"

"Sweetheart, I'd marry you tomorrow," he said. "Our house will be done by the end of February, so March sounds about perfect."

"I think so too," she said, pure joy spreading through her.

"Great," he said. "So we'll get married in March."

Nugget cawed, startling Caroline's attention over to the bird.

"Oh, go on, you," Dawson said good-naturedly. "Leave us be. You two have done what you needed to do today."

"Can they be in the wedding?" Caroline asked. "And Ruffin, of course."

Dawson looked at her with a hint of surprise in his gaze. "All right," he said after a beat or two. "They can all be in the wedding." He shifted, and Caroline stood to return to her own seat.

"Now," he said as he picked up a crispy slice of bacon. "Tell me where you want to get married."

Caroline took a bite of her toast, because she had made this decision already. She just hadn't told Dawson. She hadn't wanted to, because she'd been very clear with him—no diamonds until their year was up.

"First, I asked Belle to help me plan the wedding, and she's already got catering and flowers taken care of."

Dawson blinked, pure shock registering in those pretty eyes. "Okay," he said simply.

"Second, she's doing that, because I want to get married here. Right here, on Hidden Hills Ranch, where I fell in love with you, and where we're going to raise our family."

Everything about Dawson softened, and while he'd left this decision to her—and would likely allow her to make most of their wedding decisions—he very clearly wanted to get married at Hidden Hills. At the Rhinehart Ranch.

"Because I love your dog and the crows here," she said. "And I love this ranch, and I absolutely *adore* the cowboy who comes with it."

He grinned at her. "Well, I love Texas, and

I love this ranch, and I absolutely *adore* the idea of you at my side as we build our lives together."

She giggled, and he chuckled with her, and then they both sighed in unison too. That only got her laughing again, and when she sobered, she felt like God Himself had poured glittery stars into her bloodstream.

Caroline looked at Dawson, and he looked back at her. "I love you," she said at the exact same time he said, "I love you so much."

And that only got her to start laughing again, with Dawson joining her. She ducked her head, her eyes catching on that shiny diamond, and she felt very crow-like in her attraction to it. She couldn't wait to marry Dawson, and she lifted her toast to take another bite.

"I'll talk to your mom about where we can get married here," she said.

"Okay," he said. "I'm sure Zona and the girls would like to help too."

Caroline grinned at him. "Yes, we're going dress shopping next week."

His hand with a forkful of hash browns frozen. "Next week?"

Giddiness pranced through her. "I was hoping you'd ask me to marry you before then, but I figured I'd need a dress eventually anyway." She shrugged one shoulder and took that bite of her toast.

Dawson took his bite of breakfast too, gave her an almost-grumpy look, and said, "I suppose that's true."

"Now," Caroline said. "Can we talk about the honeymoon?"

"Please do."

"I want to go on another road trip."

"You do?" Dawson seemed surprised once again. "I didn't think you liked those long days of driving."

"Okay, not a road trip," she said. "A plane trip to the beach."

He grinned at her. "There it is."

"Can we do that?"

"Yes, sweetheart. Name the beach, and I'll get us there."

And she knew he would too. She nodded and said, "I'll work on it and let you know."

He tapped on his phone and tapped. "So... March. Do you want to get married on what? A Saturday? Sunday?"

"Saturday is fine," she said, nearing the end of her breakfast now.

"Saturday, March twelfth," he said, looking up. "Sound good?"

"Yes," she said, because she would marry him tomorrow too. "March twelfth sounds like the perfect day to become 'us.'"

I love second chance romances with my whole heart. And Texas. And enemies to lovers with a grumpy cowboy! I love Dawson and Caroline and their owl-rific romance. **I hope you did too!**

And keep reading for the first two chapters of the next book in the series, **THE COWBOY WHO WORKED LATE**, featuring the forbidden relationship between Henry Marshall and his boss, Angel White!

Did you know there are chapters and chapters of extra content in small town Three Rivers? If you're interested in deleted scenes from this book, as well as bonus chapters before it and following it, **become a subscriber by scanning the QR code below with your phone.**

Sneak Peek! The Cowboy Who Worked Late Chapter One:

Henry Marshall walked at Gilligan's flank, watching the horse pick up and put down his front hoof. "There's still something wrong," he muttered to himself. He'd been trying to get the horse to take shoes for a couple of months now, but now that they were on, he wasn't walking right.

As a farrier, Henry had several tactics to try, and believe it or not, horses didn't all wear the exact same kind of shoes. This was the third —and lightest—set he'd tried on Gilligan, and they still didn't seem quite right.

Bard wouldn't be happy about that, but Henry could come up with another suggestion for the rescue horse the owner had brought home several weeks ago. He truly believed every horse deserved the best care in the world, and he marveled that he'd been able to find such a perfect fit for him in a career.

Not only that, but Henry hadn't been on a date since he'd started at Lone Star, and he let out a sigh that left his body with more contentment than ever before. He couldn't believe that, as he really didn't like staying home at night, and being alone in the evening was even worse.

But since coming to Lone Star, Henry had been busier than ever. Still learning a lot in his field, though he'd completed his coursework nine months ago. Meeting new suppliers, owners, farriers, and horses took a lot of his energy, and he thanked the Lord every evening for the connections he was making through Bard and Angel White.

He really liked his cabinmate, a man named Levi, and they were known to leave the ranch on Friday nights, but they just went to a restaurant, ate and talked and laughed, and returned to the ranch. Nothing scandalous, and Henry hardly recognized his life these days.

A year ago, everything had been so different. Henry himself had been wildly different, and as he looked back to Gilligan, a keen sense of gratitude overcame him. His momma had taught him to acknowledge the Lord in all things, especially when the feelings struck him, so Henry said, "Thank you for this good life, Lord," as he walked.

Gilligan looked at him as he spoke, and Henry lengthened his stride to catch the equine at his shoulder. "This pair ain't for you, bud," he said. "I'm gonna take them off and put you in the pasture, okay?"

He put his hand on the horse's neck, and Gilligan crowded into him. He'd been underfed and overworked at his previous ranch, and Bard had taken him in an estate sale, along with a dozen other horses.

The horsemen at Lone Star had been rehabilitating them in the following days, weeks, and months, and because Henry's daddy owned an equine therapy unit, Henry had plenty of experience training and working with horses.

Gilligan had taken a shine to him, and only one other person could work with the horse—and that happened to be the worst person to work with Henry.

Angel White.

She'd been bringing her brother with her whenever she had to be in close proximity to Henry, something he'd absolutely noticed. He'd said nothing to her of it, and she even conducted his performance evaluations with the door open. He'd asked around, and none of the other men had to have their job skills, work ethic, or anything else critiqued where anyone walking by could hear.

Henry frowned internally, and Gilligan slowed and huffed through his lips. "Yeah, buddy, I feel the same way."

He'd not brought up the kiss from over a year ago now, and he wished God had not sharpened his memory of that moment, because he could relive it with precision any time he wanted. Asleep, awake, it didn't matter.

For Angel had kissed him back. He knew that, and he knew she knew it—which was probably why she didn't want to be in a closed-door room with him ever again.

He drew in a deep breath, getting a lot of horseflesh, the scent of fresh rain, and some notes of alfalfa as he prodded Gilligan to get moving again. The horse did what he wanted, and Henry had done more for the horses in his care than he'd ever done for any woman, for his siblings, even for his momma.

Most horsemen did the same, so Henry wasn't unique in that way. It simply surprised him, and he made a mental note to put it in his prayer journal that evening before he went to bed.

In the stable, he moved Gilligan back to the shoeing station, got the offensive shoes off, cleaned up his hooves, and turned him loose in the pasture with a few of his equine friends. Gilligan made no move to join them in the shade, where they snacked on the coolest grass.

He was a bit of an outcast still, and maybe that was why Henry connected to him so deeply.

"See you tomorrow, bud," he said before turning to return to the stable. He had a standing desk in the facility—all the horsemen and farriers did—and he found Gilligan's file and entered the notes for that day's trial.

He pulled out his phone and texted Bard. *Those shoes on Gilligan weren't right. When can I come over and chat with you about another solution?*

The older gentleman had retired completely from any administrative role at Lone Star, passing everything to his daughter, Angel. But he still liked to consult with his team leads on specific cases, and Henry and Gilligan qualified.

He wasn't glued to his phone the way Henry and others his age were, so he didn't expect Bard to answer immediately. He picked up the next folder, reviewed the notes for a pretty bay named Henrietta, and he went to retrieve her from her stall and get her feet back in shape.

Henry loved the fresh air he was privy to for his job. He loved the blue sky filled with puffy white clouds, and he loved the scratch of his gloves against his skin. He loved the view of his tools, the feel of leather along his arm, and the living, breathing animal at his side.

He chatted with Levi and a couple of other farriers throughout the afternoon, and by evening, he remembered he hadn't looked at his phone in a few hours. Bard had answered with, *Stop by whenever, son,* so Henry quickly texted back that he'd come by in the morning.

He then found several texts on his friends' group text. He appreciated his cousin for including him in the things he and his wife planned for their friends in Three Rivers, and Henry climbed the steps to his cabin and sat on the top one to read his messages.

I need a final count for game night on Saturday, Edith Ackerman had said. Finn's wife. *Depending on who's in for sure will determine what game we'll have ready. We'll also make food assignments once we know.*

She'd added a smiley face and a heart, and

Henry truly did feel like his friends in Three Rivers loved him.

We're in, Lincoln Glover had sent. He and his wife had been married for coming up on a year now, and Henry wasn't surprised at all to see his confirmation. Nor Dawson Rhinehart's. He and his fiancée would be there—and they'd be married in the next month.

Henry had enjoyed everyone's Valentine's Day pictures, and they'd all laughed when he'd sent one of him grinning next to a horse. He hadn't told them it was a male, but it hardly mattered. Everyone knew he wasn't dating anyone.

Oliver Walker had confirmed that he and his wife had a babysitter for their three kids and would be there. That made four couples, and Henry's internal frown started to form again. He'd brought a date to game night in the past, and sometimes he'd been paired with Dawson's brother. Sometimes Paul was his plus-one, but Paul had been dating someone for months now, and Henry expected to get a call from his brother any day now, telling him to clear his schedule for a summer wedding.

Not that Henry couldn't get home quickly. He could, and he wouldn't have to clear his schedule for anything. In fact, he and Finn had discovered that if Henry took a couple of back-roads, he could get to the ranch Finn owned, which bordered Three Rivers Ranch, where Henry had grown up and where his family still lived alongside Finn's.

No one else had answered, and as Henry started to text, in came Alex's message. *Nicki and I are going to the fertility clinic this weekend, so we won't be there. Hope it's fun.*

Henry's heartbeat jumped as if someone had thrown cold water in his face. He couldn't imagine wanting children and not being able to have them, and he backed out of the group text and sent one to Alex privately.

Praying for you and Nicki, brother.

Thanks, Alex said back. *We're meeting with an adoption counselor on Friday too. Nicki's not very happy about it, so any extra prayers for that would be appreciated.*

Why isn't she happy about it? Henry asked.

She wants a baby of her own, Alex said. *I think we should explore all options, so she agreed to go, but she's not too keen on adoption yet.*

Henry wasn't exactly sure of Nicki's age, but he knew she was quite a bit older than Alex, who'd just turned twenty-seven at the beginning of the year. She might be thirty-five by now, and Henry didn't know a whole lot about women, but he knew they couldn't have babies forever.

Prayers and good vibes for it all, Henry said. Then he went back to his main menu and texted Brandon Rhinehart. *Are you going to game night this weekend? Wanna be my date?* He added a laughing emoji, smiled in real life, and sent the text.

The main group string had several messages of condolences and *prayers coming* when Henry looked at it again. Brandon had not answered him, and Henry finally got up and went inside the cabin. The scent of baking bread met his nose, and he wasn't surprised to find Levi in the kitchen, an apron around his neck with flour dusted down the front of it.

"You're baking," he said as he closed the front door behind him. "Trouble with Shad?"

Levi threw him a look made of poisonous darts and went back to cutting lines in the top of an unbaked loaf of bread. "He's completely wrong about the growth rate on Berniece. That horse needs new shoes every three weeks, and it irritates me to the bone that he makes me wait four. For no reason."

He bent and put the bread in the oven, then moved to the counter, where another pile of unformed dough waited. He slammed his hands into it and continued. "Today, her hooves were all overgrown around the nails, and I couldn't get them out. I took pictures and sent them to him, and he came running right over." He rolled his eyes and abused the poor bread dough. "It's been twenty-four days, so he got after me for starting early. It's unbelievable."

Henry pulled out who barstool and sat, surveying the mess that was bread-making. "I'm sorry, Levi. For what it's worth, I'm on your side. I'd re-shoe Berniece every *two* weeks if it were me. No sense in making anyone suffer. It's not like we can't afford it."

Levi's dark eyes flashed. "Right?"

Henry's phone buzzed, and he looked at it. *I'm out*, Brandon said. *I have a date this weekend.*

He grinned at his device. *Same woman as last week?*

Yep, Brandon said. *And I can't ask for prayers after Alex's thing, so I'll just say I can't come. Sorry, bro.*

It's fine, Henry said, though he certainly couldn't show up stag. Most games they played at these parties were for couples, and Henry wouldn't go alone. His heart ached to go home for the weekend, though, so he texted Paul and asked him. Then his cousin Libby. And even his brother John.

None of them could go, and to add insult to injury, Edith messaged the group with, *That just leaves Henry. Are you in? Want to bring a date?*

He looked up at Levi, who'd gone quiet

after his rant. "Want to go to game night with my friends this weekend?"

"When? Saturday?"

"Yeah."

"Yes," Levi said, and Henry confirmed that he'd be there with "a friend." Satisfied, he set his phone aside for the evening, enjoyed the freshly baked bread with leftover chili from one of the cowboys from a couple cabins down, and kicked his feet up on the coffee table as Levi put on the Cowboy Channel and they found reruns of a rodeo out of Calgary.

He barely thought of Angel White, though the gorgeous blonde seemed to circle his mind whenever he started to get drowsy.

By Saturday, he couldn't wait for a day off, and since he didn't work Sundays or Mondays, he packed a bag with late afternoon sunshine shining through his window so he could stay with his parents for a couple of nights.

He heard the front door slam, and he called, "Hey, Levi, we have to leave in forty-five minutes." They'd planned to stop and get dinner in Stinnett before continuing on to his cousin's ranch for game night.

Levi didn't answer, and alarms rang through Henry's head when he heard boots running. *Running.* He twisted toward his open door. "Levi?" He went that way and caught Levi's retreating back as he dashed into the bathroom.

A moment later, an awful retching noise filled the cabin. Henry's pulse leapt and lunged, and he stayed where he was as he asked, "Hey, are you okay?"

"No," Levi moaned.

Henry's weekend plans flew right out the window, and he turned in a full circle. His packed bag waited for him, mocked him.

Levi moaned again as the water ran in the bathroom, and Henry moved to check on him. "I'm sorry, man," he said as he leaned over the sink and washed out his mouth. "I can't go to game night. I ate something that seriously doesn't agree with me." His skin was the pale gray color of a dry sidewalk, and his eyes seemed to sink into his face further than normal.

"It's fine," Henry said, though he now couldn't go to game night either. He wondered what his parents were doing on a hopping Saturday night on a ranch, forty-five minutes from civilization. How they lived so far out, Henry could not comprehend. "I'll just go stay with my folks. Let's get you to bed."

He put his hand on Levi's arm to steady him as he helped his friend into his bedroom. "There's loads of food here, and I'll let everyone know you're not feeling well, so they can check on you."

"Thanks, Henry," Levi said as he collapsed into his bed. He never made it, so the covers had been left where he'd flung them that morning and all he had to do was pull them over him, his eyes already settling closed.

Henry backed out of the room and returned to his, gathered his bag and his phone and went out to the kitchen. They had a group app for all the horsemen, cowboys, and farriers at Lone Star, and only the most important messages were meant to be shared on it.

This was one of those things, so Henry quickly typed out, *Levi isn't feeling well, and I'm headed to my parents' house for the weekend. Let's be sure someone comes by and checks on him from time to time, okay?*

That done, Henry needed to decide if he still wanted to grab something to eat in Stinnett, or maybe go all the way to Three Rivers and drive through somewhere there. Or he could make himself a sandwich here and stay for another couple of hours before he had to leave.

"Decisions decisions," Henry muttered as his phone lit up with affirmative responses that the others here would check on Levi for him. He was tired of making decisions.

He'd just opened the fridge when someone knocked on his door. "Come in," he called, because they never locked the door, and Henry knew everyone who lived and worked at Lone Star.

No one came in, and irritation snagged

through Henry. "Just come in," he muttered as he closed the fridge and went to answer the door. He pulled it open with, "You just walk in around here." When he saw the heavenly being on his porch, he said, "Oh," and backed up a step.

Since he'd worked with Angel White for a while now, he could recover much quicker than before. "Hey, Angel," he said. "What can I do for you?"

"Levi is ill?" She looked past him like Levi might be making dinner, the joke on the entire boarding stable.

"Threw up a few minutes ago," Henry said. "Said he ate something bad at lunch."

"What did he eat?" Her blue eyes roamed around, finally coming back to lock onto his. Henry loved her eyes, and he couldn't name the exact shade of blue they were. Stunning blue. Was that a color?

Maybe for a nail polish, he thought, and it made him smile. "I have no idea."

But a very dangerous idea had just entered his mind. He'd learned so much in the past couple of years about himself, about self-control, about his temper. But apparently, he hadn't yet learned to stop his tongue from wagging out his thoughts, because he said, "What are you doing tonight? Levi was supposed to be my date for a game night, and I can't go alone."

Angel blinked her long eyelashes at him, and blinked some more, and blinked some more. He'd never stunned the pretty woman into silence, though if he'd wanted to, asking her on a date would've sat at the top of his idea list.

What a stupid thing to do, he chastised himself, but he couldn't recall the words now. So he waited to find out what the lovely Angel White would say to his game night invite.

Sneak Peek! The Cowboy Who Worked Late Chapter Two:

Angel White gripped her cellphone so hard, she feared it might break. Only two words screamed through her head: *Game night.*

Game night, game night, game night.

Game night?

Henry stood up a step from her, a tall, imposing figure with such a handsome face. Big hands too. That deep, sexy voice, which said, "We were going to get dinner in Stinnett. We could do that, or I could—you could—we could

677

meet here and go straight to game night. It's at my cousin's farm in Three Rivers, so it's a bit of a drive." He took a quick breath. "A little over an hour."

A little over an hour, trapped in a truck with Henry Marshall. She wanted to go so badly, she almost started crying. At the same time, the rational, calm side of Angel's brain told her she'd been in desperate need of a break from this ranch for a month now. Anyone who asked her would elicit the same reaction.

Bottom line: Henry wasn't special.

He fell back a step. "Sorry I said anything," he said. "Can we forget it? Flint, Clay and Whit said they'd come check on Levi. I'll just cancel on game night and go see my folks." He pulled out his phone and started typing.

"...not going...to be able to...make it tonight..."

Angel slapped her hand over his phone, knocking it clean out of his hand. Henry yelped, and they both watched his device skitter across the floor. "What was that for?"

He turned and moved a couple of steps to pick up his phone.

He looked at her, pure accusation in those beautiful eyes. "You broke my phone."

Humiliation streamed through Angel, and combined with her sheer exhaustion and ultimate desperation for a break from everything happening in her personal life, with her family, and on the ranch, an instant, emotional tornado spiraled into existence.

"I—" Tears spilled from her eyes. "I'm so sorry, Henry." She couldn't stand to look at him, but she couldn't move either. She covered her face with both of her hands and sobbed into her palms.

Henry said something, but the words couldn't penetrate her turmoil. She fell into the warmth and safety of his arms, and she distinctly knew the door had closed, sealing her in his house.

He sat her down on the couch and pressed in close to her. He said soothing things and put his arm around her. Finally, after what felt like a long time, but was probably only a few breaths, his voice reached her ears.

"...talk to me, okay, Angel? You're okay, Angel, and you can talk to me, okay?"

She lifted her head and lowered her hands. "I'm so sorry. I'll buy you a new phone."

"I don't care about the phone."

Angel looked at him. "What?"

"I can't believe I'm going to say this, because it's so something my daddy said to me five thousand times growing up." He flashed her a smile, and her curiosity about his family life, his past, his childhood rose up the ranks. "But Angel, I don't care about the phone; I care about you. Are you okay?"

"I am obviously not okay," she said, giving him a squinty-eyed look.

"Obviously," he fired right back. "But I mean, can I help you? I didn't mean to stress you by asking you to game night. It's—"

"I want to go," she blurted out.

His eyebrows rose, and Angel couldn't stand sitting this close to him. Rather, she wanted to be closer, but she didn't trust herself. "I—"

She jumped to her feet. "I need to get off this ranch," she said, pacing away from him. Moving while she talked really helped get her brain to work better. "Things are so stressful right now, and there's so much going on with Trevor's doctor's appointments, and Daddy started coughing last week, and I have to get off this ranch."

She faced him and ran her hands through her hair. "So if you'll give me ten minutes to wash my face and get it fixed again, I'm ready to go."

Henry hadn't gotten to his feet, and he watched her from his perch on the couch. A moment passed before he said, "You can have nine minutes."

Angel blinked and then laughter bubbled up from inside her. She honestly could not remember the last time she'd laughed, and Henry had just given her a great gift. Excitement to get off the ranch—with him—flowed through her as the laughter cleansed her from the debilitating feelings that had brought on the crying.

"You might want to reconsider," she said. "I am very competitive at games."

"You might want to reconsider," he said. "It's couples game night, and we might have to do...things we don't want to do."

"Like what?"

"I honestly have no idea," he said. "My cousin and his wife pick the game, but it's been made very clear that we need an even number of people for tonight."

Angel's chin quivered, but she wasn't sure from what. Another bout of crying? The thrill of going off the ranch with Henry? Pure desperation? "I have to get off this ranch," she whispered.

"The clock's ticking," he said, and he did get up then and open the door for her. "Let me drive you back to your place."

She didn't protest, and Henry backtracked to get his truck keys. He opened her door for her, and he got her down the lane and around the corner to her house, which sat a hundred yards from her parents' homestead. Only thirty from Trevor's place, and fifteen from where their three full-time senior farriers lived.

"Six minutes," he said, and Angel flew from the truck. She could change her clothes, swipe on some deodorant, wash her face, paint some gloss on her lips, and grab some earrings and be ready to go.

Her heart pounded through all of it, and she had no idea how long she'd been inside her house before she yanked open the front door and flew out of it again. This time, she wore a pretty blue dress with white dragonflies flitting around on it, a pair of white sandals, pink lip gloss, and she carried a pair of silver hoops in her hand.

She stuck them in her pocket as she walked across her porch, and she used the remaining walk to Henry's truck to run her hands through her hair and get it settled in the right place. So many pieces of her life felt fake, and Angel vaulted back into Henry's truck with his gaze stuck to her.

He had to see her—really see her—and that idea struck Angel's heart with pure fear.

"You look great," he said simply, and then he put the truck in reverse and backed out of the small parking area in front of her house.

"Thank you." She buckled and managed to get her earrings in. "Is my hair straight?" She faced him, her pulse like a gong being banged on over and over and over again. "It's not my real hair, and I need more than six minutes to make it look normal."

"It's not your real hair?"

"No," she said, when she could've said so much more. The truth was, she was going bald. Her. A woman. Her hair had thinned considerably in the past three years, and Angel had started wearing extensions right away.

However, those only broke the little hair she had, damaging it further. So she'd moved to wigs, and she'd settled on one that looked the most like her natural hair. She'd bought five of them, and she rotated them to make sure they could be cleaned, repaired, or replaced.

With horror, she realized she'd never told

anyone she wore a wig. Not even her recent boyfriends had known. "Does it look okay?" she asked, reaching up to run her fingers through it again, trying to make sure the part sat right and the hair fell down correctly.

"It's gorgeous," Henry said, turning to look out the windshield again. He cleared his throat once and then twice. "Where do you want to go to eat?"

"Where were you and Levi going to go?"

"There's a great little pub in Stinnett," he said. "The Gas Light. It's not too loud this early in the evening, and the food is phenomenal."

"Pub food."

"They have great burgers and chicken," he said. "But they have amazing pizza too. And a really great mac and cheese." He glanced over to her. "Great big salads with roast beef. That kind of thing."

"You've ordered a great big salad with roast beef from this pub place?"

"I've been with people who have."

"Women."

"Yes," he said.

"Are you seeing anyone right now?"

"If I was, I'd be taking them to the couples game night," he shot back. "Not my cabin-mate." He glared at her. "Are you seeing anyone right now?"

She folded her arms. "No."

"Great. Neither am I. I haven't dated since I came to Lone Star, in fact."

"Why not?" From what Angel knew of Henry, which admittedly wasn't much, he'd dated a lot during farrier school.

He shifted in his seat and looked out his side window. "Maybe I don't get off the ranch as much as I should either." He faced her and cocked one eyebrow at her. Almost as quickly, he softened. His grip on the steering wheel loosened, and he reached toward her.

But he pulled back before he made it even halfway to her, and Angel had no idea what she'd do if he tried to hold her hand. Or touch her. "I'm worried about you, Angel."

"I'm okay." She cinched her arms around her midsection and watched the landscape flow toward them and around them as he drove. "I just get overwhelmed sometimes. Don't you ever feel like you're just drowning?"

"Sometimes, yes," he said quietly.

Angel couldn't get air to go down the right way. Thankfully, it only lasted for a moment, and then her lungs and windpipe worked just fine. She breathed in, swallowed, and kept her gaze out the windshield.

"What do you do when you feel like that?" She felt him looking at her, but she steadfastly refused to meet his gaze.

"Honestly?" He sighed like she was asking him to cut off a hand and lend it to her for a while. "I'm a momma's boy. When I feel like I'm drowning, I go home to my momma."

Tears pressed into her eyes. "That sounds so nice, Henry."

"I'm really sorry about your mom," he said. In the next moment, before Angel could tell him it was okay, that she'd finally accepted that her mother wasn't going to get better, he slammed on the brakes.

"Holy horses," he said. "I forgot I'm not coming back here."

"Not coming back here?" Angel had just repeated the words, but they didn't make sense.

"I'm staying at my parents' until Monday."

"I can't do that."

Henry looked at her and cocked his head. "Can't you?"

"No," she snapped at him. "I look after Trevor, and I.... Daddy likes his eggs a certain way in the morning, and Mama can't light the stove anymore."

Henry reached for his phone, which rested in the cupholder. "I'll make sure your brother and parents are taken care of this weekend."

"Henry, no."

"Angel, by your own admission, you need a break, and my momma will feed you, let you sleep as late as you want, and my daddy has the sweetest therapy horses in the world. You can go play ball with them or go riding. Soak in the sunshine. Enjoy the big, wide sky over my family's ranch." He smiled at her, and Angel could admit that everything he said sounded absolutely wonderful.

Still, she hesitated. "I don't know."

"It's less than forty-eight hours," he said gently. "And I can see you need it." He ducked his head, his eyes on his phone but his hands absolutely still over it. "Will you let me help you?"

Angel closed her eyes and let herself go. "Yes," she whispered.

"Okay, then," he said. "I'm going to send a couple of texts, and then I'm going to call my momma." He stayed stopped right there on the dirt road as his fingers tracked over his phone. A minute later, he said, "Clay, Zane, and Derrick are going to make sure your family is taken care of. Only the senior farriers, your foreman, and the team leads know you'll be off-site for a couple of days."

Henry looked at her, and Angel's insides shook with nervous energy—and so much attraction to this man. "What did you say?" she asked.

"I told them you needed a break and that I was helping you get off the ranch for a couple of days. Asked them for some help with your brother and parents, and within sixty seconds, it's done."

Angel nodded and looked away from him. "Thank you, Henry."

"My word, I'm going to say something my uncle lectured me about endlessly." He gave a mirthless chuckle. "If you need help, Angel, say something. There are plenty of people willing to help you."

"I know." She sniffled and reached up to wipe her eyes. "I'm sorry, Henry. I swear I'm going to pull myself together before we get to your cousin's house."

"If you can't, that's okay too," he said gently. She'd seen him working with horses, and he was this polite and respectful and kind to them too. His quiet, almost dormant strength spoke to them, and just as easily to her too. "It's just game night, and everyone will survive without me. You just let me know."

She drew in a breath, trying to use the oxygen to fill herself with bravery and strength. "I want to do something fun, and game night with people our age sounds fun."

"Our age?"

She heard the teasing note in his voice, but she hid her smile. "Yes," she said. "I know how old you are from your application."

"Sneaky," he teased. "How old are you?"

"Twenty-eight," she said. And Henry would be twenty-seven this year. June, if she remembered right.

"That's pretty young to shoulder all you do."

She could only nod, because yes, she carried a lot of responsibility. "Trevor is seven years older than me," she said. "He was supposed to take over."

"He's a great guy," Henry said.

"I've seen you with him." Angel released the self-hug, glad when the tension in her muscles started to recede. "You're so kind to him. So good with him. I really appreciate it."

"Sure," Henry said easily. "I've worked with quite a few therapy patients through my daddy's equine unit. He's just a person."

"Yes, well, some people don't know how to deal with or talk to a disabled person."

"Mm, sure," Henry said again, and he made the turn onto the main highway, aiming the truck toward Three Rivers and not Amarillo. "Okay, we've got better service here. Let me call my momma. She can find you some pajamas and clothes for the weekend. She'll probably need to get a bedroom ready for you."

"If it's too much—"

"It's not." He cut her a look out of the side of his eye and tapped on the screen in his truck. A loud chirp filled the vehicle, and he said in a loud, clear, slow voice, "Call Momma Chelsea."

"Calling Momma Chelsea," his truck repeated to him, and Angel couldn't hide her smile this time. Oh, and now she knew his mother's name. She'd run into the woman when Henry had moved in last summer, but she'd deliberately kept all the doors between her and him closed, hoping her insane and intense attraction to him would diminish with time and space.

Sadly, that hadn't happened yet, and now she was currently riding in his vehicle, toward his cousin's house for game night, and then a weekend away at his parent's house.

"Henry, baby, hey," his momma said. "Are you still coming tonight?"

"Yes, Momma," he said. "And I need to warn you: you're on speaker with me and a friend."

"Okay," she said.

Henry looked over to her, and Angel had looked at him when he'd called her "a friend." She would not classify Henry as a friend, and she really didn't like him calling her that. Not because they weren't friends yet, but because he hadn't used the word *girlfriend*.

And why would he? The very thought was insane—and absolutely not allowed due to Lone Star's dating policies.

"Momma, my friend is a woman in desperate need of a break from the stables. But I forgot to tell her I was coming for the weekend, and she doesn't have anything. Not a toothbrush, a stick of deodorant, or any pajamas."

His mother stayed silent for a couple of seconds. "And I'm assuming she'll be staying for the weekend."

"Yes, ma'am," he said. "It's Angel, Momma."

"Oh, Angel." His mother's voice brightened, and Angel could only imagine what he'd told her. At least it sounded like they were good things. "Okay, so you're on your way to game night?"

"Dinner first," Henry said. "Then game night. Who knows what Finn and Edith have planned, but they've got that baby now, so I'm guessing we'll get to Three Rivers by like...." He hemmed and hawed for a moment and then said, "Ten-thirty."

"Okay," his momma said.

"Is that too late? We can leave early."

"Ten-thirty is fine, baby."

"Okay," he said. "Ten-thirty then."

"I'll make sure she has what she needs."

"You're the best, Momma."

"Thank you, Missus Marshall," Angel said, leaning toward the screen where a clock ticked up the length of the phone call.

"You're welcome, honey. See you two soon."

"'Bye, Momma." Henry reached out to the screen. "Love you."

"Love you, baby."

Henry tapped the screen to end the call, and he relaxed back into his seat. "That actually went better than I thought it would."

"Did it?"

"Yeah, well, I mean—yeah, she didn't ask a bunch of questions about why you're coming with me, if we're dating, etcetera, etcetera, etcetera."

"Will anyone assume that?"

"Honestly?" He sighed, and that combined with his rhetorical question made her adrenaline spike. "Yeah, my cousins and friends and siblings will probably assume we're on a date. But I'll just tell them we're not. It'll be fine."

Angel nodded, though everything inside her writhed and squirmed. "I mean, it would be okay with me if you just let them think we're on a date. You are taking me to dinner and everything."

Henry said nothing as he drove, the ride easy and smooth along the paved road. "I guess it feels like it could be a date."

"Sure," she said, mimicking him.

"But you can't date the men at Lone Star."

"Doesn't mean I don't want to." Angel sucked in a breath when she realized what she'd just said. She tried not to, but she looked over to Henry anyway. He wore a semi-stunned look on his face, and Angel wanted to wipe it away. Say something pithy about how she had a big crush on Levi or Clay or someone other than him. Anyone *other than him.*

"Okay," he drawled. "I just need you to answer a couple of questions for me. Can you do that?"

"Maybe," she said.

"I'll take a maybe." He cleared his throat and coughed twice. "One, when I inadvertently kissed you last winter, did you or did you not kiss me back?"

Angel balked at telling him the truth, but her parents had taught her not to lie. She'd been hiding a lot, and she couldn't carry another secret. "Yes," she said. "I did."

"Mm hm. Yes, you did."

She rolled her eyes, though every cell in her body told her to smile instead. "Is that it?"

"No," he said. "If I asked you out on a real date, would you say yes?"

"That's cheating."

"What does that mean?"

"You just want me to tell you I'll go out with you without you having to ask."

"It's against the rules at Lone Star to date anyone who works there," he said. "I *can't* ask you out, even if I wanted to—and I'm not saying I do."

"Then why does it matter?"

"Because a man would like to know if the incredibly beautiful woman he's had a crush on for seemingly ever would go out with him, that's why."

"I—"

"And because if she would, and she can feel this bubbling, sizzling thing between them, then maybe some rules need to be broken."

"Henry Marshall," she admonished. "You don't break rules."

"They're *your* rules," he said, cutting her a look out of the side of his eyes. "You could change them."

"They're my daddy's rules."

The truck traveled down the road, the signs for Stinnett coming into view. Angel sensed she'd lose him and the thread of this conversation once they stopped for dinner. But she didn't know what to say.

He'd just admitted to having a crush on her, and that made warmed honey ooze through her veins.

"I can feel this thing between us," she whispered.

"Mm hm. And?"

"And." She finished drawing in her breath and blew it all out noisily. "I'd go out with you if you could ask me."

"Mm."

"You hum a lot."

"I just want you to know I heard you." He reached over and took her hand in his. Part of

Angel wanted to protest, but she looked at him and saw the determined set of his jaw.

"Henry," she said, but she didn't have the words to continue.

"I'd break all the rules for you, Angel," he said, his voice soft and powerful at the same time. "But let's not deal with it this weekend, okay? You need a break, and me adding all this too your plate is selfish and unnecessary."

"Okay," she said, her emotions teetering on the edge of sanity again.

"Okay." He lifted her hand to his lips and gently pressed a kiss to the inside of her wrist. He said something else about the pub they'd be at soon, but all Angel could hear was the sweetest words a man had ever said to her: *I'd break all the rules for you, Angel.*

So she started praying that something could be done about the no-dating rules at Lone Star. But that meant talking to Daddy about his policies, and he'd never been very open to her suggestions.

Not this weekend, she told herself. She deserved a relaxing, carefree break from the ranch, and that was exactly what she was going to do for the next two days.

With Henry Marshall at her side.

Biscuits and gravy, she thought-swore. *Dear Lord, don't let this be the biggest mistake of my life.*

Oh…biscuits and gravy! Find out in THE COWBOY WHO WORKED LATE, which you can **secure your copy by scanning the QR code below with your phone!**

The Cowboy Who Came Home: A Second Generation in Three Rivers Ranch Romance™ (Book 1): He's been serving in the military for a decade. She's been quietly grieving a devastating loss. When Finn and Edith reunite in small-town Three Rivers where they grew up together, can their second chance romance provide hope, healing, and the happily-ever-after they both crave?

Scan this QR code with your phone to see this series in eBook, audiobook, large print paperback, or regular paperback:

Be sure to check out the other three series set in the beloved town of Three Rivers too!

Meet the cowboys who started it all at Three Rivers Ranch! Scan the QR code below with your phone to check out this complete series.

Scan this QR code with your phone to see and order this series in eBook, audiobook, large print paperback, or regular paperback:

1. Second Chance Ranch
2. Third Time's the Charm
3. Fourth and Long
4. Fifth Generation Cowboy
6. Sixth Street Love Affair

Seven Sons Ranch in Three Rivers Romance™ Series

Meet the cowboy billionaire brothers at Seven Sons Ranch! Scan the QR code below with your phone to check out this complete series.

1. Rhett
2. Tripp
3. Liam
4. Jeremiah
5. Wyatt

6. Skyler
7. Micah
8. Gideon

Shiloh Ridge Ranch in Three Rivers Romance™ Series

Become a Glover Lover by reading all the Glover Family romance & family saga at Shiloh Ridge Ranch! Scan the QR code below with your phone to check out this complete series.

1. The Mechanics of Mistletoe
2. The Horsepower of the Holiday
3. The Construction of Cheer
4. The Secret of Santa
5. The Gift of Gingerbread

About Liz

Liz Isaacson writes inspirational romance, usually set in Texas, or Wyoming, or anywhere else horses and cowboys exist. She lives in Utah, where she writes full-time, takes her two dogs to the park everyday, and eats a lot of veggies while writing. Find her on her website at www.feelgoodfictionbooks.com.